THE BLUE DEMON

DAVID
HEWSON

THE
BLUE
DEMON

MACMILLAN

First published 2010 by Macmillan
an imprint of Pan Macmillan, a division of Macmillan Publishers Limited
Pan Macmillan, 20 New Wharf Road, London N1 9RR
Basingstoke and Oxford
Associated companies throughout the world
www.panmacmillan.com

ISBN 978-0-230-52936-6 HB
ISBN 978-0-230-71134-1 TPB

1 3 5 7 9 8 6 4 2

A CIP catalogue record for this book is available from
the British Library.

Typeset by SetSystems Ltd, Saffron Waldon, Essex
Printed and bound in the UK by CPI Mackays, Chatham ME5 8TD

Visit **www.panmacmillan.com** to read more about all our books
and to buy them. You will also find features, author interviews and
news of any author events, and you can sign up for e-newsletters
so that you're always first to hear about our new releases.

THE BLUE DEMON

PANTHEON

Via del Corso

Piazza Venezia

Part 1

DIVINATION

Fere libenter homines id quod volunt credunt.

Men willingly believe what they wish.

Julius Caesar, *De Bello Gallico*,
Book III, Ch. 18

- 1 -

The garden of the Quirinale felt like a suntrap as the man in the silver armour strode down the shingle path. He was sweating profusely inside the ceremonial breastplate and woollen uniform.

Tight in his right hand he held the long, bloodied sword that had just taken the life of a man. In a few moments he would kill the president of Italy. And then? Be murdered himself. It was the lot of assassins throughout the ages, from Pausanius of Orestis, who had slaughtered Philip, the father of Alexander the Great, to Marat's murderess, Charlotte Corday, and Kennedy's nemesis, Lee Harvey Oswald.

The stabbing dagger, the sniper's rifle . . . all these were mirrored weapons, reflecting on the man or woman who bore them, joining perpetrator and victim as twin sacrifices to destiny. It had always been this way, since men sought to rule over others, circumscribing their desires, hemming in the spans of their lives with the dull, rote strictures of convention. Petrakis had read much over the years, thinking, preparing, comparing himself to his peers. The travelling actor John Wilkes Booth's final performance before he put a bullet through the skull of Abraham Lincoln had been in *Julius Caesar*, although through some strange irony he had taken the part of Caesar's friend and apologist, Mark Antony, not Brutus as history demanded.

As he approached the figure in the bower, seeing the old man's grey, lined form bent deep over a book, Petrakis found himself murmuring a line Wilkes Booth must have uttered a century and a half before.

' "O mighty Caesar . . . dost thou lie so low? Are all thy conquests, glories, triumphs, spoils, shrunk to this little measure?" '

3

A pale, long face, with sad, tired eyes, looked up from the page. Petrakis, realizing he had spoken out loud, wondered why this death, among so many, would be the most difficult.

'I didn't quite catch that,' Dario Sordi said in a calm, unwavering voice, his eyes, nevertheless, on the long, bloodied blade.

The uniformed officer came close, stopped, repeated the line, and held the sword over the elderly figure seated in the shadow of a statue of Hermes.

The president looked up, glanced around him and asked, 'What conquests in particular, Andrea? What glories? What spoils? Temporary residence in a garden fit for a pope? I'm a pensioner in a very luxurious retirement home. Do you really not understand that?'

The long silver weapon trembled in Petrakis's hand. His palm felt greasy. He had no words at all.

Voices rose behind him. A shout. A clamour.

There was a cigarette in Dario Sordi's hands. It didn't even shake.

'You should be afraid, old man.'

More dry laughter.

'I've been hunted by Nazis.' The grey, drawn face glowered at him. Sordi drew on the cigarette and exhaled a cloud of smoke. 'Played hide and seek with tobacco and the grape for more than half a century. Offended people – important people – who feel I am owed a lesson, which is probably true.' A long, pale finger jabbed through the evening air. 'And now you wish me to cower before someone else's puppet? A fool?'

That, at least, made it easier.

Petrakis found his mind ranging across so many things: memories, lost decades, languid days dodging NATO patrols beneath the Afghan sun, distant, half-recalled moments in the damp darkness of an Etruscan tomb, talking to his father about life and the world, and how a man had to make his own way, not let another create a future for him.

Everything came from that place in the Maremma, from the whispered discovery of a paradise of the will sacrificed to the commonplace and mundane, the exigencies of politics. Andrea Petrakis knew this course was set for him at an early age, by birth, by his inheritance.

The memory of the tomb, with its ghostly painted figures on the wall, and the terrible, eternal spectre of the Blue Demon, consuming them one by one, filled his head. This, more than anything else, he had learned over the decades: freedom, of the kind enjoyed by the long-dead men and women still dancing beneath the grey Tarquinia earth more than two millennia on, was a mayfly, gloriously fleeting, made real by its impermanence. Life and death were bedfellows, two sides of the same coin. To taste every breath, feel each beat of the heart, one had to know that both might be snatched away in an instant. His father had taught him that, long before the Afghans and the Arabs tried to reveal the same truth.

Andrea Petrakis remembered the lesson more keenly now, as the sand trickled through some unseen hourglass for Dario Sordi and his allotted assassin.

Out of the soft evening came a bright, sharp sound, like the ping of some taut yet invisible wire, snapping under pressure.

A piece of the statue of Hermes, its stone right foot, disintegrated in front of his eyes, shattering into pieces, as if exploding in anger.

Dario Sordi ducked back into the shadows, trying, at last, to hide.

– 2 –

Three days earlier . . .

'Behold,' said the man, in a cold, tired voice, the accent from the countryside perhaps. 'I will make a covenant. For it is something dreadful I will do to you.'

Strong, firm hands ripped off the hood. Giovanni Batisti saw he was tethered to a plain office chair. At the periphery of his vision he could make out that he was in a small, simple room with bare bleached floorboards and dust ghosts on the walls left by long-removed chests of drawers or ancient filing cabinets. The place smelled musty, damp and abandoned. He could hear the distant lowing of traffic, muffled in some curious way, but still energized by the familiar rhythm of the city. Cars and trucks, buses and people, thousands of them, some from the police and the security services no doubt, searching as best they could, oblivious to his presence. There was no human sound close by, from an adjoining room or an apartment. Not a radio or a TV set. Or any voice save that of his captor.

'I would like to use the bathroom, please,' Batisti said quietly, keeping his eyes fixed on the stripped, cracked timber boards at his feet. 'I will do as you say. You have my word.'

The silence, hours of it, was the worst part. He'd expected a reprimand, an order, might even have welcomed a beating, since all these things would have acknowledged his existence. Instead . . . he was left in limbo, in blindness, almost as if he were dead already. Nor was there any exchange he could hear between those involved. A brief meeting to discuss tactics. News. Perhaps a phone call in which he would be asked to confirm that he was still alive.

6

Even – and this was a forlorn hope, he knew – some small note of concern about his driver, the immigrant Polish woman Elena Majewska, everyone's favourite, shot in the chest as the two vehicles blocked his government vehicle in the narrow street of Via delle Quattro Fontane, at the junction with the road to the Quirinale. It was such a familiar Roman crossroads, next to Borromini's fluid baroque masterpiece of San Carlino, a church he loved deeply and would visit often, along with Bernini's nearby Sant'Andrea, if he had time during his lunch break from the Interior Ministry building around the corner.

They could have snatched him that day from beneath Borromini's dome, with its magnificent dove of peace, descending to earth from Heaven. He'd needed a desperate fifteen-minute respite from sessions with the Americans, the Russians, the British, the Germans . . . Eight nations, eight voices, each different, each seeking its own outcome. The phrase that was always used about the G8 – the 'industrialized nations' – had come to strike him as somewhat ironic as he listened to the endless bickering about diplomatic rights and protocols, who should stand where and with whom. Had some interloper approached him during his brief recess that day, Batisti would have glanced at Borromini's extraordinary interior one last time, then walked into his captor's arms immediately, trying to finish his *panino*, without much in the way of a second thought. Anything but another session devoted to the rites and procedures of diplomatic life.

Then he remembered again, with a sudden, painful seizure of guilt, the driver. Did Elena – a pretty, young single mother who'd moved to Rome to find security and a new, better life – survive? If so, what could she tell the police? What was there to say about a swift and unexpected explosion of violence in the black sultry velvet of a Roman summer night? The attack had happened so quickly and with such brutish force that Batisti was still unsure how many men had been involved. Perhaps no more than three or four from the pair of vehicles blocking the way. The area was empty. He was without a bodyguard. An opposition politician drafted in to the organization team out of custom and practice was deemed not to need one, even in the heightened security that preceded the coming summit. Not a single sentence was spoken as they dragged him from the rear seat, wrapped a blindfold tightly round his head, fired – three, four times? – into the front, then bundled him into the boot of some large vehicle and drove a short distance to their destination.

Were they now issuing ransom demands? Did his wife, who was with her family in Milan, discussing a forthcoming family wedding, know what was happening?

There were no answers, only questions. Giovanni Batisti was forty-eight years old and felt as if he'd stepped back into a past that Italy hoped was behind it. The dismal Seventies and Eighties, the 'Years of Lead'. A time when academics and lawyers and politicians might be routinely kidnapped by the shadowy criminals of the Red Brigades and their partners in terrorism, held to ransom, tortured, then left bloodied and broken as some futile lesson to those in authority. Or dead. Like Aldo Moro, the former prime minister, seized in 1978, held captive for fifty-six days before being shot ten times in the chest and dumped in the trunk of a car in the Via Caetani.

'Look at me,' a voice from ahead of him ordered.

Batisti closed his eyes, kept them tightly shut.

'I do not wish to compromise you, sir. I have a wife. Two sons. One is eight. One is ten. I love them. I wish you no harm. I wish no one any harm. These matters can and will be resolved through dialogue, one way or another. I believe that of everything. In this world I have to.' He found his mouth was dry, his lips felt painful as he licked them. 'If you know me, you know I am a man of the left. The causes you espouse are often the causes I have argued for. The methods . . .'

'What do you know of our causes?'

'I . . . I have some money,' he stuttered. 'Not of my own, you understand. My father. Perhaps if I might make a phone call?'

'This is not about *money*,' the voice said, and it sounded colder than ever. 'Look at me or I will shoot you this instant.'

Batisti opened his eyes and stared straight ahead, across the bare, dreary room. The man seated opposite him was perhaps forty. Or a little older, his own age even. Professional-looking. Maybe an academic himself. Not a factory worker or some individual who had risen from the street, pulled up by his own boot laces. There was a cultured timbre to his voice, one that spoke of education and a middle-class upbringing. A keen, incisive intelligence burned in his dark eyes. His face was leathery and tanned as if it had spent too long under a bright, burning sun. He would once have been handsome, but his craggy features were marred by a network of frown lines, on the forehead, at the edge of his broad, full-lipped mouth, which looked as if a smile had never crossed it in years. His long, unkempt hair seemed unnaturally grey and was wavy, shiny with some kind of grease. A mark of vanity. Like the black clothes, which were not inexpensive. Revolutionaries usually knew how to dress. The man had the scarred visage of a movie actor who had fallen on hard times. Something about him seemed distantly familiar, which seemed a terrible thought.

'Behold, I will make a covenant . . .'

'I heard you the first time,' Batisti sighed.

'What does it mean?'

The politician briefly closed his eyes.

'The Bible?' he guessed, tiring of this game. 'One of the Old Testament horrors, I imagine. Like Leviticus. I have no time for such devils, I'm afraid. Who needs them?'

The man reached down to retrieve something, then placed the object on the table. It was Batisti's own laptop computer, which had sat next to him in the back of the official car.

'Cave eleven at Qumran. The Temple Scroll. Not quite the Old Testament, but in much the same vein.'

'It's a long time since I was a professor,' Batisti confessed. 'A very junior one at that. The Dead Sea was never my field. Nor rituals. About sacrifice or anything else.'

'I'm aware of your field of expertise.'

'I was no expert. I was a child, looking for knowledge. It could have been anything.'

'And then you left the university for politics. For power.'

He shook his head. This was unfair, ridiculous.

'What power? I spend my day trying to turn the tide a little in the way of justice, as I see it. I earn no more now than I did then. Had I written the books I wanted to . . .'

Great, swirling stories, popular novels of the ancients, of heroism and dark deeds. He would never get round to them. He understood that.

'It's a long time since I spoke to an academic. You were a professor of ancient history. Greek and Roman?'

Batisti nodded.

'A middling one. An over-optimistic decoder of impossible mysteries. Nothing more. You kidnap me, you shoot my driver, in order to discuss history?'

The figure in black reached into his jacket and withdrew a short, bulky weapon.

'A man with a gun may ask anything.'

Giovanni Batisti was astonished to discover that his fear was rapidly being consumed by a growing sense of outrage.

'I am a servant of the people. I have never sought to do anyone ill. I have voted and spoken against every policy, national and international, with which I disagree. My conscience is clear. Is yours?'

The man in black scowled.

'You read too much Latin and too little English. "Thus conscience does make cowards of us all." '

'I don't imagine you brought me here to quote Shakespeare. What do you want?' Batisti demanded.

'In the first instance? I require the unlock code for this computer. After that I wish to hear everything you know about the arrangements that will be made to guard the great gentlemen who are now in Rome to safeguard this glorious society of ours.' The man scratched his lank, grey hair. 'Or is that theirs? Excuse my ignorance. I've been out of things for a little while.'

'And after that you will kill me?'

He seemed puzzled by the question.

'No, no, no. After that *he* will kill you.'

The man nodded at a place at the back of the room, then gestured for someone to come forward.

Giovanni Batisti watched and felt his blood freeze.

The newcomer must have sat silent throughout. Perhaps he was in the other car when they seized him at the crossroads near the Viminale. Though not like this.

He looked like a golden boy, a powerfully built youth, naked apart from a crude loincloth. His skin was the colour of a cinematic Mediterranean god. His hair was burnished yellow, long and curled like a cherub from Raphael. Bright blue paint was smeared roughly on his face and chest.

'We require a sign,' the man in black added, reaching into his pocket and taking out an egg. 'My friend here is no ordinary man. He can foretell the future through the examination of the entrails and internal organs. This makes him a . . .'

He stared at the ceiling, as if searching for the word.

'A haruspex,' Batisti murmured.

'Exactly. Should our act of divination be fruitful . . .'

The painted youth was staring at him, like a muscular halfwit. Batisti could see what appeared to be a butcher's knife in his right hand.

On the table, a pale brown hen's egg sat in a saucer with a scallop-shell edge.

The man with the gun said, in a clear, firm voice, '*Ta Sacni!*' Then he leaned forward and, in a mock whisper behind his hand, added, 'This is more your field than mine. I think that means, "This is the sanctuary." Do tell me if we get anything wrong.'

The golden boy came and stood behind him. In his left hand was a small bottle of San Pellegrino mineral water. His eyes were very blue and open, as if he were drugged or somehow insensate. He bent down, gazed at the egg and then listened, rapt, captivated, as the man in black began to chant in a dry, disengaged voice, 'Aplu. Phoebos. Apollo. Delian. Pythian. Lord of Delphi. Guardian of the Sibyls. Or by whatever other name you wish to be called. I pray and beseech you that you may by your majesty be propitious and well disposed to me, for which I offer this egg. If I have worshipped you and still do worship you, you who taught mankind the art of prophecy, you who have inspired my divination, then come now and show your signs that I might know the will of the gods! I seek to understand the secret ways into the Palace of the Pope. *Thui Srenar Tev.*'

Show me the signs now, Batistic translated in his head.

The youth spilled the water onto the table. The knife came down and split the egg in two.

The older one leaned over, sniffed and said, 'Looks like yolk and albumen to me. But what do I know? He's the haruspex.'

'I cannot tell you these things,' Batisti murmured. 'You must appreciate that.'

'That is both very brave and very unfortunate. Though not entirely unexpected.'

The naked youth was running his fingers through the egg in the saucer. The man pushed his hand away. The creature obeyed, immediately, a sudden fearful and subservient look in his eye.

'I want the code for your computer,' the older one ordered. 'You will give it to me. One way or another.'

Batisti said nothing, merely closed his eyes for a moment and wished he retained sufficient faith to pray.

'I'm more valuable to you alive than dead. Tell the authorities what you want. They will negotiate.'

'They didn't for Aldo Moro. You think some junior political hack is worth more than a prime minister?'

He seemed impatient, as if this were all a tedious game.

'You've been out of the real world too long, Batisti. These people smile at you and pat your little head, caring nothing. These,' he dashed the saucer and the broken egg from the table, 'toys are beneath us. Remember your Bible. "When I was a child, I used to speak like a child, think like a child, reason like a child; when I became a man, I did away with childish things. For now we see in a mirror dimly . . ."'

Batisti recalled little of his Catholic upbringing. It seemed distant, as if it had happened to someone else. This much of the verses he remembered, though.

'But faith, hope, love, abide these three,' he said quietly. 'And the greatest of these is love.'

'Not so much of that about these days,' the silver-haired man replied mournfully. 'Is there?'

Then he nodded at the golden boy by his side, waiting, tense and anxious for something to begin.

- 3 -

The peals from the nearby clock tower cut through the muffled rumble of late-afternoon traffic. In his mind's eye Gianni Peroni could imagine the slender white campanile that sat atop the great palace on the hill above them. The Italian *tricolore* fluttered at the summit, the blue European flag beneath, both accompanied, if the president were in residence, by his own personal standard on the other. All three flew at half-mast during times of national mourning. Perhaps that would happen soon, Peroni thought with regret.

At that moment he felt every day of his fifty-three years. His hefty muscular frame ached from the hours he'd spent on the cobbled streets of the *centro storico*, his mind felt blank from staring at so many blank faces regarding him with trepidation and a little fear. He knew he wasn't the prettiest cop on the beat. The physical slashes that marked his cheeks like knife scars saw to that. No stranger opening the door to him could possibly guess that the appearance he gave – so rough, so intimidating – was nothing like the man himself, until he spoke, kindly, with a keen, bright diligence and genuine emotion.

This was a bad day in Rome, one that might so easily get worse. Peroni took a deep breath, thought about the next address on his list, and then heard the sonorous chimes of the president's campanile swamped by the thunderous roar of a police Twin Huey flying in to hover low over the Quirinale hill.

The briefing from Commissario Esposito had made plain the seriousness of the situation, and the degree of the response. Nine of the twelve Polizia di Stato helicopters from the Pratica di Mare air base south of the city were in the air, circling endlessly. They had been joined by those of the Carabinieri, the secret services, and some more shadowy security agencies Peroni cared not to think about. The combined racket they made placed a low, shrill shriek in the perfect blue sky above the summer crowds of tourists and commuters struggling through the heat.

Over the years Peroni had come to associate the racket of these machines with the state of the city's temperament. Their volume rose and fell with the general mood in the dark, cobbled alleys of the *centro storico* and the quieter, more modern suburbs to which the average Roman retreated at the end of the working day. On that basis the city's current frame of mind was uncertain, unhappy and pregnant with foreboding. A junior minister in the Ministry of the Interior had been kidnapped, seized by some band of unknown criminals just after midnight. They had casually slaughtered his unfortunate female driver, a young single mother, at the wheel of his government car. Peroni had been on duty and was one of the first on the scene ten hours earlier. The heartbreaking sight of the unarmed woman's bloodied, torn corpse still strapped in by her seat belt would haunt him for a while. There was, it seemed to him, little point in her murder, except to demonstrate its own brutality.

No ransom demand, or any other kind of communication, had been received by the authorities. Not a trace of the victim or his abductors had yet been found. But everyone knew who Giovanni Batisti was: a minor opposition politician dealing with the security of the meeting of G8 world leaders, due to begin, somewhat controversially, the following day in the centre of the city itself. An officer of the state who possessed secrets useful to the enemy, whosoever they might be. The assumption, on the part of the police and everyone else, was immediate and unquestioned. This was terrorism, a prelude to something else, something worse.

Hundreds of men and women were now engaged in trying to understand what had happened in those few bloody minutes at the crossroads in the Via delle Quattro Fontane. Yet in the end, much of the work fell to those who patiently tramped the historic streets of Rome. Helicopters and surveillance cameras, police officers in the most visible of public streets bearing arms, constant appeals to the public through the media . . . these things were fine for the cameras. When it came to the point at which good encountered evil, its discovery was usually down to a few individuals who might count themselves lucky, cursed or just plain stupid, depending on the outcome of events.

The story broke too late for the morning newspapers, which made it all the more attractive to the TV and radio stations. So, within the space of a morning, the pretty face of Elena Majewska and the kindly, scholarly features of Giovanni Batisti had become familiar icons throughout Rome, if not Italy, on TV screens, in the imaginations of ordinary people fearful about his fate and that of the nation at large. The indignation of the city was apparent everywhere, during quiet conversations in cafes and, more visibly, in the printouts of protest notices that had begun to appear in the windows of shops and private homes, on any spare space that could be found.

Peroni recalled the morning that terrorist bombs had devastated the centre of London some years before. Within the space of a few hours posters, rapidly printed at personal expense, distributed by volunteers, began appearing on the walls of the Italian capital declaring, '*Adesso siamo tutti Londinesi.*'

We are all Londoners now.

It felt that way. There was a communal howl of outrage, an instinctive reaction of shock and revulsion. Yet some inner sense of the city told him the response to Batisti's kidnap was more than a statement of solidarity born out of simple common decency. This strange and bloody act had finally breathed life into a subterranean sense of apprehension, one that had been quietly stirring for some time in the febrile, uncertain nature of the times.

Peroni had watched Commissario Esposito assemble an initial investigative team in the darkness early that morning, only to find, to his dismay, if not surprise, that the area was soon swarming with other agencies, the Carabinieri, officers of SISDE, the civilian secret service, and SISMI, their military counterparts. Foreigners too: Americans flashing badges, British men in suits who never said a word at all, French, German, Russian . . .

Rome was bursting at the seams with spooks and security officers committed to guarding the leaders who were starting to assemble inside the Quirinale. A small army of these tenebrous individuals had found their way to the narrow crossroads of the Via delle Quattro Fontane, turning it into an international scrum in a little more than hour.

It was almost, Peroni thought at the time, as if some of them had been expecting such a turn of events.

The entire area would be sealed off for another day at least, causing chaos for those trying to get to work in the presidential palace and the various ministry buildings scattered around the neighbourhood. In the tussle that ensued, Esposito had done his best to press the police case for a leading role in the investigation. Peroni had watched the most senior officer in the Questura as he fought to deal with a rapidly escalating confrontation that was slipping out of his hands. There was something quietly admirable in the man's persistent, yet polite professionalism towards the other agencies as they arrived. Nevertheless, it was an effort doomed to failure.

Once a case moved from simple criminality into the dark world of terrorism, Esposito knew, like every other ordinary serving man and woman in the Polizia di Stato, that he was merely a foot soldier destined to take orders, a tiny cog in a very different campaign, one that embraced much more than mere law enforcement. Whatever had happened to Giovanni Batisti, it would not be left to the police to take the lead in negotiating his release or trying to locate his killers, should the worst happen. The game had, very swiftly, moved on. They would become pawns on a chessboard in which the pieces were shifted by unseen hands, playing to a gambit they might never explain. This was the way of such investigations, and what amazed Gianni Peroni, a police officer of extensive experience, running back to the days of the Red Brigades, was that they were forced to confront such challenges only rarely. Bombs had devastated London and Madrid. Aircraft had tumbled from the sky in America. Rome had been lucky. It was important such good fortune lasted.

This was why he was now leading one of the many teams of police officers scouring the streets to follow up phone calls from people responding to the pleas put out by the authorities. It was the kind of routine, mindless drudgery that police officers performed much of the time: knocking on doors, asking questions, trying to judge the answers they got, expecting little, receiving nothing mostly. Every officer Commissario Esposito could get his hands on was out there, among them many men and women on holiday who had turned up determined to help. It was boring, necessary labour, and Peroni was glad he had good company for the job: Rosa Prabakaran, an experienced *agente* who was quickly turning into one of the most intelligent and reliable officers in the Questura team; and a genial trainee, Mirko Oliva, a bright young man from Turin newly transferred from uniform to plain-clothes duties.

Only Oliva, starry-eyed still with the eagerness of youth, managed to look enthusiastic after five futile responses to calls which, for the most part, had been sparked by nothing more than the innocent presence of foreigners of Middle Eastern origin. Terrorism, for the masses, still meant something from outside Italy; their memories, it seemed to Peroni, were mercifully short at times.

Now the three of them were no more than a ten-minute walk from the point at which Batisti had been kidnapped. The address they'd been given lay in a dark narrow lane to one side of the Quirinale, running from the Barberini Palace to the busy tunnel that travelled beneath the palace gardens to emerge near the Trevi Fountain. Peroni could see a phalanx of coaches fighting for space at the foot of the street so that they could discharge their cargoes of tourists for the sights.

'What are we looking for this time?' Oliva asked. He was twenty-three, stocky, like a rugby player, with close-cropped black hair and bright blue eyes.

'You're supposed to remember these things, Mirko,' Rosa Prabakaran scolded him. 'Not keep relying on your colleagues.'

'Sorry. I wish we were doing something important.'

'This is important,' Peroni insisted. He looked at his notebook. 'Or it might be.'

It was more than thirty years since Gianni Peroni joined the police, but he could still remember the impetuousness he'd felt in the early days.

Rosa Prabakaran was beyond that stage already. A slim, elegant young woman, born in Rome to Indian parents, she was dressed in a severe grey suit, the uniform of an ambitious young officer keen to take a step up, like Nic Costa, to *sovrintendente*. She was something of an enigma within the Questura: self-assured, striking, with a round, dark face, intelligent brown eyes and – a deliberate sign, he thought, of her heritage – the smallest of gold studs in her snub nose. She never mixed with her colleagues, never talked about anything personal, relationships least of all. When the work was there, she was always the last to leave. When she was off duty, no one had any idea what she did, or with whom.

'We had a phone call from someone called Moro,' Rosa told the young trainee, giving Peroni a meaningful look, one that said he ought to remark upon Oliva's sluggishness one day. 'He lives on the ground floor. He thinks he saw two suspicious-looking foreigners going up the stairs.'

'How does someone look "suspicious"?' Oliva wondered.

It seemed, to Peroni, a very good question.

- 4 -

The man Peroni regarded as one of his closest friends was only a few hundred metres away at that moment, standing outside the Palazzo del Quirinale at the summit of the hill, his head flooding with memories. Nic Costa was just starting to look his thirty years, slim, athletically built, dark-faced and handsome, his manner still diffident, with a quiet charm bordering on shyness, but sufficient professional steel to have gained him promotion to the rank of *sovrintendente*. Costa scarcely noticed his own inspector Leo Falcone and the Questura *commissario* Vincenzo Esposito next to him as the three police officers waited for clearance into the presidential palace. He'd been through the tightly guarded entrance of the Quirinale once before, as a child, when his father, Marco, a communist politician, had taken him on a private visit 'to see how the enemy live'. The place had seemed huge and fascinating, like some magical fortress from a fairy tale, one guarded by the tall, armoured figures of the Corazzieri, the presidential guard, men with shining swords and glittering breast-plates who stood a good head above most visitors.

That privileged peek behind the palace's towering stone facade was, Costa guessed, a quarter of a century before. The quiet, intro-verted child he was could never have imagined that one day he would return as a serving police officer, in a frightened Rome, a city full of trepidation, a place he barely recognized.

Not Falcone, though, or Esposito. They were older, in their fifties, and their bleak, immobile faces spoke volumes. Something that was once thought dead had returned, and for those of a certain age it bore a terrible familiarity.

The impossibly lofty *corazziere* at the gate let them through, and the moment he was inside the palace Costa found himself recalling his puzzlement as a child over his father's explanation of what a president did. This was not America. He was not the day-to-day head of government, an elected king in all but name. That job was given to the prime minister, but a republic required, too, a figurehead, an emblem of the state. History being what it was, the government had naturally decided that the place for such a man to live was the Quirinale, the very palace that was once occupied by the popes who ruled what was known as the *Stati della Chiesa*, the Republic of St Peter.

Foreigners seldom appreciated the complexities of politics in Rome. As the son of a communist politician, Costa had rarely been allowed to forget them. From the third century after Christ until 1861 when, in a brief interregnum, the pope became 'the prisoner in the Vatican', the papal hierarchy regarded itself as God's government on earth. Only when Mussolini's Lateran Treaty of 1929 gave the Catholic Church some formal recognition, and its own minuscule country set around Michelangelo's magnificent dome across the river, did the rift between pope and secular politicians begin to heal.

These were the antecedents that Costa's father had drummed into him from the earliest age, the story of the collapse of a once-supreme theological sovereign power and its replacement by a worldly, bickering and equally corrupt parliamentary democracy that had never quite found its feet. Marco Costa was born eight years after the Lateran Treaty was signed, into a nation dominated by fascism, one that would soon disintegrate into the bloodshed and poverty of war. This was all history, but Italian history, which meant that it was never as distant as one might sometimes have hoped, or completely forgotten.

Costa followed Esposito and Falcone up the broad stairs, exchanging glances, nothing more, with a group of Carabinieri officers on the way out. Very soon he found himself in a long, ornate room, with a carved-oak ceiling, tall, shuttered windows, elaborate gilt furniture and so many paintings he didn't know where to look.

At a vast ormolu table set against the wall backing onto the corridor stood the president of Italy, Dario Sordi. Seated to his left was a familiar figure from occasional high-level meetings within the Questura, Luca Palombo, the tall, heavily built grey-haired security chief of the Ministry of the Interior. Next to him was an individual Costa did not know, though something about the man's dress, a standard, expensive dark blue suit, suggested he came from the same distant and occasionally shadowy world as Palombo. At the end of the table, in shadow, was a screen displaying a blank white rectangle from a computer projector opposite.

A door in the corner of the room opened. Another familiar figure entered and Costa reminded himself that he did not normally move in circles like this. Ugo Campagnolo, the prime minister of Italy's sixty-third government since the Second World War, heir, in the space of a few short years, to Prodi, Berlusconi and, most recently, Walter Veltroni. Campagnolo was a man who had emerged from the constant, bilious flux of national politics by both courting and coveting controversy. Smaller than he appeared in the media, a handsome, slender man, with the energized, upright figure of the waiter he once was, he entered at a brisk pace, his face locked in the rictus smile the nation knew from a million photo opportunities. His wavy dark hair was a little too perfect for a man in his late fifties, though the chiselled tanned features, this close, seemed to confirm his frequent claim that he, unlike some of his predecessors, had never taken advantage of the surgeon's knife. Over the previous fifteen years, as the older grouping collapsed amid scandal and self-recrimination, Campagnolo had quietly built his own, invented party, courting the moneyed classes with promises of fiscal laxity, and the proletariat by outflanking Berlusconi's naked populism. The previous year, after the collapse of the brief Veltroni regime, brought about by a maverick communist politician, Campagnolo had won power through the most slender of margins and some dubious political double-dealing, becoming prime minister only months after the previous centre-left administration had placed Sordi in the presidency. The rifts between Campagnolo and Sordi began almost immediately. Scarcely a week went by without some new dispute appearing between the Quirinale and Campagnolo's parliament. It was an uneasy and embittered stand-off between a veteran politician who was widely admired but possessed little in the way of direct power, and a prime minister who was seen as a chancer and opportunist, without a conviction in his body, but with enough influence and cunning to win the popular vote against a fractured and dyspeptic opposition.

Costa watched the prime minister take a chair next to the security man, Palombo, without uttering a word or casting a single glance in the direction of the president. Only two days before, the papers had once again been full of the rifts between the two, over domestic and international issues and Campagnolo's decision to place the G8 summit in the heart of Rome itself, not in some country estate that might be guarded with ease and minimal disruption to everyday life.

They were two very different men.

Costa felt he had known Sordi's long, pale face, and its almost permanent expression of wry bemusement, forever. As a senator of the left, Sordi had been a close friend of his father until some unexplained fracture divided them. Even before he moved into the Quirinale, Sordi was a legend in Italy. The man himself made a point of never mentioning his distant past, though it was well mapped out in the papers and the national psyche. As a schoolboy during the Second World War he had joined the partisans fighting the German occupation. On 23 March 1944, a date engraved upon the memory of many a Roman family, Sordi had taken part in the infamous attack in the Via Rasella, a narrow street by the side of the Quirinale hill. Twenty SS men died and more than sixty were wounded. A truant from school, Sordi had personally gunned down two Germans, or so the papers said. Somehow he had escaped the terrible vengeance ordered by the Nazis, in which 355 Italians – Jews, Gypsies, soldiers, police officers, waiters, shop workers, some partisans, a few ordinary Romans who were simply unlucky – were massacred in regulation groups of five. The Germans dumped their bodies in the caves of the Fosse Ardeatine, close to the isolated rural catacombs of Callisto and Domitilla, no more than a ten-minute walk from Costa's home on the Via Appia Antica.

Sordi emerged from the war both a hero and an orphan; his father and an uncle were among those executed at the Fosse Ardeatine. Soon, the young partisan became a vocal member of the Communist

Party, only to break with it in 1956 over Hungary. Thereafter he remained a committed deputy of the 'soft' left, steadily working his way through the political process, gaining a reputation for blunt honesty and indefatigable integrity along the way, not least for his refusal to use his bravery as a teenage partisan to the slightest advantage in the polling booth.

The contrast with Campagnolo could hardly be greater. The prime minister exploited the Italian weakness for *braggadocio* and cheek. He was a buffoon of sorts, a political Punchinello, cynical, fundamentally unscrupulous, yet intelligent, persuasive and battle-hardened, a man who, through the force of his personality, had swept aside the confusion and infighting of the previous coalition administration and replaced it with his own brand of draconian leadership.

Costa could never imagine Sordi indulging in the swagger and public posturing that had put Campagnolo in power. There had once been photos of the man who was to become president in the Costa home. Usually with his father Marco, both raising wine glasses, cigarettes in their hands. Some more sober pictures were taken at the caves where the victims of the Via Rasella reprisals were murdered. The two men always looked so different – his father, seeming young almost to the last, while Sordi, with his bald head and fringe of grey hair, appeared to be set in permanent middle age. Then the friendship was gone, and all the young Costa recalled was that face looking down at him, smiling, its features extended, almost cartoon-like, with a long beak of a nose, drooping ears and wearily genial grey eyes. The 'bloodhound'. That was what his father called the man. Was this simply through the physical resemblance? Or because Sordi had a tireless dedication to the demands of realpolitik, which Marco, for whom theory was always easier than practice, found tedious?

In all likelihood, he would never know. The breach had occurred when he was too young to understand, or dare ask. Nevertheless, it was, he sensed, a separation that had caused both men pain.

More than two decades on, he stood in front of Dario Sordi, now president of Italy, and caught a pleasant twinkle in those kindly grey eyes.

'Ah, a face I have not seen in many years.'

Sordi gazed at Costa directly, then stepped out from behind the table, reaching out with his long arm to each of them, taking their hands.

'Esposito. A pleasure, always. You must be Falcone. Welcome.' Tall and thin, straight-backed, tanned with a carefully clipped silver goatee, Costa's inspector nodded, unmoved by the president's warmth. Sordi stopped in front of Costa. 'Sovrintendente. So much changed, yet still I see the little boy I used to know. Your father would be proud, even if he would struggle to tell you. Let me do that for him.'

Costa caught the look of amazement on the faces of his colleagues.

'I would like to think so, sir,' he said quietly, aware that he was fighting to stifle his blushes.

'Know it,' Sordi replied, and returned to the table, beckoning them to sit also. 'Know this too. I wish to God he were with us now. We could use men like him.' The president glanced at his watch. 'What you will now hear must not be repeated outside, except to those you both trust and believe must know.'

He glanced at Campagnolo.

'Prime Minister?'

'Are you asking me to comply also, Dario?' Campagnolo asked. 'Even in the present circumstances, this seems a little impertinent.'

Sordi's face betrayed no anger.

'I was seeking your support, Ugo. If you wished to say a few words . . . ?'

Campagnolo laughed and looked at them.

'I'm like these people. An invited guest. Here to listen. Nothing more.'

Sordi paused, then declared, 'You must understand, all of you, that we have entered extraordinary times. It is my hope and belief they will, with your assistance and a little good fortune, be brief. But until they are over you must bear with us all. This morning I have signed orders that confirm I shall exercise directly my power as head of state and of the Supreme Defence Council, and as commander of the armed forces. Commissario, you will report to Palombo here, and he to me. The prime minister is aware of this situation and,' Sordi frowned, and looked a little regretful, 'aware that he will accept it. The constitution is clear on this matter and I am exercising the rights and duties it gives me.'

'There are lawyers who would debate that,' Campagnolo cut in.

A flash of fury did enter the president's cheeks at that moment.

'For the right money, there are lawyers who will debate anything, as you surely know better than anyone, Ugo. I am grateful that you accept this is one occasion when their . . . talents . . . are best avoided. We have little time and no room for uncertainty.'

He glanced at the prime minister. Something passed between them, and it was not animosity, more a recognition that they occupied different positions, ones that were, by their very nature, in conflict.

'As all Italy understands, a young woman employee of the state was brutally murdered last night and the unfortunate Giovanni Batisti taken by her killers,' Sordi went on. 'For what reason, we can only guess. What you don't know is that we were forewarned something like this would happen.' Sordi sighed. 'The Blue Demon has returned.'

Costa happened to catch Esposito's face at that moment. The expression there – shock, fear and a sudden paleness in the *commissario*'s usually florid cheeks – was mirrored on Falcone's lean brown features.

Dario Sordi pointed directly at Costa.

'Your father warned me, and I never listened.' His bald head turned slowly from side to side. 'Though I doubt even he could have predicted this turn of events.'

– 5 –

The Blue Demon.

Costa hadn't heard the name in years, except on TV programmes about the recent history of Italy, and the tragic 'Years of Lead' when the nation had been gripped by terrorist outrages committed by a variety of outlaw bands, on the left and the right.

The Blue Demon was the most curious, the least understood of them all, even down to its name. An individual? An entity? No one knew, or even whether the entire episode was nothing more than a student prank or a myth gone wrong, some dark, violent fantasy originating in the old land of the Etruscans, in the bleak Maremma north of Rome.

Luca Palombo, the tall, dour grey-haired spook of the Ministry of the Interior, took them through the background to the present turn of events, the bloody recent past that the young knew only dimly and the old preferred to forget. Carefully, with a civil servant's measured, precise words, Palombo told of the beginning in 1969, before Costa was born, when sixteen people died in a savage bombing of the Banca Nazionale dell'Agricoltura in the Piazza Fontana, Milan. A year later a fascist coup failed in Rome. The leader, Junio Valerio Borghese, the 'Black Prince', a direct descendant of Pope Paul V, one of the first occupants of the Quirinale Palace, fled Italy overnight, never to return. In 1972 the first police officer was assassinated, in response to the death of a student in custody. Within a fortnight three *carabinieri* were murdered. Steadily, from that moment on, violence supplanted politics. Then a sudden, cathartic agony, the murder of Aldo Moro, a mild, left-leaning Christian democrat, cruelly kept captive for more than two months before being riddled with bullets beneath a blanket in the back of a car in a Rome suburb.

This was an atrocity too far. The nation rose up in horror at Moro's death. The authorities arrested and imprisoned everyone they suspected of complicity and, in some cases, nothing more than political sympathy. The wave of violence stuttered to a close as the prisons filled with men and women who regarded themselves as martyrs for a failed revolution.

'Finally, when we thought it was over,' Palombo continued, with a quiet, miserable disdain, 'we met this.'

He touched the keyboard. A familiar building flashed onto the screen: the Villa Giulia in Rome, a former pope's mansion close to the ancient Via Flaminia, now a museum so obscure that Costa had never set foot through the door.

'March the twenty-third, 1989,' Palombo noted, clicking through a series of photographs that might have been stills from some contemporary horror movie. 'The nymphaeum.'

A classical pleasure garden, built in a stone grove hollowed out from the garden of the villa. In the foreground stood a monochrome mosaic of a marine creature, half-man, half-monster, riding triumphantly across the waves, his serpent-like body snaking behind him, a long flute held playfully to his lips. Behind, beneath a balustrade supported by four pale stone nymphs, etched with algae, green ferns cascading from adjoining rock niches, ran a narrow channel of water disappearing into caves on both sides, its sinuous path drawing the eye to a bare stone plinth set in a semicircular alcove.

The mind knew what to expect: some beautiful, free-standing statue, of Venus or Diana, half-naked, enticing, an icon of beauty in a private pleasure ground built for a pope whose private life was very different from the severe countenance he maintained in public.

Instead there were two bodies, torn and mangled, contorted in a way that only death can achieve. A bloodied man and a woman, arms tentatively around one another, necks stretched awkwardly, upturned in agony. A scrawled, spray-painted message on the algaed stone behind them read, in letters two hands high, II. I. LXIII.

The victims in the nymphaeum of Villa Giulia wore only blood-stained underclothes. Their abdomens were terribly mutilated.

Costa didn't want to look. Or remember. He was only ten years old when this savage murder filled the papers for days on end one hot summer, with the fields outside the house off the Appian Way full of vines that needed tending, and no one to look after them. He could recall the way his father would snatch the morning editions off the table when they arrived, then dispose of them. There had been photos in those papers. Costa was sure of it. But not like this.

'Signor Rennick?' Palombo continued, turning to the unknown man by his side. 'Please.'

The American was about the same age as the man from the Ministry of the Interior, fifty or so, with a narrow, dark face, lined, and a head of very black hair that might have been dyed. From his seat, in good Italian, with an obvious American accent, he said, 'Mr President. Prime Minister.' The order of greeting was deliberate. Campagnolo smiled. Dario Sordi scarcely noticed.

Rennick looked more of a reserved diplomat than a spook. Not the kind for active service.

'The dead man's name was Renzo Frasca, an Italian American,' he went on. 'Born in Sicily, moved with his family to Washington when he was six years old. Degree in English literature from Harvard. Dual nationality. A good public servant. When the terrorists who called themselves the Blue Demon took him, he was an under-secretary in the US Embassy here. Nothing special.' He waited for them at that moment. 'You understand what I'm saying here? They murdered a bean-counter and his wife. Frasca dealt with minutiae. Trade agreements. Tariffs. Then one day . . .' He pointed at the screen, and the two bodies there. 'He gets this. I won't bore you with the autopsy. It's worse than you could imagine. Frasca and his wife were butchered. She was a Virginia girl. Marie. Thirty-two years old, both of them. They had a son, Danny. Three years old. From what the team could work out, he probably watched them die. We never found him.'

A new picture on the screen. A house in the middle-class suburb of Parioli, an area Costa recognized. Then interior shots: an elegant living room, the walls covered with blood. It looked like an abattoir, worse than any murder scene he'd ever witnessed.

'It was a weekend. The Frascas were due to attend an embassy social function. Partway through that there was a message.'

'What do the numbers mean?' Costa asked.

The American glanced at Palombo. The Italian officer came in and said, 'We never understood until it was too late. II. I. LXIII. Two. One. Sixty-three.' He shrugged. 'We thought it was a reference to the Bible, not that we could make that work. It didn't seem that important in the end. It wasn't . . .'

Sordi scowled.

'Others made the connection for you,' the president interrupted. 'These are act, scene and line numbers from *Julius Caesar*, the Shakespeare play. I reminded myself of them before this meeting.'

He glanced at the ceiling, then recited, in a sonorous tone:

> *'Between the acting of a dreadful thing*
> *And the first motion, all the interim is*
> *Like a phantasm, or a hideous dream:*
> *The genius and the mortal instruments*
> *Are then in council; and the state of man,*
> *Like to a little kingdom, suffers then*
> *The nature of an insurrection.'*

The president's old, cultured voice echoed around the vast hall.

' "We shall be called purgers, not murderers," ' the American murmured, in what Costa took to be another quotation from the play.

'They were murderers,' Sordi grumbled. 'Nothing else. Killers delivering a promise of what was to come. A warning that we would spend a little time in shock and then wake up to the truth: a bloody insurrection in our midst, one started by these monsters.' His eyes didn't leave them. 'We believed we'd missed the last part.'

A series of mugshots appeared, two youths, a girl, none of them much more than twenty. Happy, smiling, bright-eyed for the camera.

Rennick picked up the narrative.

'Students from the University of Viterbo, working at the Villa Giulia as part of their Etruscan studies course. From what your people put together afterwards, they got hypnotized by their course leader, some junior academic, Andrea Petrakis. Born in Tarquinia, in the Maremma, to Greek parents who'd lived in the area for a decade or so. He was twenty-two years old when this happened. Something of a prodigy. Finished his university degree when he was seventeen. Seemed set to become an expert on Etruscan matters. Then . . .' Rennick grimaced. 'The Etruscans originated from Greece. Perhaps Petrakis felt some bond with them. He seized upon their fate as a way of explaining how he felt about Italy at that time. Petrakis was very reticent for one who seems to have made such an impression on those around him. We have no background, no record of real relationships, except with those in his group. No girlfriends, boy-friends, nothing. His parents didn't mix much, either. A reclusive family. All we have is this.'

It was a blurry photograph of an unsmiling young man with long, dark wavy hair. He was gazing into the camera with a fixed, aggres-sive expression, very much in control, standing next to the girl from the earlier photograph. A pretty kid, she was staring at him with an expression that might have been adoration. Or, perhaps, condescen-sion. It was difficult to tell.

'One picture,' Rennick went on. 'They worshipped him for some reason. Maybe politics.'

'What kind of politics?' Costa asked.

'The politics of lunacy,' Campagnolo burst in. 'These people from the Seventies. All of them. Left, right . . . they were insane. We spent twenty years burying these madmen. Why are they back now?'

Campagnolo pointed a finger at Sordi.

'You take the risk here, Dario. On your head be it. You steal from me my power. My right.'

'Only for a few days,' the president replied carefully. 'In line with the constitution . . .'

'I am the elected leader of this country,' the prime minister roared. 'They voted for me, old man. Not you.'

'The constitution—'

'Screw the constitution!' His dark, beady eyes roved the room. 'I have a long memory. Do not forget. Sordi cannot maintain this position for long. If any misfortune should happen, I shall ensure the blame goes where it should.'

'Ugo,' Sordi pleaded. 'It's important you understand this situation.'

The prime minister stiffened with disdain.

'I do not need to understand that which I cannot control. Send me a memo.'

Then he got up, cast his eyes around the room and marched out, the same way he'd entered.

'I apologize for that little scene,' Sordi said when the man was gone. 'Palombo. Brief the prime minister in person, afterwards.'

Costa had barely noticed. He was still trying to understand what they'd been told.

'What did the Blue Demon want?' he asked.

'Revolution?' Rennick guessed. 'A Marxist state? A fascist one? We don't know, any more than we understand why they should name themselves after some strange Etruscan devil. They kidnapped the Frascas, killed them, and then a few days later . . .'

He touched the computer keyboard.

'See for yourself.'

Another photo. Black and white. A remote, ramshackle two-storey house in a bleak field. Carabinieri cars parked in the rough drive. Officers standing around looking lost and miserable.

Palombo took over.

'Five days after the Frascas were found dead, the Carabinieri got a phone call from someone at the Villa Giulia suggesting Petrakis was involved. The staff there hadn't liked him. He hung around when he wasn't wanted. They'd found him in the museum after hours.' He grimaced. 'Rome sent two officers to the parents' house. Both of them were dead, shot in bed. A good week before the Frascas. The couple were such recluses that no one knew, except Andrea, I guess.'

More photographs that seemed to be from the same landscape. A tiny shack in an uncultivated field strewn with tall weeds.

'They found material in the house that led them to an abandoned farm the parents owned two kilometres away. No road. No electricity. They weren't expecting anything. There was a local *carabiniere* with them to help.'

Costa could recall the story from later reconstructions on TV crime shows. These same pictures were emblazoned across the front pages. One dead officer. Three supposed extremists killed. The loss of the *carabiniere* was a national tragedy, a moment when the country's heart skipped a beat, waiting to see if the nightmare of urban terror was about to return.

Palombo clicked the keyboard and brought up a picture of a small arsenal scattered around a grubby stone floor: automatic rifles, revolvers, small handguns.

'These kids started shooting the moment they knew they were cornered. The local officer went down almost immediately. After that they turned their guns on themselves. They were all as high as kites. The place was full of drugs. LSD. Speed. Dope. Pure Afghan opium most of all – so much Petrakis had to be dealing in it.'

The photographs changed to one shot inside the house. Three bloodied corpses, faces to the ground, arms outstretched. The pretty girl wasn't pretty any more. She had a revolver in her right hand.

'Nadia Ambrosini,' the Italian security man said. 'The daughter of a bank manager from Treviso. The ones from a middle-class background are always the worst. She shot the other two, then turned the gun on herself.'

Then one final image.

It was a poster on the wall of the shack, above the contorted corpse of one of the girls: a lithe and naked devil with a pale blue face wearing an expression of pure hatred, his muscular arms outstretched, a writhing snake, fangs exposed in each hand. Blood dripped from his sharp, spiky teeth. An enormous and unreal erection, more that of a beast than a man, rose from his loins. The photograph of Andrea Petrakis they saw earlier was stuck to the paper with tape, as if identifying him with the monster.

Below, as if a caption, were the words, scrawled maniacally in tall capital letters, *IL DEMONE AZZURRO*.

The Blue Demon.

- 6 -

Peroni listened to the Quirinale campanile start to chime the quarter-hour. The house was midway down the hill, next to a small restaurant with tables on the narrow pavement. The ground-floor windows were cloudy with dust, as if the place had been empty for years.

Mirko Oliva walked up, scrabbled at the glass with his elbow and peered inside.

'This is no one's home,' the young officer declared. 'It's a mess in there. Looks like they had the builders once upon a time.'

There were just two nameplates on the door. One was for a marquetry business, an enterprise Peroni felt sure had long departed, judging by the faded card and some newspaper clippings in the window praising the quality of its work. On the bell above was a single word in scrawled handwriting: Johnson.

Oliva peered at it. He glanced at them, serious suddenly.

'Wasn't there somebody famous called Moro too?'

'Once upon a time,' Peroni answered patiently.

'Well, if the Moro who called said he lived on the ground floor, he was lying.'

It was a three-storey building. Peroni strode into the road to get a better view of the upper floors. The windows on each level looked much the same as those below: old, grimy and opaque. Except the pair at the top.

He walked to the pavement opposite to make sure. Both sets of panes had been thrown wide open. There was something else odd. Rosa came to stand next to him.

'What's that?' she asked, staring upwards.

A black swarm of insects was moving in and out of the

window. A cloud of tiny bodies buzzing angrily, as if fighting over something.

'Flies,' Peroni murmured, then looked across the street.

The young *agente* was grinning at him. His finger was prodding at the old red paint on the door and finding little in the way of resistance. Beyond it, Peroni could just make out a dark, bare hallway.

Open, Mirko Oliva mouthed.

Peroni walked back, pushed the door further and was greeted by the damp, fusty smell of rotting walls and bad drains. His fist stayed on both bell pushes as he edged into the property. There wasn't a sound anywhere.

He caught sight of Oliva with Rosa Prabakaran behind him. Her hand was already close to her jacket, feeling for the weapon there, just to make sure, the way any half-experienced officer did these days.

'I'm sure this is nothing at all,' Peroni told them. 'I go first, all the same.'

Mirko Oliva looked a little surprised.

'Shouldn't we tell the control room before we go in?'

'I was about to say that,' Peroni lied.

Oliva pulled out his secure police phone.

'What's this street called again?' he asked.

'It's the Via Rasella,' Rosa Prabakaran said immediately.

The name jogged some distant memory, but for the life of him he couldn't remember what it was.

The interior stank of something worse than bad drains. Rats, he guessed. Dead ones. Peroni walked to the half-open door of the first downstairs room, gun in right hand. No one had been in this part of the building in years. Old machinery, half-finished chairs and the skeleton of a table stood gathering dust. Oliva was at his shoulder, peering round inquisitively. Peroni took one step into the room, placed his large right foot into the grime on the floor, then dragged it backwards. The effort left a long, sweeping mark on the boards.

Oliva smiled and tipped an imaginary cap. Point taken. Rosa watched them both, as if she were in the company of children.

'We're wasting time,' she complained.

'You mean in the house?' Peroni asked. 'Or checking out the ground floor first?'

'Both, probably.'

She was a bad-tempered piece of work at times.

'If someone's still here,' he said patiently, 'they won't be hiding where we think. Now will they?'

'If . . .'

Enough, Peroni thought, and walked on with Mirko Oliva by his side, checking out the other three rooms on the floor. Two were as barren as the first. The last was locked and looked as if it had been that way for years.

It was just one call among many, Peroni reminded himself. All the same, he did something he hadn't done in years. In the absence of a key, he kicked hard at the door. The thing fell in on itself. In the dust and cobwebs lay a very old and very dirty toilet.

Rosa clapped her hands to a slow, sarcastic rhythm.

The first floor was more promising. There were marks in the dust in the main room.

'Squatters,' she declared, coming back with some rubbish from the kitchen: an empty bag from a local bread shop, a discarded tin of tuna.

'Why'd they leave?' Oliva asked.

There was an impatient scowl on her dark face.

'That kind never stay anywhere more than a week. They know we can arrest them if they hang around too long. Can't we get this over and done with, Peroni? We've six more calls to make after this one.'

'Carelessness is a privilege of youth,' he announced. 'If we need prints off anything you've handled, forensic will call you many unpleasant names, Officer, and deservedly so.'

She took the point about the potential evidence and dumped it on the floorboards.

He stepped up the dusty, creaking bare steps leading to the storey above. Three officers, two of them young, one a rank junior, the other not as smart as she sometimes thought. The old cop checked himself. He was getting jittery in his dotage.

The odd smell that was just discernible when they entered the ground floor was becoming stronger. He glanced back and waved them to a standstill. Rosa was second, naturally, right behind him, setting out her rank above Mirko Oliva.

Peroni stood there, puzzled by the pungent, resinous odour. It reminded him of hippies and foreigners.

Then Rosa tugged at his arm and mouthed the word he was hunting for.

Incense.

Joss sticks. The talismanic odour of freaks and squatters. Dead-beats from all over the world, breaking into empty houses, staying a week and then moving on. There were so many around the police never bothered much any more. Except when they got in the way.

He tried to extinguish the angry fire that was beginning to burn in his head. They were supposed to be looking for a family man who'd been kidnapped by murderous terrorists, not wasting their time on minutiae like this.

'*Polizia!*' Peroni bellowed and stormed up the remaining few steps, to find himself in a hot, stuffy room that stank of something physical. There was nothing in it but a cheap wooden dining table and a few chairs. And a man, who was seated, back to the door, head slumped forwards, like someone who had fallen asleep while eating.

Flies, too. He'd forgotten about the flies. They buzzed in and out of the windows in a black cloud, focusing on the figure at the table, hesitantly, as if there was something there they didn't under-stand either.

He kept the gun in front of him. The stench of the incense returned, renewed somehow. It seemed to be coming from a pool of darkness in the corner, where the sunlight streaming through the open windows couldn't reach.

'*Polizia,*' Peroni said more quietly, and started to work his way around to the front of the hunched form, a man of middle age, he guessed, wearing a dark suit.

'Boss,' Mirko Oliva said quietly.

'What?'

'He's not moving.'

Peroni understood that. Understood too that, though he could only see the back of this figure in a dark, crumpled business suit, it was Giovanni Batisti, huddled over the table, face in his arms.

On the wall behind someone had stuck up a poster, one so big that it looked as if it ought to have come out of one of the tourist shops around the corner near the Trevi Fountain, where you could pick up Raphael or Caravaggio, Da Vinci or some modern junk, for next to nothing.

He leaned forward, placed a gentle hand on the shoulder of the man at the table, and said, more out of hope than anything else, '*Signore.*'

No sound, no stirring, not a sign of breath, a hint of life.

He swore to himself and looked at the poster again. It was a blown-up photograph, the kind of over-imaginative thing you got in squats and communes. An ancient scrawl, like paint on plaster, depicting an evil-looking devil, teeth bared, eyes on fire, snakes writhing in his fists, skin painted a faded blue.

So many faint, unconnected memories were fighting for his attention at that moment. The knowledge that the Via Rasella meant something in itself, and this hideous picture on the wall.

Letters, Roman numerals, had been scrawled – in blood, surely – next to the vile creature's head.

III. I. CCLXIII.

Mirko Oliva swept his hand through the cloud of flies in front of him, then stooped down to tap the still, prone man at the table, getting there before either Peroni or Rosa could stop him.

What came next seemed obvious, inevitable. He touched Giovanni Batisti on the shoulder, gripped him, shook him. The politician's body lurched forward under the attention. A buzzing, billowing mass of insects rose from inside the fabric.

The junior officer said something inaudible, put his hand to his mouth and dashed for the open window. Rosa was calling for backup, forensics, everything she could think of. Her voice sounded harsh and brittle and frightened in the airless room where the only other sounds were the buzzing of flies and the distant muffled hum of traffic from the tunnel beneath the Quirinale.

'I'm too old for this,' Peroni muttered, and found he couldn't stop himself thinking about the picture on the wall.

Oliva was still retching out of the open window, heaving up his lunch into the street below.

'Get away from there,' Peroni yelled, angry all of a sudden.

From the dark corner opposite there emerged another young man, this one almost naked, his face painted blue, like the demon in the poster, his eyes wild with fear and anguish.

Words Peroni didn't recognize were coming out of his throat. In his left hand he held a bloodied dagger. In his right two joss sticks burned, their smoke curling upwards to the ceiling, through the swarming host of insects.

– 7 –

Palombo turned off the computer screen.

'The same night Andrea Petrakis's acolytes died in Tarquinia, five days after the murder of the Frascas, a witness saw a small motorboat being stolen from Porto Ercole thirty minutes north by car. A young man and possibly someone else were on board. The theory was that Petrakis tried to reach Corsica with the Frasca child as some kind of hostage. He was an experienced sailor. The parents owned a boat. He had a student pilot licence as well. He understood navigation, the weather. We never heard from him again, until now.'

'I remember something about a parliamentary commission,' Costa said. 'My father was a member.' He looked at Sordi. 'So were you, sir.'

The president nodded.

'So I was. Parliament wanted to know whether this was yet one more political terrorist group to worry about, or simply something bizarre. Something inexplicable.'

'And?' Falcone persisted, when the man said no more.

'The consensus we reached, with which Marco Costa disagreed, as was his habit, determined that Andrea Petrakis was a fantasist heading his own strange cult, one he named after this image he found in a tomb in the Maremma. The Blue Demon amounted to nothing more than the man himself and his three dead followers. Petrakis managed to make these young people murderous through drugs and any other means he could find. Perhaps his parents found out and he killed them. That was as far as we got.'

'Until now,' Rennick interrupted, tapping the laptop's keyboard, bringing the picture back to life. A map appeared. Southern Afghanistan, Helmand province.

The American indicated an area on the screen using a laser pointer.

'What you're looking at is British-managed territory near the Afghan-Pakistan border. The most unstable sector in the region, which is saying something. It's got everything. Ordinary decent people. Opium farmers. Bandits, Taleban, al-Qaeda. Cheek by jowl, indivisible, inseparable. Three weeks ago one of our teams carried out a raid on a suspect house. We found all kinds of material relating to Rome. Maps. Satellite images. Details of water and transport systems. Documents on the Quirinale hill more than anything else. They began collecting material on 13 February this year. The very day Prime Minister Campagnolo announced the G8 summit would take place here. Intelligence finally came up with this . . .'

He punched up a fuzzy photograph of a clean-shaven man in Western dress. His hair was long and grey, dirty, wavy. He was wearing sunglasses and peering in the direction of the camera, as if suspicious.

'Everything referred to an operation that was code-named *Il Demone Azzurro*. We've never encountered any kind of document in Italian in situations like this before. It took a while before we were able to make the connections. Then we got a DNA match from the house. There was still physical evidence on file from his parents. It's Andrea Petrakis. No doubt about it.'

Falcone scratched his silver goatee and looked decidedly unimpressed.

'You're saying a student wanted for murder twenty years ago fled the country and ended up working with Islamic terrorists in Afghanistan?' He sounded incredulous. 'Why?'

'His motives are irrelevant at this point,' Palombo cut in. 'Four men and one woman were spirited from Helmand into northern Pakistan in March. We have reason to believe that Petrakis is leader. In April they reached Turkey. After that we lost them, until last night.'

'If you'd shared this information with us before,' Commissario

Esposito complained, 'we might have been alert to the threat. Giovanni Batisti. That poor woman . . .'

'Batisti knew he was supposed to be careful,' the ministry official responded without emotion. 'There was nothing sufficiently concrete to warrant anything more than a heightened alert. I'm sorry, Commissario. What would you have done? What could any of us have achieved in the face of such a generalized and vague threat?'

'We can't possibly know, can we?' Falcone demanded.

'If the combined forces of the Italian and American security agencies were powerless, Inspector,' Palombo replied icily, 'I fail to see how the state police might have made a difference. The plain fact is that the Blue Demon is back with us in the shape of Andrea Petrakis. The security arrangements which were communicated to you previously have clearly been compromised. From this moment on we start afresh. In a few hours we begin building a physical ring of steel around the Quirinale Palace. A fence five metres high around the perimeter. No one comes in without accreditation. Fiumicino and Ciampino airports will close until the summit is over. No traffic will move in any of the nearby roads. We have been in touch with the Vatican authorities as a matter of routine. All public buildings, including St Peter's, will close to visitors as of this evening, until the emergency is over.'

The displeasure on Dario Sordi's face was plain.

'We'll have snipers on rooftops,' Palombo continued. 'Armed officers in every part of the city from which some kind of attack – by mortar, by rifle, by chemical or any other means – might be launched. The immediate area outside the exclusion zone will be patrolled constantly, with spot checks on anyone in the vicinity.'

'This is a city of two and a half million people,' Falcone objected. 'You can't shut them out of the place they live.'

'What choice do we have?' Palombo began.

'We?' the inspector demanded. 'Who exactly is "we"?'

'For the most part, the elite services will be in charge. Carabinieri units. Special forces. You are to be the visible presence. Your hands will be full with traffic, crowd control, the rest . . .'

Esposito shook his head.

'Don't you see how the public will interpret this?'

'Tell me,' Palombo demanded.

'They will think you're erecting special protection for the summit. A degree of security that is not afforded to the ordinary citizens of Rome!'

'This is a security exercise. We leave the public relations to you. Our job is to defend the Quirinale.' His hand pointed towards the long, elegant windows at the edge of the room. 'Beyond that wire . . .'

The atmosphere in the grand hall went down a few degrees. There was silence until Dario Sordi observed, 'I sympathize with our friends in the police, I must say. This is a disgrace. Campagnolo knew the risks when he chose to invite the world and its dog here, not some place in the country where all these great men could have talked day and night and heard nothing but the birds outside the window. I didn't even know until the decision was made.' He frowned. 'But . . .'

Those wide arms, thrown open in despair again.

'We must live with what we have. This is one reason why I am taking control. I never thought I would see fences erected around this place in order to keep out the ordinary citizens to whom it belongs. As Palombo says, there is no alternative. We must be swift, efficient and . . . careful.' He shook his head. 'I want no more casualties. Perhaps that is already wishful thinking. If so, let poor Batisti be the last.'

The three police officers on the other side of the table sat mute for a moment.

'You brought us here to tell us we're crowd control and a brick wall against which the public may vent its fury?' Falcone asked.

'We summoned you so that you might be fully informed,' Palombo responded without emotion.

'A young woman was murdered on the streets of Rome last night,' Costa pointed out. 'That's a crime. Our crime.'

'It's a crime indeed,' he agreed. 'And it will be investigated.

By the Carabinieri. No arguments, please.' He waved his hand around the room. 'If the Blue Demon should succeed in penetrating this place, can you imagine what damage they might do?'

'Palombo speaks the truth,' Dario Sordi said emphatically. 'These leaders are our guests. Their security is our first duty. In this room . . .' His eyes fell to the paintings on the walls: portraits of foreigners, ambassadors, from the Far East and Arabia, Africa and beyond, all in the dress of the seventeenth century, looking down on proceedings as if amused and interested observers still. '. . . will sit the men who rule the world. If we fail them, we fail those they represent. And ourselves.'

The president gazed at them.

'I do not expect you to like what you've heard. These are difficult and dangerous times. Every one of us knows our details are on Batisti's computer. My address is well known. Our colleagues, our friends from other nations . . .' Sordi shrugged and there was a trace of a smile on his exaggerated face. 'For me, it's odd to be under a death sentence again. The last was more than sixty years ago and came from the Germans, a race with whom I now dine, with all good grace and gratitude, as fellow European citizens I respect and admire.' His finger stabbed the table. 'We can defeat this madness if we work together.'

It was a short, self-deprecating speech, and the rare mention of Sordi's distant past was enough to silence them all.

'Good,' he announced. 'Then I will leave you to your work. Nic?'

'Sir . . . ?'

'I was abroad for your father's funeral. I've never felt happy about that. Let me make some small amends now. Will you join me outside in the garden for a moment?'

Their eyes were on him, those of his colleagues, and of Palombo and the grey intelligence man from America. None expected this. None quite understood, any more than Costa himself.

– 8 –

'Get away from the window, Mirko,' Peroni ordered again, keeping his weapon trained on the strange creature that had emerged from the shadows. 'Rosa?'

'Back-up's coming,' she said. Peroni stole a glance to his right. She had her gun on the semi-naked young man who was staring at them in silence from across the room, knife in one hand, joss sticks in the other.

He wasn't yet fully in the sun streaming from the window. Still, they could see something on his chest, a red, dappled stain. Blood, overlaying the blue dye there. Lots of it, and not his own.

'Put down the knife,' Peroni ordered.

The boy's head moved from side to side as if he were trying to comprehend.

Mirko Oliva had moved next to the older officer, his weapon up too.

'Put down the knife!' the young officer barked.

Nothing. Just the head, turning from side to side, and a look in the eye, one that said . . . *not quite right.*

'Who are you?' Peroni asked.

'I don't think he understands what you're saying,' Rosa said. 'Listen . . .'

The young man was mumbling to himself, a constant, low drone of words. None of them recognizable.

'What language is that?'

'Drop the knife!' Oliva screamed, in English this time.

A baffled look, fearful. The blade twitched in his shaking hand.

'If he can't understand us, Mirko,' Peroni muttered, 'shouting doesn't really help. Here's an idea. Let's stop waving our guns around, shall we? It's making me nervous now. All the kid has is a knife.'

'He's used it, boss,' the young officer said.

'So it would appear,' Peroni observed, and let his own weapon fall to his side, loose in his grip, then gave them the look. Rosa scowled and did the same. Oliva was the last.

The blue-painted youth shook his long, golden hair, watching them. The knife descended slowly and came to rest next to his hip.

Peroni was a father himself, used to dealing with the young, to judging their moods, recognizing their fears and uncertainties. There was something very simple and child-like about this troubled individual. As if he'd spent his entire life in fear and servitude, cowering, waiting to be told what to do, what act to perform, always seeking approval, guidance. The bright, darting eyes, constantly looking for someone, some form of comfort, spoke of dependence. Captivity even.

Out of interest, Peroni relaxed his fingers and let the service revolver slip from his grip and clatter noisily onto the floor.

He smiled, then extended his big, fleshy fist into the stab of sunlight falling through the windows and the cloud of black-winged insects swirling angrily there.

'*Mi chiamo Gianni*,' he said slowly, with confidence. Then again, in English, 'My name is Gianni. *Come ti chiami?* What's your name?'

A look of bafflement, a little less fear. The painted figure with the bloodied chest stared at Peroni's huge hand, open towards him in a gesture that was more universal than plain language. He placed the knife carefully on the table across from Giovanni Batisti's body, wiped his dirty, leathery fingers on his naked thighs, then stretched them tentatively into the dazzling shaft of yellow sunlight in the centre of the room.

He was saying something too, not mumbling this time. It was clear and utterly incomprehensible.

Rosa was making a noise. Peroni took his attention away from the figure in front of him for a moment and asked, 'What?'

'My dad's got a friend who talks like that.'

The day got stranger. Now he was more in the light, it was clear the youth's hair was an almost artificial shade of blond. Beneath the grime and the wrinkles of a harsh life he was European, surely.

'You're telling me he's talking Indian?'

'There's no such language as Indian,' she replied drily. 'He's not talking Hindi anyway.'

The young policewoman said something else and it struck a chord. A light went on in his eyes. The golden boy began babbling. She waved him down.

'I can barely speak that myself,' Rosa said. 'More than a few phrases anyway. It's Pashto. From Pakistan. Afghanistan. And so is he.'

The three cops looked at one other.

'Add an interpreter to the list,' Peroni ordered. 'Can you ask him anything?'

'I can ask his name.'

'Do it.'

She took one step forward until she was almost in the beam of golden light streaming through the window and pronounced, very slowly, very clearly, '*Sta noom tse dai?*'

The joss sticks fell from his hands. He smiled: white teeth, marked with decay, but there was something handsome, something fetching about him anyway.

'*Sta noom tse dai?*' Rosa repeated, holding out her hand this time, smiling too.

The others would be here soon, Peroni thought. An interpreter among them. They could clean up this mess, bring in Teresa and forensic, start on the long, detailed process demanded for homicide cases – one that would, he understood, result in this strange, damaged individual being charged with Giovanni Batisti's murder, probably before the night was out.

Something still troubled him.

The painted figure finally stepped closer to the sun. This close the blue dye was vivid, on his face and upper chest, and the blood was everywhere, on his hands, his torso . . .

What made it worse was the smile. He was grinning, happy, ecstatic.

A word escaped his lips. Peroni shook his head and asked, 'What?'

'Danny,' the creature repeated, with a triumphant joy, as if this were some rare privilege. 'Danny.'

He lifted his reddened arms to the ceiling.

'*Danny, Danny, Danny . . .*'

The picture on the wall behind him caught Peroni's eye again and he stared at the long, careful letters beside it, two hands high.

He doubted this strange, crazed individual dancing into the sunlight could read or write at all.

Least of all in a strange, dusty room in the Via Rasella in a country that was surely foreign to him.

Peroni blinked, half-remembering something about the street name.

The place had a reputation, a curse, one that went back to another bloody scene, another massacre, more than half a century earlier.

Perhaps that, unconsciously, was why he'd ordered Mirko Oliva to keep away from the window, and he'd never even realized.

The old cop glanced outside.

He could see a single dark shape in a room in the house opposite. A man was there, his face in shadow, with something black and deadly in his arms, aimed in their direction.

– 9 –

The palace gardens seemed to stretch forever, a sprawling formal park of geometric paths running through vast lawns, ornate flower beds and cool, dark groves of lush trees. It was hard to imagine the city beyond the high perimeter walls. Even the traffic noise seemed subdued on this high green plateau above the bustling heart of Rome.

'What do you think our friends are saying back there?' Sordi asked as they strolled away from the building behind.

'I've no idea, sir.'

'Please, Nic. You were one week old when I first saw you. There was a time – you were very young, I'll admit – when I was Uncle Dario. You won't recall . . .'

But something did come back, and it made Costa smile.

'I remember a very tall, very friendly and generous man, who brought me presents. He enjoyed . . .' it was impossible not to say this, '. . . pulling faces.'

Sordi laughed and stretched his long features into a comical expression, the kind an adult would use to amuse a child.

'When you look like this, you might as well use it. Your father didn't call me the bloodhound for nothing. Don't worry. I've had to put up with a lot worse in my time.'

He sat down on a stone bench beneath a wicker canopy covered in roses, beckoning Costa to join him. A classical statue of an athlete, fastening his sandals against a rock, stood next to this shady spot.

Sordi gazed at the figure's handsome young features.

'This is my friend Hermes. A copy, of course. The original was found at Hadrian's villa at Tivoli. He's the protector of travellers, an important fellow. Look . . .' He drew Costa's attention to the sandals. Two perfect, tiny wings projected from the sides of both. 'That's how we know he's a god. He's a good listener, Hermes.'

A pair of *corazzieri* in blue uniforms watched from the palace steps. Sordi pulled out a packet of cigarettes and lit one. His fingers were stained by decades of tobacco. The two that held the cigarette were the colour of old leather.

'Faithful, loyal servants of the state, every one of them,' the president observed, glancing at the officers. 'I don't imagine anyone can hear us. Inside those walls . . .' His long features fell into a frown, his voice to a growl. 'Every damned word in that place gets picked up by someone. I assume we may talk freely here. I have to.' His grey eyes stared at Costa. 'As you may have gathered, Ugo Campagnolo is not best pleased that I have intervened in this way. Were it practical, he would be in the courts right now trying to fight me to the last.'

'Why doesn't he?'

'He's an actor at heart, and actors always have a good sense of timing. It would take days to mount a challenge, and by then the summit would be over, his guests long gone, his moment on the world stage ruined by petulance. Campagnolo would risk everything if he went public with his displeasure, and he knows it. The man's no fool. Now he has money, friends in the media, so many politicians in his grasp . . .'

Costa remained silent.

'I'm sorry,' Sordi apologized. 'I should not say such things to a serving police officer, for whom politics have no interest. But understand this . . .' He nodded back towards the palace. 'You and your colleagues are the only ones with any sense of independence to pass through that room today. The rest, the foreigners, Palombo – they're Campagnolo's. It's only understandable. I can take control for the duration of this emergency, no longer. They will have to deal with him when he has his hands on the reins of state once more. I don't blame them for taking sides, any more than I would you, if you felt the same way.'

'I detest the man,' Costa said without thinking. 'He's made Italy a laughing stock.'

Sordi glanced at the Quirinale again and raised his eyebrows.

'Careful, Nic. Even gardens may have ears. I take tea here, you know. Every evening. A habit I learned from a friend in London. Earl Grey tea, made with good Calabrian bergamot, and a very special kind of English biscuit of which I'm fond. First sip when *Il Torrino* chimes six-thirty, at which point I pinch myself and continue to try to understand why the son of a labourer from Testaccio is sitting here, at the summit of the *caput mundi*. Old men live by habits, you know. It's all we have left. You should indulge me with a visit some time.'

Costa looked around at the manicured gardens, empty save for a workman tending to some shrubs near the northern wall. The Quirinale was a showcase for the state. The real work of government took place elsewhere, leaving the palace to Sordi and his guards.

'Why did you do it?' he asked. 'Why couldn't you work with him, instead of seizing control?'

'I was within my rights . . .'

'I don't doubt that, sir. But why?'

Sordi's arm fell on his, and it felt familiar.

'For pity's sake call me Dario. I spent the first third of my life a communist and the remainder a socialist. These formalities are enough to send a man insane. Not from you, of all people, please.'

'I don't understand.'

The president couldn't take his eyes off the palace. Palombo had come out onto the steps, with the American. Some other men too. Then Campagnolo came to join them, staring out into the garden, in their direction.

'Nor do I,' Sordi answered softly. 'Or anyone outside the circle of Andrea Petrakis perhaps. You still live in that beautiful house near the Via Appia Antica. I know. I had someone check. Are you there tonight? Alone?'

'Whenever I finish . . .'

'Be home by ten. Whatever happens. This would be a good time to be a criminal in Rome, don't you think? Every law-enforcement officer in the city seems to be chasing ghosts.'

Sordi turned so that his back was towards the palace, then spoke directly and rapidly, in a low, calm voice.

'The captain of the Corazzieri here is called Fabio Ranieri. Remember that name. He's a fine officer and a decent human being. I know the regiment are technically Carabinieri, but you can trust them. Their loyalties, at least, I do not doubt. If you need to come to me for anything, you do it through Ranieri and him alone.'

He stood up, looked around the grounds, smiled very visibly, the way that politicians did when they knew they were being watched, and shook Costa firmly by the hand.

'Your father was a great friend of mine and an honest and frank colleague in the shameful world of politics,' the president said in a firm, loud voice. Then, turning again, in a whisper he added, 'Ranieri and I shall visit you, with two men he trusts. Ten o'clock. Be there, Nic. I need friends about me now.'

'Of course . . .'

He stopped. Sordi's pallid face had lost what little blood it seemed to possess. A noise was rising from somewhere beyond the walls, down the hill, past the narrow streets clinging to the lee of the Quirinale, tumbling towards the Trevi Fountain.

It was the distant clockwork rattle of a machine gun, and he could tell from Dario Sordi's face that it was a sound the man had heard before.

– 10 –

Danny, Danny, Danny . . .

The golden boy had skipped forward into the sunlight, like some long-lost god newly sprung to life.

With that a thunderous noise filled the room, and Peroni found himself screaming over it, bellowing at the two cops with him to get down on the floor, out of reach of the deadly, shattering eye of the window.

A deafening racket shook the building. He watched a line of dust devils burst out of the ancient walls behind them, cutting through everything as the tracer line of bullets bit into the brickwork.

Rosa was on the bare timber boards already. Mirko Oliva had begun messing with his gun, looking ready to race back to the front of the room. Peroni caught him with his hand as the young officer began to move, punched him hard in the shoulder, then shoved him face first down to the floor, letting momentum do the rest.

He was still grappling with Mirko when they hit the ground so hard it made his old bones jar with the pain.

'I don't want a dead hero on my hands,' the old cop grunted, pointing a fat finger in the trainee's face.

That sentence came out without interruption. The gunfire had halted. Rosa, sensibly, was sliding backwards to the door, phone in hand, chanting a quiet demand to whoever was on the other end.

'Boss . . .'

'Quiet, Mirko,' Peroni told him, trying to think.

The figure above them was talking in his strange, foreign voice, and Peroni couldn't dispel the thought: this was not a man; it was a child, weak, defenceless, scared, baffled, exposed in the bright shaft of golden sun.

A child covered in blue paint and stained with the blood of the man he'd just slaughtered.

'Peroni . . .'

There was a note in Rosa's low cry.

He jerked his finger back towards the door and made sure Oliva saw too. Then he looked up.

The boy was wavering in the beam of light, arms outstretched, face a picture of tortured agony, standing in front of the table where Giovanni Batisti's body lay torn and bloody against the old, bare wood, something outside of him that was meant to be in.

Peroni couldn't see through the window. Maybe the gunman had gone. Maybe not. The golden boy belonged to him, to them. He had to. Was that why the man on the other side of the street relaxed his finger on the trigger, ceased spitting hot shells across the brief width of the Via Rasella in their direction?

'Get down,' Peroni called to the strange, upright creature in the sunlight, gesturing to the floor with his hands, hoping that would be enough.

He felt confused trying to weigh up the options. One thing, above all, seemed clear and significant.

They had left the golden boy behind. That said everything.

Those lost eyes, straying behind the sweaty, grimy blond curls, stayed on the window. Still, he kept murmuring, 'Danny . . . Danny . . .'

Not moving a centimetre, arms stretched out like some cheap Jesus from an Easter street procession.

'I don't have the words any more,' Peroni murmured, and knew he had to finish this.

He shuffled up to a half-crouch and wondered how strong the youth was, how easy it might be to drag him out of the target zone, back behind the relative safety of the antiquated building's crumbling brickwork.

'Don't you even dare, Peroni!' the young policewoman shrieked, with such force and vehemence he had to turn and look.

She was in the doorway in front of Mirko Oliva, her foot almost in his face, as if she were ready to kick him back into place if need be.

'Stay there,' Peroni ordered, wondering why he was taking instructions from some twenty-something female cop.

He was half on his feet when she fell on him, at a moment when his bulk was teetering off balance.

It was this, he thought later, that saved them both.

They fell, tumbling, back to the ground, and the roar of the gun was on them before they even touched the floor. Peroni grabbed her slender body and tugged and pushed the two of them across the bare, splintering boards to the far side of the room, close to the front wall, finding the dark corner, a place that offered some kind of respite because it was clear, once they got there, where the slew of bullets racking the room was aimed: through the window, directly at the only thing that was in the light.

Danny . . . Danny . . .

It sounded like a plea, sounded shocked and scared and angry.

His tall, tanned body was caught in the ripple of fire, jerking like a puppet on a string, livid wounds opening up in his bare, stained flesh.

Danny . . . Danny . . .

Mirko Oliva couldn't take it any more. He scrambled to the window, got out his gun, held it high above his head, pointing into the street, and fired off every round he had, shooting blind out into the gap.

Peroni closed his eyes, praying no one in the adjoining buildings had walked into that.

Then he waited, keeping Rosa in place with an arm, not that she needed it. He found himself looking into her brown, deep eyes, perhaps because he didn't want to see what lay in the heart of the room at that moment. She was, it seemed to him, a very smart, very private woman, one he was glad to have around, even if sometimes her presence made life deeply awkward and uncomfortable.

'Thanks,' he said, with the slightest of nods.

She didn't say anything, just scowled, but not at him this time; at

Oliva, who was trying to reload his weapon beneath the window, but was shaking so much the new shells were scattering over the floor.

'Mirko,' Peroni called to him. '*Mirko?*'

'Boss?'

The young officer's eyes were bright with shock and fear.

'It's gone quiet, son. You should notice these things.'

Dead quiet, until that nearby bell tolled again, and Peroni remembered what they called the campanile on the Quirinale Palace. *Il Torrino.*

'S-s-sorry . . .' Oliva stuttered.

'It's OK,' Peroni told him. 'Just stay still. There's nothing . . .'

Outside he heard the sound of shouting followed by the revving of motorbike engines.

He glanced at Rosa and said, 'You too.'

Before she could object he'd scrambled across the floor to the window ledge and managed to peek out over it.

'Gianni!' she yelled at him.

Mirko Oliva was beneath the frame, staring back into the room, shaking, face pale, looking ready to throw up again.

'No problem,' Peroni said, getting to his feet. 'We're too high up, and the street's too narrow.'

He clambered to his feet, got to the window and leaned out as far as he dared.

The noise of two powerful motorbikes echoed off the walls, heading down towards the Trevi Fountain and the tunnel beneath the hill. He still couldn't see the street, but at least there was something to pass on to Traffic and the CCTV people.

'Mirko . . . ?'

The young officer got up, leaned over the open window frame and began to heave out of it again, into the hot, bright day.

'Fortunately,' Peroni observed, 'I doubt there'll be anyone below just now.'

He sighed, then turned away. It was important to look, even though he knew what he was going to see.

Batisti's corpse remained slumped over the table. His killer was in front of him, prone on the floor, face down in the grime, eyes wide open, glassy, inert body shredded by gunfire, the blue paint barely visible for blood.

A thought came to Peroni: *he was the one they wanted to kill, more than anyone else, after he'd served his purpose.*

It made no sense, but then nothing did at that moment.

Something glittered at the dead man-child's neck. Peroni was surprised he hadn't seen this before. He bent down and, setting aside his squeamishness, reached for the object set against the grimy, blood-stained skin. It was a silver locket in the shape of a heart, worn and scratched, on an old and stained chain. When Peroni gently prised open the lid with fumbling, shaky fingers, hc saw there a fading photograph of a beautiful young woman with long golden hair, curly tresses of it, much like those of the corpse that lay in front of him.

Memories were coming back, distressing ones, of another case, one that was briefly in all the papers, on every police noticeboard until one final outburst of violence brought it to a close.

Gianni Peroni stared at the features of the wild-eyed blue creature plastered to the wall and felt his heart grow cold.

Then he closed the locket and turned it over. On the back, just visible after so many years in a wilderness he could only guess at, was the inscription, part English, part Italian.

To My Beautiful Marie on the Birth of Our Son, Daniel. 19 August 1986. Mia per sempre, Renzo.

– 11 –

A fierce, dry breeze arrived that afternoon. By evening the natives were complaining about the unseasonably hot weather, and much else besides. In the space of a few hours Rome had changed, become a tense, nervous city, jumpy at the site of its own time-worn shadows. Armies of workmen had descended on the area around the Quirinale Palace, erecting tall, ugly fencing and security gates at every intersection with the neighbouring streets. High, threatening guard posts were beginning to spread throughout the centre as far as the broad, open thoroughfare Mussolini had carved through the Forum, and in the open central square of the Piazza Venezia itself. The media had adopted Palombo's terminology, calling it a 'ring of steel' to protect the world leaders who were starting to arrive to attend the summit inside the palace. They forecast that the Quirinale hill and most of the area around it would become a forbidden zone for all but the most privileged of citizens, and few Romans or tourists would find life easy for several days to come.

Little of this appeared to concern the police pathologist Teresa Lupo who, thanks to her recent elevation to head of the forensic section in Commissario Esposito's Questura, had acquired a new smartphone – one that, for the moment, seemed more interesting than the present company. Costa watched her tapping frantically into her little gadget at their table in *Sacro e Profano*, a small church that had been converted into a Calabrian restaurant and pizzeria in a back street behind the Trevi Fountain. She had celebrated her thirty-seventh birthday three weeks before, though Costa felt she had scarcely aged in the six years he'd known her. Awkward, doggedly persistent, blessed with an acute intelligence that sometimes led her astray, she was, with Peroni and Falcone, one of his closest friends. Now that she and Peroni were an established couple, and his divorce had finally come through, there was speculation in the Questura that one day soon they would marry. Costa thought he would like that, that he could imagine the two of them together on the big day, both slightly gauche in new clothes, their big, shambling frames encased inside something they'd never wear again. There was an everyday honesty and devotion between the two of them, a friendship that embraced love too and made them a pleasure to be around, even when the work turned dark and relentless.

He took his attention away from Teresa, tapping away at the phone with her fat fingers, her pale, broad face entirely absorbed in the moment. Their table was on the upper level, where the organ might once have sat. This gave them a grand view of the vast wood-fired oven that seemed to provide almost everything – pizzas, meat, fish, vegetables – the place produced, and wafted the occasional wisp of smoky aromatic oak up from the nave below.

He could scarcely believe they were eating out together so soon after the afternoon's momentous and brutal events. When the sound of gunfire interrupted his curious conversation with Dario Sordi in the palace gardens, Costa had raced to the scene with Esposito and Falcone at his heels. It was easier to run than drive through the stationary snarl of Roman traffic. Whoever was responsible for the attack had been wise to rely on two wheels for their escape.

At least all three officers were safe, even if the news about Giovanni Batisti was as bad as anyone might have feared. Soon the narrow stretch of the street where the attack occurred had come to be swamped by other parties. Luca Palombo and his counterparts from America and elsewhere had arrived to take control. Not long after that, everyone in the Polizia di Stato came to understand their place in the pecking order.

Teresa, with a small group led by her assistant Silvio Di Capua, managed to spend almost fifteen minutes in the room where Batisti and the corpse of his apparent killer were found. Then they were ejected by a team from the Carabinieri, under Palombo's direction.

Peroni, Rosa and Mirko Oliva had been interviewed for almost two hours, with Commissario Esposito in attendance. After that they had been sent out into the street, where the two younger officers disappeared quickly into a nearby bar, shell-shocked and, it seemed to Costa, rather closer to one another than they had been previously. The rest of them returned to the Questura, where the atmosphere was unreal, as if they had entered a lull before some unpredictable storm.

After a few desultory attempts to work their way back into the investigation, efforts that Commissario Esposito rapidly stamped upon, Leo Falcone suggested dinner. The invitation came as such a surprise that no one objected. Strictly speaking, their shift was over – Peroni should have gone off duty hours before. They were all tired, yet conscious of an unspent nervous energy, some need to talk. Costa was astonished to discover that he was rather hungry, too. Or rather, some inner sense appeared to be telling him to eat soon, because it might be a while before he had another chance to sit down again with friends in a decent restaurant.

A diminutive waiter came over with a trolley piled high with plates of fish and vegetables and a small bowl of the scorching pepper sauce Costa always associated with Calabria.

'That's very kind,' Peroni told him, 'but we didn't order this.'

He still looked a little pale. Costa had been inside that upper room, seen what was in there. The big man was never good around blood.

Falcone, never one to be squeamish, was already prodding gently at the choicer dishes with his fork, judging the food with the studied and detached care with which he measured those around him. It was a very good restaurant.

The waiter leaned down and in a lowered voice behind his hand said, 'We know who you are. We've seen the inspector here before. It was all on the TV. We heard it.'

'Heard what?' Falcone asked as he picked at what looked like tuna and swordfish, already forking pieces onto his plate.

'That you're . . . *off the case*,' the waiter said with a theatrical flourish, visibly pleased with his own ability to produce what he thought of as cop-speak. 'So you come here. You eat, you think. All those stuck-up bastards in the Carabinieri, the government. They think they own the world.'

He put down the bottle of wine, which was still, to Peroni's visible concern, unopened.

'They close the streets. They build some wall around the Quirinale. Where are we living? Rome or Berlin in the 1950s? And when some ordinary guy in the police sticks his neck on the line, what do they do? Sit in their offices until the shooting stops, then come and take it all away from you like they know best.'

'We've still got Traffic,' Peroni said brightly. 'Didn't they mention that?'

'No.'

'You should never believe what you hear in the media,' Falcone suggested, then placed a long finger on the side of his nose and winked.

The waiter mouthed, 'Ah . . .' and made the same gesture. Peroni, getting desperate, held up the wine bottle, which the man opened, pouring four full glasses. The rich, aromatic smell of Pugliese *primitivo* mingled with the smoke from the oven downstairs.

'Haruspicy,' Teresa declared, finally looking up from the phone after the waiter disappeared.

'It's not on the menu,' Peroni pointed out.

'I'm not talking about food, you fool! It's what was going on back there. In that room. In the Via Rasella. Or so they'd like us to think.'

Peroni's fork dangled over some cold meat. A look of foreboding crossed his big, bucolic face. She glanced at him and added, 'Let's get this out of the way before we eat, shall we?'

'Oh, wonderful,' he groaned. 'If you insist . . .'

'This is exactly what Leo and Nic were told about in the Quirinale. The Blue Demon. Terrorism with an Etruscan flavour. No surprises. Well, not many.'

She held out her phone. There was a photo of some ancient, dark metal object in a museum. Costa craned forward, along with the others, in order to see better. It looked like a very odd ornament, one with a distinct and organic shape.

'The Liver of Piacenza,' Teresa announced.

'Liver?' Peroni asked weakly. He made a gesture down his front, then to the table. 'As in . . . ?'

'As in liver. Batisti was mutilated in a very specific fashion. Silvio managed to get me some old news reports about the Frascas. It looks as if they were injured in much the same way. It was a ritual. Not quite disembowelment, but . . .' She winced, from lack of facts, not something squeamish. 'A haruspex divined the future by looking at the liver of a slaughtered animal. The Liver of Piacenza was used to train people to read what they found. It divides the organ into specific areas that may or may not relate to stellar constellations. There were light surface knife marks on Giovanni Batisti that mirrored those used on the Piacenza object. To make them look like the work of an Etruscan haruspex.'

Peroni's fork halted halfway to his mouth and he moaned, 'Do we need to know this?'

'Of course,' she insisted. 'We're meant to. Someone doesn't inflict an injury on a dead man without a reason.'

They stared at her.

'A dead man?' Costa asked.

'It was all show. Batisti was killed by a bullet through the back of the head. Then they butchered him in a very specific way to make it look like haruspicy.' She pointed to the photo. 'I can't think of any other explanation. Why else would you partially remove a man's liver and run a knife over it to make a pattern based on some ancient form of divination? There was an egg in a saucer on the table as well. That was another Etruscan form of fortune-telling.'

'Why on earth . . . ?' Falcone began.

'I told you. It was a message,' she interrupted. 'A positive ID for our benefit. Like the poster of the Blue Demon on the wall. The Roman numerals. It was Andrea Petrakis leaving his calling card. A boast, if you like. He wants to make sure we know it was him, and that he hasn't forgotten his beloved Etruscans.'

'And they were who exactly?' Peroni asked, bemused.

'The people here before us. That was thcir tough luck. Rome wiped them out. An entire civilization. It was a long time ago. This was ancient history for Julius Caesar, for pity's sake. But not for Andrea Petrakis. The Liver of Piacenza was a training tool for a haruspex, like a model skeleton for a modern physician. Historians like Petrakis drool over it because it's one of the few examples of the Etruscan language. The only other of any substance is in Zagreb, on the remains of a mummy's shroud. It was made out of linen that was covered in Etruscan script. Rites, rituals, prayers. They call it the *Liber Linteus.*'

'*Linteus* means linen, doesn't it?' Costa asked.

'Who says a Latin education is wasted? Exactly. Andrea Petrakis would know all about this. The theory that went around after the Blue Demon murdered the Frasca couple was that Petrakis regarded himself as the leader of some kind of nationalist liberation movement. A lunatic looking for a revival of the Etruscan nation, who were, like him, originally Greek. Before Rome came along, those people controlled most of Italy, from the Po in the north as far as Salento in the south. The *Liber Linteus* is the only book of theirs that survives. The Romans burned the rest. If you think of yourself as Etruscan, you can understand why you might feel a little oppressed. I guess.'

The pizzas arrived and Peroni asked, 'Does the fact we're talking history mean that the liver part is done with?'

'Pretty much,' she replied, nodding. 'Petrakis was a junior professor in Etruscan studies at an age when most kids would still be working on a postgrad degree. A world-class obsessive. Maybe, in his own crazy head, it makes sense to kill people like this.'

Costa shook his head.

'I don't see it. He's an intelligent man. Who'd believe in a separatist movement based around a civilization that was destroyed more than two thousand years ago?'

'You can never apply logic to terrorism,' Falcone suggested.

'I'm not sure about that,' Costa insisted. 'This man was capable enough to escape from Italy, then hide away in Afghanistan for two decades. To deal with weapons. Money. Why would he take to pretending to read the future through butchering another human being, the way some primitive tribe did?'

Teresa Lupo frowned at him with the disappointed expression of a teacher failed by a bright pupil. Now that she and Peroni had settled into a relationship that seemed more close, and happy, than many marriages, she was in some ways beginning to resemble the big man. The same love of food was visible in their stout, healthy frames, and a similarly sceptical approach to the world in their pale, engaged faces.

'He didn't,' she told him. 'First, the Etruscans didn't indulge in human sacrifice. They would have been horrified by the very idea. Their priests slaughtered animals, not men.'

She skimmed her fingers over the phone and came across some more photos. Costa stared at pastoral scenes of dancing and celebrations, tall, elegant women, bearded, handsome men. Then Teresa turned up more that were vividly sexual in nature.

'They weren't brutal primitives just emerging from the Iron Age, either. More like colonizing Greek hippies. The Romans thought them degenerate and debauched. Uncontrollable hedonists who did what they wanted, when they wanted, to anyone they chose.'

'And then?' Peroni asked, interested now that the conversation had moved on.

'Then along came Rome. They got assimilated. We beat them at war, looked at their culture, adopted what we liked and destroyed the rest. The Etruscans were the victims of what we think of as civilization. Organized society, materialism, greed, pursued by a single-minded and fierce, war-like state. Us. The Romans marched north and eradicated their language, their customs . . . everything. It says here that sophisticated ancient Romans were bemoaning the death of Etruscan culture as early as the first century AD. They looked on it as a lost golden age, a kind of paradise, one they'd destroyed themselves.'

Peroni put down his knife and fork.

'That boy. The one we think killed Batisti . . .'

'Batisti was shot,' Falcone reminded him.

'Fine, fine.' Peroni's large, bloodless face contorted in puzzlement. 'The boy was got up as if he was in some kind of ceremony. That knife he had. The blood on him. Maybe he believed he was the Blue Demon. Whatever that was.'

'A figure from Etruscan mythology,' Teresa interjected. More taps at the phone, yet another set of photos, one of them recognizable from the briefing in the Quirinale. 'There are plenty of their burial sites north of here, near Viterbo, Grosseto, Tarquinia, in the Maremma. The early ones depict a paradise that's almost Christian. A happy afterlife, parents meeting with their children. Our idea of Heaven. Then this.'

She blew up the most vivid of the pictures: the long-bearded, blue face, the eyes that burned, fangs dripping blood . . .

'I know that face,' Peroni said.

'We all do, Gianni. It's Satan. The bringer of damnation. Before the Blue Demon came along the Etruscans inhabited a world that was either good or nothing. After this charming gentleman turned up, the place possessed evil. Someone had devoured the apple or opened Pandora's box. Or perhaps he was just a gift the Romans brought to make all those pleasure-loving Etruscans feel the weight of human guilt. The Devil was in the room and he wasn't going to leave. If you look at the wall paintings you get the picture. The Blue Demon stands between the living and Paradise. He decides who gets to live happily ever after, and who goes into a new place he's invented. Somewhere called Hell. Good name for a terrorist group, don't you think? Or its leader. No one was ever sure which it was supposed to be. There were only four in the cell anyway, as far as anyone knew. Maybe it didn't matter.'

'I remember that case,' Peroni said miserably. 'I was a young *agente*. It was all so . . . inexplicable. A decent family destroyed. Those kids in Tarquinia too. And all for what?'

'Still,' Falcone declared, 'it's not our business, is it?' He picked up a piece of ham in his fingers and stared at them. There was some kind of challenge in his expression. 'You heard Luca Palombo. We need to think about traffic. Crowds. Public relations.'

The lines of command had been made crystal clear in a series of further communications between the control room in the Quirinale Palace and the Questura on their return. The investigation into the death of Giovanni Batisti would be the responsibility of the Carabinieri and the secret-service team assembled around the man from the

Ministry of the Interior. The state police would focus on security for the coming summit, ensuring that the strict limitations on traffic and pedestrian movement in the street would be made clear to the public and maintained throughout.

'Police work is our business,' Costa grumbled. 'If I wanted to be a security guard . . .'

Falcone called for the waiter and asked for some more water. The carafe came; he waited for the man to go back down the stairs, then poured himself a glass and raised it.

'I'm very glad we didn't lose any friends today,' he said. 'Let's drink to that.'

'An Etruscan toast,' Teresa observed, watching him. 'We all lose friends in the end.'

'Really? You have a feel for these things, you know. And no evidence to look at, no forensic leads to work upon.'

'Stinking body-snatchers . . .' she hissed.

He put down his glass and smiled at her.

'There's no reason why you couldn't spend a day out of the office tomorrow. Go to the Villa Giulia. Ask a few questions about Andrea Petrakis and what happened there twenty years ago. The Frascas were that boy's parents. It would be curious if the son murdered Giovanni Batisti in the same way Andrea Petrakis dealt with his own mother and father. Symmetrical.' The smile disappeared. 'The older I get, the more I hate symmetry. It's so . . . unnatural.'

'Leo,' Peroni scolded him. 'That's police work.'

'The Villa Giulia is a museum. Anyone can go there and ask as many questions as they like.'

'It's police work, and you know it. We're not supposed to be involved.'

'That's not entirely correct,' Falcone responded, staring at the table.

'I knew there was a reason you invited us out for a meal. Is this on expenses?'

'Certainly not. I'm paying. We're merely being . . .' an expansive wave of his long arm, '. . . released from conventional duties for the duration.'

'On whose orders?' Costa asked.

'Esposito's, as far as the Questura's concerned.'

Some ideas were starting to clear in Costa's head.

'This is Dario Sordi's doing, isn't it?'

'I'm not answering that question,' the inspector replied. 'We have an office set aside. Don't bother reporting to work tomorrow. As far as they're concerned, we're on a course. All four of us. Along with Teresa's deputy and your young officers. Prabakaran and Oliva.'

He wrote down an address twice on the napkin, ripped it in half and passed over the pieces.

'That makes seven in all, with an eighth who'll join us tomorrow.'

'The Via di San Giovanni in Laterano,' Peroni murmured, reading Falcone's scribble. 'I know this place. It's that apartment in the old monastery, isn't it? The safe house?'

'It's police property that is currently going unused. Shame to waste it. We will have facilities. Whatever we require.'

Peroni picked at his pizza in silence. Teresa looked mildly excited.

'And I'm allowed into this monastery?'

'Very much so.'

'In order to do what, exactly?' Costa asked.

'Whatever we like. Let's sleep on it. Things will be clearer in the morning. Without files, or evidence, or—'

'We're in the middle of a turf war between Dario Sordi and that devil Campagnolo,' Peroni said, interrupting. 'I'd stake money on the angels losing this one, Leo. Don't put anyone else's neck on the line.'

The lean inspector stroked his beard and stayed silent.

'There were numbers on the wall,' Costa said. 'Roman numerals. Beneath the poster of the Blue Demon.'

'Oh, yes,' Teresa remembered. 'It seems to me that Petrakis is crazy in the highly intelligent and complicated way only an educated man can be. He adores games and codes and riddles, and the opportunity to show off his erudition. This is the same key as with the dead Frasca couple. Different numbers, though. III. I. CCLXIII. Three. One. Two hundred and sixty-three.'

Peroni looked at the two of them and shrugged.

'Shakespeare?' Costa suggested.

'Congratulations,' she said, beaming. 'It's the same schema. Act, scene, line. From *Julius Caesar*.'

They waited. She watched them as she spoke:

> '*Domestic fury and fierce civil strife*
> *Shall cumber all the parts of Italy.*'

Falcone pushed back his glass and said, 'San Giovanni in Laterano. Tomorrow. Eight o'clock.'

– 12 –

They were already in the drive of the farmhouse off the Via Appia Antica. The president, two bodyguards and Capitano Fabio Ranieri of the Corazzieri. Costa had checked out the regiment with Peroni. As Sordi said, they were formally under the control of the Carabinieri, though with effective autonomy. No one in the Questura had much experience of dealing with the Quirinale's equivalent of the Swiss Guards. They were regarded as dedicated soldiers committed to a single duty, the protection of the head of state. For this reason their presence beyond the palace was limited, without the contacts – official and informal – that took place in the occasionally uneasy relationship between the Polizia di Stato and the Carabinieri.

Ranieri was out of the car first as Costa arrived. He was a massive man around Peroni's age, taller than Dario Sordi himself, broad-shouldered in a black suit, with close-cropped dark hair and alert, searching eyes.

'Capitano . . .' Costa began.

'This isn't a formal visit,' the officer interjected. 'Call me Ranieri. The president does not wish news of your meeting broadcast. I expect—'

'Yes, yes, yes,' Sordi said, patting the man on the back. 'Nic – Ranieri. Ranieri – Nic. Or Costa, if you prefer. For myself, I cannot think of him as a surname, but then . . .'

He stopped beneath the porch light and gazed at the low stone villa that had been the Costa family home for almost forty years.

'. . . I have memories.'

He pointed to the long field leading back to the road.

'I helped your father plant those grapes. Before you were born.

It was back-breaking work, for which I was repaid with terrible wine. Did it get any better over the years?'

'Not much.'

'I thought that might be the case.' He held up a bottle. 'From the Quirinale cellars. Brunello. A glass now? Or would you prefer to keep it as a gift?'

'Neither,' Costa said, and opened the door.

Sordi sighed. Ranieri returned to the car with his two colleagues.

'Then I shall take a drop alone. Let's go out to the patio,' the president suggested. 'These men have work to do.'

When they reached the old wooden table he handed Costa a small mobile phone.

'If you need me, call Ranieri using this thing. Do not use any landline or mobile, personal or police.' He frowned. 'I'm sorry. I may be over-zealous. But I would not assume an indirect conversation through any other medium is secure. Campagnolo is beside himself with rage. He has many friends in the security services. We must be prudent.'

This was not what Costa wished to hear.

'I can't get involved in some vendetta between you and the prime minister.'

Sordi eyed him, half-amused.

'You really think that's what this is about? Personalities?'

'I don't know. But . . .'

'Ugo Campagnolo is a highly flawed politician who feels, with some justification, that he's been sidelined. I make no apologies for that. He should never have invited the summit to the heart of Rome in the first place. I cannot allow the man to take responsibility for the mess he's created. He's too keen to shake hands with the mighty to see the true picture, the genuine threat we face. I have a duty and I will fulfil it. As for the main issue here – the Blue Demon – he's a minor nuisance, nothing more. I would like him to remain that way.'

There was a noise from behind. Ranieri and his men were in the house.

'They're looking for bugs,' Sordi explained. 'Purely a precaution.'

'Bugs?' Costa asked, astonished.

'Bugs,' the president of Italy repeated, then pulled a corkscrew out of his jacket pocket and began to tug at the dusty bottle of Brunello. 'Now fetch a couple of glasses.'

Costa went back into the house. Ranieri's men seemed occupied. They were wandering around the living room, headphones on, some kind of electronic equipment in their hands.

When he returned, Sordi had a cigarette in his mouth and was ready to pour the Brunello. He raised the bottle to the harsh outdoor lights, three bare bulbs, an ugly feature that Costa's late wife Emily had nagged him to fix.

'This should have been opened hours ago. I'm wasting the state's wine collection. Don't tell.'

He looked at the glasses. Costa's was already filled with orange juice.

'Oh, well,' the president said, and served himself an immodest measure. 'I haven't been here in a while. Did you throw out your father's books?'

'Of course not.'

'Good,' he said, getting up suddenly. 'Let's look at them.'

Costa followed him back into the house. The library sprawled untidily across a set of shelves that spanned an entire wall in his father's study.

'Here,' Sordi said, finding two copies among the foreign novels jumbled together in a section closest to the window. 'Have you read them?'

They were by an English writer, Robert Graves. *I, Claudius* and *Claudius the God*.

'Years ago, but I don't remember them much,' Costa admitted. 'History's not to my taste.'

'They're about history only tangentially. In truth, they're about us. The human animal. About society. How it works, or attempts to. How it fails when we forget our ties to one another. Read them again sometime, properly. Your father and I . . .'

Sordi opened the covers of each, so that he could see. Inside was an identical inscription: *To my dearest friend, Marco. From Dario, the turncoat.*

'We were still friends when I gave him these. Not for much longer. Thanks to what came after – by which I mean the end of the commission into the Blue Demon case – perhaps it was inevitable we would drift apart.'

He waved the books at Costa and placed them on Marco's desk.

'These were a gift I hoped might explain a little. Your father lived for his principles. He would rather die than compromise them. I . . .' Sordi grimaced. 'A politician reaches a point in his life when he or she must decide. Do you wish to hold steadfast to your beliefs? Or do you become pragmatic and attempt to turn some small fraction of them into reality? I chose the latter, and look what it made me. A widower living in a solitary palace, with a slender grip on power and a prime minister who would send me off to an old people's home if he could. King Lear of Rome. Perhaps your father was right. I betrayed what we once stood for.'

'Dario . . .'

'These are not idle ramblings. I tell you them for a reason. As your father would have understood only too well, what you heard today was the truth, but only a part of it. The rest remains misty, to me anyway, though I have no doubt that inside that fog lies the crux of this matter.' He glanced at the door, as if to make sure no one was listening. 'I must be very careful what I pass to you. They may try to trap me the obvious way, by handing on some information that is false or traceable. If that happens . . .' He sighed. 'Then my presidency is at an end.'

He stopped. Ranieri was at the door. In his hands was something small, dark and dusty with wires attached.

'You found that here? In my home?' Costa asked.

'It was hidden in the living room, near the phone.'

The Corazzieri captain examined the thing, as if searching for some kind of label.

'Twenty years ago I could have told you the name. We used them a lot then. I wouldn't worry too much. It's long dead. Someone would have been listening in the road outside. Any nearby conversation, one half of a phone call, they'd hear the lot. It's primitive compared with what they have today. That's all we could find. There's nothing recent.'

'Take it as a compliment,' Sordi added. 'I shouldn't boast, but when I was elevated to the Quirinale, Ranieri here kindly swept my personal apartment near the Piazza Navona.' He took the bug and waved it, his face wryly gleeful, as it had been when Costa was a child. 'I had three, and every last one of them alive!'

'What's going on?' Costa demanded, hearing the rising tension in his own voice.

The president extinguished his cigarette in one of Marco's old ashtrays, then nodded at Ranieri to leave. They returned outside to the table, where Sordi reached into his pocket and took out a silver compact disc in a transparent sleeve.

'You'll listen to what I have to tell you, Nic, then read what's on this thing. In the morning pass it on to your colleagues when you meet them. Yes, yes . . .' Costa was already protesting. 'I know about what's being planned. You shall be my conduit. Discreetly. Esposito agreed to this, a little reluctantly. He seems a good man, and not in Campagnolo's power, as far as one may tell. Your friend Falcone too. I cannot deal with any of you directly. If I did, there would have to be records and minutes and formalities. This is not possible. Campagnolo and Palombo would have my hide if that became public. Our prime minister has a rare talent for delving into matters that don't concern him.'

'Politics are not my business.'

A touch of colour entered the president's cheeks.

'Is that why you think I came? To pursue some petty quarrel?'

'I don't know.'

He leaned forward and peered into Costa's face.

'I came because you're the son of a man I held in the highest esteem. I trusted Marco with my life. I assumed I could do the same with you. We face a grave threat. This Petrakis individual is in the country. He possesses resources. He's not alone and he's intent on delivering a blow to the society he loathes, our society. A blow I fear may rank among anything this damaged world has seen these last ten years. The man is . . .' Sordi shook his head, '. . . a monster. What kind one can only guess. Your father had ideas, but I was fool enough not to listen to them.'

There was a sound from outside. A phone ringing, then Ranieri's distant voice.

'This much I do know, though. Andrea Petrakis is not alone, any more than he was twenty years ago. The very idea that three students and some junior professor could have concocted the kidnap and murder of the Frasca couple is ridiculous. Furthermore, there was strong evidence that drug-trafficking was involved. I am no police officer, but I surely understand this. If you deal in drugs you must sell them to someone. Criminals, usually. Petrakis was not some solitary individual with a handful of acolytes. The fool was too young and too inexperienced to have done what he stood accused of. He was someone else's pawn twenty years ago. Logic dictates that he still is today.'

'Did you say that?' Costa asked. 'In your report?'

Sordi shook his head.

'We couldn't. We weren't allowed. This is a tragedy that goes to the very heart of who we are. Romans. Italians. Frail human beings. When your father and I tried to get to the bottom of it, we were turned back at every opportunity. I gave up in the end, and lost a dear friend as a result. Whoever set up Petrakis in the first place . . .'

He lifted his glass, as if in a toast.

'He, she, they . . . must have been here all along. While we thought the Years of Lead were gone. While we dreamed of a better future, in a world without hate or fear or poverty. Watching, waiting. In Rome perhaps, or Milan or Florence. Or beyond. Secure, undetected, unsuspected by anyone. Andrea Petrakis was a creation of the Blue Demon, not the Devil himself.'

Costa thought of the image on the wall in the poster they had seen, in the photo of the shack in the Maremma where the students had died: the hideous face, the terrifying expression of hatred. The selfsame picture that had stood next to Giovanni Batisti's mutilated corpse.

'Do you know what Gladio was?' Sordi asked.

The question came out of nowhere. A phrase came to Costa, from his schooldays.

'*Qui gladio ferit, gladio perit,*' he murmured. 'He who strikes with the sword, perishes with the sword.'

'Latin is a beautiful language,' Sordi observed. 'What we do with those words . . .'

He tapped the disc.

'You'll find here what answers we discovered before our commission was dissolved. There were some. Gladio was an organization, one designed to leave behind individuals dedicated to a secret purpose, a decent one in principle. To save us from Russia, from oblivion. Quiet men and women willing to bury their true identity, never to be noticed, never to speak of their purpose, not until they were needed. And then . . .' He glanced out at the vines, as if remembering something. 'One way or another it all went wrong. I can't help but feel it was Gladio that killed those people twenty years ago, as much as anything else – certainly as much as Andrea Petrakis.'

He reached over and poured himself some more wine. Another cigarette appeared. Costa wished he could stop the old man smoking.

'It's my belief that whoever created this myth we know as the Blue Demon was one who remained behind. Now his time has come. When they seek to kill us, Nic, it won't be with bombs and planes and distant, random acts of violence.'

Dario Sordi gripped his fist and shook it in Costa's face.

'They will murder us face to face from within, the way they killed the Frascas.' He stopped for a moment. 'The way we killed in the war, in the Via Rasella. Do you think their choice of that place this afternoon was some coincidence?'

'No,' Costa answered. 'It was a message for you.'

'A warning that they feel they are in combat, just as we were when the Germans occupied Rome. You and your colleagues must put flesh on this ghost. Whoever it is. I ask that, as your president and as the man who once made a small child laugh, here in this very house.'

He looked weary at that moment, frail and perhaps a little daunted.

'I'll do what I can,' Costa assured him.

Sordi's hand went briefly to his arm, and a smile crossed the president's face.

'I know that. I shall send you a friend tomorrow. One with some special knowledge of the Blue Demon. And Gladio too.' He closed his eyes, glanced at the bottle on the table, thought better of it. 'The one we seek could be anyone, Nic. A man, a woman, a modest, anonymous individual,' Sordi shrugged, 'running some little cafe in the city, perhaps, or delivering the mail.' His eyes gleamed. 'One of you. Or a cabal of several. In the Carabinieri. The secret services. Among those of us who pretend we are your masters. It demands courage and intelligence to devote one's entire life to appearing to be someone else. With that comes ambition, I suspect. Be wary. Do not breathe a word of this to anyone beyond those you trust.'

'Of course.'

The president hesitated. A note of uncertainty, perhaps regret, had entered his voice.

'I have selfish reasons to say this. You're the second person to whom I have confided my thoughts.'

Dario Sordi grasped the bottle of Brunello, poured himself a dash more, took an urgent, desperate sip and gazed at Costa, an expression approaching guilt on his tired, pale face.

'The first was Giovanni Batisti a week ago when the intelligence reports that Palombo spoke of first began to find their way to my desk. It was idiotic of me to tell him, but . . .'

His arms spread wide in a gesture of despair.

'Make no mistake. This is a lonely job. Mostly I pin medals on decent men and women, attend funerals and civic events. There are few people to whom I may turn in confidence. Batisti was an honest man. I asked him merely to consider my concerns and keep them to himself. Whether he did . . . You understand what I'm saying? You must not discount the possibility that he was indiscreet. It's possible the Blue Demon is rather closer to us than we might think.'

Nic Costa tried to find the right words. Dario Sordi was a kindly figure from his childhood, one who had always seemed so confident, so self-assured. At that moment he appeared lost and in need of comfort.

'Leo Falcone is the best police officer I have ever worked with. If anyone can find this individual—'

'Yes, yes,' Sordi interrupted, smiling. 'What I was trying to say was more personal. I have one death on my conscience already. I do not wish anyone to add to that burden, least of all you.'

Part 2

FALSE FLAGS

Iam vero Italia novis cladibus vel post longam saeculorum seriem repetitis adflicta ... corrupti in dominos servi, in patronos liberti; et quibus deerat inimicus per amicos oppressi.

Now too Italy was beset by new disasters, or those which it had not witnessed for many years ... slaves were bribed to turn against their masters, freedmen to betray their patrons; and, if a man had no enemies, he was destroyed by his friends.

Tacitus, *The Histories*, Book I

- 1 -

The villa overlooked the drab, flat coast running to the Tyrrhenian Sea, an untidy sprawl of industrial units and abandoned farmland not far from the main highway to Tuscany. It was a rich man's rental, eight bedrooms, an extortionate $5,000 a week paid to a property agency in Tarquinia set on the bluff above. The name was a lie, resurrected in the 1920s to boast of the sleepy medieval town's roots. Nothing hereabouts was quite what it seemed. The true home of the Etruscans was lost altogether, mere fragments, pot shards and fractured stones in a shallow valley in the hills. There, a disappeared race had turned to dust, leaving nothing but mausoleums, deep beneath the ochre earth, halls for feasting and revelry, physical joy, the life eternal, many pillaged to fill museums with vivid ceramics and statues depicting a culture built on strength and art and a stark carnal sensuality.

Andrea Petrakis could map each precious tomb in his head. The public site on the outskirts of Tarquinia where the tourists turned up in their coaches to gaze in awe and a little fear at burial halls showing men and women dancing, singing, hunting, fighting, making love, two and a half millennia before. The secret places too, graves that were whispered about in order to keep out the curious and the greedy. From Cerveteri in the south to Grosseto, Orvieto and beyond, they lay hidden beneath the parched ground, revealed only by the accident of the plough or the probing of some fortunate archaeologist, part of a lost world never to be fully rediscovered. Just a fraction of ancient Etruria had been retrieved, faded, distant hints of the Greek civilization that gave Rome everything – the olive and the grape, the Olympian gods, the makings of the Latin alphabet –

receiving only oblivion in return. The distant lives captured in the wall paintings of their tombs, so vibrant, so real, so human, seemed nothing now but the distant, wasted dreams of the dead.

There was a long, oval pool at the front of the villa, which gave out onto the coastline. A brief expanse of scrappy lawn was cut into the wilderness, filled with fake classical statuary and carefully tended topiary figures of gods and mythical beasts. Every time Petrakis looked at it he wanted to laugh. The feature that did impress him was a narrow landing strip running east–west in the adjoining field, with a set of electric landing lights and a hangar by the side. He'd made sure they could use that, and that the gardener would be told to stay away for the duration of their stay. One week before, under cover of darkness, he had landed there from Corsica in a two-seater composite microlight, laden with materials that would have been dangerous to obtain in Italy by other means, and with the man who had provided them in the passenger seat. It had taken fifty minutes in the moonlight, navigating by GPS, skimming the sea to stay beneath the coastal radar, climbing to two thousand feet after the coast, then cutting the engine and gliding to land on the hard, dry grass line etched out by the landing lights. The machine sat safe and hidden inside the hangar, ready for use another day.

Rome was less than eighty kilometres away, accessible through a variety of means. The coastal highway was the swiftest and most perilous. He preferred the back roads, skirting all the main towns, then leading to what was once the Via Claudia, close to Bracciano and its great lake, north-west of the capital. The circuitous route took twice as long, but Petrakis had insisted they return that way the previous day. It was a sound precaution; by late afternoon random checks were in place on every last main road. On the narrow country lanes they never saw so much as a police or Carabinieri car. There was a personal dimension too. The Via Claudia was built by Nero, stretching across the Alps into what was now Austria, a conduit through which to subdue the fractious tribes of Europe. Every time he followed in the footsteps of those distant legions he was reminded of what Rome had always represented.

It was a cloudless sunny morning, hot even at eight. A single jet wheeled high overhead on the approach to Fiumicino or Ciampino. Not for much longer. He'd watched the TV avidly since rising at six, happy to hear his own name mentioned alongside a photofit cobbled up from a few old images, one that would help no one. The airports would close later that morning. Road restrictions were coming into force throughout the city. Rome would slowly become paralysed by its own fear, watched over by menacing guard posts, snipers on balconies, secret-services officers mingling with the mute and angry people on the street. The authorities were advising that only those with essential duties should report to work. Shop staff and office workers knew what that meant: they were supposed to stay at home and lose three or four days' pay. The unions were threatening to strike, a response that seemed peculiarly Roman.

Andrea Petrakis completed his seventh length of the pool then hitched himself up onto the tiled perimeter by the steps and looked back at the villa. They would be visible from the nearest house, a farm a kilometre away. That made him happy. He wanted to maintain the appearance they'd given since their arrival. In the local shops, buying bread and wine, outside in the garden, by the pool, they could have been any group of foreign friends on holiday. A middle-aged Italian with a ready smile, hair that – after some time in the bathroom the previous evening – was now cropped short and dyed a deep shade of brown. A tall black African, athletic, in his twenties, who couldn't stop listening to music on his headphones whenever he had the chance, dancing along to whatever he heard. A quiet, introspective dark-skinned man, foreign perhaps, from the Middle East, with the distanced, almost arrogant air of a businessman.

And a woman. Anna Ybarra. Spanish, though she would doubtless regard herself as Basque. He'd hand-picked her from the volunteers on offer. She was of medium height, with the muscular, full body of a peasant, long dark hair and a guileless, compelling face, that of the Madonna in some medieval painting – plain, not beautiful, or pretty, yet impossible not to admire. Someone who would always attract attention, turn heads as she passed.

With her round, guileless eyes, which seemed to engage with the world and find only amazement, Anna Ybarra had an air of prepossessing innocence. She was twenty-seven but, at times, looked no more than a teenager. For all these reasons, he chose her above the other individuals trawled from the covert links they possessed around the world. Many had more talents, few more motivation. None looked less like a terrorist, and this, above all else, made her invaluable. The police and the secret services worked the way they knew, with precision and practice based on past experience. They would be looking for what their shared understanding told them to seek: a group of men hiding in the network of safe houses that the organization had acquired the length of Europe. The online news services were already talking of raids on suspected Muslim extremists in the drear immigrant suburbs of Rome, Milan, Turin and beyond. This was what he hoped for, knowing that not one of those whom the police would arrest could breathe a word about what was happening, for the simplest of reasons: none knew. This was an operation that came from on high, like 9/11, Madrid and the London bombs. No one could have expected it, because no one, outside the closest circle of those moving to and fro each evening on the Afghan-Pakistan border, was aware that the plot existed.

He could imagine the men the Italians had rounded up, locked in some grim cell, being screamed at by interrogators, wondering if the Americans might intercede at any moment, whisk them away to a private jet and a short trip to a friendly foreign country where torture was an everyday occurrence. Rendition was supposed to be banned in Italy; the politicians had demanded that after one case had resulted in criminal prosecutions against some of those involved. But in reality . . . ?

Petrakis had no idea whether it might happen or not, and he didn't care. The pain and outrage would make the detention all the more galling, and there would be mistakes, as there always were, which the media would seize upon and scream from the rooftops as evidence of the new, draconian state.

Terror was about more than the visible act. It concerned the temperament of a nation, the breaking of its spirit, the destruction of anything it could use to cling to the certainties of the past.

By the side of the pool he found his attention drifting to the woman once more. He had checked her story himself, every last detail. She had grown up in the Basque country, daughter of a simple country farmer. Married at nineteen. A mother at twenty-one. Five years later, in the midst of a police crackdown after ETA exploded a bomb at Madrid airport, killing three people, a covert anti-terror squad had stormed into the farmhouse she shared with her husband. It was a night-time raid, badly handled. In the ensuing fire-fight he had died, and so had their little boy, who was just a week away from his fifth birthday. When the sun rose on their humble home outside the village of Hernani, near San Sebastián, it shed light on a terrible mistake. The police had entered the wrong house, thinking it belonged to her brother-in-law, an ETA sympathizer. Her husband had simply been trying to defend his family against a group of armed, masked men who had hammered down the door and attacked them. He was no ETA member, not even a supporter. But soon afterwards, when she was allowed home from hospital where she was treated for a minor gunshot wound to the abdomen, Anna Ybarra was. A volunteer demanding something special, something that would give her satisfaction.

The other two were different. Joseph Priest was a member of the Kenyan Mungiki gang, half-terrorist, half-criminal, someone who could be relied upon to kill without a thought and steal everything he could find from the corpses left behind. Money was Joseph's god, though not as much as it was for the men who had sent him all the way from Nairobi.

Deniz Nesin grew up in the wild lands of eastern Turkey and was the brotherhood's place-man in the team. A front-line soldier who'd trained suicide units in Afghanistan, Palestine and Iraq, helped develop networks of supporters throughout the world, set up conduits through which cash and arms and technical equipment might be moved swiftly and securely. Never once getting caught, getting wounded, getting his face or alias out on the wires.

Petrakis liked him. Or, rather, he felt comfortable in his presence. The man was a type he had come to recognize and understand over the last two decades. A severe, dedicated fundamentalist through and through, never missing prayer, never far from his copy of a well-thumbed Koran, he was meticulous, predictable, determined and, when necessary, capable of immediate and extreme violence. With these strengths came flaws and fallibilities. Deniz was a zealot surrounded by atheists. He had accepted Petrakis's leadership because the proposal was too tempting to ignore. Still, he was unhappy in the company of strangers, and the presence of Anna Ybarra preyed upon him deeply, in part for her forthright character, but more for the reliance they had come to place on a woman.

It was of no consequence. This was Petrakis's operation. She was his choice, as were they. He'd made his position plain to the people at the top, not in person because he wasn't quite of sufficient stature to gain that privilege. But through video links and covert emails, exchanged with their shifting camps that flitted constantly, between Afghanistan and Pakistan, Petrakis had persuaded them, by the force of his argument and the strength of his position. Either the venture happened his way or it didn't happen at all. They didn't like the implicit threat in that statement. Still, they knew the truth in what he was saying. Italy would be on the alert for a conventional terrorist team, willing to lock up anyone who generated the slightest suspicion. In order to penetrate to the heart of Rome, new tactics were needed. No hijacked planes. No home-made bombs, crafted out of chemicals and fertilizer, left on commuter trains, detonated by a simple phone call.

What was required was terror on a different scale. An enormity that would send a message to the citizens of one of the most beautiful, ancient cities in the world: no one is exempt, no one is immune.

'Andrea!'

Anna's curiously accented English drifted to him from the patio.

He turned to look. Deniz and Joseph were seated at the outdoor dining table. The African nursed a coffee. Deniz was playing with the satellite phone they'd had programmed onto an illicit frequency of one of the networks the Americans supposedly couldn't crack. He wore a face like thunder.

She walked in front of the two of them wearing a full-body swimsuit that was too old for her.

'What's the water like?' she asked.

'Wet,' Petrakis called back. 'What do you expect?'

She laughed and uttered something in Spanish, a curse, probably a nasty one. He liked having this woman around. There'd been nothing in the way of real female company in Afghanistan. Just 'wives' who materialized to fill the perceived need. Anna answered back. He hadn't heard that in a female for a long time.

Deniz muttered something caustic in Arabic.

'If you want to insult me,' Anna said, standing in front of him, hands on her hips, 'at least do it in a language I can understand.'

'Show some modesty,' he grumbled in his good English.

'After yesterday you want modesty?'

Joseph raised his coffee cup.

'Good point.'

Deniz swore and went back to the phone. She shook her head, came over to the pool, dived in, swam a length underwater, then emerged next to Petrakis.

'What do we do today?' she asked.

'Relax. Stop bugging Deniz.'

She stared at him, her long hair slicked back against her head. It made her round, tanned face even more striking.

'I'm wearing a very ordinary swimsuit. This is not Afghanistan. He doesn't get to stone me to death here.'

'We don't need distractions.'

'Why do you never tell us anything?' she asked. 'Who was that man who came here in your little plane? The Greek? Where is he?'

Deniz went back into the house taking the satphone with him. Joseph had his eyes closed and was listening to some beat on his iPod, feet jogging, looking every inch the rich, idle tourist.

'I don't know what rules you had in ETA,' Petrakis said. 'But here, I tell you what you need to know, when you need to know it.'

'I don't know what rules they had, either. I wasn't a part of ETA. That's why you wanted me.'

She let her body float up to the surface, go rigid, then drifted across the rippling surface of the pool on her back. He watched her, couldn't help it. Her figure reminded him of the girl from Treviso who'd died in his parents' cottage . . .

Andrea Petrakis found himself thinking of the parties they'd held towards the end, seeing them briefly in his head, remembering the touch of warm skin, the liquid sound of doped-up laughter, the furtive, anxious sex. There'd been no rules there, either.

Very briskly, with the swiftness of an athlete, she flipped over, disappeared beneath the surface and came up by his legs.

'Deniz should think himself lucky,' she said. 'The reason I'm wearing an old woman's bathing suit is that I hate people seeing the scar. Where they shot me. Right . . .' she made a cutting gesture over her stomach, '. . . here.' She looked at him and asked, 'Why did you kill the boy?'

'I had no choice. And he wasn't a boy.'

She gave him a searching look.

'You could have let him live. He was soft in the head. Boy or man, he didn't know which day of the week it was.'

'Danny went to pieces.'

'Does that always happen the first time?' she asked. There was a cold, curious look in her eyes. He'd left her out of the seizure of Batisti. She lacked the experience, the training.

'It didn't with me. It won't with you.'

She frowned.

'Can I ask you something? You'll tell me the truth? Promise?'

'If it's a question I can answer, then I will tell you. If not . . .'

'You meant to kill him all along, didn't you? That was what he was for. A piece of the plan. Like all of us.' Her round brown eyes never left him. 'Me the innocent. Joseph the dumb one. Deniz . . .' she cast a cold glance at the house, '. . . the bigot. Is that why you chose us?'

'I chose you because you wanted this, Anna.'

He checked his watch and looked north, along the stark stretch of Maremma coastline. It was only a ten-minute drive to the excavation where they'd uncovered the original Blue Demon, the place that had captivated him when he first saw it almost thirty years before. He felt he could stare at that face forever, with its eyes that burned like red-hot coals, full of malice towards everything that lived.

'Joseph,' he yelled.

The long, lean black figure took off the headphones and looked across at them puzzled.

Petrakis thought of Rome and the tourist Mecca not far from the Spanish Steps. Ugo Campagnolo had neglected to check his diary when he booked the leaders of the world's industrialized nations for their stay in the city. It was also fashion week, an annual ritual that would not walk away easily, whatever the pressure. That morning there would be an event for the world's photographers. Models and the media. Anxious, gawping crowds, all packed around the Trevi Fountain, none of them more than a minute's walk away from the Via Rasella.

It was too good an opportunity to miss.

'I've an errand for you,' he told the African. 'An important one.'

- 2 -

Dario Sordi's CD contained the confidential report of the commission into the Blue Demon incident, seventy-nine pages on disc,
including a note declaring that Marco Costa, an original member of
the investigation, had declined to sign the findings and resigned
shortly before the remaining members reached their decidedly ano-
dyne conclusions. His son had read the entire document immediately
after the president and his bodyguards left. It was 4 a.m. before Costa
got any sleep. The intuition he'd recognized in *Sacro e Profano* – that
time might be short in the days to come – would soon, he felt, be
proved right.

But at least their new home was sufficiently distant from the
Questura to give them time to think. Esposito had provided a large,
five-room first-floor apartment in a former monastery overlooking the
narrow street of San Giovanni in Laterano, close to the vast cathedral
that was the seat of the Catholic Church before the construction of
St Peter's. Beyond the Lateran the city was a nightmare: traffic jams
in every direction, train and bus cancellations, streets full of angry,
scared people walking to work because there was no other way.
The headline in *Corriere della Sera*, over a photograph of a threatening watchtower in the Piazza Venezia, with an armed soldier at its
summit, said everything: *La città eterna, assediata*. The eternal city,
under siege. Radio chat-shows carried caller after caller complaining
about their plight, and its immediate cause: an unwanted summit at
which the aloof and distant presidents and prime ministers of foreign
nations might take cocktails with one another in the Quirinale Palace.
To Costa's surprise and dismay, much of the fury seemed to be
directed more at Dario Sordi, who had inherited the chaos, than at

Ugo Campagnolo, the man who invited it. There was an intemperate, irrational aspect to the popular mood, one that was almost palpable on the street as he walked past the everyday shops and cafes from his parking place near the hospital.

The safe house occupied a wing of the block, reached by broad stairs that curled around a rickety cast-iron lift rising to the floors above. It wasn't hard to imagine monks scurrying about the place, though – judging by the queues of pushchairs parked neatly in the lobby – most of the present occupants seemed to be ordinary families.

They had been joined by the newcomer that Dario Sordi had promised. Elizabeth Murray, born in London, raised in Italy, had been summoned from retirement to advise the small team headed by Falcone. She had arrived in Rome only the evening before, from her farm in New Zealand, and looked a little the worse for the journey. A large, beaming woman, with a very English, weathered face, she might, in another incarnation, have been Peroni's more aristocratic elder sister. She wore a khaki corduroy skirt over tan leather boots, and a blue denim shirt – winter clothing, she told them, since that was the season in the southern hemisphere. A shepherd's crook that doubled as a walking stick stood next to the largest armchair in the apartment, which she more than occupied, casting envious glances from time to time at the neighbouring desk where Teresa's deputy, Silvio Di Capua, had taken control of the only two computers in the place.

Esposito appeared to be present only as a matter of principle. He seemed uncomfortable, and anxious to flee back to the Questura.

The *commissario* gave the shortest of introductions, then asked Costa to brief everyone on what he had learned overnight. It all came down to one word: Gladio. The roots of the organization that Dario Sordi believed was the genesis of the Blue Demon lay in the paranoia among the NATO alliance after the Second World War, when Europe appeared to be one more domino about to fall to expansionist Soviet Russia. Italy, Greece, Austria, Spain, Sweden, Switzerland . . . all were seen to be countries that might, in the wrong circumstances, perhaps even by democratic vote, turn communist. To counter such an outcome, the US and the UK, in concert with domestic politicians, formed secret networks of stay-behind undercover agents, often working in affairs of state, the civil service or other areas of public life, all prepared to carry out whatever was necessary to stave off a Soviet threat.

Much of the groundwork for what would, in Italy, become Gladio was apparently in the hands of Allen Dulles, the founder of the CIA, which was the ultimate financier of most of the operations. In Germany, Dulles had helped form the Gehlen Organization. It was headed by a former *Wehrmacht* officer turned Cold War spymaster, building a secret group that would one day become a central unit of West Germany's principal federal intelligence service. In Italy, perhaps predictably in Costa's eyes, there was no such reining-in of the Cold War spooks. The stay-behind men had been sought in some of the darkest corners of the fractious post-war state, among the neo-fascists of the *Movimento Sociale Italiano*, created by the supporters of Mussolini, and from members of the P2 Masonic Lodge that was to feature in so many Roman and Vatican scandals of the late twentieth century.

The commission had uncovered evidence that Gregor and Alyssa Petrakis, Andrea's parents, far from being the hippies they appeared, had connections with Gladio's equivalent in Greece, *Lochoi Oreinōn Katadromōn*, 'the Mountain Raiding Companies'. The couple had moved from Athens to the Maremma at the urging of intelligence agents in the right-wing colonels' junta in the early 1970s. Renzo Frasca, too, did not appear to be the office bureaucrat painted by the American Rennick the day before. There was some unconfirmed evidence to suggest that he had a role as a liaison officer with stay-behind agents such as the Petrakises.

This, in itself, did not surprise Costa. The Cold War was a time for spooks of all kinds, usually conducting small, secret campaigns against one another in ways that, for someone of his age, seemed quite inexplicable. What shocked him was the report's section on the methods and aims of Gladio. The men and women of the organization were not, as Dario Sordi seemed to hint, tasked with waiting for some threatened communist take-over before moving into action. They were there to prevent such a change in the first place, by any means at their disposal.

The cold, blunt language of an internal government document made this clear. The aim of these covert groups was to achieve their purpose through 'internal subversion' and a 'strategy of tension'. In practice that meant illegal acts and support, where necessary, for terrorist movements that might sway the electorate against voting for a further swing to the left. The commission had interviewed some of those arrested from the Red Brigades trials in Italy and the Baader–Meinhof gang in Germany. All of them alleged that they had been infiltrated by members of stay-behind teams bringing arms and funds. The names differed. In Belgium the secret army was called the SDRA8, in Denmark Absolon, and in Portugal Aginter. But the intention was always the same, to counter any drift from the centre by fomenting unease and uncertainty in the electorate, in an effort to convince them that a left-wing coup was imminent, and that safety lay in one direction only, the status quo.

Political allegiances meant less than hard cash and weaponry. Renegade Gladio members quietly helped the Marxist Red Brigades kidnap and murder. At the same time they had also, Sordi's report claimed, given money to *Ordine Nuovo*, the right-wing group behind the Piazza Fontana bomb in Milan in 1969 that killed sixteen people and began the cycle of extremist violence that was to grip the country for the next two decades.

As he spoke, the older men – Commissario Esposito, Falcone and Peroni – who had lived through those years as adults, listened in gloomy silence. Costa could see the growing astonishment on the faces of Mirko, Silvio and Rosa, for whom these were, perhaps, distant fairy tales from another generation, rumours no one ever quite believed. Even Teresa, who would have been in her early teens when the Years of Lead came to a close, seemed shocked. No one spoke much when he was finished. There wasn't a lot to say. The commission had been summarily wound up before it could reach any firm conclusion – just, Costa suspected, as it was finally beginning to turn up some hard evidence. The final paragraph was a lukewarm conclusion that whatever threat the Blue Demon had posed ended with the deaths of those involved, and the disappearance, and probable end, of Andrea Petrakis.

He finished and waited. Elizabeth Murray smiled, put up her hand and said, 'A confession. I wrote that rubbish. I was the commission secretary. They moved me there from Intelligence. Does that draft Dario gave you say who else was on the commission?'

'No.'

'Thought not. Only three you need know about. The rest are either dead or in their dotage. Italians place great faith in the wisdom of age, don't they? Charming in principle, but infuriating for those who come after. Three. Dario Sordi. Ugo Campagnolo. And your late father. Who was a perfect gentleman for the most part, but could be a real bastard when he felt like it.'

'What was the rush to close it down?' Esposito asked.

The Englishwoman laughed as if the question were ridiculous.

'This was politics! Everyone had had enough. Except Marco Costa. It was . . .' she sighed, and her large shoulders heaved as she did so, '. . . like rummaging through your own dirty linen. And for what? However much we might have argued about who put that lunatic Andrea Petrakis up to his tricks, the truth was that we were agreed on one thing. It seemed as if it was all over. No reprisals followed for those three students in the Maremma. No threats.'

'These allegations,' Costa said. 'That the Petrakises were agents of Gladio. That Frasca somehow ran them, or paid for them.'

She screwed up her large, pale face in dissatisfaction.

'I was never totally happy with that idea. Gregor and Alyssa were typical Greek fascists, utterly out of control. I doubt anyone could control them effectively, least of all a junior spook from the US Embassy. Why do you think the colonels sent them over here in the first place? They were sick of all the trouble they were causing in Athens. You won't find it in the report, but we got a pretty good steer from the Greeks that both faced arrest for murder if they were unwise enough to return home. The colonels were long gone by then. There were some half-decent people in the government. The Petrakises were involved in subverting naive students, and didn't stop short of a little brutality with anyone who resisted. Some of those they talked to never came home for supper afterwards.'

She shook her head, as if puzzled by something.

94

'Very much like those three idiots Andrea roped into his scheme, if you think about it. The Greeks didn't mind taking Gregor and Alyssa back when they were dead, mind. I saw the grave for myself. They were buried together beneath the same stone in a little cemetery not far from the Plaka. I had a damned good lunch afterwards, and on expenses too.'

'The commission sent you to Athens?' Costa asked. 'Why?'

'To talk to Greek Intelligence, of course. I told you. The colonels were gone. We were all good Europeans together. The new people let me see the files, some of them anyway. The Petrakises were career criminals who worked as hired hands for anyone who paid them. When they weren't doing the dirty work for LOK, they were busy robbing, stealing, buying and selling dope. Not a nice couple at all.'

Mirko Oliva sat on his chair, wide-eyed, speechless. Elizabeth Murray leaned forward and smiled at him.

'Yes, children. All of this happened, here, not long before you were born.'

'And Frasca?' Falcone wanted to know.

'The Americans stonewalled us,' she said. 'As they stonewalled you yesterday in the Quirinale. Frasca was Intelligence, probably CIA. A thoroughly decent government officer from what I could gather. It's possible, I say no more, that he was trying to dismantle the nonsense he'd inherited. This was the late Eighties. The collapse of the Eastern Bloc was just around the corner. Anyone with half a brain could see that coming. The Cold War was in its death throes. Who needed a bunch of right-wing crazies running around Europe handing out guns and banknotes to any passing terrorist they could find? Just to keep out a Russian regime that was crumbling from within anyway, with that very nice man Gorbachev at the helm?'

She hesitated, thinking.

'I suspect the smart money was already on the next threat coming from the east. From Afghanistan, Pakistan. Washington got the message first. Makes sense. They put the mujahideen through college in the first place. By the late Eighties the CIA had started cutting up Osama's company Amex card. Dealing with thugs and terrorists in Europe didn't matter any more. That battle was won. It was only a question of waiting for the Berlin Wall to come down. Though that's partly conjecture, which is entertaining, but ultimately futile. The truth is, I don't know what Renzo Frasca did exactly. Except he was no bean-counter.'

'False flags,' Teresa murmured.

Elizabeth Murray smiled at her and nodded.

- 3 -

'False flags,' Elizabeth Murray agreed. 'Gladio. All of those networks. That's exactly what they were. They existed to convince the people who were shot and bombed, who'd lost family and friends, that they'd better sit tight and make sure nothing changes, because the wicked bogeymen were waiting round the corner with their balaclavas and Kalashnikovs.'

'This is outrageous,' Rosa complained, visibly upset. 'You're saying these atrocities were sanctioned. By the Americans? By our own politicians? That they killed people here in order to keep themselves in power?'

'No, no, no,' the Englishwoman said quickly. 'It's not that simple. "Sanctioned" isn't the right word. No one phoned back to Rome or Washington or wherever to get permission. They didn't need to. They were spooks out in the wild, on their own, working to the rules they invented. But Gladio existed. Just a few years after this report was killed, your own prime minister, Giulio Andreotti, confirmed its existence to a rather more weighty parliamentary commission than ours. It makes for awkward reading, I know. Perhaps that's why so many have forgotten what went on. False flags have been around for centuries. Japan invaded Manchuria by fabricating the Mukden incident. Hitler set fire to the Reichstag to blame it on the Jews and seize power in Berlin. There are those who think the attack on the World Trade Center was a false-flag incident. The Madrid bombings, Pan Am 103. Are you starting to see the world you've entered?'

'Not exactly,' Peroni complained.

'It's a hall of mirrors. The truth seems as likely, or as improbable, as the absurd. Personally, and I have no particular information to support this, I do not believe for one moment that the Twin Towers fell through the actions of anyone but the murdering bastards in al-Qaeda. Equally, I know for a fact that paid agents of NATO provisioned and guided the men who planted bombs that killed ordinary Italian citizens the length of this country during the Seventies and Eighties. The difficulty is . . .'

For the first time, an expression of doubt crossed her face. 'Why would any of them stay behind so long? Who, exactly, is the enemy?'

'Petrakis thinks he's fighting what he always fought,' Costa pointed out. 'Us. Rome. Society.'

'Andrea was someone's plaything back then, and probably still is now,' she said, with absolute certainty. 'An interesting man, even when he was young. But all this . . .' She waved at the window. 'It is beyond him. Without a little help from his friends he'd never be here. Didn't Dario make this clear?'

Commissario Esposito held out his arms, exasperated.

'We're police officers, not spies. What are we supposed to do?'

She shrugged and said, 'Find the answers that eluded us twenty years ago, perhaps? Or at least provide some insight. You're not a part of the Great Game. That could be an asset. You may see something I'd miss.'

'If you couldn't find the answers,' Esposito began, 'what makes you think—?'

'I came here because Dario Sordi begged me, Commissario. He thought . . .' she grimaced, '. . . perhaps there was something I'd overlooked. Or forgotten. And that you . . . I don't know.'

She shook her head, got to her feet, took the stick and hobbled to the window. Elizabeth Murray was older than he first thought, Costa realized. Not well, either.

The woman threw up the pane, took out an unusual packet of cigarettes, with a black cover bearing some heraldic emblem. She lit one and blew the smoke out into the hot, rank city air. The sound of angry car horns drifted into the room.

Costa walked over and stood next to her. She was scanning the narrow street, up to the Lateran, down to the Colosseum.

'Old habits,' she muttered, holding up the cigarette. It had a gold tip and a dark body. 'They're called Russian Blacks.' She took another look out into the street, seemingly seeing nothing. 'Apologies if I appear paranoid. I did surveillance for a while. No one ever suspected. A batty Englishwoman. Why should they?'

'Who for?' he asked.

She turned and looked at him. An icy, deprecating stare.

'Sorry,' Costa said quickly. 'Foolish of me to ask.'

'No one's watching us anyway. At least as far as I can see. Perhaps they realize we're chasing phantoms.'

Falcone was next to them. He bent down and leaned out of the window too, then waved away the cigarette smoke.

'What do you find most puzzling about this, signora?' the inspector wondered.

'That's an extraordinary question,' she said, laughing. 'Where do you start?'

'Sometimes with something you've dismissed already, because you feel you'll never know the answer, and therefore it's not worth pursuing.'

'You are an interesting bunch, aren't you?' she replied, gazing at him. 'I can see why Dario picked you.'

'And the answer?' Falcone persisted.

She frowned.

'Why on earth would Andrea Petrakis take Frasca's son in the first place? He was fleeing Italy, en route to God knows where. Who would want a three-year-old child in tow while he was on the run? As a hostage? Possibly. But why keep him for twenty years in that case? Just so that he could teach the poor bastard a little Etruscan handiwork with a knife, then bring him back to Rome and shoot him like some wild animal?'

'We're sure it is Danny Frasca?' Teresa asked.

Peroni said, 'He called himself Danny. He had that locket. He did that thing to Batisti, he spoke Indian—'

'He spoke Pashto mostly,' Rosa cut in.

Esposito waved her into silence.

'Palombo says they have a confirmed DNA link with samples

from the Frasca couple,' the *commissario* told them. 'He was their son. There can be no doubt about it.'

'That was quick,' Teresa observed. 'A DNA match from a sample twenty years old doesn't normally turn up overnight.'

Elizabeth Murray nodded at her.

'And a sample that matched what? The Frascas are buried outside Washington. Would you keep physical evidence all that time? For a closed investigation?'

'We would,' Esposito insisted. 'So would the Carabinieri. This was their case.'

'Bodies,' Elizabeth muttered, then walked over to the computer, took Costa's CD off the desk and thrust it into the machine. 'That bothered me back then.'

She shuffled through the report until she found the photos of the shack in the Maremma, after it was stormed by the two remaining Carabinieri men.

'I only put three or four photos into the report, but we had twenty, thirty to go on. And real graves. Two young men, one young woman, dead. Grieving parents. I talked to some of them.'

'What did they say?' Costa wondered. 'About why their children did what they did?'

'The usual. Their kids could be a little wild. Easily led. But . . .' She was running through the report on the screen. 'It was the disparity. They gave me just two photos of the Frascas. Two of the Petrakises. You can see them here.'

Teresa was at her elbow immediately.

'You're the pathologist,' the Englishwoman said. 'What do you think?'

'I think I don't make snap judgements. Not without more information. Where are the autopsy reports? Where's the rest of the paperwork?'

'It wasn't in our brief. I had a couple of pages on each. They didn't tell us anything.'

Teresa looked at her, wide-eyed.

'A couple of pages?'

'The case was closed! We weren't trying to reopen it.' The

Englishwoman looked briefly guilty. 'We were trying to understand why.'

Falcone harrumphed and said, 'You can't hope to find an answer without understanding the question. Are you telling us you saw no contemporary accounts of what actually happened in any of these places?'

'I was an intelligence officer,' she complained. 'Not a cop. It was a dead case. The Carabinieri had solved it, hadn't they?'

'With their customary zeal,' Falcone observed. 'Nic. Go to the Maremma immediately. Take Prabakaran and Oliva with you. Find someone there who remembers all this. Perhaps a local police officer from the time. We'll see if we can track one down while you're on your way. It would be interesting to know their version of events.'

The inspector turned to Esposito and Silvio Di Capua.

'I need all the information you can find on both the Petrakises and the Frascas. Sir?'

Commissario Esposito shuffled on his feet, looking as if he couldn't wait to flee back to the Questura.

'What is it?' the senior officer asked miserably.

'I want your permission to ask for the Carabinieri files. And for the names and whereabouts of all the officers who dealt with the case twenty years ago.'

'Do you honestly believe none of this has occurred to them?' Esposito demanded.

Falcone's tanned face was starting to turn a deep shade of red.

'I have no idea what has or has not occurred to the Carabinieri over the last twenty-four hours. Nor are they likely to tell me, if I call and ask. You have the power to do that. We need to know. If the president wants—'

'No!'

The force of his voice was such that it echoed off the walls of the high-ceilinged room. Even Elizabeth Murray looked a little shocked.

'I don't report to the president and neither do you. He'll be gone in a few years and we'll still be here. Once this little adventure is over, we go back to being under the wing of the Ministry of the Interior. They'll be here until we're in the grave. Don't make me regret indulging Dario Sordi and his theories. They may turn out to be fantasy all along. There will be no approaches to Palombo or anyone else in the Quirinale.' He nodded at Di Capua at the computer. 'Use the resources you have here, and nothing more. If they are insufficient, then pray that Palombo and the rest of them are doing their job. That is my final word on the matter.'

He left, leaving a puzzled silence behind.

'Wonderful,' Teresa snapped. 'He wants the job done so long as we don't use anything obvious.'

Silvio Di Capua's fingers were rattling the computer keyboard. Elizabeth Murray stumbled across on her stick to stand behind him, then took a seat, her eyes glued avidly to the screen.

'I suspect,' she observed, 'you may have been picked precisely because the obvious isn't going to get anyone anywhere. Don't you?' Di Capua was still typing. 'We never had toys like this in my day. What on earth are you looking at?'

'More than I expected,' Di Capua answered. 'Who set us up with this system?'

'Esposito,' Falcone responded.

'Interesting.'

'Because . . . ?' Teresa asked, sliding behind the pair of them to gaze at the monitor as it filled with records: names and numbers, dates and file names.

'I thought I was just going to get what we have back in the Questura. I was wrong . . .' He turned and grinned at them. Di Capua had matured of late. The geek ponytail was gone. He wore a suit most of the time. Rumour had it he had acquired a live-in girlfriend and taken to playing squash, which Teresa found deeply troubling on the rare occasions she thought about it. 'We're straight into the records system of both the Ministry of the Interior and the Carabinieri. In deep too. I don't know where the shutters are going to come down, but I've never seen stuff like this before.'

'Can we have that in words I might understand?' Peroni asked.

Di Capua said, 'Esposito may not want us to talk to Palombo directly. But we can read a lot of their reports. Quite senior too.'

'Esposito fixed that?' Costa asked, surprised.

Di Capua shrugged.

'Someone did.'

'Get in there quick before someone spots the hole,' Teresa ordered. She reached for a stool to sit next to him.

'No,' Falcone said. 'Miss Murray and I will work here. You and Peroni can go to the Villa Giulia. See if you can track down anyone who remembers the Frasca incident. Or Andrea Petrakis.'

Teresa Lupo's nose wrinkled.

'Me? With him? Together? Like a team or something?'

Peroni looked just as horrified.

'Best get going,' the inspector added. 'The traffic's terrible out there.'

- 4 -

Joseph Priest didn't argue when Petrakis said he had a job in Rome. He was determined to go back to Nairobi in one piece, and with some raised authority in the Mungiki. Extortion, beatings, blackmail, robbery – these were habits he wanted to confine to his past. His future lay in the upper ranks, among those who controlled the Mungiki army throughout Kenya and, increasingly, neighbouring parts of Africa. The firm was growing, and with that came opportunities. There'd be plenty of money waiting for him when he got home, maybe enough to take a stake in some small tourist hotel on the beach in Mombasa. A step up the ladder. Something that set him apart from all the other slum kids trying to claw their way up in the world.

But the Mungiki had rules, and obedience was one of them. He had to return with the job done. Victorious. So he hung on every word Andrea Petrakis said, even the history, since, to an African – a man who didn't take the ready supply of drinking water for granted – it seemed important. The *Acqua Vergine* was one of the city's oldest supplies, one of its purest too, as the name suggested. It rose in the east, fed by rain from the Alban Hills, dividing into two channels, the *Antica* and the *Nuova*, which between them supplied, without artificial pumps or pressure, almost every important fountain in Rome, from the toothy dolphins in the Pantheon's square to the grim-faced lions overlooking the Piazza del Popolo. Even in the twenty-first century, older members of the dwindling local population would fill their plastic bottles with the flow from these public fountains, Petrakis said, flattered to drink from the same supply that had once slaked the thirst of emperors.

The *Antica* ran in a subterranean channel under the park of the Villa Borghese, through the gardens of the Villa Medici, winding beneath the busy cobbled streets around the Spanish Steps. Its journey from the quiet Lazio countryside ended at a spectacular *mostra*, an endpoint for the water system constructed for a pope emulating the architectural habits of the emperors he had succeeded.

Priest was getting a little weary of the history lesson by that stage, but his interest picked up when Petrakis did something very clever – namely, provide context. All this information, the young Kenyan discovered, had a point. The Italian needed him to understand how important the *Acqua Vergine* was to Rome, how its public display, in fountains and features, was a source of both pride and comfort for citizens beginning to stew in the summer heat, able to take a sip in the street, knowing the water would be fresh and good. History had a familiar face. The *mostra* where the *Antica* concluded its journey was the Trevi Fountain, a place Joseph Priest had visited himself, since it was a mandatory sight on the itinerary of any tourist, even a terrorist in disguise.

Two hours after he left Tarquinia he found himself striding towards the pedestrian street, not far from the Via Rasella, that he'd visited the previous week. A bunch of women's bags were slung over his right shoulder. He was practising his basic Italian in his head. To the people around, he must have looked like one more African hawker about to pester tourists in the city centre. The narrow cobbled lanes were less crowded. The TV channels had made much of the murder of the Polish woman driver and her passenger, and the statement from the president about an imminent terrorist threat. Tourists were trying to scramble onto the last departures from Fiumicino and Ciampino before the flights ban came into force. The mainline train stations were choked with travellers fighting for the few remaining seats. Hotels and restaurants were already wailing about the economic effect. The mayor had been on CNN, speaking in good English, claiming no one need fear, that security was good and the necessary measures would not interfere with any holiday in Rome.

He hadn't seemed convincing. The straggle of visitors walking cautiously through the city centre looked less carefree than a week before. Some had no choice about being there at all. Petrakis had told him why. This wasn't just a time for world leaders. The city was engaged in a fashion-week spectacular too, one scheduled long before Ugo Campagnolo invited the leaders of the G8 to the Quirinale Palace. It was an annual affair that attracted thousands of people in the rag trade, spawning a series of shows and catwalk events, some private, some public, all organized with the extravagant flair for publicity that went with the business.

Security fences and guard posts seemed to be springing up everywhere, in the Piazza di Spagna and outside subway stations and public buildings. Armed uniformed police toting ugly black automatic weapons lounged on street corners, surveying the passers-by. But the fashionistas brought their own crowd. Bright and garish, loud and unmissable, untouched by the threat, or so they wished to believe.

When he turned the corner he discovered the Trevi was swamped by a garrulous mob, all eyes on a line of brightly clad women stepping through lines of photographers held back by uniformed police. They pranced through the mob, then lined up to stand on the low wall that fronted the fountain, posing, pouting, stretching themselves into the curiously androgynous pose that models seemed to like. This was one of the most-photographed scenes in the world and he was now a part of it, someone who would alter the way the place would be perceived from this point forward, forever.

Priest strode across the street, pushing his way through, head down. He paused to glance left, towards the Via Rasella, remembering what had happened there the previous day. He had helped scout that location with Petrakis. The Italian had been insistent for some reason; no other street would suffice for their first blow in Rome. Then he found a squat stone bollard on which he was able to perch, leaning against the wall, and turned to look at the place that Petrakis had chosen for their second act.

A single statue, the regal figure of Neptune, dominated the scene, erect before the pillars of some kind of palace, bestriding a fantastical scene of imaginary sea creatures, tritons and horses and serpents, frozen in stone, yet somehow full of motion. The waters of the *Acqua Vergine* emerged from some invisible outlets at the sea god's feet as he rode, triumphant, in a seashell chariot. The fountains burst forth with a constant force and gusto, falling into a semicircular blue pool behind the line of models posing for the cameras. The surface circulated constantly, as if the force of the stream that began so many kilometres away, in the Alban Hills, was angry to find itself trapped and constrained beneath the constant gaze of a milling, garish mob.

As he watched, the perimeter of the pool became entirely surrounded by models and cameramen, TV crews and eager members of the public. None took much notice of the water or the statuary with its great, sweeping figure of the god above them.

They think they're more important, Joseph Priest said to himself quietly.

As Andrea Petrakis had instructed, he took out the camera phone, an expensive model, set it to video, checked the picture, dialled the number he'd been given, then stared at the lens, waiting for them to answer the call.

He could just make out three of them by the pool in a tiny frame on the screen. Through the shaky picture Petrakis raised his glass. Beer, Priest realized, and couldn't wait to taste one too. His mouth felt dry. He was more scared than he'd ever been since the first job that got him into the Mungiki, muscling protection money out of street traders in some dangerous Nairobi back street. Deniz Nesin was there, what looked like a clear glass of Arabian tea in his hand, his face serious as always. Deniz had fixed all this camera stuff, and the rest. The man was happier around toys and gadgets than people.

The Turk leaned forward and said, the words audible even as Priest looked straight into the eye of the phone, 'Do you remember what to do?'

'Yes, boss!' he replied, and tried to make some small salute.

Then the camera shifted position and he saw Anna Ybarra. She was still wearing the same dark swimsuit. He'd found it hard to dispel the image of her in the pool that morning. She wasn't beautiful. Not really. But she had something that worked on him, and she knew it.

'Be careful,' Anna said in her husky English.

Priest grinned and pulled out the mounting apparatus Deniz had given him. It was black metal, fitted the phone perfectly and had some kind of sticky adhesive base that was supposed to adhere to anything – brick, metal, plastic. There was a road sign by the bollard: pedestrians only. He fixed the phone in the mount, reached up and attached both to the metal front, pointing the lens towards the sea god and his strange retinue, human and stone, opposite. When it was seated firmly, he stretched up to adjust the focus and the frame, making sure the three of them back in Tarquinia would see everything, and could pass it on everywhere, over the Web, in seconds.

'Be careful . . .' he murmured, thinking of Anna Ybarra again.

The time before, after they checked out the empty houses in the Via Rasella, Petrakis had taken him to a good ice-cream shop just a few metres away, down a side street between the Trevi and the busy Via del Tritone that ran from the Corso to the Piazza Barberini. It was in the right direction. Priest thought he might buy something there, afterwards, when the panic had taken hold and he was able to walk safely away, back to the rented Moto Guzzi Nevada parked in a back road behind the Villa Borghese.

He elbowed his way through the crowd, not looking at anyone – the cops, the photographers, the models even. They were all so self-absorbed that no one noticed another African bag-seller. Even the police, with their big, ugly guns, couldn't take their eyes off the women in their bikinis and skimpy clothes, arching and angling on the wall in front of the Trevi Fountain.

The device lay hidden beneath Neptune's feet, buried there somehow by Deniz Nesin two nights before. A bitter, cruel surprise slumbering under the rocks and the waters of the *Acqua Vergine Antica*. It was a clever idea, and one that had only a single drawback. Radio waves weren't as subtle or insistent as water, Deniz said. Hard marble was almost impervious to their power, unless one found a way to get very close indeed.

The little remote control they'd given him needed to be within twenty metres of the sea god's torso in order for its signal to reach the detonator and the explosive hidden beneath the stone. He hoped he had enough leeway to be around the corner from the statues when he hit the button.

There was no way he could return to Nairobi a failure. Joseph Priest knew he'd be as good as dead the moment he left the airport. He might as well have stayed in Rome, trying to sell cheap bags for real.

– 5 –

Teresa Lupo had worked alongside Peroni many times before, but not like this. He was a cop, big, gruff, amiable, in spite of his brutish, damaged appearance. She was a forensic pathologist, fifteen years younger than him. He'd brought stability, love and some genuine companionship into her life. Professionally, their jobs meshed but never competed, much like their shared private lives. That was, she thought, for the best.

They had to take the long route through the city, driving over to the Trastevere side and then on to the Vatican, before crossing the Tiber again in Flaminio. The *centro storico* was gridlocked because of Palombo's security measures. Not that they could avoid them altogether. Close to the Vatican, from the Castel Sant'Angelo to St Peter's, the scaffolding and guard posts were beginning to appear, and the streets seemed full of uniformed men nursing weapons.

The Villa Giulia was a former papal residence near the Viale delle Belle Arti and the National Gallery of Modern Art. The place was a compact palace, grandiose but a little faded, its frescoed colonnades in need of some restoration. The grounds were well tended and possessed the kind of follies she associated with the Vatican hierarchy of old when it was at leisure: fake temples and, in the mid-distance, a balustraded ground-level feature in faded grey stone. It could only be the nymphaeum, the artificial cave harking back to pagan times where the mutilated bodies of Renzo Frasca and his wife had been found two decades before.

The museum director was called Pietro Conti. He was short, frail and elderly, beyond retirement age she thought, with pallid, blotchy skin, perhaps indicative of illness, and a pinched, grizzled face bearing a meagre salt-and-pepper moustache. Conti greeted them in his office, a capacious, sun-filled room on the first floor. He listened to Peroni's brief explanation for their visit, then said, 'Ask away.'

'You were here?' Teresa asked. 'You knew Andrea Petrakis?'

'Briefly.'

The man volunteered nothing else.

'What was he like?' Peroni asked.

Conti shrugged.

'All this was a long time ago. You read the reports, surely. You're police officers. Why ask me?'

Peroni looked at him and said, 'You've seen the news. You know Petrakis has returned. We need to try to understand this man. To comprehend why he's come back, now. In this . . . frame of mind.'

'Don't ask me about his frame of mind. I never understood it then. Why should I today? Andrea Petrakis was arrogant, wilful, disrespectful of authority. Obsessive about everything that interested him, which seemed to be Etruscan principally – and Shakespeare for some reason, which I suspect gives you a clue to his view of history.'

'What clue?' Peroni wondered.

'That he saw it all in dramatic terms,' Conti replied, as if the answer were obvious. 'Ordinary lives didn't interest him. Only great ones, or those he regarded as great. This is dreadful arrogance for any historian. Politicians merely steer the ship. Real people, ordinary people, row it. I found him lacking in insight, though highly intelligent, which at least set him apart from most of those around him. The people in Viterbo had given him some kind of junior professorship, which was a mistake. He believed he understood the subject matter rather better than was the case.' He frowned. 'That young man was indulged, which is never good for one so inexperienced and with such admiration for himself. Where he got this crazy idea . . .'

The director waved his fragile right hand in the air. It seemed so thin Teresa wondered if it might break.

'What crazy idea?' she asked.

'That he possessed some kind of empathy with the Etruscans. That they were not simply a lost race suitable for study, but a kind of metaphor one might use to explain the modern world. He had Greek blood. He thought this gave him some special insight. But . . .'

Conti glanced out of the window.

'If you'd told me he was capable of such things . . . Those poor young idiots in the Maremma. I taught them. The girl, Nadia Ambrosini, was very pretty, if somewhat vapid and lacking in academic focus.'

He pointed a short, wrinkled finger at them.

'I was merely a curator then. Had I thought anything untoward was on the cards . . .'

'You would have acted, sir,' Peroni assured him. 'No one foresaw what would happen. You've no need to feel any guilt.'

'Easy for you to say,' Conti responded. 'When they come here as students, they're in our charge. We're responsible for them. We have to be, since so often they refuse to be responsible for themselves.'

'Why did the other students worship him?' Peroni asked.

Pietro Conti looked puzzled.

'Who said they did?'

'They followed him. He was the leader of their group. They went to that place of his parents, near Tarquinia. There were photographs . . .'

'You shouldn't believe everything you see in the gutter press. I read those stories too. How he was some sort of Svengali. I assumed they were the fantasies of a desperate reporter. You think otherwise?'

Peroni said, 'Possibly.'

'Well, I can't say I noticed. I rather felt they were laughing at him most of the time. Or taking advantage. The girl in particular. Female students can be like that. Cruel.'

Teresa found herself glancing at Peroni, reassured to see he found this just as baffling.

'But they went to that place in the country,' she pointed out. 'They died there.'

'Yes,' the director agreed. 'They did.' He wriggled uncomfortably in his seat, as if steeling himself to say something unpleasant. 'Look. I was never asked this before. I find it odd that I am going over this subject now, twenty years after those children were put in their graves.' He cleared his throat. 'Andrea Petrakis was a very clever, very unusual and rather unpleasant young man. One of his talents, I came to gather, was that he knew how to provide his peers with whatever they wanted. A place where they could go and . . . hang out, was the phrase back then, I believe.'

'Hang out?' she asked.

Conti glared at her.

'Oh, please. I'm no fool. They used to talk about it, quite openly. They were little more than provincial children, most of whom had fled very traditional Catholic upbringings. Petrakis offered them a place where they could do whatever they liked. If they adored him – and I have my doubts about that – it was for purely practical purposes. He provided them with what they sought, which is the easiest way anyone can win popularity with the young.'

Teresa tried to work this out.

'You're saying they didn't even like him?'

'I'm saying . . .' He tried to find the right words. 'They were two parties who knowingly exploited one another. Petrakis fed their needs. He provided them with drugs. Many drugs. We had officers in the Carabinieri crawling over this place afterwards. Quite why such mundane crimes were of interest to them, in the light of what hap-pened to that unfortunate American couple, is something I'll never understand.'

'You mean he was their dealer?' she asked.

'Precisely. In return, they indulged his strange ideas about the Etruscans, and gave him rather a lot of money too, I imagine.'

She was starting to get hot under the collar. The briefing from the Quirinale was plainly inaccurate or deliberately misleading.

'Is that what drove them?' she asked. 'Not politics, but dope?'

'I never heard a word of politics discussed in those circles. I would have welcomed it if I had. They all seemed remarkably . . .' he searched for the word, '. . . dull, to be honest with you. Petrakis apart.'

'That's what these kids wanted? The chance to behave the way they never could at home with Mamma around? To be hippies, like the Etruscans?'

Pietro Conti regarded her contemptuously and asked, 'What?'

'Hippies,' she repeated, feeling uncomfortable beneath the heat of his gaze. 'Or so I read . . .'

He adopted a pose – fingers tented, head to one side – that appeared very much that of an indignant academic.

'Where did you read this? In some history book for infants? The Etruscans possessed half of Italy for more than two hundred years. They provided at least three kings of Rome. This was a proud and independent warrior nation that showed its enemies no mercy whatsoever.' He nodded at the door. 'You should see some of the exhibits we have. They had a society, a culture, that didn't fit in with our ideas on morals. But they were no . . . hippies.' He shrugged. 'And in the end they were defeated. Now, because all that Rome has left us is a few tombs and some rather risqué objects, we regard an entire civilization as some fey, lost race of aesthetes. Poets bearing olive branches, too delicate for this rough world of ours.'

The old man folded his arms.

'Andrea Petrakis was a decent scholar. He certainly knew enough to reject such nonsense. You'll have to do better with your theories than that, my dear.'

'Sorry,' she muttered, feeling a little humbled.

Peroni came to her rescue.

'Can we see where the Frasca couple were found?'

A practical, straightforward question, she realized. Unlike her, he was a cop, someone who thought in straight lines. Sometimes it was the best way to be.

'If you must,' Pietro Conti groaned and struggled out of his chair. 'But before we leave the subject, I will tell you one thing.'

They waited.

'Licentious, weak, self-obsessed, flawed – a people waiting on oblivion, almost inviting it,' the museum director went on. 'Should anyone fit that description, it's us, surely. If an old man like me can see that, so can a younger one as bright as Andrea Petrakis. He gave those children what they wanted. The place in Tarquinia. Their . . .' his mouth wrinkled with disgust, '. . . fun. But he knew it was a vulnerable debility on their part and he hated them for that. Hated us too. That I saw in his eyes. Now, let me show you our nymphaeum, such as it is.'

- 6 -

The device Deniz gave him looked like the remote from a video camera. Small, black, plastic, it sat in Joseph Priest's hand, wriggling in his sweaty grip. There weren't just models and photographers and a small crowd of gaping locals and tourists crowded round the Trevi Fountain. There were *carabinieri* too, as if they knew – or at least suspected – something might happen.

The Kenyan let slip a quiet curse and told himself not to be so stupid. It was a famous place. There'd be pickpockets and street people, hassling, looking for a purse or a camera to steal. The cops would be there, always. Except that these men and women held weapons, modern automatic rifles, the kind the Mungiki never managed to get, even in Nairobi. They weren't watching the half-naked women on the perimeter wall fronting the fountain's foaming waters any more. They were scanning the crowd, peering hard at anyone they felt deserved it.

Priest was as close to Neptune as he could get. He could have thrown Deniz's little remote and hit the sea god on the chest, if only that would work. He didn't give the idea more than a passing thought. Weeks of training in rough itinerant camps on the Afghan-Pakistan border had left him in no doubt about the nature of the people he'd joined. Bad luck wasn't going to serve as an excuse.

One of the *carabinieri*, a thickset man with sunglasses, no more than two strides away, was staring at him, cradling a black rifle in his arms.

Priest surreptitiously stuffed the detonator control back into his pocket and smiled, the big, open grin he imagined he ought to use. Then he removed a counterfeit designer bag from his shoulder, dangled it in front of the man, laughing, trying not to tremble.

'Special cop discount,' he said, aware of the nervousness in his voice. 'What you think? Huh?'

'I think you should go somewhere else. You know the rules.'

Priest nodded. He didn't understand the first thing about being a street hawker.

'Cigarette, boss?' he asked, raising his fingers to his mouth.

'No. You got a hearing problem?'

He laughed, cupped his hand to his ear and shuffled off into the crowd, trying to think. The cop's eyes were surely boring into his back, still. Priest knew he couldn't wander too far. Deniz's little control wouldn't be able to talk to its partner, buried beneath all that contorted stone, in whatever ancient supply system fed the teeming waters of the *Acqua Vergine* into its *mostra* at the Trevi.

Priest bumped into someone, apologized, tried to smile again and found himself looking into the face of a very pretty, very pale woman, of perhaps thirty. She wore a grey business suit with a black leather handbag over her left shoulder and stared at him, straight-faced, almost miserable, as if he'd come from another planet.

'I can sell you a nicer bag than that,' he said in English, looking her in the eye. 'Something a little brighter.'

'Beat it,' she shot back.

American.

He held up the same one he'd shown the cop.

'For you, a really good price. You're like me. You got a Third World currency now. And . . . yeah . . .'

He grinned. She was a looker. Much more so than Anna Ybarra.

To his surprise she didn't swear at him. She simply turned back to watch the models jigging away to some music from a system set beside the fountain. There was a big man by her side. She spoke to him. The way the guy nodded in tune to her words told Joseph Priest he was hers to control.

He had a dark suit, close-cropped dark hair, shades. White shirt and tie. Muscular, with a tanned face and a thin-lipped mouth that seemed to run in a near-straight horizontal line from one side of his face to the other.

Joseph Priest really didn't like this guy.

'*Scusi*,' he murmured, then pushed his way through the mob until he turned the corner into the narrow street leading back to Tritone.

A quick glance back confirmed what he'd hoped for. The video phone was still there, high on the sign behind the crowd. Andrea, Deniz and Anna ought to be watching everything on the patio of the villa outside Tarquinia, relaxed, laughing maybe, while he risked his neck, alone, without so much as a weapon to help him, since Andrea said that could only increase the danger.

'Always the same,' Priest muttered to himself. 'Give the black guy the shit job.'

He closed his eyes for a moment, breathed deeply, wondered how big an explosion Deniz had planned, and whether the Turk had been truthful about his chances of escaping its effects.

There'd be lots of flying masonry, he guessed. Lots of smoke and noise and damaged bodies. Getting away didn't worry him. In Nairobi and Mombasa he'd crawled out of any number of violent encounters, sometimes right under the nose of the law.

What he didn't want was to get hurt by his own actions. There'd been some fighting in Afghanistan, a quick escape in the night when the British got too close to where they were staying. A couple of people died in that, and it wasn't the other side's soldiers who killed them, but some crazed Taleban kids, firing off their rifles wildly, at anything that moved. To lose your life that way seemed so . . . unfair.

He leaned up against the wall that ran to the side of the fountain. Neptune's street show was now a good ten strides away. The stone seemed so solid it ought to survive anything. Joseph Priest checked round, made sure no one was watching, looked up and did his best to nod discreetly to the phone set high on the wall beyond the fashion mob and the bored, rude cops. He wondered if the three of them would notice, whether they were even looking at anything except the heaving sea of bodies that lay just a few seconds away from some bloody oblivion.

They made a strange team. This wasn't the kind of work Priest relished, not that he had any choice in the matter.

Timing was essential, Andrea said. Eleven-thirty exactly, because at that moment the big men of the G8 would be posing for the cameras on the piazza outside the Quirinale Palace, kicking off the summit for the privileged pack of photographers allowed into their secure and private lair to record the event.

He watched the second hand on the fake Rolex that Andrea had given him that morning as it ticked round to the right time.

It didn't seem quite right to pray at that moment. So he took a deep breath and then, his legs stiff from expectancy, sweat starting to prick his brow, pulled out the control once more and thrust his strong, dark thumb onto the button.

- 7 -

They walked through galleries of objects that amazed her: glazed ceramics, statues, jewellery. Scenes of a disappeared past, of war and love, feasting and mythical creatures, some in agony, some coupled together in strange, unreal forms of ecstasy. The Villa Giulia was a world within itself, one she could hardly believe she had missed in all her years in Rome. Then they were outside, striding through the grounds to the place where Renzo and Marie Frasca's bodies had been left like store dummies posed for posterity.

The nymphaeum didn't seem to have changed much in two decades. All it lacked was two horribly disfigured corpses stretched out on the plinth beneath the gaze of the four stone muses support-ing the balustrade above.

The place had been dug out of the dank Roman earth and it smelled of damp and algae. Lily pads filled the narrow channel of the stream that ran in a winding channel behind the empty platform. Ferns and moss tumbled from the alcoves. The mosaic in front, a sea triton playing the pipes, was grimy with dust and dirt from the feet of tourists wandering around this small subterranean folly, one that, close up, lacked the grandeur and taste Teresa Lupo had come to associate with the imperial-era grottoes that it sought to imitate. There were no mythical fairy creatures here. Only the ghost of a monster.

Peroni turned, looked at the staircase, thinking, in the plain, logical way cops did, one she wished she might, one day, emulate.

'Two corpses,' he said. 'Adults. Hard work dragging them in from the street, down those stairs. One man alone—'

'Could not do it,' Pietro Conti agreed. 'That is, I think, obvious.'

'Did you come here, the weekend it happened?' she asked.

He shook his head.

'The museum was closed to the public for some much-needed building work. I was in Cambridge. A small conference organized by the Fitzwilliam. But . . .' He shrugged. 'I heard enough on my return. By then it was all over.'

'Is there anyone left who was around when it happened?'

'There's a caretaker. Gatti. Ordinarily he would have been in the apartment. But the place was closed for renovation. There seemed no need.' He pulled out a mobile phone and called for the man. 'Andrea Petrakis had a key to the main areas. It was his right. He was a junior professor. The people in Viterbo said so.'

Peroni pulled out his pad and looked at the notes there.

'They were murdered at their home in Parioli, almost two kilometres from here. He had to transport them by car, drag them in from the street, take them down those stairs, leave his message . . .'

'Shakespeare, as it turned out,' Conti grumbled. 'It took a lot of cleaning to get rid of that. Nor do I feel it's an act that a professor, even a junior one, ought to countenance. Spray-painting on the walls of a museum.'

He glanced at them.

'Andrea was rather fond of tricks and riddles and codes. That play in particular. I think it mirrored his view of the world. The wrong people were in control, you see. Caesar, the dictator posing as a democrat. The heroes were those who would depose him, and found themselves cast as villains. And in the end they would lose.' He sniffed and looked around him at the grimy stones. 'As did everyone concerned, I rather thought.'

'Shakespeare,' Teresa repeated, thinking. 'Why write a message like that in the first place?'

A burly middle-aged man was striding down the steps. Gatti looked like a wrestler, newly retired. He wore a grimy T-shirt and faded jeans, and had a round, bristly bucolic face, ruddy from sun or labour or drink.

'Angelo . . .' Conti said, standing back as the man arrived. He had a powerful smell of sweat about him, and an expression of surly

120

bafflement. 'These people are from the police. They would like to know what you remember of the Petrakis incident.'

'Why?'

Peroni gazed into his face.

'You must have read the papers.'

'Better things to do.'

Conti retreated a little further and commented, 'Reading is not to Angelo's taste.' A fiery glance came from the hefty workman, one that made Peroni take notice. 'Nor,' the director added, 'need it be.'

'Twenty years ago . . .' Teresa began.

'Two dead people there,' Gatti grunted, pointing at the empty flat stone beneath the four grimy nymphs.

'Did you see them?' Peroni asked him.

'Yes.' Nothing more. This was going to be hard work. She felt her temper rising, then bit her tongue. Peroni was so much better in these situations.

'Tell me what happened, Angelo,' he said quietly. 'I know these things are upsetting and we shouldn't be here asking, after all this time. But we've no choice.' He eyed Conti, in a way Gatti couldn't miss. 'We've got bosses too. They're all the same.'

The man laughed a little at that. Angelo Gatti was smarter than he wanted to appear.

'I saw what you saw. *Exactly* what you saw. Two dead people. Lots of blood. Some words on a wall for me to clean up.'

'Nothing else?' Peroni persisted.

'What? To clean up? No. Nothing else. They'd done that. All those cops and people in suits. The photographers. You know what I thought when I got here?'

He wanted to be asked.

'What did you think?' Peroni said.

'I thought there was a wedding going on. So many people with cameras. So many suits and uniforms. No one looking happy. Just like every wedding I ever went to.'

She couldn't help herself.

'What did you see?'

'I told you! The same as everyone else. A bunch of pictures in the paper. I bought one that time. Seemed only right. Only way to find out what was going on. All the bosses . . .' he looked askance at Conti, '. . . were at the seaside or somewhere. The Carabinieri didn't want the likes of me around. Went crazy the moment I appeared . . .' he nodded towards the steps that led to the terrace above, '. . . up there. As if they belonged here. Not me.'

'The bodies . . .'

'Saw them in the paper. Just like you.'

'Just in the paper? Not here?' Peroni asked. 'You're sure of that? Absolutely?'

'Sure I'm sure. All I saw was a lot of men in suits looking like they were going about their business. Then there was me. Up there. Getting marched off like I'd broken the law or something. Americans. Italians.'

Peroni wasn't listening to the man's moans. He was focusing on detail.

'Let me get this straight,' he said. 'There were two murder victims found here. You're telling me none of you saw them? No one from the museum at all?'

'The people we deal with have been dead rather longer than a few hours,' Pietro Conti replied rather pompously. 'Why would we want to be involved? He only came because he heard something was going on. Isn't that right?'

Peroni watched the squat, muscular man.

'Where did you hear that, Angelo?'

'Cafe in Flaminio. Someone saw all the cars turning up. I got curious. I'm the caretaker. Job means what it says.'

Teresa took Peroni to one side.

'We're wasting our time here,' she whispered. 'They know nothing. We need to get Silvio and Elizabeth Murray to trawl through the documents and see what they can find.'

'Computers,' he muttered. She felt small and inexperienced at that moment. 'They're going to do that anyway.' He glanced at the subterranean hollow around them. 'Something odd happened here. We're not going to find out what it was from some idiotic machine.'

Her voice rose.

'So what's the point if no one remembers a thing?'

The caretaker from the Maremma heard and bridled at that. He jerked a stubby finger covered in dirt and earth in Teresa Lupo's direction.

'I remember lots. Not my fault it's not what you want to hear.'

'Angelo has a very good memory,' Pietro Conti added. 'That's one reason I thought he might be able to help. As much as anyone, anyway. If you'd asked in my office, I would have told you. We weren't involved. None of us were. The Carabinieri and all those gentlemen who came with them. They didn't want us around. It's understandable, isn't it? What did we have to offer, other than the name of Andrea Petrakis?'

'And who gave them that?' Teresa demanded.

The two men exchanged an odd glance.

'Not us,' Conti answered eventually. 'They had it already. These people were remarkably unpleasant. They took over this place as if they owned it. None of us felt much minded to pose awkward questions . . .'

'I asked them,' Gatti announced. 'The Carabinieri told me to mind my own business.'

'This was our business,' Conti cut in. 'Petrakis was attached to the museum. I've no idea where they got his name from. If they'd been asking about drugs, possibly. But not in relation to something of this nature. It wouldn't have occurred to me. He simply seemed to be one more arrogant young man, not a murderer.'

'The Carabinieri,' Peroni growled. He gazed at Gatti. Teresa could imagine these two in a bar somewhere, moaning about the state of the world over beer and *panini*. 'I don't suppose any of them gave you their names, did they?'

The caretaker shook his grizzled head.

'You think they'd have told the likes of me who they were?'

'You could have asked,' Teresa said with a sigh.

'I could have. But I didn't. They told me to get lost and I wasn't in the mood to argue. Who wants to see a couple of dead bodies anyway? What's the point?'

'Thanks,' Peroni began to say, and started to turn away from beneath the gaze of the four stone nymphs who had been watching their conversation, as if quietly amused.

'I said they never gave me their names,' Gatti added. 'Doesn't mean I don't know.'

The big cop stopped and stared at him.

'One of them anyway. Saw him on the TV. Only yesterday. Same long, miserable face as he had back then, when he was young and throwing his weight around. Big man now. Important.'

'So you do watch TV?' Teresa said. 'Saw who? Where?'

'The *carabiniere* who kicked me out of here when I came looking. He was at the Quirinale Palace when Sordi was laying down the law to us all, about where we can go, what we can do. Two steps behind that cunning old bastard he was, pulling his strings too these days, I guess.'

'Who?' she asked.

'The TV said he was important. Something to do with security . . . They called him Palombo.'

– 8 –

The Trevi Fountain didn't look any different. Nothing had happened. Still, he felt everyone was looking at him. The three of them in their nice, comfortable villa outside Tarquinia most of all.

Joseph Priest put his head down, slipped the detonator back into his pocket, wiped his sweaty hands on his jeans, took the thing out and tried again. Twice.

What was it Deniz said? If at first you don't succeed . . . get closer.

Which was a very easy statement from someone sitting on a rich man's patio miles away, laughing at all this down a mobile phone line.

He tried to imagine what it would be like to be loose and penniless in Italy. He could do better than sell cheap bags. He could steal and bully, wriggle his way into any number of scams. Except that he would be just one more penniless black African among the tide of *clandestini* trying to scrape a living off the street. Even if he managed to escape the wrath of the Mungiki forever – and that he somehow doubted – Joseph Priest wondered what he might achieve in a world where, at the age of twenty-eight, he had to begin again from scratch, just as he had as a nine-year-old beggar in Kibera, Nairobi's slum, the biggest in Africa they said, almost as if it were a matter of pride.

'Deniz, Deniz,' Priest murmured, taking a couple of strides nearer the fountain, checking his watch, seeing he was now a minute late, and the second hand seemed to have picked up speed. 'You'd better not be kidding me, my man.'

He dried his fingers once again, took a deep breath and pushed the button. Then again. One more step forward. A third try.

It was dumb. The only phone they gave him was on the wall opposite, recording his failure. He'd no way of calling them, telling them the truth.

It just doesn't work. I tried. Really. I did.

Maybe the batteries had gone flat. Maybe the ancient stone beneath Neptune's feet was so thick the twenty-first century couldn't penetrate it. Or the waters of some imperial-era aqueduct had seeped into the electronics the Turk had managed to smuggle into the fountain system a few nights before.

The bomb didn't work and it never would.

Joseph Priest knew that somehow. Just to prove it to himself he barged back through the crowd, elbowing everyone out of the way, a cop at one point even, and the American woman – the looker, the one who'd told him to beat it a few minutes earlier.

He got to the edge of the fountain and found himself giggling for some reason. Priest pulled out the remote, leaned over the stone wall, grinned at the people round him. Goggle-eyed teenagers, serious fashion types. Photographers. A few tourists too. He pumped the button again repeatedly. It was dead. As dead as they ought to be.

He looked at the young girl next to him, grinned and said, 'I guess it's your lucky day.'

Then he threw Deniz Nesin's little black toy into the foaming waters of the Trevi Fountain, where it sank beneath the surface to join a glittering collection of coins.

He turned. The American woman and the big guy with the shades were there, up close, staring at him.

She threw back her head. Her hair was blonde going on ginger. Long and soft.

'Sadly,' she said, 'I don't think it's yours, Joseph.'

He managed to elbow the young kid next to him hard in the ribs, and the way she recoiled from the blow, shrieking in pain and shock, at least gave him a body in the way.

Running was never a problem. He'd been doing that most of his life. But when he got to the edge of the crowd, going back the way he came, towards the ice-cream place he'd never revisit, he was shocked to see they were following him, with weapons in their hands. They were close and all they were looking at was him.

Joseph Priest felt, at that moment, scared, and a fool. He dumped the bags, dumped everything in his pockets, all those items that might incriminate him, then took to his heels and started to flee, wondering where he could hide now, knowing there was no way home.

– 9 –

'Am I the only one who finds it remarkable that Luca Palombo was there twenty years ago too?' Teresa Lupo wondered. They were back in the apartment, with Falcone, Silvio and the Englishwoman, and the pathologist was astonished to discover no one seemed much interested in what she and Peroni had found out at the Villa Giulia.

'I'm sorry, I thought you knew already,' Elizabeth Murray said. 'Of course Palombo was part of the investigation. He was a senior Carabinieri officer. It was pretty obvious to everyone he was going places. If a man like that hadn't been part of the Blue Demon case, that would have been odd.' She looked at them, a large, exhausted figure clutching her walking stick, immobile in one of the threadbare chairs. 'Well, wouldn't it?'

'It would have been very odd,' Falcone agreed. 'You really must try to avoid seeing conspiracies in everything.'

'Then why didn't he tell you at the briefing yesterday?' Peroni wondered.

'Because it wasn't relevant,' Elizabeth replied. 'Is that all you found out at the Villa Giulia? I'm sorry. I could have saved you the journey. I was rather hoping . . .'

'No, it's not all,' Teresa snapped.

'Well?' Falcone asked when she said nothing more.

'It's the fact that all we can see about this case is what people choose to put in front of us. There's no . . .' she fought for the right word, '. . . no dust. No traces left behind. No stray pieces anywhere, not a single witness, not a photograph that hasn't come out of Palombo's album. Or even one member of staff at the museum who saw a thing.'

Elizabeth Murray gave her a sympathetic look.

'There were renovations. The place was closed to the public. It was the weekend, so there were no academic staff there.'

'The caretaker turned up not long after they found the bodies,' Peroni cut in. 'He didn't look the sort to keep his nose out of anything.'

Teresa felt grateful for his intervention. She could tell what they were thinking, the Englishwoman and Falcone. She wasn't a cop. She was out of her depth, flinching at shapes in the shadows that no one else could see.

'They kept him away from the bodies,' Teresa added.

'We always keep civilians away from the bodies,' Silvio Di Capua said from the computer, then shut up when she glared at him.

'I'm telling you,' Teresa insisted, 'something about this is just plain wrong. Two dead people in a museum. No one sees. No one has a story to tell. Not a report on file anywhere. How do you explain that, Silvio?'

'It was a long time ago,' he said straight away. 'From what I can see, the Carabinieri don't have anything on their present system from then. Unless it's live, of course. Why should they? We wouldn't.'

'Are you serious?' she shrieked. 'Eight people died in all. For a week or so everyone thought Italy was back in the terror years again. Someone killed the Frascas. The Petrakis couple. Those three kids in the farmhouse near Tarquinia. The *carabiniere*. And you're telling me there's nothing anywhere on their system, on ours, on the ministry's . . . ?'

'You're judging them on the basis of how we work now,' Di Capua declared. 'Twenty years ago they used different standards, different methodologies. Trying to fathom out what they were doing – it's the same kind of thing Petrakis was trying to work out as a historian. Looking at fragments, hoping to decode them.'

Peroni came to her aid again.

'At least he had some fragments. It's very unusual to have nothing at all. Don't you think?' He frowned, as if worried by what he was about to say. 'Leo? We could approach Palombo and ask for some background. There's got to be some sly way of doing it without letting him know what's going on here. Just a request for information. I can handle it. I just act dumb and ask for some clarification. He'd never know . . .'

Falcone shook his head. He looked tired, Teresa thought. His tanned features were gaunt, his silver beard less than perfectly trimmed. They were locked out of the heart of the operation, stranded in a strange, cold place none of them quite understood. The inspector was never beneath a little intrigue. But he wanted to be the perpetrator, not the victim.

'And what would you ask for? If it was useful, Palombo would realize why we were asking. Then we'd compromise ourselves, Commissario Esposito, the president himself. You know our orders. We can't approach anyone in the team at the Quirinale under any circumstances. I will not break that promise, or allow any of you to do so, either. We can't take the risk.'

Teresa slammed her fists down on the table. Silvio Di Capua's machine jumped, as if to attention.

'I don't believe this. So how are we supposed to pass the day, Leo? We can't talk to anyone. We can't access any contemporary reports apart from some ancient inquiry that got stifled before it could get anywhere.'

A thought struck her. She looked at Elizabeth Murray.

'Who did kill your report?' Teresa asked her straight out.

'No one *killed* it,' the Englishwoman insisted. 'There was an agreement to go no further. It seemed pointless. Everyone concurred. Except for Marco Costa, as I said.'

Falcone was staring at her.

'These things don't just die of their own accord. Someone must have planted the idea.'

She looked a little out of sorts. The discomfort didn't sit well on her.

'Who?' Peroni insisted.

'It was just gossip. I was the secretary. They kept me out of the room when they wanted to talk privately. But . . .' She glanced at Teresa, who was unable to read the woman's expression. Relief or resentment? It was impossible to tell. 'Marco told me it was Campagnolo who kept pressing for the commission to be wound up. He was very insistent. He had powerful friends, even back then.'

Teresa felt like screaming.

'So that's two people you met yesterday who were directly involved in the Frasca case and never bothered to mention it.'

'Rome is a small place . . .' Falcone began.

'So I can see. Silvio. Did you look up that detail on the boy?'

Falcone seemed bemused.

'What detail?'

'Show him,' she ordered.

Di Capua pulled up a photo she'd snatched with her phone in the bloody room in the house in the Via Rasella. Danny Frasca dead on the floor, a bloody mess. The assistant pathologist zoomed in on a patch of skin on the upper chest.

'Palombo's people snatched the body away from me before I could look properly.' She stared at the screen, and the conviction kept growing. 'A convenient locket round the neck apart, what evidence is there that this is the son of Renzo and Marie Frasca?'

'DNA,' Elizabeth Murray told her. 'The best evidence there is. Or so I thought.'

Silvio Di Capua glanced at his boss, as if he was beginning to understand where this was going.

'That's not evidence,' he pointed out. 'It's hearsay. Palombo told us it was a fact. He hasn't shown us any report. I can't find one on the system either, and it ought to be there.'

'There's a tattoo of a rose on his shoulder,' Teresa went on. 'Judging by the appearance, I'd say it was old. So old that I'd hazard a guess it was put there when he was a young boy.'

Peroni said, 'The Frascas wouldn't do that to their own child. No one would.'

Di Capua shook his head.

'Not many people. I did a little hunting. The only place I can see that it's recorded is in Russia. Among the criminal classes. The tattoo was a sign of their lineage.' He looked at them. 'The rose meant, "This is the child of a Mafia member."'

No one spoke for a moment. Then Teresa added, 'Afghanistan

was under Russian occupation from 1979 until 1988, when they retreated. It wasn't a rout. In the beginning there was some loose Russian support for the Najibullah government in Kabul, but pretty soon Russia itself was falling apart. By 1991 Moscow had enough problems of its own. There were Russians still there, though. In Kabul as advisers. As criminals too, helping run the opium trade. When the Taleban arrived in 1996 . . .'

She fell quiet, remembering. The return of the Blue Demon had sent her back to her own computer the night before, to revive her memories of this tumultuous time, a period not so long ago when the world seemed to shift on its own axis.

'The first thing they did was torture, castrate and then hang Najibullah from a lamp post in the centre of town. After that they rounded up everyone they didn't like and the killings began.' The link made sense. It had to. 'Any Russian criminals who got left behind wouldn't have lasted five minutes. A young boy with a tattoo . . . who knows? They might have kept him in case he was useful later.'

'This is far-fetched,' Elizabeth said, though with little conviction.

'As far-fetched as the idea Petrakis took the Frasca boy all the way to Afghanistan in the first place? And then back again? You were the one who said that didn't make sense. Not that picking up some local Russian orphan and returning him to Rome as Danny Frasca does, either. Particularly . . .' she felt her own head begin to spin, '. . . if he needs the covert support of some Ministry of Interior hack to make the trick work. I don't know if this is crazy or not, and I can't find out. We don't have forensic. We don't have access to the body. Or Palombo's report. It's almost as if they exiled us out here as a joke. They know we can't make any progress trapped in this place. We don't have the resources. We can't prove or disprove anything.'

This was Falcone's call. It had to be.

The inspector looked lost for a moment. She knew him well enough to understand that his own mind was working in this direction too.

'You could call Esposito,' Peroni suggested. 'Tell him this is some set-up.'

'He sent us here,' Di Capua reminded them. 'Or Dario Sordi did. Or . . . who?'

Unconsciously, Teresa realized, they were all looking at Elizabeth Murray at that moment.

'Sorry,' the Englishwoman said with a shrug. 'I just got a call asking me to come out of retirement. I did warn you. This world is a hall of mirrors. More than I counted on, to be honest.'

'We stay, we work, we talk to people,' Falcone insisted. 'We're not sidelined. Nic's out there. Let's find some more names for him to chase. What about the three *carabinieri* who went to the farm-house in Tarquinia? Who were they?'

Di Capua's fingers began to clatter the keyboard again.

'The one who died was called Lorenzo Bartoli,' he announced. 'The other two were Ettore Rufo and Beppe Cattaneo.'

'What?' Peroni asked. 'Cattaneo?'

'That's right,' Di Capua answered, running his hand across the screen. 'The dead man came from Tarquinia. The other two from Rome. Cattaneo . . .'

Peroni scowled.

'Cattaneo was a crook. We found him with half his face shot off in a car out near Fiumicino ten years or so ago. I was on the case. The guy was as crooked as they come. Some Sicilian drug gang had him on the payroll. We had word he worked as a hit-man for them from time to time. He liked that kind of job. Never did find who killed the bastard, but there were plenty of people with good reason.'

Falcone nodded and said, 'I remember.'

'And also,' Peroni added quickly, 'what the hell were two *cara-binieri* from Rome doing out there in Tarquinia? They've enough local people on the ground. Elizabeth?'

The Englishwoman sighed.

'I don't know. I never asked. It didn't seem—'

'Relevant,' Peroni interrupted. 'You got anything on Ettore Rufo? The name means nothing to me.'

Di Capua pointed at the screen.

'He took early retirement one year after the case. No trace of him on any of the systems after that.'

'Find the man,' Falcone ordered. 'Find me . . .'

'Behold!' Di Capua cried, and turned to them with a broad grin on his face, flourishing his chubby hand at the monitor with glee. 'Bartoli's older brother was in the Carabinieri too. He quit two months after his brother died. The system says he's now a coastguard in some place called Porto Ercole. Where's that?'

'North of Tarquinia. Just over the Tuscan border. Nic can get there.'

'We're not supposed to go into Tuscany without permission,' Peroni pointed out.

'No,' Falcone agreed. 'We're not.'

- 10 -

Anna Ybarra sat in silence next to the two men huddled over the laptop computer in the dining room of the villa, trying to understand what was happening. It seemed impossible to her. There was nothing like this in the little village of Hernani. Nothing at all.

Somehow Deniz had managed to hook the mobile phone to the computer screen. They saw the scene at the Trevi Fountain unfold in miniature, moment by moment. It felt wrong, like watching a bad home-made movie. Joseph working his way through the crowd, turning from a visible dark spot to little more than a pinprick and then disappearing, only to return. And still no explosion.

Did Joseph really throw the remote into the fountain? She thought so, and so did the two men with her. Deniz sighed when they saw the movement of the Kenyan's arm, a gesture that seemed to indicate, even through this shaky, indistinct medium, a sense of despair and surrender.

'Might have known,' the Turk said, and took a sip of his water.

'It didn't work, did it?' she told him, feeling more than a little angry on the part of the Kenyan. She hadn't liked him much, hadn't appreciated the way he stared at her, openly, lasciviously. He'd taken the risk, though, while they sat around drinking, swimming, waiting. 'He tried. What else could he do?'

'He did try,' Petrakis agreed, then picked up his own phone.

'Who are those people?' she asked, pointing at the picture. 'In the crowd. There's a man and woman there. They look interested in him.'

'It's a fashion show,' Petrakis told her. 'You'd expect security.'

She was sure of what she'd seen.

'He spoke to them. They followed him. Why?'

'You just can't get the staff . . .' the Italian murmured.

Then he keyed a short number into this phone and turned to smile at them, waiting, his finger over the button.

'Tell me what you think of Joseph,' he said.

'He was a comrade,' she answered straight away. 'One of us.'

'Really,' Petrakis said.

She felt a red flare of anger in her head.

'Why do you keep us in the dark, Andrea? How can we work together if we know nothing?'

'I'm a general. You're a soldier. You know what you need to know. Now . . . Deniz?'

The Turk did something to the keyboard. The screen split into two windows. One was the shaky video of the Trevi Fountain. The other appeared to be a live newscast from the piazza of the Quirinale Palace, with all the G8 leaders lined up for the cameras, smiling, silent in the sun.

Andrea Petrakis hovered his finger over the phone.

'Watch.'

He pressed the key. After a long second the picture at the Trevi Fountain changed. A dust cloud began to emerge, shakily, from beneath the group of statues at the back, obscuring everything. Then it was cleared in part by a violent crimson geyser gushing forth from the mist, raining down gory liquid and rubble on the gathering in the cobbled piazza, sending them shrieking into one another, turning a half-orderly crowd into a yelling, terrified mob.

A single drop of what appeared to be blood landed on the camera lens. She watched as it slowly began to streak downwards, smearing everything a lurid and filmy shade of red. She could still see beyond. When the storm that had roared out from the Trevi subsided, the fountain was transformed, wrecked, ruined as if by some sudden internal earthquake.

Neptune lay in pieces, a stone corpse, face down, limbs torn asunder amidst a gushing scarlet stream. Everywhere the water had taken on a familiar livid hue.

Sweat started to dampen her palms, a pain began to bite at her temples. In the window on the screen next to this terrible scene they could see the famous figures of the summit, less than a kilometre away, on the hill, recoiling in shock at the noise of the nearby blast. Their faces were bloodless, their eyes blank with anger and fear. Dark-suited men with coils emerging from their perfect, standard-issue haircuts were beginning to usher them swiftly away from the podium, back into the palace behind.

Terror had arrived in Rome – not the private kind, reserved for the likes of the politician they had kidnapped in the dead of night, but a different sort of beast, one so bold and vicious it felt free to roam the city at large in the bright, clear light of a summer's day.

She looked at the fountain again, fearing to see the injuries, knowing she had to look. Desperate shapes stumbled through the dust cloud, hands to heads, shrieking, unable to see properly. A few bodies lay on the floor, though they seemed to be moving. A couple of police officers had placed handkerchiefs over their mouths and were trying to make their way into the howling mob to help. Yet, as the storm of dust began to settle, it didn't look like a massacre somehow, and the damage to the familiar landmark seemed limited to missing stone limbs and cracked frozen waves at the foot of the figures where the bloodied water had burst upon the crowd.

Anna Ybarra watched carefully, trying to understand. She formed a picture in her own mind of what might have happened. It was as if someone had placed a blood clot in the Trevi's thrashing, flowing vein, then punctured it, despatching a pressurized burst of fake gore out onto the models and photographers and curious, gawping bystanders in the crowd.

It was a piece of theatre, a visual political gesture, one that possessed a vicious, cruel streak of brilliance.

'Did you kill anyone?' she asked quietly.

'Probably not,' Petrakis said without looking at her. 'That wasn't the point.' He scowled at the screen, as if trying to clarify his thoughts. 'I don't want their fear clouded by hatred. Not yet.'

'You never needed Joseph there, did you?' she asked quietly, almost meekly, in fear of him for the first time.

Andrea Petrakis watched the mayhem on the screen, amused by his handiwork.

'Of course I did,' he responded, casting her an icy, disappointed look. 'Just not for the reason he thought.'

She glanced at her watch, realizing the truth, though she didn't dare say it, even though she knew, from the expression on his face, that Petrakis understood what she was thinking. The explosion was perfectly timed to match the appearance of the world leaders on the temporary podium outside the Quirinale. She'd watched Andrea give Joseph the Rolex that morning before he set off. The time was wrong, too fast. It had to be. The Nigerian had attempted to detonate the blast a good two minutes before the correct time. He was as much a part of the show as fake blood and the hidden explosives.

Petrakis turned to Deniz Nesin.

'You can email that to the right people? Al-Jazeera. The BBC. CNN.'

'In a moment . . .' the Turk replied.

'And they won't be able to trace it from here?'

Deniz gazed at him, offended by the question, and said nothing.

'What about Joseph?' she demanded. 'If he talks . . .'

Petrakis wasn't even listening.

- 11 -

Something happened just after he started to run, something loud and shocking and deadly. Joseph Priest wanted to turn to the pair pursuing him and scream: *It wasn't me.*

It really wasn't. The soft, dull roar of an explosion sent flocks of grubby pigeons scattering into the bright blue sky, shaking the windows of the stores he ran past, putting fear and anticipation on the faces of the men and women he bumped into as he fled. Within the space of a few seconds a cacophony of sirens began to rise from the streets around the Trevi Fountain. Joseph Priest raced as quickly as he could in the opposite direction, determined to find sanctuary somewhere, anywhere.

Another narrow cobbled alley. Another line of fashion shops and stores selling cosmetics. Huge photos of beautiful women, smiling down at him, their flawless suntanned flesh seemingly so real, so exposed he felt he could reach out and touch the soft, stray cloud of gentle down on their forearms.

As he fell deeper into the fashion area of the city, becoming ever more lost with every step, he began to feel he was drowning in the modern world he had, for so long, coveted. He stumbled, panting, through the streets that ran from the Spanish Steps to the Corso, a tangle of medieval alleys that had metamorphosed into temples for shoppers who'd pay more for a tiny scrap of denim, manufactured in some distant Third World sweatshop, than he could dream of earning in a month. A universe of brands and trademarks consumed him from every angle, totemic symbols of a materialism he had craved as long as he could remember. The faces of international supermodels and sportsmen grinned down at his flight from the clothes stores in the Via

Condotti and beyond, as he fought to lose the scary couple who'd picked him out at the Trevi Fountain and known his name all along.

This was not his world, he thought, gasping for breath, too afraid to look behind him for fear of what he might see.

He dashed past an ancient statue, reclining in a fountain, green and algaed, surrounded by water that still bore the clear, untainted sheen of the *Acqua Vergine*, upstream perhaps of whatever strange device Deniz had placed in the flow near the Trevi. He glanced at the sign on the wall – the Via dei Greci – and realized he understood enough Italian to know what it meant. *The Street of the Greeks.*

The face of Andrea Petrakis popped unbidden into his head, bigger and scarier than the gigantic soccer players and beautiful women leering at him from the store fronts.

Priest dashed into a dark side alley, close to a book shop, knowing he had to catch his breath.

A sharp, agonizing pain began to stab at his stomach. He doubled over. As his head went down he realized he'd blundered into a dead end. The cul-de-sac was full of public rubbish receptacles, green and blue, overflowing with trash. A few metres away stood the grimy, smoke-stained wall that must have marked the rear of some building in the adjoining alley.

He took three deep breaths, then looked up, half-guessing what he'd see.

They were out of breath too, anyway. And angry, the woman more than the man. Her face was shiny with sweat, her eyes were popping out.

There was nowhere to run, even if he had the strength.

Joseph Priest knew when he was beaten. He raised his hands in the air, closed his eyes briefly, tried to collect his thoughts, then looked at them and, with all the sincerity and conviction he could muster, said, 'I got no gun. Nothing.'

They had, though. Two small pistols low at their sides, and they were walking towards him, the merest glimpse of doubt and fear in their eyes.

'You listening to me?' Priest added, shoving his arms as high as he could stretch.

From somewhere nearby came the sound of another siren, its tone descending the scale as the source disappeared down some unseen street.

'No gun,' he emphasized. 'No nothing. You understand?'

They stopped in front of him and he knew for sure this time: she was the boss.

The burly man looked at her, as if waiting for some kind of instruction.

'Listen,' Priest began to plead. 'I can tell you where they are. I can tell you what they've got. What they plan to do. Everything.'

Not a word, not an emotion.

'E-e-everything,' he stuttered. 'They're crazy. Animals. Lunatics.'

Very slowly, to show there was no ill intent, no concealed weapon, he took down his left hand, placed it on his heart and looked the woman in the eye.

'I swear, lady. Whatever you want, it's yours. The Mungiki made me do these things. I hate those bastards.' He glanced out at the street. 'I can take you to these people. To Andrea Petrakis right now. You never get a problem again. Not from Joe Priest.'

It was as good a performance as he'd ever given. He felt proud of it. The hefty man with the gun was still watching him, hesitating. But the woman . . .

There was something here he didn't understand.

She flashed her eyes at the figure beside her and said, 'Do it.'

Then she turned on her heels.

Joseph Priest, who wished he'd had time to tell them this was his real name, whatever everyone thought, looked up at the guy and found he had to shield his eyes against the light because the sun was that bright, that insistent.

'Do what . . . ?' he began to ask, until he realized it was a stupid question, and he knew the answer already.

Part 3

THE TOMB

Facilis descensus Averno;
noctes atque dies patet atri ianua Ditis;
sed revocare gradum superasque evadere ad auras,
hoc opus, hic labor est.

The gates of hell are open night and day;
Smooth the descent, and easy is the way:
But to return, and view the cheerful skies,
In this the task and mighty labour lies.

Virgil, *Aeneid*, Book VI

– 1 –

They were passing Civitavecchia when Falcone called with the lead. Costa turned off the radio to take it. Aldo Bartoli, the brother of the dead *carabiniere*, was still at work, unwilling to discuss the case with a stranger over the phone, but agreeable to a personal approach on the understanding that his name would not be attached to any resulting report.

So they kept driving, past Tarquinia, a solitary town in the Etruscan foothills to their right as they followed the coast road, listening to Mirko Oliva at the wheel, talking of his childhood holidays when his family swapped urban Turin for Monte Argentario, the rocky peninsula where Porto Ercole lay. The mood changed as every passing minute took them further from Rome. The young officer was a good conversationalist, happily chatting about the fishing, the swimming, the hiking. The radio stayed off. It was against the rules. But so was sneaking into Tuscany without authority.

Rosa sat in the back, following Mirko's tales, asking questions from time to time, laughing. Costa watched the countryside slip past and the landscape become ever more bleak and bare as they entered the flatlands of the Maremma. He couldn't get their destination out of his head. Porto Ercole was where Caravaggio died a pauper in a charity hospital, a place that had existed in his mind for years as a harsh, cold coastal hamlet, unwelcoming towards visitors, neglectful of strangers who arrived sick and penniless. Then they crossed the causeway that linked the mainland to Monte Argentario and found themselves on a narrow road winding through lush green country-side, Mirko still talking about holidays and his childhood. And Nic

Costa began to realize how foolish it was to judge a place by its history alone.

The Guardia Costiera building was little more than a two-storey pink-washed villa on the sleepy, picturesque harbour front. It looked more like a plain residential home than an outpost of the law-enforcement agency tasked with surveillance of the port and the Tyrrhenian Sea beyond. The national flag fluttered red, white and green by the steps at the entrance. There was the sound of a television set from behind shuttered windows thrown open to the breeze. Rich yachts filled the tiny port. Luxurious homes dotted the surrounding hills. Mirko Oliva said that his father's old place just outside town, little more than a country cottage, was now worth more than one million euros, and would probably wind up in the hands of some rich financier from Milan. This was not the bitter, poor outpost of a shattered Italy that had turned its back on a stricken Caravaggio, leaving him to a beggar's death and an unmarked grave. Times had changed.

They walked into the coastguard post and found that Aldo Bartoli was the only officer there. He was sitting beneath an old-fashioned ceiling fan in front of a small TV, watching the news, sucking on a cigarette, a thin, wiry man in early middle age, with close-cropped silver hair, a mournful face and a downturned, immobile mouth that didn't look as if it often broke into a smile. His eyes were watery and red-rimmed, like those of someone who drank too much, and had done for a long time.

The coastguard listened to their introductions and then stated, without emotion, 'You don't know, do you?'

'Know what?' Costa asked, suddenly guilty about the radio.

'There's been a bomb. In Rome.' Bartoli thrust a hand at the TV. A familiar reporter was standing in front of the Trevi Fountain. It appeared to be awash with blood, more than was physically possible, even in the most vicious of blasts.

'No one dead,' Bartoli added. 'It's a miracle. They shot the terrorist. That's something anyway. Maybe there are more bombs in the city. Poison in the water supply. God, am I glad to be out of all that crap!'

'Excuse me,' Costa apologized, then stepped to one side to call Rome.

It was a brief conversation, an unwelcome one, judging by Falcone's testy response.

'You can't get back here, Nic. They've closed every route in and out. Make arrangements to stay in a hotel somewhere. Do some digging. Ask this Bartoli individual where you should start. Take a look around Tarquinia.'

Costa walked outside and watched a palatial yacht edging slowly across the peaceful harbour. It was impossible to imagine that, little more than ninety minutes by car to the south, the capital of Italy was paralysed by chaos, waiting for the next outrage. He wanted to be there, more than anything.

'What good are we here? We can make it back. I know roads . . .'

'There's nothing for you to do. Don't you understand?'

He could see Rosa and Mirko Oliva seated beneath the slowly revolving fan in front of the TV next to the dour-faced Guardia Costiera officer, silent, watching the newscast.

'How bad is it?' he asked.

He was sure he heard Falcone utter a short, grim laugh.

'That depends on what you mean by bad. You can't move anywhere, except on foot, and that's not easy. The city council has warned everyone to drink nothing but bottled water until they know the public mains is free of contamination. Whatever this device was, they planted it in the domestic supply. There may be others. So there's panic in the shops. For bottled water and food. Most people won't be able to get home from work for hours.'

'It feels wrong we're not there, Leo. I'm sorry.'

'I know it does. But there are a million people – ours, the Carabinieri, Palombo's secret-service agents – tripping over each other at the moment. They don't need three more bodies to get in the way.'

'What was it?'

'Some kind of explosive device hidden inside the Trevi Fountain. A small bomb and a lot of red dye. It's almost as if they didn't want to kill anyone. As if it was some kind of a prank. There's a handful of models and photographers in hospital with minor injuries. This was for show, not to kill. The only fatality . . .' there was another pause on the line, '. . . is the terrorist. The news says some unmarked officers saw him planting the thing on CCTV. There was some kind of confrontation near the Via Condotti. He was shot dead by two agents.'

'Ours?'

'No. We knew nothing about it until the bomb went off. Palombo's people, I guess. I talked to Esposito, briefly, not that he was in the mood for conversation. He's no more in the picture than we are. There's been an unconfirmed email claiming responsibility. It says this is just the beginning. We have to work on the assumption the dead man planted several devices. Esposito's sent out everyone he can lay hands on. They're searching everywhere. Every tourist site. Every station. Every bus and train. Let's leave them to it.'

Costa tried to picture his native city brought to an angry, futile halt in this way.

'Who's claiming responsibility?' he asked.

'The email went straight to the Quirinale Palace. The president's office. They haven't released that detail yet. Nic . . .' Falcone's voice took on the note of embarrassment that it always possessed when the subject became personal. 'There are aspects of this case that are beginning to trouble me. Please. Take care. See what Bartoli can tell you. Pass on anything you find straight away, and do nothing else. We're not entirely masters of our own fate at the moment. I don't want you thinking we can try to track down these people. That was never our brief. Try to find some facts.'

'And then?' Costa asked, when the conversation dried up.

'Then Commissario Esposito calls the president and asks him what to do next. If we get that far. We're a handful of officers up against . . . what? I've no idea, and nor have you. Now listen to me.'

There were some questions the inspector wanted answered. A second warning not to try to return to Rome. Then Falcone hung up.

Aldo Bartoli still sat grim-faced and immobile in the office, watching what was happening in Rome, Rosa and Mirko by his side. Costa could hear sounds from the apartments nearby and they were all the same: the racket of TV sets, tuned to the same terrible news. It was a scene he knew was being repeated everywhere throughout Italy at that moment. Perhaps the world. This was what Andrea Petrakis had sought in the first place, twenty years ago: attention, fear, the ability to instil some deep and haunting doubt in the nation about what the remains of the day might bring. Back then he had failed in everything except the murder of two young Americans. Now he was making amends. This bloody act, a foretaste – it seemed to say – of what was to come, had attracted an audience of millions, brought together by the same sense of outrage and trepidation.

'Jesus!' Bartoli's outraged voice broke through his thoughts with a stream of florid curses. Costa strode back into the office. There was a new picture on the screen: a shaky video, the kind taken using mobile phones. He watched as the familiar statues at the Trevi Fountain disappeared in a storm of rubble and dust, and a livid red spume of liquid burst out from the cloud, soaking the cowering, screaming crowd in fake blood.

'The bastards handed out that thing themselves,' Bartoli exclaimed. 'Put it on the Internet, as if it was some kid's video for all the world to see.'

'Who?' Costa asked. 'Did they use a name?'

Bartoli turned and glowered at him.

'You know who. That's why you're here.'

He turned up the volume. The announcer was speaking rapidly, blurring his words with an unprofessional haste. The caption was running across the bottom of the TV, looping over and over.

'The president's office has announced that the terrorist group known as the Blue Demon have claimed responsibility, and say this is the first act of many . . .'

Familiar images began to fill the screen, of a young Andrea Petrakis, the Frasca couple's corpses in the nymphaeum at the Villa Giulia, the bloodied shack near Tarquinia where the three students died, alongside a member of the Carabinieri.

'So they really are back,' Bartoli said. He looked at his watch. It was approaching four. 'I need a beer. And you,' he nodded at the three of them, 'will not believe a word I'm about to tell you.'

- 2 -

'Lorenzo was an infant,' Aldo Bartoli insisted. 'A child. Why do you think I joined the Carabinieri in the first place? To look after the young idiot. I did a good job, too. Until those bastards from the city turned up.'

They sat in a cafe by the harbour, Mirko Oliva and Rosa Prabakaran still quiet and shocked by events back home. The TV in the corner was locked to the news. A small group of locals sat around it, watching in silence. Costa couldn't take his mind off Rome. He ached to be there, to do something useful, that had meaning.

Bartoli's younger brother was alone on duty the day of the trip to the shack near Tarquinia. The two visiting officers, Ettore Rufo and Beppe Cattaneo, only stopped by the town Carabinieri head-quarters to ask for directions. Aldo Bartoli was sure they hadn't wanted his brother along.

'The kid was like that. A pest. He wanted to be a part of everything. He would never have let them go there alone. He phoned me. It was my day off. He said some big guys from the city had turned up looking serious. They had weapons. Not the usual kind. They wanted directions to some shack in the countryside belonging to the Petrakis family. Lorenzo said he'd show them. That was the only way.'

Bartoli nursed his beer, his eyes misty, his face full of grief.

'That was the last time I ever spoke to him. Next thing I knew there was a call telling me I had to go and identify a body.'

'I'm sorry,' Mirko Oliva said quietly.

'Yeah. Well . . .' He called for grappa. Costa put a hand over his glass. The others did the same. 'He should never have been there.

150

He was useless. Couldn't shoot straight. Couldn't think straight. If I'd been on duty . . .'

'Wait.' Costa was trying to get the sequence of events straight in his head. 'According to the files, Rufo and Cattaneo came to the local station after they'd found Gregor and Alyssa Petrakis dead.'

The man looked incredulous.

'Says who?'

'The files.'

Bartoli shook his head.

'Even Lorenzo would have called for help if that had happened. The way I heard it, those guys were just asking directions.'

'When did you know the parents were dead?' Costa asked.

He thought for a moment, then said, 'Afterwards, I guess. It all got complicated. All these people turned up from Rome. I was just thinking about my brother.' He stared at Costa. 'It kind of happened all at the same time.'

'Tell us about them,' Mirko suggested. 'The Petrakis family.'

The coastguard shuffled on his seat, looking uncomfortable.

'No one liked that pair. They never did a stroke of real work that I could see. Had enough money to keep a little plane down at Civitavecchia, though. The kid liked to fly it. Used to buzz the town sometimes. Flying low. Thought it was some kind of joke. I had words with him. With them. They laughed in my face . . . didn't give a damn.'

'Did you have any idea they might be involved in terrorism?' Costa asked.

Bartoli shook his head.

'Course not. I would have reported them. I kept my eye on them, though. They were always going places they weren't welcome. Those tombs. The scary place they found the Blue Demon. They had a thing about all that stuff. The museum people got nervous once or twice and called me. The kid thought he knew everything.'

'How did he get on with his parents?' Rosa asked.

The man shrugged.

'Fine, as far as I could see. The son was probably the only person they didn't argue with. Everyone else – us. The police.' He hesitated.

'Look. Afterwards, when they told us what had gone on in Rome.' Bartoli scratched his grey head. 'It never made sense to people. Why would someone name themselves after some painting in a tomb somewhere? All that Etruscan stuff is history.'

'Not to Andrea Petrakis,' Rosa said quickly.

'In that case he's crazy.'

'Where did Gregor and Alyssa Petrakis get their money?' Costa asked.

Bartoli grimaced.

'I asked myself that question a lot. Before all this happened. Every time I tried to get permission to get serious with the Petrakises, someone on high told me to mind my own business. I wondered if it was to do with drugs. There was talk about that in the town. People in Rome were watching them. I was beginning to wonder if maybe they were informers. And then they were dead. Killed by their own son, supposedly.'

He slammed his glass hard on the table. Strong spirit spilled over his shaking hand. The barman walked over without being asked and placed another grappa on the table. He knew Aldo Bartoli, knew what he needed.

'Why am I wasting my time telling you all this? I told the big people who came up from Rome after Lorenzo got killed. When they buried my poor, stupid brother . . . I told them then something wasn't right. When they didn't listen, I went to the police. When you kicked me out I tried to tell the newspapers, until someone got hold of the reporters and whispered in their ears that Aldo Bartoli was a little soft in the head.'

He downed the drink in one shot.

'My mother went to her grave and I don't think I ever saw her smile again. My old man drank himself to death. So I got the hell out of there, found myself a job watching rich people bump their yachts into each other, sticking tickets on them for bringing in too many cigarettes from time to time. This story's dead. As dead as Lorenzo. You can't do a damned thing to change that.'

Costa looked at his watch. It was close to five. There would still be people around in Tarquinia they could talk to.

'So what do you think?' Aldo Bartoli asked. 'Does it sound like I'm a lunatic?'

'We need facts . . .' Costa began.

'Facts. I saw the parents' bodies in the morgue,' Bartoli said. 'They'd been dead a week or more. Andrea was living in Rome. He didn't come home at all during that time, not as far as I could see. Why kill them anyway? What was his motive? He didn't look like the most loving son around. He didn't look like he wanted them dead, either.'

Bartoli grinned. He looked a little drunk.

'Maybe the Carabinieri were just cleaning up the statistics, huh? Putting the deaths of the parents at the kid's door so they didn't have to report it as one more unsolved crime?'

Rosa Prabakaran brushed away a strand of long brown hair from her dark, thoughtful face and said, 'It wouldn't be the first time.'

'Bullshit,' Bartoli mumbled. His eyes looked redder, mistier. 'There's something else. This is the one where you start to know I'm crazy.'

'Try me,' Costa suggested.

'They didn't want us to see Lorenzo when he was dead. The big men in the Carabinieri said it was a bad sight. Not for a mother or a father. Mine being the nice, trusting people they were, they believed that too.'

Aldo Bartoli was beginning to enjoy this, Costa thought, as if he had something to say that had been waiting for years.

'Being a country *carabiniere*, I'd got used to dead bodies. Usually in pieces inside a car stinking of drink, smashed up against a tree or a wall. I wanted to see my brother before they buried him. Whatever he looked like. A friend of mine worked in the morgue. He got me in when no one was looking. Five minutes. Was enough.'

Someone at the bar was getting bad-tempered. The TV news went off. It was as if no one wanted to see any more.

'The story,' Bartoli continued, 'was that Lorenzo and the two *carabinieri* from Rome, the special guys, were walking up the front path of this crappy shack of the Petrakises when the kids inside opened fire. Lorenzo was hit straight away. The other two got lucky, fought back, and by the time they got to the shack, the kids inside had killed themselves.' He raised a long, skinny finger, as stained by tobacco as Dario Sordi's. 'One problem. Lorenzo didn't look bad at all. I'd seen much worse out on the roads on a Saturday night. He had just one bullet wound . . .'

Aldo Bartoli swivelled his head and indicated the nape of his neck.

'Close up, from what I could make out. Here. In the back. The way the mob used to execute people. Which is funny, when you come to think of it, since he was walking forward at the time. These were university kids, mind. They must have been real clever to have killed him like that.'

The coastguard officer pushed back the beer, pleased to have said this.

'A cynical man might have thought those students didn't kill him at all. Those two *carabinieri* from Rome did, and then went on and murdered those kids, which is what they came for in the first place.'

'Why would they do that, Aldo?' Costa asked him.

'I've no idea. But I talked to someone who said they'd seen those two before. A week or so earlier. Around the time the Petrakises got shot, I guess. There's a coincidence. If those guys were good at murdering my brother, maybe they were good at murdering those Greeks too. Nothing to do with Andrea. He just got the blame, because someone decided that was what was going to happen.'

Costa shook his head and didn't say a thing.

Aldo Bartoli blinked, then added, 'And you know the funny thing? A few years later they found one of those *carabinieri* – Cattaneo, I think his name was – shot dead. Bullet through the back of the skull, though for some reason this one came out a little messier than it did with Lorenzo.'

He gazed at them and grinned.

'They never did find out who did that. I guess it's like my kid brother. There's no knowing now, is there? I'd like to ask the other guy. Rufo's his name. Except I never managed to find him to talk to, not that I haven't tried. If you get lucky there . . .'

Costa glanced at the two young officers with him. They looked glassy-eyed, a little shaken.

'I need names in Tarquinia,' he said.

'I don't know any worth talking to.' He leaned forward. Costa could smell the strong spirit on his breath. 'Did you understand what I just told you?'

'I think so,' Costa replied, getting up and throwing some money on the table for the drinks.

- 3 -

They spent an hour in Tarquinia, trying to find someone who would talk. In the local police offices, in the Carabinieri station, the council. It was as if they were intruders at a funeral. No one had time for anything except events in Rome. An uneasy silence grew between the three of them. Costa was still quietly hoping he would be able to sneak back to the city late that evening, after dark, when the roads might be more manageable. The younger officers had their doubts. Rosa had called a local hotel and booked three rooms as a precaution. Mirko Oliva was making noises about food. They recognized a wasted trip when they saw one, understood instinctively when it was time to take a break and hope the following day would be more promising.

Costa insisted on one final visit, out to the tourist tombs on the edge of town. They found only a couple of women closing the site for the day, one tall and surly, one dumpy and pleasant, shooing out the last straggle of visitors. Costa left Rosa and Oliva talking to the pair and took out the mobile phone that Dario Sordi had given him.

It seemed to take forever for someone to answer. It didn't sound like Sordi's voice, and there was no name.

'Who's that?' Costa asked.

'The president told you I'd answer this call, Sovrintendente. Ranieri of the Corazzieri. You remember? The man who found that microphone in your house last night.'

Dario Sordi's visit seemed an age away.

'Can I speak with him?'

A pained sigh briefly filled the earpiece.

'The president is with his guests, welcoming them to Italy. If one can call it that, in the circumstances. I doubt he would appreciate the interruption. On a day like this . . .'

'I'm sorry. I'm not in Rome.'

'Oh . . . where?'

He wondered what to say, whether he had made a stupid mistake already.

'I'm in Tarquinia.'

'Indeed.' Ranieri didn't sound surprised.

'Do you know the area?' Costa asked.

'Only as a place in the distance, from the road when we drive north to see my wife's parents in Livorno. It looks beautiful. Is your visit proving . . . educational?'

'Not very.'

'Perhaps you would like me to pass on a message?'

He couldn't think of one. He wasn't really sure why he called.

'Where were you twenty years ago?' Costa asked the Corazzieri officer.

There was a significant pause on the line.

'The NATO offices in Brussels. Military liaison. A cold place, but the food could be quite good if you knew where to eat. I missed the Blue Demon episode, I'm afraid. Those years . . .' Ranieri's voice sounded hesitant, almost guilty. 'I was scarcely in Italy at all. Reading about what happened in the papers – it was as if it was a different country. One I would prefer not to meet again.'

'I'm sorry to have bothered you.'

'No,' the man said emphatically. 'You were told to call when it was necessary. You must. I will tell him you will get in touch some other time. If you make it after nine-thirty tonight, then the formal proceedings will be over. Perhaps . . .' There was an unexpected silence, as if Ranieri was waiting for someone to leave the room. 'Once the food is cleared away, the evening is Campagnolo's. An appropriate time for the cabaret, don't you think? I feel sure the president will not wish to linger.'

Costa walked back to the gatehouse and the tombs complex. Mirko Oliva was still talking to the two women. Tempers were rising.

'Why can't we see the tomb?' he asked.

'Because it's closed,' the tall woman insisted. 'Permanently. If you want access, you've got to talk to the museum. Why do you want to see it anyway?'

'Why do we?' Costa asked, trying to bring down the temperature.

'Because,' the young officer stuttered, 'it's the Blue Demon.'

He paused and looked lost for a moment.

'The thing we're supposed to be looking for,' Oliva added quietly. 'Let's face it. We don't have much else. Aldo Bartoli's off his head.' He looked searchingly at Costa. 'Isn't he?'

'It's not worth it,' the other attendant cut in before Costa could reply. 'Trust me. I've been down there.'

She waved across the site. The burial mounds rose like gigantic anthills, most with explanatory signs next to them. The woman was indicating somewhere else, closer to the little country road that led out of the town, along the line of the hill. There was another archaeological area covered in corrugated iron and plastic sheeting, running through what looked like an abandoned car park.

'Aldo Bartoli thinks that's scary?' Rosa Prabakaran asked.

'Like you said,' the tall one declared. 'Off his head.'

She made a gesture: swigging back a bottle. The other attendant scowled at her.

'That man lost his brother. Then his parents,' she snapped. 'You leave the poor soul alone. He's gone, isn't he?'

'Good riddance . . .'

Costa watched the friendly one. There was something she wanted to say.

'Did you know the Petrakis couple? The son?' he asked.

'We all knew *of* them,' she answered.

'Signora,' Rosa pleaded. 'We've spent hours here, elsewhere in the Maremma. Trying to get people to help us. And . . .' She swept the warm early-evening air with her hand, and for a moment Costa found himself imagining her in this place two and a half millennia before, dark-eyed, attractive, an Etruscan, someone from a different world. 'It's as if the Petrakis family never existed.'

'They didn't,' the first attendant said. 'Not for us. Foreigners.

Greeks. Selling drugs to our children. Getting up to God knows what in that place of theirs – not that you or the Carabinieri ever took much interest.'

'None of us understood them,' her colleague added, more calmly. 'That's the honest truth. If people tell you nothing, it's because they know nothing. The Petrakis family spoke to no one except to insult us. Then, one day, they were gone and all we could do was read the papers and think to ourselves: these were the monsters that lived among us, and we never really noticed. I suppose you never do.'

Costa found himself looking at the tomb, with its corrugated-iron roof and air of abandonment.

'How on earth did Andrea become obsessed by that?' he asked.

'He didn't,' the tall woman declared. 'That's our Blue Demon tomb. The one he used to hang around is on the road to Monte Romano. Middle of nowhere. You'd never know it was there unless someone told you. Just a heap of earth near the wood. No one goes near.'

Her colleague was thinking.

'Someone does. I saw people there two days ago, when I went to my sister's. From the museum, I imagine. They were . . .' She scratched her cheek, remembering. 'They looked as if they were going inside.'

The other woman drew herself up to her full height.

'I am the senior assistant here, Felicia. I know what the museum is doing. No one has been inside the Monte Romano site for years. Not since . . .' She grimaced. 'Not since we used to have to chase the Petrakis boy out of there.'

Felicia was not budging.

'I saw someone. Two men. In the afternoon . . .'

Costa picked up a map of the area from the ticket counter.

'Where?' he demanded.

She drew a circle by the side of a narrow country road leading inland, three kilometres away.

'It's in the wood off the Strada di Santa Amaia. No one goes down there except a few farmers.'

'Thank you,' Costa said, and looked at his two officers. 'We have one more call to make.'

'That'll be five euros,' the tall woman said, holding out her hand. 'For the map.'

– 4 –

Around five Anna Ybarra went back to the palatial living room and sat next to Deniz Nesin, who was glued to the television. All the afternoon programmes – the cartoons and the kids' features, the contests and the old-fashioned song-and-dance shows, with their ageing singers and prancing, half-naked dancers – had been cancelled. There was one story alone, and that was Rome: a city in agony, shaken, living off its nerves.

The Turk didn't want to talk so she went outside. It was still burning hot, even though early evening was now approaching. The garden, with its dainty bushes and too-new white statues, was empty. Finally she found Andrea Petrakis by accident almost, noticing that the doors to the aircraft hangar – a gigantic garage-like structure built next to the parched grass strip – were half-open.

She walked in, not caring whether or not he would be offended. The plane looked like an exaggerated child's toy. High wings, a slender, shiny wooden propeller, and a tiny engine that might have seemed more at home on a motorbike.

He was poking at the silver metal behind the propeller with a spanner. She opened the flimsy cabin door – the window was little more than polythene sheeting attached to a bare metal-tube frame. Then she eased herself into the right-hand seat and played with the joystick in the centre, aware of the intense way Petrakis watched her from the other side of the windshield.

'Don't touch anything,' he ordered.

'I've never been in a little plane before.' She found herself avoiding his eyes. In truth she had never been in a plane at all until they spirited her away to Pakistan.

The panels and instruments were in front of the left seat, the pilot's, she guessed. There weren't many. It didn't look complicated.

Petrakis was eyeing her avidly, and there was something soft, something intriguing in his eyes that she liked.

He put down the spanner.

'I need to check the engine. The way everything is rigged. There's only so much you can manage on the ground. You can come along, if you like.'

'Oh.'

She was surprised by the sound of her own voice. It possessed a note of excitement.

'It's got a little autopilot,' he added. 'Just a couple of cheap servos hooked up to the ADI. The only way to work out if it's accurate is to take the thing up.'

'I don't know what you're talking about.'

'Put on your belt,' Petrakis ordered.

She began to wrestle with the buckle. He took hold of the little plane's nose and pulled the aircraft out of the hangar, hauling it until they stopped next to the brown grass of the strip.

'Don't you need to swing the propeller or something?' she asked as he clambered into the pilot's seat.

'This is the twenty-first century,' Petrakis said, smiling so freely at that moment Anna Ybarra felt she was in the presence of a stranger.

He climbed into the left-hand seat, strapped on his belt and brought the engine to life. It had an odd, high-pitched whine and sufficient power to make her grip the seat tightly in anticipation. Then he edged the push–pull throttle forward and they moved onto the makeshift runway. The miniature aircraft picked up speed with a rapidity that threw her into the back of her seat. Its tiny frame was shaking around her, as if it might fall to bits. The volume rose, the vibration made her feel giddy. He watched the dials and then, when some magic moment was reached, jerked back on the stick, bringing up the nose, and they were airborne, free of the earth, unhooked from gravity, climbing more rapidly than she thought possible, as if on some fairground ride that didn't know when to stop.

It only took a couple of minutes for them to reach a height where she felt as if she were in a real plane, high above the earth. To the north she could see the flat Maremma coast stretching towards the outline of Monte Argentario, a place they'd visited four days before, to eat fish at some fancy restaurant in Orbetello. In the distance, to the south, was the ugly smear of smog that was Rome.

'Here,' Petrakis shouted over the engine noise, giving her the stick. 'Fly straight and level. No sudden movements.'

She gripped the control between them. It shook in her hands, as if the plane wished to resist. Petrakis wrapped his fingers round hers and taught her how to manage the thing. It was obvious really. She kept the stick stiff and immobile and the aircraft followed, as if in harness to it.

He looked pleased. Almost impressed.

'How does it feel?' she yelled over the wind and the engine noise.

'What? Flying?'

'No. Knowing they're afraid of you.'

'Of us,' he said, watching her.

'Of us.'

'It feels good,' he answered, and abruptly grabbed the control from her.

She didn't know what he did then, but it felt wonderful. The tiny plane turned and became locked into some steep circling turn. Her body was thrust down into the cheap plastic seat by the force of the manoeuvre. They were both giggling like kids, though he was checking things too: tapping panels, looking at readings there, getting through the jobs he had in mind all along. He was never far away from that, even a thousand feet or so above the Etruscan countryside in little more than a motorized kite.

'I wish I could fly,' she said softly, hoping he couldn't hear.

'You did fly, Anna. You have.'

'Not really,' she murmured, and found herself hoping he hadn't noticed the doubt she felt, the uncertainty that was never far from the surface.

He wasn't listening. Andrea Petrakis was staring down through the open side window, onto a shallow, bowl-like stretch of dry farmland – olive groves and empty fields, stretching behind the town of Tarquinia that sat beneath the left wing.

'We need to go back,' he said, and his voice sounded the way it did on the ground, hard and determined.

'No,' she said, looking at the blazing horizon. 'Not yet.'

He looked at her and it was the old Andrea.

Without saying another word he moved the stick. The little plane turned on its axis, then rolled into a steep, curving descent, towards the coast and the villa in the lowlands.

– 5 –

It took them more than an hour to find the place, tracing and retracing the tiny rural lanes that criss-crossed the hills leading inland behind the town. The site turned out to be a bosky tract of land in a dip along a winding single lane to the hill village of Monte Romano. The main road was half a kilometre away. Few people would pass by, and even fewer would see the archaeological site that was located in a shady rectangle cut out from lines of straggling trees.

Costa told Mirko Oliva to pull in to the verge. There were three torches in the boot. The light was failing. The dying sun hung as a bloody red disc sinking towards the hidden Tyrrhenian Sea past the line of the ridge.

'Can we eat something after this, boss?' Oliva asked.

'Yes, Mirko,' he said patiently.

Rosa took the torch he offered. She looked wiped out. Events in the city seemed to hang over them all, impossible to dismiss or discuss in any meaningful way.

'Why are we here, Nic? Exactly?' Rosa asked.

'If you'd been living in a foreign land, a distant one. For twenty years. Among people from a very different culture. People who didn't speak your language . . . Then one day you came back to the country where you grew up. Wouldn't you want to take a look around the places you used to know?'

'He'd be happy out there,' Oliva said. 'In Afghanistan.'

They both stopped and looked at him.

'He thinks he's an Etruscan, doesn't he?' the young officer explained. 'That long ago . . . They must have been hard men. They all were. Maybe Andrea would feel more at home out there than here. We're all Italians now. We're soft, aren't we?'

'That's an interesting idea,' Costa observed.

'Pleased to be of assistance, sir,' the young officer said with a little bow.

Rosa was laughing at him. Costa looked at her and smiled.

Mirko Oliva nodded at the clearing in the woods and said, 'So is this is where the Blue Demon lives? The real one? The scary one?'

'Guess so,' Rosa agreed.

His genial face fell.

'Can I ask a favour, boss? If this involves going down there . . .' He coughed and looked around them. 'You need someone to stay up here. Let it be me. I don't much like being underground. I get claustrophobic. It's like being in the grave. If you really need me . . .'

'Did you mention all this at the interview board?' Rosa demanded, staring at him.

'Yes,' the young officer answered, 'but they sounded desperate.'

Costa had no idea whether or not that was a joke. He called Falcone to brief and be briefed. Then he agreed that Oliva would remain outside, in touch with Rome if need be, keeping an eye open for anything that might be useful.

After that he and Rosa went off with their torches to the tomb in the woods.

– 6 –

They continued to work in the apartment in the Via di San Giovanni in Laterano, listening to families return to the neighbouring homes, grumbling vocally out in the corridor, resigning themselves to days of uncertainty and disruption.

Teresa Lupo had rarely been so close to the hourly grind of investigative research and fact-checking, and it both surprised and impressed her. Peroni and Falcone would take a single name attached to a report on the Blue Demon investigation, then try to forge some connections. If there were none in the computer systems, they would look through whatever online news-service reports they could track down. When that failed, they turned to the phone directories, calling people with the same last name, asking if they knew of someone who'd been involved in the case.

It was a painstaking, hit-and-miss process. One that should have been undertaken by a substantial team of officers. Not two middle-aged cops who were struggling to make any headway at all. Peroni's pale, damaged face seemed more bloodless than usual. Falcone's lean, tanned features had lost their customary urgency and his eyes, usually so sharp, were fast becoming glazed and weary.

Around six they took a call from the team in Porto Ercole. Falcone put Costa on the speakerphone, and so they listened to the story of Aldo Bartoli, the drunk who had, perhaps, confessed to murdering the *carabiniere* he believed had killed his brother. Why had Lorenzo Bartoli died? No one had any good answers, and Costa wanted to be on his way. The information gave Falcone some focus, though.

Teresa was making one more round of coffees – the best support she felt able to give at that moment – when Peroni whooped with something close to joy.

'What is it?' Elizabeth Murray asked, lifting her head up from the file reports that Falcone had given her.

'Ettore Rufo. I tracked down a relative. Rufo moved to America within a year of leaving the Carabinieri.' He waved a piece of paper in the air. 'Got a restaurant now. In Chicago. Called it after himself.' Peroni looked at Falcone. 'You want me to ask about a reservation?'

'Do it,' the inspector ordered.

Elizabeth Murray watched him, worried.

'This might get back to Rome,' she cautioned.

'It's the only name we've picked up all day,' the inspector complained. 'I'll take that risk.'

Peroni was on the phone already. Teresa Lupo sat next to him, playing with the computer keyboard, listening, a little in awe, as she always was when he turned on both the pressure and the charm, switching from Italian to English and back, talking his way past whoever answered the phone. It was lunchtime in Chicago, and by the sound of it Ettore Rufo had wound up with a busy restaurant.

She did a search on the name and found out that her instincts were right: Rufo's looked big and popular on its website, full of leather seating and shiny tables, pretty waitresses bearing cocktails, a couple of chefs holding steak and lobster aloft. It was all a long way from a bloody shootout in the Maremma. The obvious question rose in her head: would a pay-off from the Carabinieri really fund a venture of this scale?

'Ettore?' Peroni cried, when he finally got through. 'It's Martelli. Calling from Rome. You remember? We talked twenty years ago when we were on the Blue Demon case together.'

Then he hit the speaker button so they could all hear.

'Twenty years ago . . . I don't remember much,' said a cold, unpleasant voice. 'No one called Martelli, either. Who are you?'

'I was a cop then.'

'Weren't no cops involved. Who the hell is this? Gimme your number.'

'Sure,' Peroni answered and passed on something imaginary. 'You want to call me back?'

'No. I wanna make sure you don't bother me no more.'

'Why's that? You're in Chicago. It's all safe there, Ettore. I'm in Rome. You don't watch the news? That bastard Petrakis has popped up again. I thought you'd want to help.'

'Petrakis, Petrakis . . .' Ettore Rufo sounded as if he never wanted to hear the name again. 'I got a restaurant to run. Who are you?'

'Still a cop. Still looking for answers.'

'Some cop. You didn't even ask me a question.'

'You sure about that? Also, I wanted to pass on some more news. We found the guy who killed your friend Cattaneo.'

There was silence on the line.

'You remember Beppe?' Peroni went on. 'The two of you went to Tarquinia. Got in a shootout with those three kids in the shack that belonged to the Petrakis family. Some local officer died.'

'I remember. Who the hell . . . ?'

'The brother killed your friend.'

'Whose brother?' the voice on the phone yelled.

Peroni sighed, as if exasperated.

'What is this? Does the catering business make you slow or something? Lorenzo Bartoli's brother. Seems he came to believe those kids in the shack didn't shoot Lorenzo at all. You two did. So Cattaneo got it in the head in his car a while back. I have the pictures here somewhere. You think I should email them? Not pretty. Best you finish your lunch first.'

'What do you want?'

Peroni took a deep breath and said, 'I'd just like to know the truth, Ettore. It might help us stop him coming at you. Can't pick him up 'cos, to be honest, his confession is a little shaky, see. Not one he will repeat for the lawyers, even if we had some means of bringing him in. Which we don't, not right now.'

'This thing is closed . . .'

'Don't they have TVs in Chicago? You've watched what's happening here and you're telling me it's closed?'

'For me it is.'

'Not if Aldo Bartoli finds you, Ettore. He's a dedicated man. Real angry too. If someone was to point his attention to some nice restaurant in Chicago . . . What does an airline ticket cost these days? You get my point? If I can find you, so can he. With a little help. This is in your interests, just as much as ours.'

'You don't have the first clue what you're into,' Rufo grunted, then the line went dead.

'He may have a point,' Elizabeth Murray said quietly.

'I've a good mind to call up Aldo Bartoli and give him the bastard's address,' Peroni grumbled. 'This guy's a Roman. He knows what's going on here. And he doesn't even ask what it's like. How bizarre is that?'

The phone on the table rang, so loud it made Teresa jump. Peroni stabbed the speaker button again and said, 'Ettore?'

It was Costa again, calling from the car.

'You found Rufo?' he asked.

'Don't be so quick off the mark. It makes us old guys feel, well, old.'

'Where is he?'

'Selling pizza in Chicago. Too busy to talk to the likes of us. You got something?'

After the visit to Tarquinia, Costa wanted Falcone to consider the possibility that Petrakis and his team were not in Rome at all, but out in the countryside, dashing in and out of the city as they pleased.

'Unlikely,' the inspector commented. 'They need resources. Good transport access. Speed. Terrorists tend to work from urban locations.'

'That,' said the voice on the line, a little sharply, 'is conventional thinking. It's not going to get us anywhere. All I'm asking is that you consider the possibility they're in the Tarquinia area. That . . .'

The call became muffled. She thought she heard something competing with the sound of Nic's voice, a high-pitched drone, like that of a far-off scooter somewhere in the background. It blanked out half the sentence.

'. . . we're going to take one last look anyway.'

'Nic . . .' she found herself saying.

But there was nothing there any more. The line was dead. The three young officers were out in the bare, empty Maremma. Teresa could picture some of the places she'd visited out there: beautiful sights, old and rich in history, separated for the most part by long stretches of desolate wilderness.

'I'm going to call that bastard Rufo again,' Peroni said with some vehemence.

'No,' Falcone told him. 'He won't talk. We've done enough. Go home and get some sleep.'

'Can we even get home?' Teresa asked.

'You can,' Silvio Di Capua said. He showed them a map on the computer screen, the Carabinieri's official ruling on where the public could and could not go. A red line marked out a lozenge-shaped forbidden zone in the centre, from the road past the Forum to the Quirinale hill, then down again to the Piazza Venezia. Teresa Lupo couldn't imagine the constantly bustling centre of her native city depopulated in this way. It was eerie, wrong.

'We can go by the river,' Falcone pointed out.

'Silvio?' she asked. 'You can stay with us, if you like.'

Her deputy lived way out in the suburbs and had left his car at the Questura. Even if he managed to retrieve it, there was no guarantee how long it would take to drive home, or get back in the morning. The Englishwoman – she had no idea.

'Silvio and I discussed this,' Elizabeth Murray told them. 'There's plenty of space here. And these machines . . .'

Her eyes gleamed at Di Capua's computers.

Outside a siren sounded. Almost immediately another, more distant, appeared to answer its call, then a third, then another. This was not their city any more. They were simply one more group of civilians, trapped by the machinations of Andrea Petrakis and the state's response.

'What is it?' she asked, seeing an odd expression on Peroni's face. Half-interest, half-guilt.

'The Petrakis couple were messing around with drugs,' he said, looking at Falcone. 'Or so Aldo Bartoli seems to think.'

'So?' she asked.

'They wouldn't dare do that without permission.' Peroni reached for the old, battered address book he kept in his jacket pocket. 'Let me call a man with a past. See if he's hungry.'

– 7 –

There was a single humpbacked mound, much like the ones they had seen at the public site on the outskirts of Tarquinia. Around the perimeter was a low, rusty barbed-wire fence, broken in parts. Tall, parched grass surrounded the grave site. A narrow path of bare earth ran from an unlocked gate to a metal door set against the nearest side of the knoll that rose ahead in the trees.

'Someone's been here,' Rosa said, looking at the ground.

'We know that already,' Costa replied. 'It could just have been sightseers.'

'Out here? Have you ever been inside one of these things?'

'No.'

Closer up it looked as if a small house had been buried by some prehistoric landslide, leaving nothing but the roof extending above the surface.

'I did a school trip from Rome when I was a kid,' Rosa said. 'To the ones in Tarquinia that we saw first. It was . . . scary, but thrilling too. They're huge. They go deep and, when you get to the bottom, it's not a grave at all. It's like a room, two rooms sometimes. The sort of place you'd go for a banquet or a wedding. They believed they were departing for something good, a place to meet their family, their lovers. Drinking, dancing, feasting . . .'

And then along came the Blue Demon, Costa thought, remembering what Teresa had told them. The worm of doubt worked its way into the Etruscans' safe and comforting credo, spreading insidiously the notion that death was not an automatic invitation to an eternal paradise. That there was another destination too.

He walked up the path and took hold of the handle on the metal door. It opened freely, screeching on dry hinges. On the ground were a padlock and chain. Costa picked the chain up by the end. The metal where it had been snapped by bolt-cutters was clean and shiny, even in the dying golden light of the day.

'Whoever was here,' he said, 'they weren't just looking.'

He turned on the torch, told her to do the same, and flicked the beam forward, beyond the open door, into the black mouth of the tomb. Ahead lay a long line of steps, descending at a steep angle into the earth, with a single, flimsy banister to the right.

'I go first,' he announced before entering the inky pool swimming beneath their feet.

It seemed an endless descent, one pace at a time, gripping the dry, splintery rail at the side. Finally, after more footholds than he could begin to count, the torch beam fell on bare earth. Costa found himself standing on firm ground once more, in a subterranean cavern of some size, so deep beneath the surface that he could hear nothing of the world above, not a bird, not a night insect.

Rosa joined him and shone her torch around the space in front of them.

'It's huge,' she said.

'And empty.'

There were marks in the floor, niches carved out of the brown soil, where once, he guessed, at least two sarcophagi had lain. The archaeologists had been there already, or perhaps the grave-robbers before them. Not an item remained in the centre of the chamber. He shone his light further in front. There was a small archway carved in the stone ahead, and a dark, seemingly smaller chamber beyond.

'Where's the Blue Demon, Nic? Are you sure this is the right place?'

'It's the place the woman gave us.'

Costa knew why she was asking. The beam of her torch had flickered sideways, coming to rest on the frieze running round the nearest wall. What was painted there, with some skill, seemed to have no connection with the dark terrors he had expected. It was a Bacchanalian orgy: naked men and women, with wine cups overflowing, running through a wood that must have been much like the one in which the tomb was built. Some wrestled. Some made love. Some performed more perverse sexual acts. There were animals too, and violence. One cruel, explicit scene in particular seemed more in keeping with the kind of pornography that Costa had occasionally seized from the seedier shops around Termini.

'You can see why they didn't open this one up to the public,' Rosa muttered, sounding a little shocked. 'No one's going to be bringing any school trips down here.'

'I wouldn't argue with that,' he said, then moved on towards the smaller hall.

The tone of the frieze to their left altered as they neared the low, narrow door that led into the further chamber. The expressions on the faces of the characters shifted subtly, from ecstasy to, first, surprise and then doubt, bordering on fear.

He felt Rosa following him and knew, from the sound of her tense, short breathing and the way she kept close by him, her shoulder occasionally brushing his in the gloom, that she was noticing this change in the paintings too. Then he was through the opening. She followed him and the two of them turned both beams of their torches on the wall to the left.

A brief, pained shriek escaped Rosa's throat. Costa felt his own blood run cold. It took a moment for him to think straight, to remind himself that this was nothing but paint on ancient plaster, placed here 2,500 years before.

The frieze had disappeared. The images ran the full length of the wall, larger than life, the product of some terrible and vivid imagination. The trick the long-dead artist had played was both devious and sinister. Seen by the visitor walking through from the larger chamber, it was as if the lines of giddy revellers were tumbling ecstatically towards Hell.

Still in each other's arms, in congress, dancing, fighting, eating, drinking, they appeared to fall through the slender opening into the second chamber like unwitting victims slipping into a nightmare.

The Blue Demon was there to meet them: the same hideous devil, recreated time and time again, sharp fangs dark with gore, his eyes like coals, his tail whipping like a serpent, an inhuman erection rising from his loins. The creature seized the cavorting figures as they stumbled into his domain, then feasted off them, tearing the unwitting Etruscans to pieces, handing the remains to lesser demons to shred and gorge upon. It was a horror from Hieronymus Bosch, but shorn of the aesthetic licence of the artist who would come almost two millennia later. There were no fanciful, dream-like sequences here, just flesh and blood and entrails, and the all-powerful figure of the azure lord, the master of ceremonies, his talons slicing at the hapless victims as they made the transition from light to dark, blinded by bliss, unaware of their fate until there was no going back.

Costa felt Rosa's fingers grip his arm.

'Get me out of here, Nic,' she whispered, her voice almost unrecognizable.

'When we're finished,' he said, then moved the beam of torchlight away from the red-eyed monster on the wall and on to the tiny chamber itself.

It was no larger than a child's bedroom and, unlike the adjoining room, it wasn't empty. On the floor, in front of the wall facing the entrance, there was a group of objects, dark – metal by the looks of it.

Modern too.

He told Rosa to keep her light on them, bent down and looked. They were munitions boxes, with NATO markings. The latches were easily undone. Beneath the lid lay packs of material neatly stacked like sets of playing cards. Costa retrieved one and saw the telltale word on the side.

'Do you know what Explosia is?' he asked her.

'Can we discuss this outside?'

He put the pack back in the case and stood up.

'It's the commercial name for Semtex these days. They changed it after all the bad publicity. It was Semtex back when Czechoslovakia was behind the Iron Curtain. Now that we're all as free as birds . . .'

Explosia. He remembered the course well, and the female instructor who had taken them through the history of the means terrorists used to wreak havoc on the world. Most Islamic groups relied on simple, home-made fertilizer-based devices. Gaining possession of real explosives had become hard, and the genuine material now possessed chemical tags and metallic coding that meant it could be traced to the original buyer.

Next to the boxes lay several automatic weapons wrapped in clear plastic, as if straight from the factory, and boxes of shells.

'Using traceable material like this, it's . . .'

Nothing Andrea Petrakis did matched up to the template of twenty-first-century terrorism from the East.

'. . . strange,' he began to say, then stopped.

Something had moved in the darkness. Something small. Something close.

He felt Rosa's body come close to his, saw the shaking beam of her torch edge towards the black space in the corner. The sound was coming from there.

Her screams rent the darkness, her terrified shrieks sounded like the cries that might have come from the dead Etruscans shuffling in drugged rapture from the chamber outside into the bloody, flailing arms of the Blue Demon.

In the bright light of her torch beam lay a body, slumped against the corner wall. A middle-aged man in jeans and a shirt that had once been white. His mouth was open, his eyes black and sightless, staring up at them. Rats ran over him, making rustling sounds as they scurried beneath the fabric. His dead hand clutched at his chest and what looked like a wound there.

Rosa's cries were wordless, mindless, and the small, enclosed space made them sound so loud he felt the walls might cave in. She dropped the torch. There was his alone now. Costa took her arm, coaxed her back into the first chamber, pushed her to the stairs, helped her up slowly, one foothold at a time, listening as her choking sobs began to subside.

It seemed to take forever to climb the rickety wooden steps. She took the last few on her own to get there ahead of him. When he reached the top, he could see that evening had arrived, a bright clear Mediterranean night, lit by stars. Her dark cheeks were stained with tears. But she had control of herself again, and there was a glimmer of shame in her intelligent, pretty face that told him she wished he'd never seen her this way.

'We need to call Falcone,' he told her and stepped outside. 'Mirko?'

There was no one there. He took two more steps towards where the car ought to be. Then something pounced on him, and for a moment he wondered whether he'd met the Blue Demon itself. Costa found himself on the ground trying to defend himself from a flurry of vicious and furious punches. Something dragged the weapon from his shoulder holster. As he lay, aching on the hard earth, arm in front of his face, trying to make sense of this, his head turned and he saw Rosa next to him, hand to her mouth, where a faint trickle of blood had emerged.

A dark, foreign-looking individual was kneeling over her, his hand drawn back, recoiling from a punch. As Costa watched he snatched the gun from the young officer's holster, cast it to one side and then, for no reason whatsoever, swiped her hard across the face with the back of his hand.

Costa looked up at the man who'd brought him to the ground. Behind stood a woman, whose expression seemed much like those of the long-dead Etruscans he'd seen on the walls of the tomb. Confused. Frightened. Expectant.

'God punishes the curious,' the figure above him said, pointing a pistol straight into Costa's face.

– 8 –

Teresa Lupo gave Peroni the look. The one that said, 'Only you could pick a place like this for meeting the mob.'

He'd taken her and Falcone to a small, intimate and rather expensive-looking restaurant called Charly's Saucière only a few doors away from the apartment, in the same road, near the Lateran piazza. They were the only customers in an elegant dining room, depopulated, the elderly waiter said, by the state of affairs in Rome. He looked decidedly disappointed when Falcone ordered a single bottle of mineral water between the three of them.

Ten minutes later a dapper middle-aged man in a dark suit arrived. He gave no name, and didn't ask theirs, but immediately ordered a glass of Barolo and a plate of foie gras with truffles as if he were a regular. He looked like a well-paid accountant or lawyer, though Teresa couldn't help noticing the missing two fingers on his left hand.

The visitor stared at Peroni as if she and the lean inspector next to her didn't exist.

'We're here to talk history? In company?'

'I'm training a new assistant,' Peroni replied, and she only just stopped herself kicking his shins under the table. 'You OK with that?'

'And him?'

'Management,' Falcone said simply. 'I'm here to pay the bill.'

'Good.'

He watched the antipasti arrive. When the waiter was gone, he picked up a piece of fat goose liver with his fingers and shoved some into his mouth. Appearances could be deceptive. The suit, the shirt, the red silk tie . . . the immaculate black hair, dyed naturally, and moustache trimmed to perfection . . . Whoever this hood was, he'd spent a lot of money on his appearance. But he still couldn't get rid of the peasant in him, not entirely.

'This conversation don't exist,' the man announced. 'Never happened. You not eating? Onion soup's good. Snails. Steak tartare.' He tried a little more foie gras. 'I'll go for the steak. Come on. It's not polite to eat alone.'

The big man shook his head.

'We lost our appetites somewhere along the way. It was that kind of day.'

The man glared at him, called over the waiter, placed his order, then waited until they were on their own again.

'Shame. And once this is done, we're even?'

Falcone didn't even blink. Teresa looked at Peroni and the man and asked, 'Dare I ask what kind of favour you're repaying here?'

They didn't respond, didn't even look at her, which was an answer in itself.

'Twenty years ago,' Peroni said. 'A Greek couple called Petrakis. They were killed in Tarquinia. From what I gather, they'd been dealing dope. Maybe upsetting some people you know. I need to understand what happened and why.'

'Petrakis, Petrakis, Petrakis.' The well-dressed hood rapped his fingers on the table. 'Greek, you say?'

'Toni . . .' Peroni sighed.

He did have a name and, judging by the flash in his eyes, he didn't like to hear it out loud.

'We don't have time. This is important.' Peroni nodded at the door. 'You know what's going on out there.'

'Nothing's going on. Thanks to you people mainly. And the Carabinieri. Those idiots you got wandering round looking like they're in a movie or something. Who are you kidding?'

'A politician and his driver have been murdered,' she pointed out. 'We're lucky someone didn't die at the Trevi Fountain today. It may just be the beginning.'

Toni stopped eating for a moment, furled his heavy black

eyebrows and said, 'Wait. Are you trying to tell me these two things are linked? Some Greek bums who got what was coming to them years ago. And this?'

'I assume you read,' Teresa snapped. 'What's going on now is the work of Andrea Petrakis. The son of the couple who got murdered. We'd assumed, at least some of us, that he was responsible for that, and a lot else besides. Now . . .'

'Now what?' he wondered.

'Now we're not so sure.'

He sniffed the wine, making out he was some kind of connoisseur.

'Greeks. What kind of kid would kill his parents? Never get that in Italy.'

Actually, she thought, there were at least four cases she could name in which Roman offspring had murdered one or more parents. But Teresa Lupo didn't mention this.

'Is that what happened here?' Falcone asked.

Toni shrugged.

Peroni leaned over the table and pulled away the plate. The hungry hood held his knife and fork over the empty space. He looked hurt.

'We think what's going on now has to do with what went on then,' Peroni repeated very slowly, very patiently. 'We think it might get worse unless we can do something to stop it. To achieve that, we need to understand what happened. This is nothing to do with your business, Toni. It's about people. Ordinary people. We need to bring it to an end. Quickly. With no one else dead.' He watched the man opposite, whose knife and fork stayed in the air. 'Or do you like seeing Rome this way?'

The cutlery went down. Toni glared at the two of them and there was outrage in his dark, glassy eyes.

'Do not insult me, Peroni. I grew up on the streets here. This is my city. More than yours.'

'Then help us.'

'With what?'

'The Petrakises,' Teresa said quietly, wishing Falcone would do something, say something, instead of just watching this overdressed creep behave like a jerk. 'Who killed them? And why?'

The plate with the half-finished foie gras went back over to his side of the table.

'You sure know how to ruin a guy's appetite.'

Peroni swore and got to his feet.

'Let's go,' the big man told Falcone. 'I was an idiot. I thought these scum still had an ounce of decency in them.'

'Hey! Hey!' Toni yelled. 'That's just plain offensive.'

There was a commotion from out back. A howl, as if someone was in pain. Then the old waiter came out, his hands to his grey face, babbling about something on the TV.

Peroni strode through into the kitchen and watched what was happening. After a few seconds he went back into the dining room and called the others through.

They only watched for a minute or two. It was enough. The TV stations had found fresh footage of the outrage at the Trevi Fountain. It came from the mobile phones of some of those who'd been around at the time. These shots were clearer than anything they'd seen before, much more vivid than the shaky video the Blue Demon had posted on the Web. It looked as if somehow the fountain itself had burst a vessel, soaking everyone nearby in gore. As if Rome herself were bleeding profusely into the street. People were screaming. A few were hurt, seated on the ground, covered in dust and rubble, clutching shattered limbs.

Falcone turned to the mob man and asked, 'Are you really going to walk away from all this? And feel nothing?'

Toni grunted something wordless.

'Or are we back in the Years of Lead?' Falcone asked. 'Where the mob plants bombs the moment any rotten politician stuffs money in your pockets?'

The man in the flashy suit shook his head, reached out, took a couple of stems of asparagus from a serving dish in the kitchen and stuffed them in his mouth.

Without another word he went back to the table and picked up his glass.

When they got there Teresa said, 'These are not ordinary times, in case you hadn't noticed. If we weren't desperate . . .'

'She's good,' he told Peroni. 'The lady's melting my heart.'

'Oh, for Christ's sake.' Teresa wanted to scream.

'You ever see anything like that?' he interrupted. 'Who could do that kind of thing? Why?'

'That's what we're trying to find out,' she said.

He looked at her, and for the first time seemed interested.

'You really think these dead Greeks might help?'

'That's why we're here,' Peroni replied patiently.

'Huh! You know what channel conflict is?'

'Marketing bullshit,' Teresa responded.

Toni shook his head. His hair moved oddly. She wondered if it was a rug or not. He picked up his fork and started eating again.

'No. It is not. Imagine you've been selling something, say . . .' he played with his wine glass, '. . . some decent Barolo. You've been selling it for years. Spending time developing distribution, marketing. Establishing demand.'

Falcone poured himself another glass of water and raised it in a sarcastic salute.

'I'll ignore that, Mr Inspector. You buy it from the people you always did. Pay a good price too. Then one day you go out to sell some more and they're there. The wine-makers. The ones who took your money in the first place. They've opened up shop in your street, selling the thing you already bought from them. Selling it cheap. Saying, "Don't buy from those old guys any more. They're yesterday. Buy from us." What's a businessman going to do?'

They waited. He waved to the waiter, who came out with the steak tartare. The man looked as if he'd been crying.

'I'll tell you,' he went on eventually. 'Hypothetically. First, you sit down and talk to them. You try to reason with them. You explain that this has been a good business for everyone. We've all made money. We never had no fallings out. So why not keep it that way?

183

We can cut a deal. Manage the margins a little, maybe. Act like decent human beings, the way grown-ups do . . .'

'This was dope, hard drugs. Not Barolo,' Teresa interjected.

'Wasn't nothing, it being hypothetical and all. Then, if the talking doesn't work, you get a little more direct. You tell them how it's going to be.'

He looked idly at the dessert menu, as if this all needed to be planned in advance, screwed up his face and said, 'Nah.'

'And when that doesn't work?' she asked.

'Then you go round and pop a bullet in someone's head. Stop the trouble right in its tracks. Before it gets out of hand. That's what I'd guess might happen anyway. What do you think?'

Falcone thought about this.

'So Andrea Petrakis didn't kill his parents. Even though it says the exact opposite in an official parliamentary inquiry.'

'I wouldn't know anything about that,' Toni replied. 'I'll tell you one thing, though. This kind of thing doesn't happen often, thank God. You know why?' He grimaced. 'It's messy. Usually, it ends in a war. People get angry. People get dead.'

Teresa cut in, 'The Frascas died. Those kids in Tarquinia . . .'

'Who the hell were they?' Toni growled. 'Bystanders. Children. What kind of people do you think we are?'

'Best we don't go there,' she murmured.

'Your charm is short-lived, lady. Something else you need to know?'

'The war,' Falcone kept on. 'You're saying it didn't happen.'

Toni clicked his fingers and grinned.

'See,' the man said to her. 'These two guys are smart. They're listening to what I'm *not* saying. If you want to make it as a cop, you could do worse than learn from Peroni. Though it's a little late for a career change, I'd guess.'

'There was no war?' she asked him. 'No retaliation. No comeback from the . . . wine-makers?'

He raised his glass.

'The thing about wine is . . . there's always another supplier. Or even the same supplier, once you make them see sense. You should be grateful for all this, by the way. Proves the old saying: Nothing beats self-regulation. Most effective form of policing there is.'

'Nothing happened?' Peroni wanted to know. 'Nothing?'

Toni shrugged.

'Two lying, cheating scumbags lost their lives. The son went crazy and got himself into all kinds of trouble. None of it to do with us. Then . . . life went on.' He put down his knife and fork for a moment, which seemed to Teresa a sign that something surely baffled him. 'You tell me how that came about. I'm just a little guy. Was then. Still am now. Makes no sense. It was like . . .'

The mob man shook his head, then wound some of the raw meat from his steak tartare into the egg and shallots and capers on the side.

'Hypothetically, it was as if this was the way it was meant to be. Those stupid Greek bastards screwed us around, then got handed over on a plate. It was like there was a sign on the door saying: Shoot here. As if we were doing someone else a favour.'

He took a mouthful.

'You know what? Looking back, I'm not even sure it was true. We told them good the first time. They knew what was gonna happen if they screwed around again. What the hell!' He shrugged. 'We got word they were still dealing. Consequences ensued.'

'Who told you?' Falcone demanded.

'What? That they weren't listening? I don't recall. Long time ago. Not the kind of detail you keep.'

His bleak face froze for a moment.

'All that stuff the son got into afterwards – none of that was about business, was it?' he insisted. 'Not ever. It was about something dirtier, something we wouldn't touch, nor anyone I respect either, not in a million years. Not directly anyway.'

'Which was?' he asked.

'Politics,' he said, his mouth full of raw pink beef. 'Excuse the language.'

'So what was the Blue Demon in all this?' Teresa asked.

The mob man put down his knife and fork, picked up a napkin

and wiped his mouth, never taking his dead, emotionless eyes off her for a moment.

'It was interesting talking to you all,' he said, then got up and walked out of the door without uttering another word.

- 9 -

Costa couldn't think straight, couldn't imagine any way out of this. There was no doubt in his mind that the man above him was Andrea Petrakis. He looked older, wearier, more dangerous, but this was the same individual he'd seen in the photograph they had from twenty years before.

Three against three, under the bright moonlight, though they were now disarmed, disorientated. Mirko Oliva, his face bloodied and ashamed, looked hurt. Rosa had ceased struggling under another kick from the man above her.

'I put a call into base when I saw them, boss,' Oliva said quickly, desperately. 'There's back-up men coming . . .'

'Liar! Liar! Liar!' Petrakis yelled, so loud he couldn't care who might hear.

'We're police officers,' Costa said calmly. 'We're not alone. You'll be found. What my colleague says . . .'

Petrakis turned and kicked Oliva hard in the chest. The big young officer took it with scarcely a flinch. There was a look of thunder in his face Costa didn't want to see. They had nothing to fight with but their bare hands. There would be no back-up. There was only one way to get out of this alive, and that was through talking.

Petrakis came back, leaned down and stared into Costa's face.

'What were you doing here?' His eyes strayed back to the tomb, his hand indicated the open metal door. 'You had no right . . . no right . . .'

'You need to think about what we do now, Andrea,' Costa said calmly. 'How we get out of this. All of us.'

'I do?' he asked, laughing.

'Listen to me,' Costa began, then saw, to his horror, what was happening.

'Mirko!' he yelled.

Oliva wasn't waiting for anything. He'd launched himself off the ground, his big, burly rugby player's body aimed squarely at Petrakis. The impact was sudden and painful. The young officer had his arms round the man's torso, might have got somewhere if Costa had the time to get upright himself and help.

The other man, the dark one, intervened, pistol-whipping the figure beneath him round the head, brutally, with undisguised force. The young cop yelped in pain, then slumped to the earth on his knees, hands cradling his hurting skull.

Petrakis danced round and round like a crazy man.

'We can still talk about this,' Costa began.

'Talk! *Talk!*' Petrakis shrieked.

He walked up to Mirko Oliva, nursing his wound on the ground, placed the barrel of his weapon against the young cop's skull, then shot him through the head.

Oliva's body jumped as if hit by an electric shock and fell in a heap on the dry ground. There was a single gasp of pain and shock, and then he was gone.

Rosa began screaming again.

Mirko, Mirko, Mirko . . .

The words rose towards the velvet Mediterranean sky, to the stars and the bright, heedless moon. Then the man crouched above her delivered another slap and she was silent.

Nic Costa watched Mirko die, knowing that he'd seen such an act before. Too many times. On the TV, over and over. It was the way captives were executed in war. Suddenly, without compunction or compassion, or a single reflection that in an instant a human life would be snatched from the world forever, before its time.

Andrea Petrakis was walking back towards them, the gun still in his hand.

There were no prayers, no actions for a time like this. Costa kept his eyes open, though, and watched.

The man was one step away when the sound leaped out of his shirt pocket like an electronic insect bursting out of its cocoon.

For some reason – and Costa wanted to remember this, because he knew it had to be important – the phone call made Andrea Petrakis crazier than ever. Crazier than three cops straying into his private temple. Crazier than the realization that, whatever he did to his captives, it would soon become clear where his team had been lurking as they stalked the citizens of Rome.

Petrakis began screaming, louder than Rosa ever had. Costa rose to a crouch, wondering, waiting for an opportunity.

The other man must have seen, because in an instant he was over and the side of some weapon fell hard against Costa's head, sent him clattering, dizzy, to the cold, hard earth.

He wasn't sure what he heard after that. He thought someone had done the same thing to Rosa. He wanted to fight. To argue. To struggle. A line from a piece of poetry came into his head, a snatch of an English work his father had loved towards the end, a paean to rage, a war cry against the dying of the light.

The sound of his own breathing rose in his ears until it was so loud he thought it might deafen him. He could feel the blood alive in his veins. With a final effort he tried to move, but his head – pained and confused – intervened, and the agony sent him tumbling back to the ground. After a moment Rosa's damp, warm fingers reached out and clasped his hand.

A gunshot sounded close by, followed by a shriek. It could only be her, making a noise like the yelp of a child or a young animal. Her taut, terrified grip on his fingers, something that meant so much at that moment, became still and lifeless. He tried to turn his head to see, and it was impossible.

'Do not go . . .' Costa found himself whispering, feeling no rage whatsoever, or fear, only a sense of failure and despondency.

There was another noise, closer this time, loud and long and booming, and then darkness.

Part 4

THE NIGHT

Voici le soir charmant, ami du criminel;
Il vient comme un complice, à pas de loup; le ciel
Se ferme lentement comme une grande alcôve,
Et l'homme impatient se change en bête fauve.

Behold the sweet evening, friend of the criminal;
It comes like an accomplice, stealthily; the sky
Closes slowly like a great alcove,
And impatient man turns into a beast of prey.

Charles Baudelaire, *Les Fleurs du Mal*

- 1 -

Dario Sordi had never seen the Salone dei Corazzieri look more magnificent. Beneath Agostino Tassi's fresco *Allegoria della Gloria*, before a gathering of the world's most powerful men, and one or two women too, a string quartet played Haydn's *Sunrise*, a bright, optimistic piece that failed to match the president's mood.

So, after introductions and polite, brief conversations, he contented himself with staying at the periphery of proceedings, chatting with those he found more interesting: waiters and musicians, security personnel and household staff. When they were too busy he watched his guests, mingling, shaking hands, talking in the guarded way politicians did, feeling, for his own part, that he had at least performed his duty, even if he'd learned little in the process. Sordi was head of state and no one shared confidences with a figurehead.

When the president's attention returned to the room, he was depressed to see the prime minister walking towards him bearing a glass of what appeared to be *vino santo* and a plate full of Tuscan biscuits and sweets.

'I've eaten my fill, thank you,' Sordi said quickly when the man arrived.

Campagnolo jammed a couple of tiny stuffed figs into his animated mouth.

'I wasn't bringing this for you. I don't wait table any more.'

Before Ugo Campagnolo entered the world of television he had spent some time working in a tourist camp in Sardinia, as a restaurant hand and night-club singer. In the early days of his political career this was frequently mentioned in the press, though now that much of the media had shifted to Campagnolo's camp, the story was less well known. Nor did anyone repeat another tale from those times, of how he had bought the entire enterprise when he came into money, abruptly firing every manager with whom he had fallen out. A good few were in that category, and, in Sardinia, where work was scarce, they did not find new jobs easily.

'So . . . ?' Campagnolo asked. 'It was a good evening, don't you think?'

Sordi felt his blood run cold.

'We're making merry in a velvet prison. Out there,' he indicated beyond the salon's shuttered windows, 'the city is dead. Empty streets. People sitting in their homes wondering what next outrage will come their way. And you . . .' He scowled as Campagnolo swigged back his wine and held out the glass, without saying a word, waiting for someone to come and fill it. '. . . you don't seem to care.'

A dark anger rose in the prime minister's beady eyes. He let the attendant depart before answering.

'Never say a thing like that in public. I will crucify you. Already the people out there blame you more than they blame me. You took responsibility.' He waved his hand, as if this were a small matter. 'Besides, all will be well. Trust me. In a little while this will simply be a bad memory. Petrakis is a madman. We will have him before long. Rome will go back to being Rome. Come August, everything will be forgotten. The public have short memories, thank God.'

'I doubt the parents of that poor Polish girl or Giovanni Batisti's widow would agree. By the way, I enjoyed your visit to the Trevi Fountain.' It was an excruciating moment: Campagnolo wandering around the rubble and the stones, still soaked in fake blood, shaking his head, hugging the survivors, eyes moist with tears. 'You never miss an opportunity, do you?'

'I'm a politician. What do you expect?'

Dario Sordi wondered when he could make his excuses and retire to the solitary quarters he occupied in the palace, leaving the guests to depart in their armoured convoys, tracking through a dead and ghostly city. His own rooms were magnificent, fit for a pope, and quite lacking in all of the attributes – small personal items, a fragrance, a long-cherished view – he associated with the word 'home'. He longed for the modest two-bedroom apartment near the Piazza Navona that he'd shared with his late wife for nearly forty years. Though Nic Costa didn't remember, he had slept there for a few nights as a child, when his parents were going through one of their difficult patches. The Sordis, if only for a few brief days, had discovered what it was like to be parents, something fate had denied them. Memories of that nature were irreplaceable. Next to them even the hidden microphones that the secret service had placed in their bedroom seemed no more than minor inconveniences, like mosquitoes in summer or the occasional stray intrusion of a mouse.

The last few nights in the elaborate apartment in the Quirinale he had not slept well. The dreams were bad and relentless. One in particular, in which he was back in the Via Rasella, little more than a child, gun in hand, in front of the two young German soldiers, ready to shoot, but unable to pull the trigger. In the nightmare one of the Nazis kept leaning down and asking, 'So you're a coward now, boy, are you? A little late for us, isn't it?'

'You know Palombo's people still answer to you,' Sordi said with a sigh. 'This is a charade, a play with a single short act. As you said yourself, I have simply deprived you of the culpability. You should be grateful.'

The prime minister glowered at him.

'You stole away my powers.'

It was a ridiculous charge, one that grew more false by the day. Only that morning, in a spare moment, Sordi had run through the list of new appointments to the judiciary. It was an open secret that they were, almost to a man and woman, Campagnolo's creatures. The same steady process had been occurring in the police and the civil service and, thanks to the prime minister's friends in the corporate world, throughout the media. In the absence of any concerted, organized opposition from the fractured parties of the centre and left, Campagnolo was steadily building himself a power base throughout the nation.

'No, Ugo. I merely borrowed one or two, for a little while, and for the best of reasons. We need the administration to survive. Not yours necessarily. But some authority. A process in which people can believe. A president is just one man. He can easily be replaced. A system of government . . .' It had been part of Sordi's thinking all along, though he was unsure why he was bringing Campagnolo into his confidence at this moment. Against his own wishes Dario Sordi found he was unable to stifle a brief, wry smile. 'It's ridiculous. We are Romans. We've been trying to solve this riddle – how does, how *should* one govern? – for so long. Two millennia or more. Still the answers elude us, and we have failed our people so often they begin to despair. If I can avoid one more scandal, one more collapse in public confidence . . .'

'Poor Dario,' Campagnolo declared as his gaze swept the room. 'You speak so beautifully. You're so clever. Yet you miss the obvious. No one wants to be governed by intellectuals. It makes people feel inferior. They want one of their own. A honest man with . . .' his face creased in a showman's smile, and he winked boldly, '. . . a side to him. It was a lonely and pointless talent that led you here.'

Sordi nodded.

'I believe you may be right, Ugo.'

'I am! I like this place too. One day, when I am old and weak and impotent, like you, I shall ask for it as payment in return for . . . something. We get what we deserve in this life. I assume you earned your time here yourself.'

'I assume so too, though what . . . ?'

'Your gift for the gab, I imagine. And this . . . art.' The prime minister's arm extended to the glorious frescoes. 'This place will suit me one day. It makes me feel at home. At one with those who commissioned it, and those who executed it. Politics is an art too. Sometimes highbrow. Sometimes low. Mainly the latter, if I'm honest with you. Some are better at it than others.'

'Do you have a favourite?' Sordi asked out of genuine interest. 'Among the paintings?'

'All are my favourites!' He indicated the *Allegory of Glory*. 'That one in particular. It's wonderful. To be able to paint like that . . .'

'Agostino Tassi,' Sordi said, recalling the delightful hours he had spent walking the palace in the company of the pleasant and attractive female curator of paintings. 'He's from the first half of the seventeenth century, one more follower in the footsteps of Caravaggio. Agostino collaborated with Orazio Gentileschi.'

'Never heard of them.'

'A shame. Agostino was like so many of his peers, a talented though damaged man. He raped Gentileschi's daughter, Artemisia, another gifted painter.'

The prime minister became interested.

'Artists, eh? What do you expect?'

'When the young woman complained, she was herself taken into custody. The authorities . . .' This thought refused to evade him. 'Our predecessors . . . examined her physically. Internally, with some brute force. They then tortured the girl by crushing her fingers, a peculiarly cruel torment for a painter, I think.'

'Women . . .' Campagnolo muttered. 'What happened?'

'Agostino went to jail briefly. Afterwards Artemisia became celebrated for painting, repeatedly, the same subject. An Old Testament scene. Judith decapitating the infidel Holofernes, a woman's revenge on a lustful man. They're spectacular canvases. If you compare the one in the Uffizi with Caravaggio's similar work in the Barberini here . . . There's something personal in them, some fierce female anger that a man – even Caravaggio – could never reproduce. You would see this instantly.' He thought of Campagnolo's reputation as a serial womanizer. 'Especially you.'

Campagnolo sniffed and looked back at the crowd.

'She got something out of it then? You make a good tour guide, Dario. If you're still breathing when I move into this place, you can have a job showing around the visitors. Your pension will cover it.'

Then he raised his empty glass, said 'Ciao' and, to Sordi's relief, departed.

The president walked outside, down the steps into the garden, to the stone bench beneath the wicker canopy by the side of Hermes, the place where he'd spoken to Nic Costa the day before. This was one part of the Quirinale that Dario Sordi loved. Early each evening, work permitting, he retired here and drank a single cup of Earl Grey tea, alone with his thoughts and a plate of special biscuits he had sent from England – ones that, in spite of their name, Garibaldi, were unavailable in Italy.

When he first moved into the palace, in an early flush of enthusiasm, he had harboured a fantasy about starting his own kitchen garden in the grounds, one he could oversee himself, growing the Roman vegetables of his youth: artichokes and *agretti* and, more than anything, the wild chicory he had once gathered in the suburbs near the Porta San Sebastiano during the war, when food was scarce and every family sought its own. The taste, sharp and bitter, remained with him still, and the joy with which his meagre pickings, little more than scraps of weed, were received when he brought them home. To have raised this simple vegetable in the gardens of the Quirinale would have brought a smile to the faces of his parents. The same straggly plant grew near the Ardeatine caves where Sordi's father and uncle were among those slaughtered by the Nazis after the attack in the Via Rasella. Its green leaves seemed to struggle from the brown earth in defiance of the climate and the poorness of the soil. Sordi liked this persistence against the odds, though perhaps its proletarian plainness would have looked out of place in the grandiose avenues of a palace.

As he lit a furtive cigarette, a shape moved in the darkness. He found that his heart bucked its usual rhythm at that moment.

'Who is it?' Sordi demanded. 'Show yourself.'

Fabio Ranieri emerged from the shadows.

'I'm sorry, sir. I was taking another look around. It is my job, you know.'

Ranieri came further into the light. He was a tall, strong man and his face, handsome and sincere, was a welcome sight.

'We're here to look after you,' the Corazzieri captain told him. 'Not . . .' he nodded back towards the brightly lit palace, '. . . them. I couldn't help but hear some of the things that bastard Campagnolo was saying. Lord knows he makes enough noise for ten.'

'No!' Sordi scolded him. 'I will not listen to another word. The men and women in that building are more important than an old wreck like me. Your care is for an office, not a person. You should view Ugo Campagnolo in the same light. Whether you respect the man or not, at least respect what he represents. The aspirations of several million of your fellow countrymen.'

Ranieri cleared his throat and stared at the ground.

'Oh dear,' Sordi muttered, with genuine regret. 'Things must be bad if we're beginning to argue.'

'I hate seeing Rome like this. While they . . .' another angry glance at the Quirinale, '. . . feast like Nero watching the city burn.'

'Bad history. That never happened. Nero wasn't even here at the time, or so I was always taught.' He stepped forward, keen to see the captain's face. 'Listen to me, Fabio. I will not be here forever. When I go, you must work with the people who come after. Whoever they are, and your part in their choice is no greater or less than that of any other Italian.'

'I am a captain of the Corazzieri,' Ranieri replied, bowing his head a little. 'My job is to protect the president.'

'And you do it very well. Any news?'

'Nothing.' He thought for a moment, then added, 'Except that Costa called. I told him you were busy.'

'What did he want?'

'He was in Tarquinia. He wanted to know where I was twenty years ago. Apart from that, I'm not sure he knew himself.'

'He must have his reasons. The phone, please.'

Ranieri handed him the private mobile that he had organized at Sordi's request. The president stumbled over the buttons, feeling foolish.

'I don't remember the number now.'

'Here . . .'

Ranieri helped and handed the mobile back. There was a ringing tone. Sordi put the thing to his ear, and as he did so a strong female voice said, '*Dígame.*'

Dario Sordi replied, automatically, 'I fear you're in Italy, not Spain, signora, and I have misdialled. My apologies.' He found himself thinking. Nic was a young man, now single. 'Unless you have Sovrintendente Costa with you.'

He waited.

'Signora? *Signora . . . ?*'

- 2 -

They'd needed a drink after the strange meeting in the restaurant with Peroni's hood. Falcone chose the location, naturally, which was why they were in the Via della Croce, drinking Falanghina in the Antica Enoteca, staring at some of the best cold food in Rome, trying to work up an appetite.

The inspector had decided he didn't want to walk all the way from San Giovanni, and instead had tried to drive them home in his Lancia. Four armed *carabinieri* turned them back at the barricade by the Colosseum, looking at their police IDs and laughing. That did nothing to improve his temper. Now his sleek saloon was abandoned halfway up the pavement of a side street on the opposite side of the Corso, near the Mausoleum of Augustus, in the shadow of an ugly fascist-era marble office building. Rome's shaky traffic-management system had collapsed under the pressure of the street closures and the panic to get out into the suburbs. Much of the *centro storico* was deserted, isolated by a multitude of barricades. Beyond them jams stretched in every direction. They were slowly beginning to clear, and as they did they revealed a city almost devoid of humanity, as if it were living under some kind of curfew.

The old wine bar should have been bursting with people fighting to get to the counter, yelling for their glasses of good Italian wine, from Tuscany and Puglia, Sicily and the Veneto, picking at plates of food. There were just two couples in the place. The waiters looked bored and a little scared. Peroni had chosen the dishes automatically, his favourites whenever they came here. Three generous plates, one of roast pork with prunes, a second covered with cheese, and a third of antipasti, sat on the bar, largely untouched.

'Was that a good day?' Teresa asked. 'As far as the work is concerned, I mean.'

Falcone scowled and held the Falanghina up to the light. It was perfect: cold and fragrant.

'I've known better. If it weren't for your assistant and the Englishwoman . . .'

'Silvio and Elizabeth are quite a team,' she agreed. 'I hope they manage to get some sleep. There's a limit to how much a computer can tell you.'

The two men stared at her.

'I know, I know!' she objected. 'I'm learning, aren't I? I'd like to think our trip to the Villa Giulia provided a little useful intelligence.'

'I suppose so . . .' Falcone looked thoroughly miserable. She found herself feeling sorry for this solitary, difficult man. He hated being excluded from the centre of events, and it was only in part due to his arrogance. More than anything he detested the idea of losing. All the men she'd come to admire, and in some ways love, did. It was a peculiarly damaged form of heroism on their part.

'Leo?' she asked, carefully. 'There's something I need to get clear in my mind.'

'Ask away,' he responded.

'Our new friend Toni. Walking out like that just because I asked him about the Blue Demon.'

There was a canny look in his eye.

'What about it?'

'Well, why? It's not as if it's a secret that they're the people we're looking for. Why did he suddenly get so touchy?'

'I didn't understand that, either,' Peroni began. 'It was as if it meant something different to him.'

Falcone's phone made a noise. He glanced at it, then turned the handset to face them. It was a short text, one that came, the screen indicated, from the private mobile phone of Mirko Oliva and read, simply: *They're here.*

'Is that it?' Peroni asked. 'Where are Nic and those kids now anyway?'

'Tarquinia,' Falcone told him. 'They should be at the hotel by now. I told him to do nothing but ask questions. I *told* him . . .'

Teresa walked outside, muttering something about indecision and men.

It was still hot. The street was empty. There ought to have been late-night shoppers and couples going out for dinner, arm in arm, laughing. Instead two *carabinieri* wandered past toting automatic weapons, their chests enveloped in heavy bulletproof jackets, and stared hard at a couple of forlorn street musicians, one with an accordion, the other with a trumpet, who were counting their few coins in the light of the fashion store on the far side of the street.

She called Nic's number. The phone rang for a long time before the automatic answer-message kicked in. The same thing happened with Rosa Prabakaran's phone, and Mirko Oliva's.

Peroni and Falcone were with her by then.

'We can ask someone in Tarquinia to go looking,' Peroni suggested.

'Look where?' Falcone asked.

Teresa rang Silvio Di Capua. They had an arrangement with the phone companies. When necessary they could try to track down the location of the cell from which a call was made. It was inexact. But it was something.

Peroni listened and when she was finished asked, 'When will they be back with an answer?'

'An hour. Maybe more.' She stared at Falcone. 'It's going to take us longer than that to get there, isn't it?'

He didn't answer straight away. She knew why. Nic wasn't supposed to be near Tarquinia.

'Are you going to tell our people there or not?' she asked.

'Tell them what?' Falcone demanded. He held up his phone. 'That we've had a single, obscure text message from a young and inexperienced police officer who's somewhere he doesn't belong?'

Peroni shrugged.

'It's not like Nic to be out of touch like this. Or Rosa.'

'I know that,' Falcone replied, exasperated. 'I also know what the cost will be to them if Palombo finds out where they've been. I don't care about my career.' He glanced at them. 'Is it worth risking theirs for two words on a phone?'

'There's only one way to find out, Leo,' Peroni said.

Falcone didn't say a word. They followed as he strode to his Lancia on the other side of the Corso.

It was the worst journey out of Rome she'd ever known. The main route to the coast, past Fiumicino, was closed. So was the Autostrada Azzurra, which should have been the obvious way north, past the airport's silent runways.

Falcone fought and argued his way through jams and road checks until they found the Via Aurelia, and followed it until they began to hug the shoreline, past the old Etruscan towns of Ladispoli and Cerveteri, and the choked modern port of Civitavecchia, which took almost an hour to navigate. It was as if everyone wanted to hide at that moment, to get home, get indoors, try to believe that safety lay in being outside Rome, behind the walls of one's own house, joined to the world outside by nothing more than a TV set and a phone line.

Driving through these dead, empty towns and villages, Teresa felt as if she were entering a wasteland, some kind of desert.

It was almost a comfort when, as they finally navigated Civita-vecchia and the road turned inland, away from the sea, towards Tarquinia, a sign appeared that there was someone alive in the night.

They stopped in a lay-by. Peroni needed it. From somewhere over the steady roll of the waves came the noise of an engine. A fishing boat trawling for a catch, she guessed, though it sounded louder than she might have expected, and more highly pitched, and the source of the noise seemed to come as much from the sky as from the dark, shifting waters of the Tyrrhenian.

– 3 –

The night reminded him of the East: bright and clear, with a luminous moon set against a sky punctured by a million starry pinpricks. The same sky he'd watched for two decades on the run, always waiting, always thinking. Of home and the Blue Demon, his parents, and what had happened. Lives that had been diverted from their natural courses, turned by events towards unexpected, unforeseen paths.

For twenty years Andrea Petrakis had dreamed of his return to the place of his birth. Not Italy, but Etruria, a place of freedom, a land where one's future was mapped out by the strength of human will, where everything was possible for those who dared. His father had taught him all this at an early age, and that it was his legacy, a destiny deep within the blood. He learned how the Greeks prefigured the Romans, establishing a world built on individual freedom, power from a man's personal fortitude, not birth or position or luck. How they had crossed the Ionian Sea, colonized the south, the Magna Graecia of modern Sicily, Apulia and Calabria, home to Pythagoras, an outpost of Athens in Italy. This was the base from which the men of Greece spread north, occupying the land from Naples to the Po, forging the Etruscan identity, bringing philosophy and art, politics and culture to the primitive tribes that lived there, giving meaning to their little lives. Until Rome grew ever stronger and, in the Pyrrhic War, might defeated right. The Greeks fell everywhere, becoming little more than slaves to the newer, duller, more mundane civilization they had themselves created. Zeus was toppled by an army of bureaucrats and mediocrities, men whose first response upon finding themselves in the foothills of Olympus was to pillage everything that went before.

When he was ten years old he read Virgil's paean to Arcadia, an homage to a lost pastoral Greek ideal written for a Roman emperor, Augustus, who himself rued the disappearance of the past. Virgil was an Etruscan too, they said, and Andrea Petrakis didn't doubt it for a moment.

His father had first taken him to see the Blue Demon not long afterwards. The tomb hidden in the woods of what was once the real Tarquinia seemed like a sanctuary, somewhere holy. Even fleeing the NATO troops in Afghanistan, hiding out in the mountains, in fear for his life, Petrakis could never forget the fire burning in the eyes of the devil who tore apart the Etruscans as they danced and made love on their way to eternity. Or what the creature truly stood for, the identity of the beast.

Something caught his attention and dragged him back to the present. The headlights of a car flickered through the blackness below his little plane, as it cruised a precise two hundred and fifty feet above the dark, gleaming waters north of Civitavecchia. Petrakis responded immediately, gunning the two-stroke Rotax to feed some power into a sharp turn to the right.

The port was busy, even in times like this. There would be radar and shipping, coastguards and other more shadowy security services. In Afghanistan he had sought intelligence during the planning stages, when he was determined that every eventuality would be thought of, every possible twist in the scheme considered and dealt with. It was easy in the modern world, *their* world, to discover the facts. They could scarcely resist boasting about them, on the Web, through sites he could find with a satellite connection on his laptop, in a poppy farmer's tent in the Helmand valley. Marine ground-radar scanned up to a hundred feet above the sea. The active aviation systems of Fiumicino and Ciampino would detect anything above five hundred, whether it carried a transponder or not. There was a slender gap of invisibility between the two, a layer of darkness into which his tiny microlight could flit undetected.

With his flimsy machine he was able to take off and land from a short, hidden country strip, to evade their radar, to fly slowly down the coastline, south towards Rome, cruising at a modest sixty knots, the craft trimmed out and kept straight and level by the cheap, simple autopilot that maintained altitude, direction and speed.

On the passenger seat and in the small space in the rear of the cockpit lay as much explosive from the Etruscan tomb as the weight and balance limits of the microlight would allow. Strapped to his back, bulky and uncomfortable as he flew the plane, was a $2,000 BASE ram-air parachute secured from a specialist supplier in Milan, delivered to the villa the week before.

Petrakis had undergone illicit training in BASE jumping at a small airfield near Karachi. A rogue member of the Pakistani air force had taken him aloft three times to teach him the technique, on each occasion reducing the height from which they exited the jump plane. This was no ordinary system. The rectangular chute was designed to cope with low-altitude jumps that were impossible for the conventional skydiver.

There was no room for error, no secondary canopy that could be deployed in the event of failure. These were the devices that BASE jumpers used to leap from buildings and cliff tops. They could function in a descent of five hundred feet or less, a distance a man in free fall would cover in less than six seconds.

He thought of the Blue Demon, and the legacy in his blood. Then Petrakis placed his hand on his back and felt the straps there.

As he got closer he wound down the trim a little, until he sat at just over two hundred feet above the sea. The moon was bright and serene, its rippled reflection lying on the surface of the gentle waves as if beached there. Petrakis watched as the mouth of the Tiber approached, with the town of Fiumicino to the north and Ostia on the other side of the river.

There was not a plane in the sky above him. The city, twenty-five kilometres inland, marked by a halo of light, was cut off.

After passing the narrow mouth of the shining Tiber winding its way inland, he followed the coast as it turned south-east, marking fifteen kilometres, still at the same height, waiting for the moment. Once he had passed the long, straight road of Via Cristoforo Colombo, named after one more Italian pirate, he was clear. That was the final route from the nearest shore back to Rome. There was nothing afterwards but flat, empty farmland, all the way to the second airport, Ciampino, where Air Force One and the planes of most of the G8 leaders sat on the asphalt.

When the marker beeped on the GPS he turned, setting the final destination of the plane: the apron at Ciampino, directly in front of the terminal building, now full of politicians' private jets. Latitude 41° 48′ 4.76″N, longitude 12° 35′ 21.49″E. He could picture the destination in his head as he locked the cheap autopilot to the handheld GPS unit.

The modern world was, he thought, like ancient Rome in many ways. It invented the means of its own destruction, in the name of science and knowledge and prosperity, blind to the threat of its own overwhelming arrogance. Twenty years before, when he'd learned to fly in a battered old Cessna 152 near Civitavecchia, nothing like this existed. No power on earth would have allowed him to penetrate to the inner sanctum of the state in the way he now planned.

Five kilometres short of Ciampino, the airfield clearly visible ahead, outlined by runway lights, Andrea Petrakis unfastened his pilot's harness and took out his second GPS unit, a tiny handheld model meant for walkers. It had long since seized the position. He waited for the waypoint he'd agreed with Deniz Nesin and Anna Ybarra before they left Tarquinia: the long, perfectly straight line of the old Appian Way, running almost parallel to Ciampino's runway, just a kilometre short of the field.

He looked down. A car was there, where it was supposed to be. He watched as it flashed its headlights close to the circular tower of the tomb of Cecilia Metella, the monument's outline clear in the moonlit night.

Petrakis fed in more power, brought the plane up to six hundred feet, aware that somewhere in the control room of Ciampino an air-traffic control officer would notice a blip on the radar screen at any moment.

It was too late for them to do anything. Even if a military fighter was in the area, it would now have little more than a minute in which to act. No jet could manoeuvre onto a previously unseen target in such time. They worked the way they had always worked, on the basis that both opposing parties fought to the same rules.

He'd calculated the glide path, the rate of descent. He knew the simple autopilot was working as intended. The laws of physics applied to everyone, equally. Petrakis trimmed the plane down into a steady, accelerating descent – one that would soon rise to a hundred knots or more – checked the autopilot was locked on the GPS coordinates one final time, then ripped open the flimsy door of the plane and half-fell, half-leaped, out into the black fury of the night.

- 4 -

There was a voice somewhere. Female, tremulous, familiar. It spoke his name, it made him feel human. Marooned somewhere between wakefulness and dream, he wanted to turn towards the source of the sound.

'Nic . . .' it said more insistently.

A hand shook his shoulder. Costa found himself being turned upright. He didn't know where he was for a moment. Then the memories came back, full of pain and despair. Rosa Prabakaran was staring at him, bleary-eyed, exhausted, frightened.

He said the first words that came into his hurting head.

'Why are we still alive?'

'I don't know,' she whispered. Then, as if she hated to say the words, she added, glancing backwards, to some unseen place behind him, 'Mirko isn't.'

Costa dragged himself upright, fighting the crashing stab of hurt the effort brought on. Someone had slugged him hard on the back of the skull. Someone . . .

Memories. A gun fired close to Rosa. Andrea Petrakis – a man who, they assumed, was working as part of a lone hit-team – had taken an incoming phone call, one that had enraged him much more than the presence of three police officers entering his private lair. These things were important, though at that moment he lacked the energy and the intelligence to understand why.

He walked over to look at the slumped, inert figure visible beneath the intense, prurient moon. The young police officer's corpse lay where Petrakis had shot him, stretched on the dry summer grass, arms akimbo, face bloodied and blank. In death he looked like a teenager.

She was by Costa's side, shaking a little.

'They took the car. They took everything. What do we do?'

He looked up at the sky, thinking.

'Are you all right?' he asked her.

'My head hurts.'

He stepped forward so that the silver light fell on her face and said, 'Show me.'

She turned. He reached forward and touched a matted patch of fine hair behind one ear.

'Ouch!'

'Sorry. It's not so bad. They . . .' He fought to remember those last moments. One recollection stood out. 'I thought they'd shot you.'

'He fired into the ground. Then they hit me. I was too scared to do anything. I was trying to find the courage to run. Then . . .' Her voice broke. 'Mirko . . . how could someone do that? As if he didn't really matter?'

'He didn't,' Costa answered straight away. Mirko Oliva's life carried no more weight, no more meaning than that of the golden-haired young man whose body had been riddled with bullets in the Via Rasella. Petrakis had a mission. Nothing could stand in its way.

Yet, somehow, they had survived.

He checked his jacket. Nothing. No weapon. Not even a wallet. His police mobile was gone. So was the tiny phone Dario Sordi had given him.

'Do we have anything else?' he asked.

'Just this.' She had one of their torches in her hand. 'It was Mirko's, I think. He must have dropped it when they got to him.'

'Stay here.'

'You're leaving me?' she asked, outraged.

'I'm going back into the tomb. Do you want to come? It may be a waste of time. Your choice.'

She didn't blink. Rosa Prabakaran said, 'I'll come.'

It seemed shorter the second time around, step by step, every one taken with care. He didn't look at the paintings on the wall, in the large chamber or the small. He walked on, feeling Rosa's arm attached to his for safety, for comfort.

When they got to the corpse slumped in the corner, in the room of the Blue Demon, the rats scurried away once more.

Costa bent down to look at the man. He'd been shot through the mouth and the chest. It was the same kind of death that had been delivered to Mirko Oliva. Sudden, deliberate, unthinking. He wore a cheap dark suit and a white shirt, now stained with gore, open at the collar.

Costa reached inside his jacket and recovered a wallet. There was a little money and an ID card. It said he was a Greek national called Stefan Kyriakis.

In the other pocket was a very new-looking mobile phone. Costa glanced at Rosa as he pushed the On button.

'Wish us luck,' he said.

A light came on the screen. Almost immediately the low battery warning began to bleep.

The two of them got back up the wooden steps as quickly as they could. Beneath the Mediterranean moon, by the corpse of Mirko Oliva, Costa found the weakest of signals.

He called Falcone. The inspector's familiar, bad-tempered voice barked, 'Pronto.'

'Petrakis found us,' Costa said quickly. 'They killed Mirko Oliva.'

'And you?' Falcone demanded.

He couldn't get this out of his head.

'We got knocked out. We'll live.'

'Where are you?'

Costa told him as best he could.

'This is not what I asked for . . .' Falcone began.

'I'm sorry. You need to tell Palombo. You need to bring in everyone you can. They're here, Leo. Not Rome. Here. This is . . .' he thought of the Blue Demon in the earth beneath his feet, '. . . their home. Where they came from. What made them.'

He could hear talking in the background. Then Falcone said, 'I somehow doubt that. We'll be there in five minutes.'

'Five . . . ?'

'Five. Mirko Oliva sent us a message.' He heard the anguish in Falcone's voice. 'He's dead?'

It wasn't like the man to repeat himself.

'I'm sorry.'

'Stay where you are. Don't—'

The last milliamp of power in the phone he'd found on the corpse in the Blue Demon's tomb expired. The thing fell silent in his fingers.

- 5 -

It took longer than anyone expected to locate the tomb in the parched grass knoll in the woods. An hour perhaps, even more. Costa found it difficult to speak when they arrived, but he answered the inspector's questions as best he could. Teresa had her arms around Rosa, who was weeping openly. Peroni stood over the young officer's body, grim-faced, furious.

After listening to what Costa had to say, Falcone took a torch and went down into the tomb. The rest of them waited. Costa didn't want to see that face on the wall again.

When the inspector came out again he demanded, 'Who is he?'

Costa took out the wallet and the ID card he'd found.

'Stefan Kyriakis.'

'No, Nic,' Falcone insisted. 'Who *is* he?' He looked close to losing control. Costa had rarely seen the man in this state before. 'Who are any of them? The Blue Demon? Jesus . . .'

'I don't understand,' Costa replied weakly.

He felt faint. He needed food. And sleep.

'We're not supposed to,' Peroni interjected, walking over with his hands in his pockets, looking thoroughly depressed. 'We're not supposed to understand any of—'

He didn't finish the sentence.

Something had arrived in the night sky, something so large it began to block out the moon. The thing wasn't alone.

The air was rent by the slashing of vast rotor blades. Hulking black shapes began to descend around them, landing on the spare flat ground by the road. Men raced from their bellies, bright, hard beams of light emerging from their heads, weapons tight in their arms, at the ready.

A voice barked through a loudhailer, issuing all the familiar commands he knew so well

Get down on the ground. Arms outstretched. Don't move.

Falcone didn't budge an inch. He glared into their bright beams as if he could stare them down with a single glance.

'We'd best do as they say, Leo,' Costa murmured, and put a firm hand on his inspector's arm, pushing him down to the hard, dry earth.

- 6 -

The visibility was better than anything Andrea Petrakis could have hoped for. In the snatched seconds available to him between tumbling out of the microlight and opening his ram-chute, he was able to orient himself with some precision and aim squarely for the target area: the large patch of flat, open grassland next to the tomb of Cecilia Metella.

He'd briefed Deniz Nesin and Anna Ybarra thoroughly. Their torches were clearly visible, sweeping to make two arcs that met at the safest, flattest point of the zone. Petrakis scarcely needed them. The moon was so bright it was like descending under floodlights. His chute opened with perfect precision at four hundred feet above the ground. Petrakis gripped the stays, taking the strain as the deployment fought the wind beneath the fabric and briefly dragged him upwards once again.

For a few delicious moments he found himself suspended in the hot summer air, seemingly free of the perpetual drag of gravity altogether. The lights of Ciampino glittered beyond the line of lamps on the highway. A bird – an owl, or so it seemed – squawked somewhere near his head, as if resenting the intrusion of man into its private world.

Then, slowly, he began to fall earthwards, into the centre of the ranging beams of light below.

The glittering horizon was still visible when the tiny plane, loaded with explosive, hit the apron of the airport. Just a little more than a kilometre away the sky burst into flame, as if some deadly hothouse flower had suddenly shot blooming from the earth.

He watched and laughed and clung to the chute stays all the way down. It was a gamble. Everything was. There was no way of knowing the precise alignment of the aircraft parked outside the terminal, no certain scheme to ensure one was hit. The little plane could as easily crash into bare asphalt, causing minor damage and a little inconvenience. Yet, watching the searing orange petals of gasoline fire rise into the night sky of Ciampino, he knew immediately this had not occurred. Guided by the amateurish autopilot, the microlight had hit home like a makeshift guided missile, finding the enemy, igniting the combustible fuel in the belly of some grounded leviathan on the apron.

The noise of the explosion came after the beautiful angry flames. Then another, and a third.

At that point the horizon disappeared and Petrakis found himself fighting to regain control of his descent. The ground loomed up, with a shocking alacrity. He fought to ease the rate of fall, bent his legs, crouching for impact. Their lights found him, dazzled him. He rolled. The earth slammed into his shoulder, sending him tumbling, turning, spinning like a child's top.

He wondered if something might break. If the whole escapade might come to nothing more than a fractured bone.

Then the world ceased turning. He found himself on his back, the ram-chute wrapped round him like a clumsy shroud, staring up at the insistent sky. His entire body hurt, but, as he gingerly tried to move his limbs and measure their response, he realized it was a familiar pain, that of nothing more than a bad fall.

By the time the two of them arrived – out of breath, panting, looking at him in amazement – he was on his feet. The sky above the gently sloping hill that led to Ciampino was now a livid line of orange and red. They could hear the sound of secondary explosions bursting in the unseen distance. The smell of burning gasoline was beginning to become faintly noticeable over the scents of the Appian Way: grass and wild herbs.

'Brother,' Deniz Nesin said, and came forward to embrace him, arms around his shoulders.

Anna Ybarra just stood there.

'Congratulations,' she said quietly.

'Congratulations? Congratulations?' Deniz was ecstatic. He raised his arms to the glowing sky. 'This is a wonder, brother. We have struck them deep in the heart. We have brought them the fruits of jihad. They know fear now. They know terror. They know what we have borne all these years.' He thumped his chest with his fist. 'We – all of us.'

Petrakis laughed and wondered what was really happening at the airport, how much damage he had truly caused.

'It was just a plane and some explosive, Deniz. None of them were there. No presidents. No politicians. If we have killed anyone then . . . who? A few cleaners and security guards. A mechanic perhaps and a couple of cops.'

Cops. The memory of what had happened in the tomb of the Blue Demon refused to leave him. From that moment forward he would, he knew, have to improvise everything on his own. To take unexpected risks, and not listen to them any more. To decide, swiftly, without compunction, which path to take.

'It's a beginning,' Deniz told him. 'A great one. See . . .' He indicated the bright, orange sky behind them. The smell of burning fuel was beginning to overwhelm everything else, and behind it they could hear the crackling of distant fires and the wailing of sirens. 'Tomorrow we bring them something better. Tomorrow . . .'

'They knew,' Petrakis cut in. 'How else did the cops get there?'

Anna Ybarra and Deniz Nesin were quiet immediately. This he found interesting.

'The Kenyan,' Deniz interrupted. 'The bastard must have told them.'

Petrakis shuffled off the parachute and walked free of the ropes.

'Joseph never knew about the tomb, Deniz. Only you and I did. We took delivery of the explosives there. Remember?'

The woman stepped back, looking at the ground.

There was an expression on the Turk's face Petrakis had seen only once before. The day he had, out of nothing more than pure curiosity, pushed them too far in training in Helmand. It was a curious kind of anger, one that Deniz wished to be seen, but not taken into account, merely acknowledged.

'What are you saying?' he demanded. 'The Kenyan could have followed us. And so,' he nodded at the woman, 'could she. Anyone might have seen . . .'

Petrakis took him by the arm.

'All this is true. And yet . . .'

He put his hand inside his light summer anorak. The weapon was there, in its holster.

'I must ask myself, Deniz. Are these things possible?'

'No!' the Turk yelled. 'Do not say this. Not even in jest. Do not . . .'

Andrea Petrakis stepped forward, wound his hand around Deniz's tanned, bony skull and jerked the weapon close to the man's temple. Anna Ybarra took another two strides away from them, hands by her sides, eyes downcast, seeing nothing.

'Even if I'm wrong,' Petrakis said slowly, calmly. 'If . . . I must ask myself this, Deniz. What use are you now? With everything changed. With no purpose for your . . . toys which, if I'm candid, are your solitary skill?'

He was a commander. A general. He had decisions to make, challenges to face.

'I beg you,' Deniz Nesin said, squirming in his grip. 'I would not betray you, Andrea. Ever.'

'Possibly.'

'Ever . . .'

There was a fresh explosion somewhere off in the distance. It was a good night. There was no guarantee their luck would continue.

'Then I shall be forced to apologize in Paradise,' Petrakis murmured.

He relaxed his grip enough to be free of the man, fired – only a single shot since that was all it took.

She watched all the while, trembling as the Turk fell, briefly thrashing, to the ground.

Anna Ybarra had her own weapon in her hand, pointed, half-shaking, in his direction.

'You won't kill me,' she said in a tremulous voice.

It seemed a ridiculous statement. Petrakis stood his ground.

'Of course not. I have need of you. As you have need of me. We shall drive to Ciampino and see what we can. Then I shall show you our new home.' He shrugged. 'It's not so magnificent as Tarquinia, I'm afraid. But we won't be there long.'

Her gun went down. She still refused to look at the body of the Turk.

Andrea Petrakis smiled and said, 'Good. Did you bring some food, like I asked? I'm hungry.'

– 7 –

They were face down in the earth, feeling the down-draught of the helicopter blades cutting slowly through the night air, just able to glimpse the teams of hooded, armed men spreading through the area around the tomb.

Costa waited, his head hurting once more. Then he heard a familiar voice, one he recognized instantly, though he had heard it only once.

Luca Palombo, the chief Ministry of the Interior spook, was storming towards them, speaking loudly and rapidly on the phone, distracted, it seemed, by events that – from the tone of his speech – were much worse than those he had somehow come to discover out in the wilds of the Maremma.

Rosa was on Costa's other side, close to him. He could feel her hand tighten on his arm, as if she were willing him to be ready for something again.

'Get up,' Palombo ordered. 'Get up.'

Falcone was first to his feet and stood straight in front of the man from the Ministry of the Interior. Palombo listened to something else on the phone, scowled, then put it in his pocket.

'How did you get here?' he demanded.

'It's called police work,' Falcone answered. 'How did you . . . ?'

'I ask the questions. Not answer them. How did you find this place?'

Costa went and stood next to his inspector. The rest of the team joined them.

'We were following up on a report that someone had been seen near the tomb of the Blue Demon. It was routine.'

'Here?' Palombo bellowed. 'In Tarquinia? You heard my orders. You're supposed to be in Rome, dealing with the kind of work you're fit for. Keeping order. Watching the streets.'

Teresa Lupo leaned forward and said, 'The streets are empty. Didn't you notice? People daren't go out. If they do, they can't get home. You've closed Rome. There's nothing for us to do there.'

Peroni added calmly, 'We've got a dead officer here, friend. Don't push it.'

The big man's intervention, and his angry, ugly face, got some reaction.

Palombo glanced at the shape on the earth some distance away and said, 'I'm sorry. We will deal with him.'

'He was a colleague of ours,' Rosa said, her voice cracking. 'We deal with him.'

'Not on this occasion,' Palombo ordered. 'What else is here? I need to know now. I don't have much time.'

No one spoke until Costa said, 'There's a corpse in the tomb. Shot. Petrakis had hidden some explosives. Firearms. Munitions. Whether they're still there . . .'

He held out the phone he'd retrieved from the hall of the Blue Demon.

'This was on the dead man.'

Palombo snatched the handset from his fingers, then ordered some of his men to go down below to take a look, while another group took care of the fallen officer.

A couple of the figures in black came over and began lifting Mirko Oliva's body onto a gurney. There was a commotion near the entrance to the tomb. Two men had brought the body to the surface. A second gurney was on its way to deal with it.

'I don't imagine Stefan Kyriakis was his real name,' Costa said quietly.

'I don't imagine it's any of your concern,' Palombo replied.

'What is?' Falcone asked without emotion. 'We don't have any-thing else to guide us. If you'd care to shed any further light on what's happened here . . .'

Palombo's phone was ringing again. He looked at the screen,

swore once, answered and then barked into it, 'I'll call when I'm back. We'll be in Rome within the hour.' A moment of hesitation, listening, then, angrily, to the phone, 'No. I don't know. Do you?'

The conversation ended. The man from the Ministry of the Interior stared at them under the moonlight, his face haggard and weary.

'I will say this once and once only, and I shall expect Esposito to remind you of it when you finally crawl back to the city. Your duty lies in Rome. Nowhere else. It's confined to the streets. To keeping people safe and the traffic moving. And staying out of my way. The death of your *agente* is unfortunate, but it will remain secret until I deem otherwise. The Carabinieri will investigate, not you.'

'He was a police officer!' Peroni roared.

'This is the Carabinieri's case. You will not mention his death to anyone. You will not inform next of kin or any other party until I allow it, and that will not be for another day at the very least, until the summit is over.' He glared at Costa. 'You're lucky you're not dead too. If you breach that order I will, I swear, ensure that you wish you were. I could throw the whole bunch of you into jail for as long as I damned well feel like.'

'This is not a police state,' Teresa yelled at him. 'You can't just imprison innocent people for no good reason. It's not—'

'Listen to me! Earlier this evening Ciampino was bombed. They flew some kind of light aircraft laden with explosive straight onto the apron. Two aircraft were destroyed. We think there are fatalities. The president has issued the decree. He didn't have any choice. We're now in a formal state of emergency. With the anti-terrorist laws I have at my disposal . . .' His face was grim, yet bore the mark of some satisfaction too. 'I can do anything I like.' He glanced at a couple of the armed men dealing with the body from the tomb. These people weren't even looking for evidence, Costa thought. It was as if they already knew what had happened.

'So what do you expect of us, sir?' Costa asked.

'Go back home. Stay inside. Order a pizza. Turn on the TV. If any of you cross my path again, I shall not be so lenient.'

He watched the second gurney make its way to the nearest helicopter.

'Good evening,' Palombo said, and then followed it.

They hadn't even cut the engines. The machines stirred into life, found their voices, began to bellow once more, their rotor blades chopping through the black night air.

As quickly as they came Palombo's team was gone – dark, diminishing shapes against the stars, moving south towards Rome.

Peroni picked up a torch and marched back into the tomb. He came back a minute later, red-faced, livid.

'They didn't just take the body, Leo. They took everything. The explosives. The weapons. The ammunition. The evidence, for God's sake.'

'Screw them. I can find things,' Teresa told him. 'You can't clean a crime scene in a couple of minutes. Give me time—'

'We don't have time,' Falcone interrupted. 'He knows that. If I bring in a unit . . .'

The sequence had already run through Costa's head. They would need to liaise with the local *questura*. To establish a forensic team. To involve so many people – it would be impossible to keep the case quiet. Palombo knew what he was doing. There was nothing they could accomplish easily over the coming twenty-four hours.

Falcone was looking at him, and at Rosa Prabakaran.

'This has been a long night,' he said. 'Palombo may be right. We could put you in a hotel somewhere nearby. Back in Porto Ercole perhaps. You could stay out of this.'

'I want to go back to Rome,' Rosa said, watching the inspector.

Falcone sighed and murmured, 'Nic?'

'Someone can fetch a change of clothes to the apartment.'

He pulled the little object from his pocket. He'd managed to extract it while they were on the ground, waiting, wondering what the helicopters might bring.

'Silvio can take a look at this,' he added.

They looked at the piece of plastic in his hands.

'It's the SIM from the phone I found in the tomb,' Costa said. 'I don't think Luca Palombo needs it. Does he?'

– 8 –

They left Deniz Nesin in the field where Petrakis shot him. This was the last day. She understood that now. By fleeing Tarquinia they had broken some part of a plan she'd never been party to. A scheme that entailed the steady diminution of the team. First Danny, the strange kid who baffled her with his bad English, Russian and Pashto. Then Joseph Priest, slaughtered in the street after the outrage at the Trevi Fountain, for which he was not truly responsible.

Now the Turk. She wondered when her turn came, whether Petrakis really thought he could attempt the final part of the job – the hardest, penetrating directly into the Quirinale itself – on his own. This seemed impossible. She was, she thought, meant to die, just as he was in all probability. But it would be at the end, as part of achieving what they came for.

They took the hire car Deniz had rented at a deserted Hertz depot on the outskirts of Fiumicino and drove up a narrow lane until they joined the main road running directly past the airport, almost parallel with the single runway. It was impossible to get close. The police had blocked the highway. Flames still engulfed the horizon. Fire engines and ambulances fought one another to get through the crush of vehicles. Crowds of bystanders and newspaper photographers were out of their cars, on foot, trying to get closer to the scene.

Petrakis turned the car round, retraced their tracks down the little lane to the Appian Way and pulled into a farm entrance. There he took out his phone, the fancy one Deniz had given him, and called up the RAI mobile news service. There was video footage of a plane in flames. She moved closer to him from the passenger seat, trying to see. On the tail of the aircraft, burned almost beyond recognition, was the Stars and Stripes, and beneath it a number. The charred outline had the bulbous nose of a 747 and what looked like a blue flash around the cockpit.

'It's Air Force One?' Anna Ybarra asked.

He grinned like a schoolkid. The phone said three aircraft ground staff were already confirmed dead, and another five were missing. All Italian. The crew of the plane, and everyone else in the American party, were in the city when the bomb struck.

'The little people have died,' she murmured. 'Again.'

Petrakis snapped the phone shut and glared at her. She remembered the way he'd killed Deniz Nesin and didn't say anything else.

He turned round, took another lane behind the Via Appia Antica. Somewhere along the way he pulled off onto a narrow track. She noticed it wasn't far from a church with a name that rang a bell. *Quo vadis?*

Some distant memory of church rose in her head. It was Latin: *Where are you going?* She remembered the connection too. St Peter fleeing Rome, in fear of crucifixion, only to find a ghostly Jesus waiting for him on the road south, asking this very question. *Where?*

The track ended. There was a caravan stranded in a field. It was old, small, the kind of thing a tramp might inhabit.

Petrakis parked the car by the side, got out and unlocked the heavy padlock chain on the door. She followed him inside. There was an electric light system. When the dim bulbs came on, she saw that the place was as tidy as an office. A single bed in the corner. A desk, with a computer. A small gas stove, a refrigerator. Petrakis reached inside and immediately found a bottle of champagne there.

She looked at the label: Krug, 1995. From the expression on his face she guessed she was supposed to feel impressed.

'I thought we might need something to drink if we wound up here,' he said, nothing more.

Anna Ybarra glanced at the desk. There was a set of passports there, shuffled like a pack of cards. So many: British, American, European, South African, Australian.

She flicked through them and saw mugshots of herself and Petrakis, pictures taken in Afghanistan. No one else. Not Joseph Priest or Deniz Nesin anywhere.

Three of the passports were sets, made for a couple who would pose as man and wife.

'I have a name already,' Anna Ybarra told him.

'A good general plans for all eventualities,' Petrakis said, watching her. He'd poured the champagne into two cheap glass beakers, the kind you'd use as tooth mugs. The drink was the colour of straw. She let him hand her a glass and took a sip. Vintage champagne didn't taste like anything she'd ever tried before. It made her throat feel a little numb, made her head spin for a moment. She took one more sip and put the glass down.

'The passports . . .' she murmured. 'My photo. Anyone would think I get out of this alive, Andrea.'

He toasted her with the tooth mug.

'Is there any reason you shouldn't?'

'Three I can think of so far.'

'They were drones. There's something different about you.' He took a long draught of the drink and briefly closed his eyes. 'You don't care, do you?'

'Not much.'

'That makes two of us.'

'Where would we go? Afterwards?'

He shrugged.

'Where would you like?'

'Somewhere there's not many people. A desert island. Antarctica.'

'I'll book the tickets.'

He took one step forward and chinked his glass against hers.

Petrakis placed his hand against her jacket and began to unfasten the buttons. Then he bent down, pulled her into him with his arm, placed his face in the nape of her neck, kissed her neck with an amateurish roughness.

She put the passports back on the table.

Anna Ybarra couldn't get their faces out of her mind. Joseph, the stupid Kenyan, thinking he was working his way to a different kind of life. Deniz, miserable, cold-hearted Deniz, who had no love for anything.

And the man-child Danny, which was not his real name and never had been. She'd heard him chattering in his sleep, frightened murmurings, the product of nightmares she could only guess at. In those extreme moments he used one language and one alone: it sounded like Russian, and it had the plaintive, pleading tone of a captive.

Petrakis was working at her clothes, with awkward, fumbling fingers. She let him. She'd allow him anything at that moment, however much it revolted her. Anna Ybarra knew she was lucky to be alive and somehow, for the first time in ages, this seemed to matter.

– 9 –

It was past three in the morning by the time they got on the road: Falcone at the wheel, Peroni in the front seat, Costa squeezed in the back between Teresa and Rosa, both of whom began to doze as the car worked its way back to the highway on the coast.

He couldn't sleep. He couldn't stop thinking. About how Mirko Oliva died and they survived. And the way the black helicopters of Luca Palombo had descended from the night sky unbidden, only to disappear just as quickly once the Ministry of the Interior spook had found what he was looking for.

As they drove from Tarquinia towards the coast and the glittering sea beyond, Costa pulled Teresa's phone out of her bag and called the Quirinale Palace, asking to be put through to the duty Corazzieri captain.

'Nic . . .' Falcone began to say testily from the front.

It was too late. The palace switchboard sounded alert and a little frightened. He had to talk his way past three people before Fabio Ranieri answered, sounding tired and close to the end of his tether.

'It's Costa. I can't talk to you the usual way. Sorry.'

Ranieri went quiet for a moment, then asked, 'What was I doing twenty years ago?'

'Working for military liaison with NATO in Brussels. And looking for somewhere decent to eat.'

'Let me call you back on another line.'

The phone rang again almost immediately.

'This time I do need to speak to him,' Costa insisted.

'Do you have any idea what happened tonight?'

'Some. That's why.'

There was a moment's silence, another attempt at prevarication, which Costa ignored. Then he heard a familiar voice and a face rose in his memory: the long, extended features of the 'bloodhound', a friendly, inquisitive countenance that seemed to have been ever-present in his childhood.

'This is not the best of times, Sovrintendente,' Sordi said in a tone of mild irritation.

Costa kept the narrative short and to the point, and found he was able to imagine the shock and outrage on Sordi's sad, pale face as he spoke. He left out nothing that had happened at the site of the tomb of the Blue Demon. Not Mirko Oliva's sudden end or Luca Palombo's threats.

When he was done there was silence. Then Dario Sordi said, with a sigh, 'I blame myself. I should never have asked you to undertake this task. You must stop immediately. Let me call Esposito. It's . . . busy here, as you may imagine.'

'We can't stop,' Costa interrupted.

There was a pause. Sordi was unaccustomed to being refused something.

'Why not?'

'Because we lost someone.'

'I'm deeply sorry about that, Nic. I don't want any more casualties on my conscience.'

Costa sat up straight and was aware of the charged atmosphere in Falcone's Lancia.

'It doesn't work like that, Dario. You can't turn these things off and on when you feel like it. You can't . . .'

'I am the president of Italy!'

'You're one more individual under the law. No different to any of us. You gave us this job. We haven't finished it, and we've more reason than ever to do that now.

'No!'

He was aware that the car had stopped. Falcone had pulled into a lay-by on the highway. They were all staring at him.

'What?' Costa asked, looking at the four faces peering in his direction.

'Do we get a say?' Peroni demanded.

'Do you need one?'

'Not really,' the big man answered. 'But it would be nice to be asked.'

Falcone held out his hand for the phone. Sordi's voice was coming out of it, a tinny, angry shriek. The inspector waited and then introduced himself, listened for a moment and said, 'Mr President, you heard the *sovrintendente*. We have a dead colleague, and Luca Palombo thinks it's none of our business. He is wrong. If you agree with him, you are wrong too. Now kindly answer my colleague's questions.'

He handed the phone back.

Sordi let loose an old and uncommon epithet, then bellowed, 'Who the hell do you people think you are?'

'We're the police,' Costa responded. 'We ask the questions you want answered, but are too polite to ask. We go to the places you want to know about, but daren't enter. You started this, Dario. Don't think you can call it off now. You can't.'

'Jesus! You are your father's son. What was I thinking?'

'I was under the impression you were trying to find out the truth.'

'I was, Nic. I am. But not at any cost . . .' He listened to Sordi's long intake of breath. It was slow, a little wheezy, the sound of an old man. 'Tomorrow morning – *this* morning – is the principal meeting of the summit. I have the most important men and women in the world under my roof. Sucking up to Ugo Campagnolo because they know he's the man with the real power, and I'm just some old has-been with the keys to the front door. Good God.' A note of self-contempt entered his voice. 'What am I talking about? This is to do with Rome. She's like a ruin in the wilderness. Full of frightened people, wondering what they did to deserve any of this. And somewhere . . .' Another long sigh. 'Petrakis and his people are still out there, planning. Do you have any idea where they are? What they really want?'

'No.'

'Can you find out?'

'We can try. If you can stop Palombo getting in the way. Why do you think I called?'

'Palombo is Campagnolo's man, not mine. Now that we have a state of emergency . . .' There was desperation in his tired tones, something Costa had never heard before. 'I'm head of the armed forces. But there are limits. You have to understand. In times like these the power lies with those in the field. Even a commander has little control over individual events, hour by hour. Luca Palombo is much more the master of Italy than I am at this moment, and through him Ugo Campagnolo.'

'Do what you can,' Costa suggested.

'Yes, sir,' Sordi answered drily.

One question bothered Costa.

'I tried to call earlier.'

'Ranieri told me. I'm sorry. I was talking to our charming prime minister, of art and other things he doesn't understand.'

'I'm sure you meant well when you told Palombo we were in Tarquinia, but in future . . .'

'Excuse me?' Sordi interrupted.

'Palombo came straight to us – I assumed . . .'

'I never told anyone, Nic. I would never dream of such a thing. No one was aware of your work for me, outside the people you know already.'

It was the middle of the night. Costa felt exhausted. He couldn't think straight.

'I'm sorry. I didn't mean to accuse.'

'I must go. We have a security briefing. Palombo will believe you were simply over-zealous police officers who refused to know their place. If the subject comes up, I shall defend you and insist we have more important matters to deal with. This is true, by the way. Is there something else I can tell you?'

Probably, Costa thought, if only he could find the right question.

'Then good night,' the president said. 'And take care.'

They were all wide awake and looking at him.

'How did they find you?' Falcone wondered. 'Who knew you were there?'

'The women at the tomb in Tarquinia. It seemed inconceivable. 'I can't believe it was them.'

'Look for links,' Teresa suggested.

Rosa moaned, 'There aren't any.'

'There are always links,' the pathologist said patiently. 'The hard part is finding them.' She thought for a moment, then said, 'How many phone calls did you make from the tomb?'

'Two. One to the Quirinale on that private mobile Sordi gave me.' Costa shook his head. 'Dario isn't lying. He's adamant we can trust Ranieri.'

'And the second?' she persisted.

A little light came on, and with it a memory: Luca Palombo snatching from his fingers the phone he'd taken from the corpse in the Blue Demon's chamber.

He retrieved the phone SIM he'd got from the handset in the tomb, looked at her, grateful she'd got this out of him.

'This wasn't about us. It was about tracking Stefan Kyriakis. For whatever reason. They picked up my call when they were listening for him.'

She nodded.

'Good guess. Let's get that thing to Silvio, shall we?'

- 10 -

It was a long, slow drive, one in which Costa drifted in and out of a fitful sleep. Close to the city he awoke, suddenly alert, to find Falcone driving down some long, winding road, one that finally emerged at the gigantic subterranean car park hidden beneath the earth just a short way from St Peter's. There was an all-night cafe there. The man behind the counter nodded at Falcone as if they were old acquaintances. Costa wondered how well he really knew this man, even after all these years.

They got coffee and pastries in paper bags, returned to the car, and then he drove them somewhere they all recognized, the summit of the Gianicolo hill nearby, and Garibaldi's monument, a place every Roman child was taken to once at least. It was a picturesque spot, with wonderful views back to the city. Listening to his father's tales of the patriots, fighting a desperate battle they would come to lose, Costa, as a child, had found it difficult to equate these bloody stories with the verdant, lovely park to which ordinary Romans retreated of a weekend, seeking a little peace and quiet. He had, he now realized, yet to learn the lesson of adulthood: that evil was a mundane thing, present everywhere, even in places of beauty.

Falcone got out of the car and walked to the balustrade of the viewpoint, popping open his coffee, biting into a *cornetto*, looking as if he'd done this a million times on perpetual sleepless nights.

The city looked dead, but a ray of light was breaking in the east, rising over the distant Sabine Hills. There was scarcely any traffic on either side of the river. The *centro storico* seemed devoid of life.

'They might go away, you know, Leo,' Peroni said without much conviction. 'Petrakis. Whoever his sidekicks are. They might look at what they've done to Ciampino and think, "Mission accomplished." They were never the Red Brigades, really. Those bastards lasted years. With the Blue Demon it was over and done with in a week.'

'And isn't that curious in itself?' the inspector asked.

'It could be it's over already.'

Falcone eyed the horizon. His face was grim and determined.

'And walk away from that? I wish I could believe it. They're here to destroy what we cherish, Gianni. That's more important than how many people they kill, how much damage they wreak. They want to make their mark, to have us cower at our own shadows. They haven't left. Perhaps, after a fashion, they never will. This is the world we inhabit. Best live with it.'

Costa thought of the way Andrea Petrakis had spoken in the bloody dark in Tarquinia, the urgent determined fury in his voice when he took the unexpected call after he shot Mirko. Falcone was right. They were here already, hidden somewhere among the empty streets and piazzas, the echoing subway stations and vacant churches.

Falcone's phone squawked. The inspector seemed, suddenly, absorbed. He pulled out his pocketbook with his free hand, walked to the Lancia and began to make notes on the roof. The others recognized the change in his mood and walked over to join him.

'*Grazie*,' Falcone said, and ended the call. He looked at Costa.

'That was Di Capua checking something for me.'

The last thing he'd done before they left Tarquinia was to make one more visit to the tomb. Something there had caught his interest. Not that he'd been willing to discuss it with anyone.

'This was on the wall next to the figure of the Blue Demon. Scratched in some bare paint. Someone had tried to rub it out. Palombo, I imagine. He didn't have time to get rid of it all.'

He held up the page from his notebook. More Roman numerals, this time XII. II. I. CLXXIII.

Costa remembered the cryptic message painted on the wall of the Villa Giulia, behind the bodies of Renzo and Marie Frasca.

'Shakespeare?'

'I assumed that. I asked Di Capua to check. It doesn't work. Too many numbers.'

'A phone number . . . a code . . . something.'

He was out of ideas. They all were.

'Something,' Falcone agreed. 'Let's go back to San Giovanni, get some sleep, then start again.'

Part 5

EVENTS

Sat celeriter fieri quidquid fiat satis bene.

Well done is quickly done.

Suetonius (quoting Augustus),
The Twelve Caesars, Book II

- 1 -

'You want what?' Bernie Stackler yelled into his phone.

The cafe in the Via dei Serpenti was empty except for a couple at the end of the room. The anonymous contact who'd promised to meet them there had never materialized. It was that kind of day.

The TV cameraman listened to his distant producer, cupped his hand over the handset and turned to the reporter they'd given him, Julia Barnes.

'You know what this is? This is JP Two all over again. Getting jerked round Rome looking for fairy dust while these fat bastards in New York sit on their butts laughing like baboons.'

He'd hated the funeral of the pope. The Vatican's security had got so heavy with the media that they'd ordered him and a female reporter to buy a high-def camcorder, dress up as tourists, pose as mourning Catholics and sneak in past the guards. It worked, almost too well. They'd got right up to the bier, filmed mourners, talked to everyone, got material that was so close, so personal, the network baulked at using some of it. Not that New York was happy. Dan Fillmore, the selfsame producer who was on duty now, had been on his case throughout, whining, 'But where's the . . . *grief*?'

Stackler hadn't managed to get it across to the moron. A very old, very well-respected old man had died, after a long illness. People were sad. They weren't desolate. It wasn't Princess Di. The Rome that the foreign camera crews wanted – 'a city in mourning' – didn't exist outside the imagination of headline writers. Beyond the lines of sad, resigned Catholics bunched together in the streets around the Vatican, life went on pretty much as normal. The only way they could get 'grief' was to pay for it, from anyone willing to act. Which was what Stackler resorted to in the end. Not that it would work now.

'What exactly is it you want?' he demanded, trying not to think of the smug smile he knew would be creasing Fillmore's clean-shaven, executive baby face at that moment. It was so easy to be a desk man these days.

'You need me to tell you?'

'Yes, Dan. Frankly I do. You see I'm here. You're there. I see what I see. I don't see what you want me to see. So you be a little clearer and let me try to understand.'

'Incredible,' the voice on the line grunted. 'I can't believe I'm saying this. We want something exclusive, Bernie. Remember that word? Long time since you heard it, I guess.'

Stackler fought hard against his rising fury.

'You do *watch* the material we send you, don't you? All the stuff about how this is a ghost city now? How none of us can move anywhere for all the goddamned security? Three people died when they hit Ciampino. There may be more before the day is out. Plenty in hospital. I could try and talk to some of them . . .'

'Sick foreigners in a bed. That's going to go down big.'

'They're part of the story.'

'They're extras. I want the stars. I want pictures of the First Lady looking scared. I want to feel her fear. I want—'

'Funnily enough, they're not giving interviews right now.'

'We can't air excuses, Bernie. Sadly. Just do the usual thing. Pay someone to get inside a neighbouring building. Go on the roof. Get an overview of the palace or something – people walking the grounds.'

'No one is going to open their door to a stranger today.'

'Helicopter?'

'Oh, please.'

'You could at least try,' Fillmore whined.

Stackler thought of the armed officers with their automatic weapons wandering the streets. The guard posts. The way every roof-top was being watched.

'I am trying. I got a call from someone who said they could get me something. That's what I'm waiting for.'

'Get you what?'

'If I knew that I'd be there, not here, wouldn't I?'

'A call?' The disembodied voice sounded sceptical.

'Someone phoned and said they'd meet us with a lead. No, I don't know who. Occasionally life works that way. I leave my card in the strangest places.'

'Yeah. Normally ones with a liquor licence. If your new friend doesn't show, you've got to come up with something else. Find some viewpoint.'

He groaned.

'That would be really smart, wouldn't it? I stick a camera lens out from some building and get my ass shot off.'

'Oh, I understand . . .' There was a long, sarcastic drawl in his ear. 'You want the safe jobs now. What would you prefer? The Emmies? Skateboarding dogs?'

'Ha, ha.'

Julia Barnes sighed, went over to the counter and came back with two more coffees and some *biscotti*. She was as sick of the situation as he was.

'Let me get this straight,' said the voice in New York. 'This is the biggest story in the world. Rome is paralysed. You got some terrorist team carrying out stuff on a daily basis. No one's coming out of their houses. No one's allowed to walk down the street much any more. And what you got to give me? Local colour. Wallpaper. Empty street scenes. For Christ's sake, Bernie. There's nothing you've filed for the last two days I couldn't have got off YouTube. Sometimes better.'

'Enough,' Stackler said, with what he felt was remarkable restraint. 'We have media credentials. There's one arranged photo shoot outside the palace, in the piazza. You get that. Then anything else we can find.'

'YouTube . . .'

'Kindly do not say that word in my presence ever again.'

'YouTube.'

Stackler blinked and was grateful several thousand miles separated him and Dan Fillmore.

'Listen,' he went on, trying to sound reasonable. 'When I go to Iraq. Or Afghanistan. Or some other hellhole you wouldn't dare set foot in, there I risk my ass for the corporation. In Rome . . .' It wasn't right. He knew the city well. He loved the place, had even thought of moving there once upon a time, until he realized he'd never be able to earn a decent living. 'Here, you don't get that privilege. We're going to play this the way I want. Cautious, meekly. It's not right out there, and I can't begin to tell you why.'

'Then I guess we'll have to hope someone else has got the guts to do a professional job.'

Stackler could picture the man slamming down the phone at that moment. He'd done it so many times, on so many teams around the world.

Julia Barnes was holding out the cup of coffee. He didn't want it. They'd drunk too much already, wandering the deserted streets, trying to talk their way in through the cordons. The Quirinale was just up the hill, blocked off from everything by closed roads, guard posts and ranks of armed officers. Come eleven-thirty they'd be able to get through briefly for the media event – if it still happened. But it wouldn't be anything great. Just a line of distant faces outside the palace, he guessed. It was that kind of assignment.

He nibbled at one of the *biscotti* and looked at her.

'You know what I'd really like to do?'

'What?'

She was pretty. New to the network. Maybe thirty. Someone who'd worked her way up through the grind of little city outfits.

'This guy who phoned isn't going to show. I say we do the photo call. Then afterwards we go get lunch at this restaurant I know in the ghetto. Artichokes and lamb. A bottle of white wine. An afternoon doze.'

He couldn't not look at her when he said that.

'That would do my career no end of good, wouldn't it?' Julia Barnes said, looking at him as if he were slightly soft in the head.

They weren't alone any more. The other couple in the cafe had stood up and come over. For some reason Stackler glanced at the counter. The old man who'd served them was no longer there. Even this bright, clean city-centre coffee bar seemed to have been emptied by the fog of fear that had descended on them all.

'We couldn't help overhearing,' said the man, a handsome, middle-aged Italian, about Stackler's age, wearing sunglasses, even inside. 'You're American media? You need a camera angle or something? On the Quirinale? If you go out back . . .'

'You bet,' Julia said straight away, getting up. 'You got one? We can pay.'

'Wait, wait, wait,' Stackler tried to say, but she was following them already, out to the door at the rear of the place. 'Did you phone us or something? Was that you?'

'Phoned?' the man said. It was impossible to judge his expression. The shades . . .

Stackler didn't mind. Not if it was easy. Not if it was safe.

He tried to think this through. He travelled so much, to so many different parts of the world. But he kept a mental picture of each in his head, a map he could use to find the best place to be. It was part of the job. The most important part sometimes.

The Via dei Serpenti, the street of the snakes, some stray thought told him, lay in Monti, downhill from the Quirinale Palace. There'd be views back to the Forum and over to the ruins of Trajan's Markets. Not that they'd be of any use. But a clear line of sight uphill . . . He couldn't imagine it.

The Italian couple stepped back and let him and Julia walk through the narrow door. Then the pair followed and closed it behind them.

There was another door, open – one that led to the cellar, down a long flight of old stone steps. At the bottom, visible under a single naked light bulb, was the old man who'd served them when they came in. He was trussed up like a chicken, gagged, hands behind his back, frightened eyes staring at them behind a pair of wire-framed spectacles, one lens of which was broken.

Something cold pressed against Stackler's neck.

He put up his hands, not daring to look, and said, 'I got a wife and kids. Two daughters, four and two. Please don't make them lose their daddy.' He thought of all the times he'd rehearsed this line, in Baghdad, in Pakistan, in Kabul. 'You guys have got a point. We all know it.'

The words sounded weak and stupid the moment he said them, and Stackler couldn't avoid the fury he saw rising alongside the fear in Julia Barnes's dark, attractive face.

'I want your money and your credentials,' the man said.

Stackler waved his arms higher and nodded, 'Take anything you want.'

The contents of his jacket were gone in an instant. He waited, wondering. The barrel of the gun never moved.

'Little people,' the woman said obscurely, and somehow he felt it was a compliment.

A foot connected with his spine. He felt himself falling down the stairs, hands against his head, thinking of home.

When Bernie Stackler came to, he was trussed like the cafe guy next to him. Julia Barnes was in the same state. The solitary light came from a narrow line of glass at the rear, which surely only connected with a courtyard at the back of the building. But he didn't feel too bad. A part of him wanted to laugh, to call Dan Fillmore in New York and boast, 'See, kid. This kind of shit never happens to you.'

But they'd gagged him too, as they'd gagged his reporter. He shuffled upright and made himself as comfortable as he could.

- 2 -

There was no broken circle of noisy, angry vehicles backed up by the Colosseum, no choking line of traffic behind the bus and tram lines. Falcone found a parking space near the hospital in San Giovanni with ease. They walked to the apartment without passing a single living soul.

Silvio Di Capua had sent out for a change of clothes. Costa tossed him the SIM card from the phone, then he and Rosa went to sleep for a few hours, at Falcone's insistence. When he got up, Silvio, Teresa and Elizabeth Murray were already around the computer chattering and pointing at the screen. Falcone was in the kitchen. Commissario Esposito was there with him, talking quietly as the two men sipped coffees. It could have been any ordinary surveillance scene, were it not for the state of the city outside.

Rosa came in, fresh from the bathroom, her hair still wet and wrapped in a towel. She looked older than a day before, Costa thought. There were signs of a new, unwanted wisdom and dark shadows beneath her eyes. He recalled the journey to the Maremma, Mirko Oliva amusing them all with his stories of a wild childhood on Monte Argentario, raising a rare sparkle in her serious face. He had wondered whether there might, one day, be something between the two young officers. Hoped so, if he were honest. She'd never had a relationship – not that anyone in the Questura knew of, at least, and it was a place with few secrets. Rosa Prabakaran deserved a little happiness in her life. The years she'd spent with the police had been far from easy.

'Take a look at this,' Teresa said.

Something popped out of the printer in front of her. He picked up the page and shared it with Rosa. It was a familiar item: a police report, this one dated from five years before. The name of Stefan Kyriakis sat at the top. The dead man he'd stumbled upon in the tomb of the Blue Demon was pictured in a standard Questura mugshot. With a rough moustache and an unpleasant, aggressive scowl, he wasn't a pretty sight. The charges were ugly too: smuggling weapons from Corsica into Italy through the main port of Monte Argentario. Six pallets of automatic rifles, with accompanying ammunition.

'Porto Santo Stefano,' Costa said. 'That's a fifteen-minute drive from Porto Ercole. It keeps coming back to the Maremma, doesn't it?'

'What happened to him?' Commissario Esposito asked. He and Falcone had joined them silently. For once they didn't look at loggerheads.

'He was charged with arms-smuggling, and beating up a couple of the officers who apprehended him,' Silvio Di Capua responded. 'Never came to court. No reason given. The man doesn't appear in our records ever again.'

The *commissario* scratched his head and stared at Falcone, as if looking for help. He was in full uniform. His face was grey and tired. It must have been a long night for everyone.

'So?' Esposito asked. 'What about this phone lead you have?'

'A SIM card?' Silvio Di Capua said. 'That's a lead?'

'You can find out who he called,' Costa began.

'It's a SIM card, Nic. The phone logs the calls. Not the card. All that keeps is the network, the number and any texts. Of which there are none, by the way.'

Teresa gave him a filthy look.

'We must be able to find out something.'

'I've passed on the details to a couple of phone geeks I know. If we're lucky we may be able to track down the account holder. That's not strictly legal, by the way . . .'

'Don't tell me this,' Esposito warned him. 'Do you have no answers at all?'

'We've got plenty of questions,' the inspector replied. 'Why did those two *carabinieri* come up from Rome intent on killing those kids in the Petrakises' shack?'

'You don't know that,' Esposito grumbled.

Falcone shook his head.

'What other explanation fits? They murdered those students, and the local officer who happened to be fool enough to go along with them. Nic and Rosa spoke to his brother. He saw the body in the morgue, even though they tried to keep it hidden. The bullet wound was in the back of the neck.'

'It's not just him,' Teresa intervened. 'There was the girl. Nadia Ambrosini.' She hammered at the computer until she found what she wanted: the photograph of the dead students after the attack. 'Nadia is holding the gun. The story is that she shot the other two, then killed herself when she realized they were going to be captured. Why? She was a bank manager's daughter. The director of the Villa Giulia knew her. She was an airhead. Into dope and disco. Not theatrical suicides. Come on . . .' she waved at the photo on the screen, her face the very picture of disgust, '. . . a weapon in the hand? Please. This is posed. An act. A riddle. Like Giovanni Batisti, shot dead, then butchered to make it look as if he's some kind of human sacrifice. Like . . .'

She picked up a piece of paper. It was a page from a police notepad, with Falcone's writing, and the Roman numerals.

'Like these.' Teresa shook her head. 'Twenty years ago Andrea Petrakis leaves a cryptic message about *Julius Caesar* after he's butchered Renzo and Marie Frasca at the Villa Giulia. He does the same when he kills Batisti. And next to the body of this arms-smuggler, who's clearly just made some kind of delivery.' She stared at them. 'Am I the only one thinking this?'

It had occurred to Costa too.

'It's a message for the same person. Whoever was supposed to read it back then is still here to receive it now.'

He turned to Esposito and said, 'We need to know the schedule for the summit. At least that might help us understand what they're planning to attack.'

Commissario Esposito, a good man at heart, but a politician too, shook his head and stared at them glumly.

'They could be planning to attack anything. Besides, do you think I'd get an answer?'

'There are questions we need to put to some of those people,' Teresa told him.

Esposito picked up his car keys. He wanted out of this conversation.

'We're in the middle of a national emergency. Palombo is one of the most senior security officials involved. You want me to call him in for an interview in the Questura?'

'If that's what it takes,' Rosa began. 'Mirko—'

The commissario glared at her.

'Do not dare to use the death of an officer in that fashion, Agente. I answer to those above me, and they answer to Luca Palombo, who has already decreed that Oliva's death is a matter for the Carabinieri. Find me some facts that will allow me to question that position and I will drag the bastards responsible in front of a magistrate myself.' Then, more quietly, 'But a set of numbers scrawled on a wall, a host of suppositions – these do not represent evidence, and on a day like this I will not waste time trying to pretend they do.'

He regarded each of them in turn.

'Find me something of substance. If not, then Palombo will have his way and we will see what happens when this madness is over.'

'They buried it once,' Teresa cut in. 'They'll bury it again.'

'Some things are best buried,' Esposito replied. 'It's less painful that way.'

Then he took a theatrical look at his watch and declared, 'I have a meeting at the Ministry in thirty minutes. We have nothing else to discuss here. If you find something, come first to me.'

They watched him leave.

Peroni leaped in.

'I can try Cattaneo in America again . . .'

'It's four in the morning over there,' Teresa complained.

'I don't care,' the big man replied.

Silvio Di Capua was printing out another page.

'I've a name for the Frascas' housekeeper. A woman. She must be elderly now. Lives in Testaccio. Is that any—'

'I'll do it,' Costa said, and realized Rosa was watching him. '*We'll* do it.'

'Good,' Falcone observed. 'We'll go through what we have and see if there's something that's been missed.'

Peroni was on the phone already. Di Capua and Elizabeth Murray were printing out more pages from the computer.

Costa went and located the clothes Silvio had got for them, cheap ones bought from a store round the corner, to save time and avoid any security people Palombo might have placed on their homes. He had jeans and a T-shirt. When Rosa came out from her room she had on a simple lime-green skirt, shorter than anything he'd ever seen her wear, and a skimpy halter top. Big shades too, and a white plastic handbag.

She followed him down the stairs. Outside she glanced up and down the empty street and said, 'We must look like the only two tourists left in Rome. Is this meant to be a disguise?'

Probably, he thought. The address Peroni had found was near the Via Marmorata, a short drive away. Silvio had got them a scooter too, and a pair of fluorescent crash helmets.

'Nic?'

He watched her fasten the helmet.

'What is it?'

'I still don't understand why we're alive and Mirko's dead.'

'Perhaps we were lucky. Petrakis got distracted. Or careless.'

'Careless?' she repeated, staring at him.

'Sorry. That was a stupid thing to say.'

'We're missing something, and you know it.'

'We're missing lots.'

She watched him get on the scooter.

'These people don't know what's true, what's real any more.'

'We're real,' Costa said, and brought the little machine to life.

She climbed on behind him, holding his waist tightly as they rode out into the Via San Giovanni in Laterano.

- 3 -

'Signora Barnes?'

The *carabiniere* at the barrier barely glanced at her press ID card, with its new photo carefully inserted beneath the plastic.

'*Si?*' Anna Ybarra said automatically as she stepped into the scanner arch erected to deal with the long line of media queuing for the brief press conference. She passed through without so much as a beep.

'*Grazie,*' the officer said and waved her on to join the snaking queue of bodies working their way onto the piazza and the rectangular space marked out for them in front of the palace.

It was just as Andrea Petrakis had said. There were two ways in. The narrow Vicolo Mazzarino that led from the Via Nazionale, the route she'd taken. And, on the opposite side of the square, along the Via della Dataria, which led down the steep hill, towards the Trevi Fountain and the main shopping street of the Via Corso, the way she'd use to leave.

She was wearing the clothes Petrakis had provided, an outfit waiting for her in the caravan: a thin wool pinstriped suit in charcoal grey. The kind of clothes a TV reporter might want for work. He was prepared. Had been prepared. And he'd briefed her too. Quickly, thoroughly, professionally, as they'd dressed that bright, clear morning, in a field where rowdy blackbirds were trumpeting another sunny day on the outskirts of Rome.

The media event went the way he said. Five speeches, mostly in English, for the benefit of the international media. The first came from the Italian president, Sordi, an upright, distinguished-looking man with a pendulous, sad face and an air of gravity that was impossible to ignore. She had read about him on the little computer they provided

250

in Afghanistan, discovered he had an interesting, intriguing past that was difficult to connect with the august, calm figure she saw on the podium outside the Quirinale Palace. Next came some politics from his own prime minister, the familiar, theatrical figure she had seen so many times on the TV in Spain, younger, snappier, more lightweight, yet somehow more powerful.

The British leader then spoke, since his country held the current presidency of the European Union, and afterwards the American, and finally the Russian, the only one who needed an interpreter.

She stood there, mesmerized. All of these men talked of the same thing. Of their sorrow at happenings in Rome, their sympathy with the relatives of those who had lost their lives, the determination such acts instilled in them to fight the good fight, for as long as it was needed.

Anna Ybarra never thought she would be so close to those who ran the world. Close up, even separated by a barrier and a small army of soldiers, police officers and plain-clothes security personnel, they looked quite ordinary as they began to sweat beneath the keen summer sun. They sounded sincere. They looked grave and stern and serious. There was conviction in the air. She could feel it, touch it, see it acknowledged by the nods of the reporters around her, whose questions, when they were allowed, seemed sanitized and predictable, organized in advance, tame invitations to an answer waiting to be delivered.

It took no more than fifteen minutes. Then the leaders stood still, barely smiling, for the cameras. It was over, too quickly, before anyone had said anything that mattered.

She found it impossible to dismiss from her head some of the things she had read about Dario Sordi. These mattered, yet not a single professional journalist around her had thought fit to raise them. Or perhaps they were simply too scared.

Before she knew it, Anna Ybarra found herself pushing to the front of the crowd, a question rising in her head, one she had to voice, though she accepted it was not part of the plan, and that Andrea Petrakis, if they ever met again – and that she doubted somehow – might kill her for its utterance.

'Mr President! Mr President!'

They were turning to go back into the palace. It was a stupid thing to shout. There were so many presidents there at that moment, and she really only wanted to talk to one.

'Presidente Sordi?'

The tall, elderly figure on the podium turned, hesitating.

Without thinking she exclaimed, '*Dígame!*'

He gazed in her direction. There was puzzlement in his eyes, and perhaps something else. Then he walked back to the microphone and asked, 'Do I know you, signora?'

'No, sir,' she shouted, heart beating quickly, her mind full of fear that she had gone too far. 'Not at all.'

'You have a question?'

'I wondered . . .' The reporters around her were staring. She was out of line, asking something that was unexpected, unwanted. The security guards were closing ranks between the barrier and the figures outside the palace. There was so little time.

Anna Ybarra held up her media badge for all to see and said, 'Of all the men and women here, you alone know what it is like to be called a terrorist. You've killed men in the street for no other reason than their nationality. How is this different?'

Dario Sordi gazed across the bright space between them and shrugged, an ordinary, humble gesture.

'I killed soldiers in uniform, with rifles in their hands. Not ordinary men and women struggling to get by. It's a small difference, though not an insignificant one, I think. This was many years ago, when we were a nation at war, occupied by the enemy, fighting for our own freedom.' He thought for a moment, then added, 'For what it is worth, there is not a day goes by when I do not see the faces of the two human beings I murdered, do not remember the surprise I saw in their eyes. They did not expect their lives would come to an end at the hands of a child. As a fellow man I regret this constantly. As a former soldier . . .' his face grew longer, '. . . I did my duty. But I repeat,' he waved a finger at her across the piazza, 'that was in a time of combat, and this is not the case now, however much my colleagues here, with their so-called war on terror, may wish to disagree.'

She wanted to ask something else, but the words refused to form.

'Are you sure we've never spoken before?' Dario Sordi added, his old grey eyes closing on her.

'That's not possible, sir,' she answered, and slunk to the back of the crowd, disappearing into the huddle of bodies already marching towards the exit, chanting into mobile phones, talking to their newsrooms, in Italy, Europe and beyond. Some, she could hear, were starting to mention the comments she had elicited from Sordi, words that would never have been spoken if an interloper, an impostor, had not sought them.

Petrakis had taken her through the next part, step by step, using a map of the city. It was easy to follow his instructions, leaving by the steps on the palace side of the square. She found the alley he'd told her about, narrow and shadowy, partway down the hill. It ran for a short distance, then there was a right fork into the Via della Panetteria. To her right ran the old palace stables, and after a little way the street named after them, the Via della Scuderie, running beneath the Quirinale walls to the Via del Traforo, with its tunnel beneath the palace, the stopping point for coaches visiting the Trevi Fountain.

Look for a stable door, he said, marked with a red paper circle, the kind a child might use at school.

It was one of many similar entrances, halfway along the narrow street. She checked up and down the road to make sure no one was looking. Then she turned the worn brass circular handle on the door and walked through.

The room beyond was vast and dark. Anna Ybarra took out the small torch he'd given her and found herself in what looked like a stable set into the barracks at the back of the Quirinale Palace: a bare stone chamber like the nave of some tiny country church, with a couple of saddles on the wall, and the brittle remains of an ancient carriage.

In the corner, beneath a broken cartwheel, she found what she was looking for. In a cheap suitcase lay another change of clothes: a long, flowing evening dress, floor-length, cut low at the front, and a pearl necklace. By its side was a large instrument case. It contained a large, shiny baritone saxophone the colour of gold. The name 'Yamaha' was stamped on the bell.

She took out the instrument, reached into its mouth and removed the package hidden inside. Petrakis had briefed her on this too. It was the kind of weapon she could never have imagined until they took her to Afghanistan. Now she knew its name. Somehow his sources within the palace had provided a black Uzi Para Micro, a tiny machine pistol developed for Israeli special forces and counter-terrorist units. The magazine was hidden in the accessory area of the case along with a slender shoulder stock. Petrakis, who had coached her through the task of learning about firearms, said it contained thirty-three shells. There would be no spares. The entire load of ammunition could be expended in under two seconds, if she wanted. This was a weapon for slaughter, not marksmanship.

Anna Ybarra put on the evening dress, which fitted a little awkwardly around her strong shoulders. Then she cradled the Uzi, stock against her arm, practising, trying to imagine what it would be like in the room he'd mentioned, the Salone dei Corazzieri. Standing on the platform with the musicians, pretending she was a last-minute replacement for someone who couldn't show. Letting them play a few notes, then stepping off the stage, walking into the melee of dinner suits and glamorous dresses, wondering which way to arc the weapon in the single burst she'd be allowed.

Her head was full of questions. Too many.

She pulled out her phone, found his number and sent him the single, one-word message they'd agreed.

Inside.

Less than a minute later came his reply.

Wait.

She sat down on an old, rickety chair, next to the wrecked carriage. There was a single, small high window through which the bright summer day streamed, illuminating the dark, dusty interior of the stable. The shaft of light fell, almost deliberately she thought, on something that must have stood there for years: a crucifix attached to the side wall, a tortured bronze figure of the dying Christ, head bowed, awaiting release.

– 4 –

Letizia Russo's home was a neat third-floor apartment in a block by the river in Testaccio. She was an unsmiling, pinch-faced woman, thin and bird-like, with a sharp, spinsterish manner.

They sat on an old-fashioned sofa. She watched them from an armchair in the window, the light falling so that the shadow of the curtain fell on her face.

'You do know why we're here, signora?' Rosa asked.

'I can guess. What do you want of me?'

'Memories,' Costa answered.

'Is that all?'

'For now. We're trying to picture what happened. It's not easy.'

'No. It wasn't.'

'The Frascas. What were they like?'

'Not the best family I've worked for. Not the worst. I was just the housekeeper. I came in and cleaned. Looked after the little boy from time to time. They were kind, after their fashion. I was,' she stabbed her skinny chest with a finger, 'a servant. I never forgot that.'

'The boy . . .'

'Daniel was beautiful. I taught him to talk like a Roman. They didn't like it. They said,' her voice changed accent, became hard, 'we don't want him speaking like some cab driver. Huh! Daniel was as bright as a button. And now . . .' The sour look came back. 'The papers say the poor boy was shot dead somewhere only the other day. That he killed someone and was soft in the head. Not my Daniel.'

'No,' Costa agreed. 'Perhaps he wasn't.'

Her expression never changed. She asked, 'Then where is he?'

He shrugged.

'I don't know. There's so much we don't understand. We're trying.'

The old woman nodded at the window. There was scarcely any traffic running along the riverside road. On the Tiber itself he could see two high-speed Carabinieri launches racing towards the city, armed officers upright at the bows. Overhead the clatter of a helicopter flying low rattled the rooftops.

'Not doing much good, is it?'

'Would you prefer we did nothing?' Rosa asked tartly. 'What happened on the day they were killed?'

The corners of Letizia Russo's thin-lipped mouth turned down in a gesture of ignorance.

'It was the weekend. I was visiting a relative in Civitavecchia. First I heard was on the news.'

Costa asked her the usual details. What she found in the apartment. What she was asked by the investigating officers. She listened, staring at him.

'Why don't you know this, if you're police?'

'Because it was twenty years ago and the investigating team then – they were from other agencies.'

'I didn't get into the apartment for a week. By then they said these animals who called themselves the Blue Demon were dead or gone. Daniel too. When they finally let me in . . .' Another casual frown. 'It looked the way it always did.'

Costa recalled the photographs they'd seen in the briefing in the Quirinale.

'The blood on the walls . . .'

'I saw no blood.' She stopped, thinking. 'They said they'd cleaned up before me.'

Rosa was staring at him.

'Why would they do that?' she asked. 'Daniel Frasca was still missing. Could they cover all the points?'

'Maybe,' he responded, unsure himself. 'What was different, signora? About the apartment?'

'Nothing.' She hesitated. 'Especially that room they said they'd cleaned. It was the way it always was. Signora Frasca was not the most house-proud of women. There were always things left for me to tidy away. Things another woman would have dealt with herself. Coffee cups. Danny's toys.'

'Their friends?' he asked.

'There weren't many. Not that I saw. A few Americans came round. English. All foreign. Mainly embassy business, I think. I never understood this. Signor Frasca spoke excellent Italian. He was Italian. By ancestry. I never knew him to have Roman friends. They were not the most sociable of couples. They adored Danny, I'll say that for them.'

Her face hardened.

'Then one day they're dead. Buried in America, the papers said. Not so much as a memorial service in Rome. I was only a house-keeper. This was none of my business, I imagine. All the same, I would have mourned, if anyone wanted it.'

Letizia Russo seemed to be struck by some stray thought.

'What is it?' Rosa asked.

'When people die, there are decisions you have to make.'

'Who gets what? Who does what?' Costa said. 'Anyone who loses someone—'

'I asked if I could help,' the woman cut in. 'I asked what might become of the Frascas' things. Police. Carabinieri. You never think of such matters. This was a family. They had a home. Belongings. Items that would be precious to someone, some relative. Some of it – you would never have shipped everything all the way to America. So I asked for a memento . . .' Her skinny hand waved through the air. 'They cut me dead. The embassy would take care of everything. How? Daniel's little paintings? He loved to draw. Who would want them? Who would pay to send them all the way across the ocean?'

A low Roman curse escaped her bloodless lips.

'I am not a thief! I asked for nothing that anyone might want. Many foreign families have employed me. Once the ambassador of Egypt, who has a beautiful house on the Aventino. No one has ever accused me of stealing something. It's unthinkable. Always, when I finish service I receive a gift. It's tradition. If the family is dead . . .'

Costa tried to imagine the scene.

'You wanted something to remember them by,' he said. 'Nothing more.'

'Exactly! I played with young Danny. He loved me. No one else took any interest in what was in that apartment of theirs. What was a photograph? A simple family picture? They had plenty. All of them better than that thing they gave to the papers.'

'You took it,' Costa murmured, thinking. 'They found out.'

'Just the photograph. And a vase too.'

She got up, walked over to the mantelpiece and removed an old-fashioned piece made of blue porcelain.

'Delft,' the woman said, stroking it. 'Dutch. Not worth much. I checked. A week – maybe more – later, when Signor Frasca and his wife are on their way back to America in their coffins, there is a knock on the door. Four big men. Police or security, or something. I don't remember. They treat me like I'm a criminal. They say, "Where is it? Where is it?"'

She held up the vase.

'I tell them. Here. Take it. They look at me like I'm an idiot. They don't want that. Only the photograph. I ask you. Why?'

'What did it show?' he asked.

'It was a picture. A snap! The father, the mother, that lovely little boy. One day in the Forum. Smiling. Happy. A sunny day. Danny had a *gelato*. I can still see his face today. That little boy loved me.'

'Did you give it to them?'

She scowled.

'I had no choice. They were threatening me with the courts. With prison! Me! All for a memento no one wanted.'

Rosa was looking at him, interested.

'You didn't keep a copy, I suppose?' she wanted to know.

'What am I? An idiot? They threatened me! Who wants to employ a housekeeper who steals? No one. Why should they?'

'The only photograph of the Frascas we've ever seen . . .' Costa began.

The old woman nodded.

'The one in the newspapers. I saw it too. Did them no justice.

Terrible, old picture. Even I wouldn't recognize them from that.'
She blinked. 'Or that other photograph. At the Villa Giulia. It's a
scandal. How can the newspapers print such things? Two human
beings, butchered by that terrorist animal . . . that poor boy stolen
away into slavery, or whatever.'

'What was Renzo Frasca like?' he asked again. 'What did he do?'

'Talked on the telephone. Read books. Went to the theatre.' She
frowned. 'A lot of meetings too. He travelled much. In Italy. Not
abroad. The north mainly. I remember that.'

'Tarquinia?' Rosa asked, a little breathless.

'Somewhere north,' she agreed.

'What kind of books?'

'History. Roman history.' Letizia Russo thought for a moment,
then added, 'And the Etruscans. Like that Petrakis animal. He and
his wife went to the Villa Giulia to see those statues there. They took
me once, with Daniel. Disgusting! A child should never have seen
such obscenities. But,' she shrugged, 'Americans.'

Sometimes one found answers in the most unlikely of places. He
had no idea why he asked the question. It was probably no more
than desperation.

'Shakespeare . . .'

'Hah! Shakespeare!' she shrieked. 'Sometimes you'd think there
was nothing else in the world but that man. Every time there was a
play. A book. A movie . . .'

'Nic?' Rosa asked. 'I don't get it.'

'Me neither.'

His phone was ringing. It was Silvio Di Capua and he had
something.

'I take it back. What I told you about the SIM being useless,' the
young pathologist said quickly.

'And . . . ?'

'We traced the account to the Ministry of the Interior. It's a
spook phone. This magic little computer system we've got can log
into the account records.'

'Give me the last five people he called,' Costa ordered, pulling
out a pad and pen.

'Can't do that, Nic. This is a new phone. Apart from your call to Falcone, it was only ever used for one other number.'

Di Capua read it out, said thanks, then cut the call.

The women were looking at him. He excused himself, went to the window and dialled.

A voice he recognized answered.

'This is Sovrintendente Nic Costa. We have to meet in thirty minutes. In San Carlo alle Quattro Fontane. I think you know where . . .'

Words of protest, of outrage.

'This is important, sir, or I wouldn't be bothering you. We have uncovered something very disturbing about the Blue Demon. Something I feel you should know. Thirty minutes. Please . . .'

He finished the call. The two women were still watching him. He wondered whether any of these connections could possibly make sense. Then he looked into Letizia Russo's cold, sharp eyes and said, 'I would like you to come with us, signora.'

'Why? Am I under arrest? For stealing a vase twenty years ago?'

'No. I simply need your help. Please. We will organize a car.'

'There are no cars. No one moves in Rome. Not now Dario Sordi has turned the city into a prison while he and his cronies drink champagne in the Quirinale Palace!'

'I'm sure that pains President Sordi as much as it does the rest of us, signora.'

'Don't be ridiculous! Let me—'

'Your coat, please.'

There was a muttered curse, then she went into the next room.

Rosa stared at him and asked, 'Where are we going?'

'To church.'

– 5 –

There were flowers on the meagre remains of the Tempio del Divo Giulio: roses and chrysanthemums scattered over the dun pile of earth where, more than two millennia before, Mark Antony had read his notorious ovation for an assassinated dictator.

The noblest Roman of them all.

Great Caesar, Divine Caesar.

Now tourists from parts of the world that the tyrant could never have imagined ambled past the place where his bloodied corpse was reduced to ashes.

Not many today, though. Petrakis found himself virtually alone on this baking summer's afternoon. The broad thoroughfare through the Forum, from the Piazza Venezia to the Colosseum, was as empty as a Sunday when the city closed the road to traffic. Soldiers, *carabinieri* and all manner of police officers, local and state, wandered around the foot of Via Cavour and the narrow streets in front of the ruined Trajan's Markets. Armed men scanned the area from temporary watchtowers built of plain, ugly scaffolding. Hideous, loud signs had been erected at every possible entrance into the forbidden zone, the government's much-vaunted 'ring of steel', warning that no ordinary citizen was welcome beyond these points, and all who disobeyed would face instant arrest under the emergency legislation.

He sat, phone in hand, on a piece of ancient, displaced marble, staring at the spot where Caesar's pyre had stood, amused by the scattering of fading blooms. There was always some stray bouquet there, thrown by a gullible visitor. Petrakis wished he could have been present when they deposited the flowers on the tyrant's altar, wished he could have told them just a little of the true face of Rome.

Of its brutality and hatred of anything, any race, it failed to understand or command. He closed his eyes and thought of the ranked exhibits in the Etruscan halls of the Villa Giulia: men and women locked in a joyful existence, fired by passion and pride, beholden to none, frightened of nothing. He'd wanted to be like that since he could first think, ached to feel that selfsame fire, that release from the daily ritual of routine. His father had promised such gifts and then been snatched away. Nothing had ever come close.

And one day the Devil arrived. For the Etruscans, on the wall of a tomb in Tarquinia, a blue shape capering like a malicious fiend newly released from Hell, an arbiter, standing between life and death, bringing misery and torment to anything it might catch.

For him . . .

Petrakis knew the moment, had captured it forever. Bad news, the worst. An explanation, an urgent need for a solution. It took place in a nondescript office in Rome in a place he could no longer remember. There was a man in a suit, making promises Petrakis didn't understand, sealing bargains that came with hidden conditions, invisible until they were triggered by the relentless, cruel tide of events.

He was the Devil of Faust, a sly, compelling creature, offering the world to all who would listen, in return for something that seemed so slight and insignificant.

He was the Blue Demon, the vicious, feasting animal that sought to conquer and devour everything.

He was Rome, all-powerful, all-commanding. Rome, the heartless monster before which everyone knelt in obeisance. Europe was a land of lost races, disappeared civilizations. The Etruscans were nothing more than exhibits in a museum, their tongue eradicated, their culture reduced to objects in glass cases. In this way the kingdom of Caesar grew to become the empire of the pope, spreading its ideology everywhere until it was the spirit of the age. From the drab site of a dead dictator's funeral pyre to the Lincoln Memorial, from the altar of St Peter's to the Palace of Westminster, the despotism became insidious, ubiquitous.

Petrakis glanced in the direction of the Quirinale. The high priests of the religion now feasted and praised one another in the pope's palace, behind the tower above the markets of Trajan, the one that the lying, cheating tour guides said was the viewpoint from which Nero had watched Rome burn.

In the wastelands of Afghanistan, trying to work his way to the al-Qaeda leadership, as the man in the suit had ordered all those years before, he'd seen something – a light, a beacon. One bright, cold day in September they had gathered around a portable TV set and watched in amazement as the Twin Towers fell in New York, pillars of the old world tumbling to the ground, to be replaced by fear and chaos, panic and uncertainty.

At that moment something in him had changed. He had seen through the Blue Demon's lies, all of them; had known, for sure, that the empire that began with Rome was no longer beyond defeat. Helmand and the bandit lands on the Pakistan border had finally taught him to ride a horse like an Etruscan, to kill an enemy with a simple, short dagger, to take what one wanted from life before the inevitable darkness fell, and with it oblivion. He never converted, he never pretended to. They accepted him for what he was: some kind of elemental force, created by events, by nature.

On that sharp September day those few years before, Andrea Petrakis metamorphosed into the man he had pretended to be for so many years, as easily, as naturally, as an insect emerging from the chrysalis, hungry, expectant and ready.

There was a short, straight line from that instant to the present. He had watched it form, shaped it, directed it with all his might and vigour.

Petrakis stared at the phone, waiting for it to ring.

The call comes. He gets up, stretches, yawns under the hot sun and spits, with all the phlegm and force he can muster, directly onto the roses that cover the place where Julius Caesar turned to ashes.

'You'll have company soon,' Petrakis whispers, wondering if there is some kind of magic in the universe after all, whether Caesar's shade might hear his words in some distant twilight realm where dead dictators muster, still pretending they are gods. And, if the blood-thirsty old bastard listens, whether he might understand.

– 6 –

Ben Rennick didn't look pleased that he'd been dragged out of the Quirinale. He was wearing a lounge suit and a dark tie. There was a bulge beneath the right-hand side of his jacket. But he didn't seem like the kind of man who would use a weapon easily. It was more of a badge, Costa thought.

'This had better be important,' the American said.

'It is,' Costa told him. 'I would have broached it with Luca Palombo, but . . .' He stopped, and looked at this man, wondering what was going on his head.

'But what?' Rennick wanted to know.

'But I don't think it would be a good idea. Not yet.'

They were in Borromini's church, San Carlo alle Quattro Fontane – San Carlino to the locals – just a few short steps away from the crossroads where Giovanni Batisti had been kidnapped and his driver, the young Polish woman, Elena Majewska, murdered. Costa had forgotten how beautiful this compact place of worship was. The interior seemed alive, organic somehow, a flowing mass of convex stone curves wrapped around a Greek-cross floor plan. It was a five-minute walk from the Quirinale Palace, but the closest point Costa could reach, given the security on the streets. Any nearer, even as far as the neighbouring church of Sant'Andrea, by the architect's bitter rival, Bernini, and the armed officers would have turned him back.

'You're lucky being a foreigner,' Costa told him. They were alone. It seemed the best way. 'I grew up around places like this. A Roman takes them for granted sometimes. This city has so much. Too much perhaps.'

'I don't have time for chit-chat.'

'Yet you came,' Costa said, smiling. 'Even though I've never seen you outside the Quirinale since we first met. Not even in the photo calls.'

Rennick scowled and looked at his watch.

'Curiosity, I imagine,' Costa added. 'Do you like the dome?' It was astonishing to witness how Borromini had placed so much ingenious, complex beauty in such a small place. Seemingly incongruous geometric shapes – hexagons and crosses, ovals and circles – interlocked to point the way to the centrepiece, a glass window depicting a pure white dove, a symbol of peace, of redemption, crowned with a halo, about to descend to earth.

'Cute,' Rennick agreed. 'So we have to go through this small talk. Fine. Didn't Borromini commit suicide, if I remember right?'

'You know Rome well.'

'Well enough. Why am I here?'

'Did Palombo tell you what happened last night? Near Tarquinia?'

He nodded. The tall security-services officer looked grey and tired, as if he hadn't slept much in a while. Miserable too.

'I'm sorry about your colleague. You shouldn't have been there. You were told.'

'If I'd known one of my officers might die in front of my eyes . . .'

Rennick took his arm and led him into the fluid shadows of the columns to the left of the high altar. It felt as if they were inside the belly of a cold stone beast. There was no one else there, not even the usual church official.

In the half-light the American peered into his face and it occurred to Costa that, in different circumstances, he might enjoy getting to know this man. He seemed sincere and serious. The weight of the years had left its mark.

'Listen to me. These are difficult times.' Rennick spoke in a low, authoritative voice.

'I'd gathered that.'

'No. You haven't. Not at all. In situations like this, smart people do as they're told. Nothing more. Nothing less. No improvisation. No peeking. This is not the moment to be inquisitive, my friend. I know you're close to Dario Sordi. Maybe he's put some ideas in your head. Dismiss them, now. For your own sake and that of your colleagues. We're in control here, as much as we can be. Anything you try on the side just muddies the waters, and that's not helpful. That's what leads to people getting hurt.'

'Did Giovanni Batisti confide in you?' Costa asked straight out.

Rennick's narrow eyes screwed up in puzzlement.

'What?'

'Did Batisti tell you that Sordi never believed Andrea Petrakis was behind the Blue Demon? That it was the creation of someone else, someone who never left for Afghanistan or anywhere? Someone who stayed behind: invisible, silent, waiting, the way Gladio operatives were supposed to? Maybe in Rome or somewhere else, a city, a job in which a man might hide out in the plain light of day.' He paused. 'America, say.'

Costa touched Rennick's arm and leaned in to speak, glancing at the door, nodding to the distant figure he saw there.

'Did you create the Blue Demon, Signor Rennick?'

The man closed his eyes for a moment as if the question pained him.

'The Blue Demon's a myth. A character from mythology. Andrea Petrakis used the name to cover his tracks, to make himself appear more than the simple, bloody murderer he is. Don't think the world's more complicated than it is. And stay out of our way. In a couple of days everything will be normal. I guarantee it.'

'"We shall be called purgers, not murderers,"' Costa recited, looking into his eyes, wondering what he saw there.

'What?'

'A line from Shakespeare. You mentioned it in the briefing with the president. I was impressed. Not many men can quote something as obscure as that. A specific play too, *Julius Caesar*, so easily . . .'

'You shouldn't spend all your time in the company of cops.'

Costa pulled out a sheet of paper from his pocket.

'This was scratched on the wall of the tomb in Tarquinia. Next to the corpse of a man called Stefan Kyriakis. Did you know him?'

'Never heard of the man.'

Rennick's eyes wouldn't leave the paper and the numbers there: XII. II. I. CLXXIII.

'Twelve, two, one, a hundred and seventy-three,' Costa said. 'We thought it was Shakespeare too. But . . .' He shrugged. 'There are too many numbers.' He watched Rennick's face. 'What does it mean?'

'I haven't a clue. You've got to excuse me . . .'

'Palombo didn't tell you about these numbers, did he?'

'I . . . don't have time for this,' Rennick said, shaking his head.

'Who did he tell?'

Rennick had turned to leave. Costa put a hand on his arm.

'One last question, sir. Why did Stefan Kyriakis, an arms-dealer who supplied weapons to Andrea Petrakis, possess your phone number?'

'What?' Rennick murmured. '*What?*'

'How do you think I reached you? We have the SIM from his phone. Your number is on it. We have evidence that links you to him, directly. How is that possible, sir?'

The American remained immobile, unable to speak.

From the door opposite, open to the street, a woman was striding across the floor, her eyes on the tall figure standing in the light beneath Borromini's dome. There was a stream of Roman epithets emerging from her mouth, the volume rising as she approached.

Rennick looked trained for these situations and was already reaching for his weapon. Costa leaped on the man, wrenching the pistol from his grasp, sending it rattling across the marble floor.

'Bastard!' Letizia Russo yelled, then raced up and slapped him hard around the face. 'Bastard!'

The American didn't say anything. For a moment he tried to laugh it off, then she slapped him again.

'I think you've mistaken me for someone else, signora,' Rennick muttered in perfect Italian.

'Bastard! I cried for you. For your wife. For that child I used to hug in my arms. They said you were dead. Murdered. And Danny gone . . .'

Falcone was leading the rest of them through the door: Peroni, Teresa, Rosa. They stood in front of Rennick, blocking the way. Costa relaxed his grip. The American was going nowhere.

'Signora Russo?' Falcone said.

The old woman stood erect and furious in front of the man.

'*Si?*'

'Do you recognize this man? If so, will you identify him for us, please?'

'Renzo Frasca!'

'Frasca died twenty years ago . . .' the American began.

'I worked for you!' she yelled. 'I did your washing. I changed your child's nappies when you were too lazy to do it yourself.'

Rennick glared at the inspector.

'Listen, I don't have time for this nonsense and nor do you. The Frasca case is dead. There's a headstone over a grave in Washington that bears their names. The DNA on that kid killed in the Via Rasella the other night—'

'You made up that report!' Teresa cried. 'Give me the body. Let me run my own tests.'

He shook his head and murmured, 'I can't do that right now.'

Peroni took a photograph from his pocket and gave it to Letizia Russo. Costa caught a glance: a handsome young man with long blond hair.

'I have some good news, signora. This is what Danny looks like now. We got pictures from his Web page. Daniel Rennick is a student at Harvard. Bright kid, it seems. His subject is English literature, just as it was for his father.'

The big *agente* leaned towards the American.

'I don't imagine he remembers a thing about Italy, does he? Just three years old when you switched identities. You can change a lot about yourself. But not a kid's first name. Not if everyone called him Danny from the start.'

The Russo woman clung to the photograph, took one more look, then put it in her bag.

'Bastard!' she murmured, her eyes filling with tears, then turned on her heels and walked outside into the bright day.

'I'm an officer of the US government, with diplomatic immunity,' the man they still knew as Rennick insisted. 'I've got things to take care of today that you people can't even begin to imagine. I am walking out of here now . . .'

Costa grabbed his arms behind his back and slipped on the cuffs. Rennick began to howl with fury.

'Don't make so much noise,' Falcone growled. 'We can hold you on that phone number alone. Put him in the car and take him to the Questura.'

Peroni took hold of him and headed for the door.

'How long have we got?' Costa asked.

The inspector grimaced.

'Palombo will hear the moment we get him in an interview room. Maybe before. If we have an hour before they spring him, we'll be lucky.' He glanced at Peroni shuffling the American out into the daylight. 'Did he know what the message meant? The numbers?'

'He said he didn't.'

'Was he lying?'

'I don't think he even knew there was a number. Or that Giovanni Batisti was set up.' He frowned. 'Either that or he's a well-trained liar. An hour? Is that all?'

The nave of the tiny church went dark. Black-clad figures were swamping the doorway, blocking the light. They wore masks and bore automatic weapons. He'd no idea who they were: some special police unit, Carabinieri, military. Or something else altogether.

Luca Palombo strode through the mass of bodies, his face red with fury.

'Apparently not,' Falcone murmured.

- 7 -

Silvio Di Capua sat at the computer desk staring at the numbers on the page, on the screen, and now etched deep inside his head too.

XII. II. I. CLXXIII.

'You'll go mad if you look at that any longer,' Elizabeth Murray told him. 'How much sleep have you had over the last twenty-four hours?'

'Probably more than you.'

She patted the laptop computer and grinned.

'I'm still enthralled by these things. We never had toys like this in my day. You are so lucky.'

He wished he found her words cheering.

'Teresa thinks we're in danger of relying on this stuff too much. That one day the cops will sit back every time there's a crime, look at us and say, "Fetch the DNA, link the criminal records." Then go out to lunch. And if we don't have an answer . . .'

There'd been a case not long before where all standard DNA techniques had been snatched from them, albeit briefly. It was not an experience he wanted to live through again.

'Data is data,' she observed. 'It's what you do with it that counts.'

Elizabeth was a little behind the game. She'd gone out for an hour that morning, to take a break, see an old friend, remember Rome, a city she'd lived in for twenty years, she said, and scarcely visited after retirement. She didn't know about Peroni's fruitless attempt to get more information out of Cattaneo in America.

The others had left by the time she returned. This seemed to surprise her.

'Where's everyone else gone?' she asked.

He thought of the way they'd bustled out with barely a word.

'Some wild good chase, I guess. I was working on these numbers. Or trying to. Nic thought he might have something worthwhile.'

'To do with what?'

'Probably nothing. Guesswork. I deal in detail, not hypothesis. I don't do all that faux cop stuff Teresa thinks she's good at. I like looking at numbers, at facts, at words and pictures. Not . . .' this thought came from nowhere and he knew it ought to shock him, '. . . at people.'

'People commit crimes, Silvio.'

'And they rarely get caught unless you come up with a case that's based on the kind of facts people like me dig up. Evidence. Numbers . . .'

Numbers were solid, indisputable, unchanging, even if they were open to interpretation. XII. II. I. CLXXIII. Twelve, two, one, a hundred and seventy-three . . . or 1221173. There were any number of ways the figures scratched on the wall of the Blue Demon's tomb might be read.

'Did they look hopeful?'

'I'm sorry,' he murmured, shaking his head.

'Falcone and the others. When they left?'

'I didn't really notice.' Di Capua stared at the screen again and said, 'It can't be Shakespeare, can it?'

He'd been through every play there was. None of them could be broken down in this way. The works were divided into acts, scenes and lines. There was no fourth element, and nothing that could be interpreted as the number twelve. Even Julius Caesar ran to just five acts. So the initial idea that had struck him – using the first number for the act, and the final one for a particular word somehow – hadn't worked at all, and he'd wasted two hours on that.

'A phone number?' she guessed.

'An attractive idea. Falcone, like all cops, misses detail. All we have is what he scrawled down on a piece of paper in an underground tomb. We don't know if there was punctuation between the numbers, spaces, anything else. Or if he got it down correctly in the first place. It would be easy to make mistakes.'

But eight digits – so many phone numbers fell into that format. He'd liked the idea, until he researched it.

'I can't find any phone-number system in Italy that would follow that format. It could only be the number itself, anyway, without country or city code. So that presumes that whoever got to read the message would know the location.'

He looked at her. She didn't seem tired at all. Sitting on the office chair next to him, in her check country shirt and moleskin trousers, Elizabeth Murray appeared bright and interested, holding on to her walking stick like a shepherdess making an occasional visit to the city.

'Would Andrea Petrakis – who hasn't, as far as we know, been in Italy for twenty years – assume that someone would have that kind of information?' he said.

'Unlikely.'

'So it's not a phone number. It's not a reference to a Shakespeare play. It's not,' he took a long swig of the tepid coffee on the desk, 'anything I can imagine.'

'Roman numerals,' she said. 'The classics . . .'

'Virgil, Homer, Tacitus, Suetonius. That's what I thought. There's nothing that breaks down into the right subdivisions. The *Aeneid* – yes, it has a twelfth book. But no acts, no scenes, just line numbers, and they won't work. Tacitus – there are books and chapters and line numbers, but again no scenes, and not enough books, either. Suetonius – at least there we've got something obvious. The book is called *The Twelve Caesars*. But the twelfth Caesar is Domitian, and where would he come in?'

He flicked up a hidden window on the screen, one of so many he'd lost count.

'Section twenty-one might fit.'

Di Capua read out from the translation.

' "He used to say that the lot of princes was most unhappy, since when they discovered a conspiracy, no one believed them unless they had been killed." And here, the following paragraph, "He was excessively lustful. His constant sexual intercourse he called bed-wrestling, as if it were a kind of exercise. It was reported that he depilated his concubines with his own hand and swam with common prostitutes."' The young pathologist sighed. 'At least you have to say Ugo Campagnolo is conforming to type. But that's as far as the connections go.'

'It's a long time since I read *The Twelve Caesars*,' she confessed. 'What happened to Domitian?'

'Murdered by his own courtiers,' Di Capua told her. 'Stabbed to death in his bedroom at the hands of a bunch of civil servants. You can see why Shakespeare never bothered with *him*.' He glanced at the screen. 'Sounds as if he deserved it, though. Bloodthirsty bastard . . .'

'Weren't they all?'

She placed a large forefinger on the paper and said, 'Let's take this one step at a time. If these numbers are separate digits, why do you have to assume they all refer to the same thing?'

'Because . . .' he began. The answer was so stupid he couldn't say it. *Because that was the only way they would make sense to someone who didn't know the secret.*

Anyone who had the key wouldn't think that way. They could decode the answer easily, by splitting the different parts into some simple system they understood already.

'I'm an idiot,' Silvio Di Capua said softly.

'You don't know I'm right.'

'You have to be. Nothing else can possibly work. These don't refer to just one thing. It's more than that. So the question is . . .'

He thought about this. They all had a feeling time was growing short. It was important to be focused, to go straight to the point.

'What do we have if we treat these as separate numbers, not some contiguous code?' he mused.

Elizabeth Murray pulled up her chair and stared at the screen. He felt happy in the presence of this woman. She was intelligent, methodical.

Suddenly she picked up the paperback edition of the collected works of Shakespeare he'd bought at the book store round the corner and flicked through a few pages. Then she shook her head, patted his shoulder and said, 'I can't help you here, Silvio. I need to call my friend. She's a classicist. Let me talk to her over lunch.'

'Enjoy it,' he said, hammering the keyboard. 'I may be a while.'

A question occurred to him. What kind of sentence would begin with a number? What might that number indicate?

'Elizabeth . . .' he began to ask.

He swivelled round in the desk chair, wondering for a moment if he wasn't becoming a physical part of the thing. But she was gone.

- 8 -

It was impossible to guess the number of masked, armed men crammed into the doorway of Borromini's little church. Teresa Lupo was yelling at the faceless squad there already. Falcone stood, unmoving, in front of Luca Palombo, the man from the Ministry of the Interior, with Peroni and Rosa alongside him. Rennick – he couldn't think of him by any other name – was now secure in Costa's grip again, cuffed behind his back, not saying a word, listening to Palombo shout down the incandescent pathologist, then start to read the riot act.

Letizia Russo was nowhere to be seen. Perhaps she'd encountered these anonymous figures with rifles and feared the worst. Perhaps Palombo had already taken custody of the one witness who could testify to the American's true identity.

The security man's lecture was short and caustic. When he was done reminding them that they had no place being where they were, Palombo turned to Costa and ordered, 'Now release him.'

Falcone remained stock still in front of their prisoner and said, very calmly, 'We have a witness who has identified Signor Rennick as Renzo Frasca. We have reason to believe he was involved in the murder of the Petrakis parents twenty years ago.'

'That's ridiculous,' Rennick objected.

'We have evidence that he had knowledge of the Blue Demon tomb, where a colleague of ours was murdered last night,' Falcone insisted. 'At the very least, we must take him in for questioning. It's a matter of the law.'

'The law says he has a diplomatic passport,' Palombo replied. 'Along with that comes immunity.'

Peroni put his big face in the way.

'It's a passport issued under a false name. Sir. In my book that makes it invalid.'

'I wasn't aware it was the job of some has-been *agente* in the state police to decide immigration policy. Release him. That's an order.'

'We don't take orders from you,' Falcone snapped.

The tall, lean spook stepped back into the doorway and made a phone call. They waited. He came back and handed over the handset.

The inspector's face fell.

'Sir,' he murmured, listening. Then, when there was a pause, he added, 'You asked for evidence, Commissario. We have it. A positive ID of Signor Rennick as Renzo Frasca. His phone number on the person of the arms-dealer killed in Tarquinia. These raise many, many questions. I cannot . . .'

They could hear the voice rising out of the phone, both tinny and furious.

'You're ordering me to release an identified suspect in a case involving several murders and terrorist acts, including the death of one of our own colleagues,' Falcone said with a stony face. 'May I know why?'

A single scream emerged from the handset. Then nothing.

Falcone pocketed the phone. Palombo held out his hand towards the American.

'Allow me to say this one thing first,' Falcone pleaded, looking him straight in the eye. 'I understand your position, Palombo. This is a crisis. We are simply police officers who do what they see as their duty, without access to all the facts. There are ramifications here we do not understand, nor should we. This man,' he indicated Rennick, 'is an impostor. He is at the very heart of your operations. He knows as much as, or more than, Giovanni Batisti, who was seized just a few metres from here, by an individual that I suspect Rennick – or Frasca, you choose – must know personally.'

'Speculation, Inspector,' Palombo said with a bored sigh.

Teresa was on him so quickly that one of the hooded soldiers intervened to push her back.

'Of course it's speculation, you moron,' she yelled. 'That's why we need him down the Questura to answer some questions.'

Palombo gestured towards Costa.

'You will release Signor Rennick into my custody. I order that. Your own *commissario* has told you the same thing. Capitano?'

One of the masked figures came closer, his weapon half-raised.

'Oh, brother!' Teresa shrieked, pointing a finger in his face. 'What brave boys! You daren't even show your faces out in the daylight. A bigger bunch of brainless, dickless idiots . . .'

'Please,' Falcone intervened, and moved between her and Palombo. 'Let me deal with this. Nic?'

He turned and nodded. Costa got the message. He found the keys and took off the cuffs. Rennick shook himself free and turned to stare at them. The man, to his credit, looked guilty. Upset. Apologetic even.

'I intend to see you again before you leave Italy,' Costa said. 'When you're without your friends.'

'Don't jump to conclusions,' the American said with a low, sorry sigh.

'I'll pass that on to Mirko Oliva's parents when we're allowed to tell them their son is dead . . .'

Palombo had his hand on Rennick's arm. The man removed the Italian's long fingers, as if he felt some distaste at their touch.

'None of us here,' Rennick nodded at the soldiers and Palombo, 'means you or Italy any harm. When the fog clears, it'll be fine. You'll see.'

Costa looked at him, wondering how he could have been so slow. He recalled Elizabeth Murray's stories of a world shaped by the dying days of the Cold War. Letizia Russo had painted a picture of a tight little family that never went out of the house much, never made friends, but kept itself close and would one day make an astonishing sacrifice, for no obvious reason. There was, he understood, only one possible explanation.

He stood as close to Rennick as he could, under the gaze of four or five long black barrels, and said, 'This is your own private false-flag operation in the middle of our city, isn't it? You've been waiting for this moment for twenty years or more. These acts are the price you expect us to pay for some greater benefit that ordinary men and women cannot see. Elena Majewska. Giovanni Batisti. Mirko Oliva . . . What's that neat little euphemism you use? Collateral damage?'

Palombo marched in between them and barked, 'Enough.'

'No!' Rennick cried.

The two men faced up to each other, and it was the Italian who backed down, reluctantly, with ill grace.

'These officers have lost a colleague,' Rennick said. 'They deserve something. They deserve more than we can give them.'

He glanced behind him at the doorway and ordered the men there to leave. Luca Palombo stood where he was, clearly unhappy with Rennick's actions.

'I'm no happier with these deaths than you are, nor do I understand why they occurred,' the American said, shaking his head. 'But how many people died on 9/11? In Madrid? Bali? London? Thousands. Perhaps thousands more in the future unless we win this war.'

'Ben,' Palombo murmured. 'This isn't necessary . . .'

'Yes, it is,' Rennick insisted. He gazed at each of them. 'Imagine we could place an operative in their midst. Not in the training camps. Not with the middle men. We're there already. I mean at the very top, a place we've never penetrated before. Imagine we could fake some event that persuaded them they could trust someone who was ours. Take him straight into their lair. You know their names. We all do. You know we've been trying to find them for years, and we never will, not without some traitor in their midst. A man who has their absolute confidence because of what he's done.'

'For that you'll sacrifice Rome?' Rosa asked him.

'For that I'd sacrifice my life. And a few others too. We all pay a price, one way or another. Willingly or otherwise.'

He checked himself, as if knowing this was too far, too soon.

'This is how things stand. Not pretty or tidy or safe, and that's why we told you to stay away. For your own good. There will be one more event. It will be spectacular. It will not cost a single innocent life. Come tomorrow,' he glanced outside, towards the empty street, 'things will start to return to normal. Here anyway. This I promise. And in a little while, a month perhaps, a year . . . we will find them, the men we've been looking for all these years. The seed we plant here will bear fruit.'

'Twenty years is a long time to be a stay-behind man, isn't it?' Teresa asked. 'Twenty years among people you're supposed to hate. Have you never heard of Stockholm syndrome? How do you know Andrea Petrakis is still yours?'

Palombo intervened. He pointed at Costa and Rosa and said, 'It's thanks to this man you two are still alive. Do you imagine that was an accident?'

'You were lucky,' Rennick said simply, looking at them. 'I was worried when he didn't call in. I'm sorry I didn't get there soon enough for your friend. I tried to tell you. This is a field operation. You step into it at your own risk. This is done with. We're going now. No more questions. No more answers. Good day.'

Palombo lingered as he left.

'Do not repeat one word of what you heard here to anyone,' he told them when Rennick was out of earshot. 'I will deal with you people later.'

They watched the two men join the masked officers in the street, climbing into their armoured black vans with shuttered windows and not a single descriptive word painted on the side. The vehicles rolled down the streets to the barricade, then passed through and headed towards the tightly guarded piazza of the Quirinale Palace.

– 9 –

Early afternoon. A time for events. Men and women flocking from their offices, walking to a favourite cafe or restaurant to sit down with a coffee and a *panino*, a plate of pasta, a dish of meat and vegetables from some neighbourhood *tavola calda*, discuss football and politics, work and the cost of living. New friendships and enmities would begin, old ones blossom, fade and end. Everywhere, from the drab commercial streets of Parioli to the tourist quarters of the Campo dei Fiori and the little alleys of the ghetto, there would be life, with its awkward idiosyncrasies, its argumentative logic and irregular serendipity.

All of this was gone now. The church bells tolled over a city that was waiting, timid, apprehensive, and in its heart quietly mutinous. No lovers walked hand in hand through the peaceful green park that hid the subterranean remains of Nero's Golden House. No students chattered happily on the steps of Ignatius Loyola's Collegio Romano in the *centro storico*. Among young and old, rich and poor, there was a sense of resentment, a growing loathing, of the criminals who had engendered this state, the politicians whose arrogance had invited their presence, and the masked, black-clad figures who had usurped their familiar police officers in blue – men and women who, though flawed, fallible and somewhat weather-beaten much of the time, were somehow all the more reassuring for that.

Rome stood still, as if holding its breath in anticipation of what might happen in its midst, regardless of the cares or intervention of any ordinary citizen. For the oldest of all, those who remembered the Forties, the atmosphere was bleakly reminiscent of the war, the German occupation, the mood of foreboding that preceded a cathartic outburst of violence by one party against another, turning everyday streets into bloody battle grounds.

Events . . .

In a quiet field by the circular tomb of Cecilia Metella, daughter-in-law of Crassus, who was in turn both nemesis to Spartacus and patron to a lowly politician named Julius Caesar, a family from Ciampino, aware of the smell of burned avgas still drifting from the nearby airport, sit down for a picnic, only to find that their dog, a Dalmatian cross, makes a discovery that means their bread and cheese and sausage go uneaten, and their bottle of cheap, weak Frascati wine untouched during the long hours it takes for the police to make their way to the Via Appia Antica.

Events . . .

Deep in the underside of the Quirinale Palace, in a stable built for the soldiers of a pope, a young Spanish woman, widowed and made childless by tragedy and misfortune, feels she can hear the minutes tick audibly by as she awaits the appointed moment, unable to take her eyes off the crucifix on the wall, or to extinguish from her mind the memories of a Basque plainchant in the Franciscan sanctuary of Aranzazu near her distant home, and the words, translated to her as a schoolchild by the parish priest who organized the visit.

> *Ne irascaris Domine, ne ultra memineris iniquitatis.*

> Be not angry, O Lord, and remember no longer
> our iniquity.

Events . . .

In the solitary Forum, hidden in the shadows of the towering ruins of the extant northern aisle of the Basilica of Maxentius and Constantine, Andrea Petrakis meets a ghost from the past, and finds there are no words to say after such a passage of time and circumstance. When his visitor departs, he has something to covet. He opens the large, expensive suitcase the visitor has brought and casts his eyes on the items there, the key that unlocks the final door.

It is the uniform of a serving cuirassier, a member of the

Corazzieri. The *tenuta di gran gala*, reserved for the most serious of occasions: white trousers and gauntlets, knee-high leather boots and a black jacket with epaulettes. The helmet is gleaming gold with a *criniera* mane of dark horse hair and a high, vivid red fabric flash on the left side. The breastplate is silver, etched with gold emblems, held at the shoulder and waist by leather straps.

By the side of the clothing lies a fine sword, the height of a man almost, encased in a silver scabbard.

Eyes gleaming, Andrea Petrakis unsheathes the weapon and runs the inside of his right index finger along the blade. A thin line of blood appears instantly on his skin. His fingers slip inside the boots to feel the padding, which will take his height close enough to the regulation 190 centimetres required of each *corazziere*. He licks the redness from his hand and thinks of the afternoon ahead.

Then he places everything back into the suitcase, picks it up and, when the time is right, steps out into the deserted Via dei Fori Imperiali, close to the guard posts at the foot of Trajan's Markets.

The route back to the Quirinale is still open to pedestrians, some of the way at least. He takes out his phone and, with steady fingers, sends a text.

A single word.

Now.

Part 6

IL DEMONE AZZURRO

We're an empire now, and when we act, we create our own reality. And while you're studying that reality – judiciously, as you will – we'll act again, creating other new realities, which you can study too, and that's how things will sort out. We're history's actors . . . and you, all of you, will be left to just study what we do.

Unnamed White House senior aide,
believed to be Karl Rove,
speaking to *New York Times* reporter Ron Suskind, 2002

- 1 -

Now.

Anna Ybarra had sat in the stable for what seemed like hours, staring at the little screen of the phone, waiting for the message. When it arrived she found herself transfixed by the single word there, one that took her mind away from the judgemental, twisted figure on the crucifix looking down at her from the wall, pleading, accusing through the dusty air.

It was important to concentrate on two things alone: the face of her husband, Josepe, and their little boy, Zeru. There were times that would never leave her. The three of them sitting on the thick grass in the hills on a hot summer's day, when the acres of farmland below were rich with crops and animals. Walking to the shop in the village through freezing winter gales and the downpours of spring, the boy's small gloved hand tight in hers.

Zeru growing from baby to toddler to little boy, yet with a bond, always – a special one – to her alone. It was as if some part of the umbilical cord remained, invisible yet real, a tie that only death could sever. She was a sensible, level-headed woman. That day would come. But not, she always believed, for a long time. Nor in the way it did, in the night, unexpected, full of noise and screaming and hatred.

She had never, not even in a nightmare, believed she might one day witness his tiny wooden coffin enter the hard ground alongside that of his father. Two still corpses hidden beneath soft white pine, the ones she loved most snatched from life by a cruel, faceless fate, ignored by the embarrassed state that bore responsibility for their deaths.

Zeru meant sky. She and Josepe had picked the name together

the very afternoon the doctor's scan told them the child would be a boy. A Basque name. One full of light and hope. A name that would last a lifetime, never shortened, never changed.

Holding his tiny, fragile body in the hospital bed in San Sebastián, she had imagined him old, wrinkled, weather-beaten, still living on their family farm, long after she and Josepe had departed the world. Later she would sometimes dream that she had seen him with children and grandchildren of his own, gathered round in his fading years, listening to stories, of life, the Basque land of Hernani, and the much-loved family that went before.

At some point he would gesture to the sky – sometimes bright and sunny, noisy with birds, sometimes the night, illuminated by a scattering of stars.

'That is my name,' the dream Zeru Ybarra said, in a voice that was strong and kind. 'That is me.'

The Euskaldunak, those who spoke the old, true language, would diminish in the decades to come. So Josepe said. Or perhaps that was his brother, the ETA man, talking, through him.

She wasn't so sure. They had given their son a true name, a good name, one that had stood their little community and the broader family that the Spanish called the Vascos in good stead over the centuries.

A name helped give meaning to a life. Sometimes – not always – it offered the consolation, the hint that something persisted, the way the plainchant of a distant monastery might linger in the memory, long after it should have been forgotten.

In the darkness of a stable in the palace of a pope, she murmured, 'Zeru . . .' and wondered, as the two syllables died in the air, whether there was a god anywhere to hear. She'd believed that once. But she'd believed many things, most of which had turned out to be nothing more than cruel lies, fantasies for the gullible.

Anna Ybarra did not look at the crucifix on the wall again. She picked up the saxophone case and opened it, checking and rechecking the weapon inside, the way the dark, silent, frightening men of the Taleban had shown her. Then she glanced at the instrument itself, gleaming gold, a complex machine, intricate with levers and strange, contorted workings, all to produce nothing more than a single musical note, one that a human being might utter through breath alone.

Now.

She took out the map Andrea Petrakis had given her. Even though she was inside the Quirinale complex, it was a long walk from the stable in the Via delle Scuderie back to the palace. He had stressed how important it was to take the right route, one that would avoid the guard posts as much as possible and take her into the staff quarters of the palace, then to the broad corridor along-side the Salone dei Corazzieri. The guests, presidents and prime ministers, spouses and civil servants, would be in that grand hall, he said, listening to music, sipping champagne. This was her moment, there for the taking.

Without looking back, she walked outside. There was a cobbled courtyard that cried out for horses and men in bright, anachronistic uniforms. No one was there. She scurried beneath the promenade at the edge of the square, staying in the dark, walking quickly, swinging the instrument case with her right arm, aware that the dress – dark velvet, probably more expensive than any she had ever worn – was so long it caught on her shoes as she strode towards the palace.

Two more courtyards. Then the smell of cooking and the noise of a kitchen. She checked her map. High on her right was the clock tower, its curious campanile reminiscent of Spain. Flags fluttered there. So many colours. So many different nations.

'Zeru, Josepe . . .' she whispered.

Another walkway beneath a vaulted ceiling, with arches to the side. On the far side of the patio beyond there was a small flight of stone steps up into the Quirinale proper. The corridor by the Salone dei Corazzieri lay only a few steps beyond.

The lilting tones of stringed instruments came to her over the din of kitchen sounds, arguments, plates and pans banging against one another, the half-remembered music of family. She could delay no more. With quick steps she walked out into the strong daylight.

'Signora, *Signora!*'

It was a man's voice. Strong and firm. She stopped, wondering at the source.

A figure emerged from the shadows. He was tall and muscular, a picture from a child's storybook: gleaming silver and gold breastplate, a polished helmet with a mare's-tail plume, high leather boots.

'Stop!' the officer bellowed as she continued to walk.

There was no alternative. She came to a halt in the middle of the patio, beneath the bright sun, conscious she was beginning to sweat a little.

He marched over to stand in the shadow of the bell tower, peering into her face. It was impossible to see what he looked like.

'Papers,' he ordered.

'I'm a musician, sir,' she said, fumbling for the envelope Petrakis had given her.

'You're late. The band's started already.'

'It was difficult getting here. No buses. No transport.'

'It's the same for everyone.' He examined the sheet of paper. It bore, she saw, the official seal of the president's office. 'I must see your ID.'

Her mind went blank. The only proof of identity she possessed was the press card of the American TV reporter.

'ID,' he insisted.

'I left it at home,' she said finally. 'I thought . . . a letter from the president's office was enough. I'm a musician. I'm late as it is. If I let them down again . . .'

She hated lying – and liars more than anything. Yet, when it was necessary, deceit seemed to come so easily.

'Please. They'll fire me, and I need the money. Playing an instrument,' she held up the case, 'is no way for a single mother to earn a living. Please . . .'

He sighed.

'You're not Italian.'

'Spanish. My husband's Italian. Wherever he is.'

He waved the letter Petrakis had given her.

'Don't walk around Rome without an ID. It's the law.'

'Thank you, thank you.'

He laughed, a little anyway.

'Why anyone would rush to be in a room with those people is beyond me. Play well. What's it they say?' He gestured with his arm, theatrically. 'Music has charms to soothe the savage breast.'

'They're the leaders of the world,' she replied primly.

'And we're their subjects. Quite.'

In a moment, heart still beating wildly in her chest, she found herself in the long, broad corridor that Petrakis had described. Just to be sure she checked her map once more. It was all as he had said. A palace more grand than anything she had ever seen. Tapestries hung from the walls like everyday drapes. Paintings decorated every spare inch so that scarcely a fraction was left bare. A line of long, open windows gave out onto the green gardens of the Quirinale that seemed to stretch forever, as if they were a private park made for a king.

The music grew louder as she walked, a light dance tune, the kind old people listened to, tapping their feet. It came, she knew, from the adjoining room, and was accompanied by the low murmur of voices.

She walked on towards the door he'd marked on the interior map, holding the instrument case firmly, feeling the handle grow slippery in her sweating fingers.

Zeru, Josepe . . .

Nothing can bring back the dead, she thought. But one might mark their memory in a way others would not forget.

The door she wanted looked as if it had been carved from old gold. Mythical creatures, dragons and unicorns, danced the length of the frame. She could see her son's face, clear in her memory.

Then a flash of recollection, cruel and relentless. It was the day they'd found a baby thrush in the garden, too young to fly, too weak to feed.

Josepe had quietly taken the creature to one side and, out of kindness, smothered it in an old blanket. Zeru had not witnessed this, had not been told, and yet, when he became aware of its disappearance, he knew somehow, understood intuitively what had happened, feeling the small creature's agony somewhere in the recesses of his young heart, crying for its loss.

What would he say now? her inner voice asked.

'Zeru was a little boy,' she answered softly, speaking to the window and the empty park beyond, feeling tears beginning to prick her eyes. 'A child is a child. What they know is a truth for them, a fairy tale. Not for the rest of us.'

She heard a sound from behind. Anna Ybarra's blood ran cold.

Turning, her hands still tight on the instrument case, with the primed Uzi inside, she found herself facing a solitary figure she recognized. The old man from the podium. He was now standing erect, amused, smoking a cigarette, slyly blowing the smoke out of the neighbouring window.

'Another truant I see, signora,' Dario Sordi, the president of Italy, remarked. 'Enjoying the view when you should, by all rights, be playing. Unless I'm mistaken.'

At that point something clouded his eyes and she knew immediately what it was. Recognition. Astonishment. Yet not alarm, though she failed to understand why.

'Perhaps I am,' he added.

– 2 –

Teresa Lupo wondered what kind of spectacle they made, sitting on the steps of the little church near the Quirinale looking miserable as Hell. They bunched together on the hard stone, silent, downcast, watched by the sour-faced saints high on Borromoni's curving facade. It wasn't a thinking silence, either. That was what worried her most. For the last couple of days she'd started to consider herself a cop, not a pathologist, and this blank inactivity bothered her. Cops were meant to rationalize, to discover, to snatch ideas out of thin air, then seize them, turn fancy into fact, something concrete, something one could act on. Not sit around waiting. Peroni hadn't done this, not quite. He'd disappeared round the corner for some unannounced reason. A hunt for the bathroom, she guessed. But the rest of them . . .

She turned to Falcone, whose long, tanned face was in his hands as he stared down at the empty street, and asked, 'So what do we do now? Just sit here like tourists waiting for the bus to turn up?'

'Short of any better suggestions . . .' the inspector murmured.

'But it's not supposed to be like this!'

Rosa was watching her.

'What is it supposed to be like?' the young police officer wondered.

'We're supposed to be finding things out. *Working* things out. Seeing some . . . rational link between what's going on.'

'"Rational link"?' Falcone demanded. 'What an extraordinarily old-fashioned view of police work.'

'What else is there?'

His lean face wrinkled with distaste.

'I sometimes wonder if you've taken a moment's notice of anything I've tried to teach you over the years.'

'You? Teach me?'

'In terms of policing,' he deferred. 'When it comes to . . . *science*,' he said the word as if it had a bad taste, 'I value your advice immensely. Not that science is doing us many favours.'

'Leo!' She pointed in the direction of the Quirinale Palace. 'Over the road a bunch of faceless grey spooks are concocting some kind of fake terrorist incident. Here, in our city. All in the hope that the so-called perpetrator will then be allowed to return to the bandit lands of Afghanistan and lead those selfsame spooks straight to the evil bastards they've been chasing, with no success whatsoever, for years. Which seems pretty unlikely if you ask me, not that I'm an expert in such matters, thank God.'

'It would seem that way,' he agreed.

'Well? People have died because of this nonsense. One of our own included . . .'

'You heard the American's apology for that. We were warned not to interfere.'

'These are criminal acts.'

He shrugged.

'Would you like me to arrest someone?'

'Yes!'

'How? Esposito won't countenance it. Palombo would overrule it if I tried. Besides, if they're right . . .'

'Don't you try that on with me for one moment,' she retorted. 'The ends cannot justify the means.'

He frowned.

'It's easy to say that, isn't it? But what if you could turn back time? What if,' he scratched his silver goatee, 'you could prevent New York, Bali, all those other enormities? Just by torturing a single human being? A guilty man. A murderer who would murder thousands more if he could . . .'

'Doesn't work, and you know it. You'd have to torture a thousand human beings, and most of them wouldn't be guilty at all.'

'If you could have killed Hitler before he ordered Auschwitz?' Rosa asked.

'Any argument that requires the mention of Hitler in order to succeed is doomed from the start, as far as I'm concerned.'

'Then what?' he asked.

Peroni was walking up the street, his hands filled with cones of *gelati*.

It was beautiful ice cream. Her favourite: pistachio. A thin green line of it had melted down his lapel and he hadn't noticed. She wiped it off with a tissue as he sat down next to her.

'Your job's nothing like mine, is it?' she said.

'I never claimed it was,' Peroni answered, looking puzzled.

'Our occupation, such as it is,' Falcone cut in, 'principally consists of assembling unseen shapes in a darkened room, then waiting for the arrival of daylight to see if any of them resemble, in some small way, what we expected.'

Peroni looked around at them and said, 'Normally I would ask you to bring me up to date on things. But in this instance . . .'

She patted him on the knee, so hard he shut up.

'I was simply coming to realize what a rotten police officer I'd make. Spending all this time running your hands through meaningless dust . . .'

Peroni considered this and said, 'I think you mean dust for which we have yet to find a meaning.'

Teresa laughed and then pecked him on the cheek, not minding that they saw. She loved this man, for all the right reasons. In a way, she loved all of them. They were a team. A family. A group of people bound to one another by invisible, yet forceful ties. This was one more reason why it hurt so much that there were no shapes to work with, no darkened room, no prospect of daylight. It was such a joy to see the spark in their faces the moment some glimmer of revelation appeared.

The pathologist finished her cone, got up and stood beneath the grim stare of Borromini's stone saints. It took Silvio Di Capua a second to answer the phone, no more, and a minute to fill her in on his thinking.

'Where's Elizabeth?' she asked.

'Gone out.'

'Gone out where?'

'She said she was meeting a friend. I'm a forensic scientist, not a bodyguard. Besides, she can look after—'

'Shut up, Silvio! I'm trying to think.'

'You called to tell me that?'

'No.' She remembered now. 'I called to talk to Elizabeth.'

'Ask me.'

'You're a man. You think the wrong way. Like me.'

'Intellectual cross-dressing can become very confusing, whether you're watching or taking part.'

'Very clever.' She thought of the numerals. There had to be something there.

'When you start a message with a number, it usually signifies either a time or a date,' she suggested.

'Been there, looked at that. It can't be a date, not if it refers to the summit. The twelfth of the month is already past. And if it's time . . .'

'It can't be today, since we're past midday. But it has to be.'

'Why?'

'Because the big men in the Quirinale Palace say so. Don't ask for an explanation. You wouldn't believe it.'

'Then it's not a time and it's not a date. So what is it? Can I pair it with the following numeral and make something?'

'You tell me,' she demanded.

'No. I can't.'

'Thank you for that.'

'*Non è niente.*'

'These are Roman numerals. Latin.'

'No arguing there.'

'So why do you assume that the number twelve would mean back then what it does now?'

'Twelve is twelve,' he said with a long, pained sigh. 'Numbers are numbers. Gloriously immutable. That's why we do what we do. That's why the sky never falls.'

'You're missing my point.' Two points actually, the more she thought about it. 'Petrakis thinks he's living in the past. Maybe part of the joke is that he writes that way too. What did the number twelve mean to Julius Caesar? Midday? Possibly. But they weren't walking around with watches on their wrists, were they? I don't know. Check it out.'

'Good one,' he agreed. 'Will do.'

'And, also, check out the obvious.'

There was a pause on the line. The two of them had this discussion from time to time. About the way Silvio Di Capua was an astonishingly learned and sharp individual, one so clever that occasionally he was unable to see something that stood directly in front of his own face.

'The obvious?' he asked, sounding a little scared.

'Even if we don't know what the first number stands for,' Teresa said patiently, 'this would signify that the second set possesses some separate meaning. Not time. Not date. Not . . . I don't know. Perhaps just the same as the other numbers we've had to deal with.'

Somehow she could sense fear inside his silence.

'Silvio,' she asked, growing a little hot under the collar. 'You have looked, haven't you? Shakespeare? The text Petrakis used for the other codes?'

'The other codes had three numbers,' he said hesitantly.

'So has this one, if the first number refers to something else. What is it?'

'II. I. CLXXIII.'

'Act Two. Scene One. Line one hundred and seventy-three. Possibly. Check out the time. Check out the verse. Get back to me as soon as you can.'

'On it,' he said quickly. 'Anything else?'

There was nothing she could think of and she said so. The others were watching her. Peroni had a new blob of pistachio ice cream on his suit.

'Well?' Costa asked hopefully.

'Science,' she told him. 'Boring old integers. Nothing you philosopher-types need bother your clever heads about at all.'

– 3 –

'*Dígame*,' Dario Sordi murmured, looking at the young woman in the long velvet dress, a large, closed instrument case in her hand, an expression of fear and anticipation on her plain, intense face.

The corridor by the Salone dei Corazzieri was empty. The room beyond, one he knew so well, every glittering inch engraved upon his memory, reverberated to the sound of light music and the low chatter of voices in many languages. He had been glad to escape. Smoking was an enjoyable excuse, nothing more.

'Sorry?' the young woman said.

'I was under the impression we'd met before,' Sordi answered before throwing his half-finished cigarette out of the window, into the gardens beyond, with only the faintest feeling of guilt.

'I don't think so, sir. I'm a musician . . .'

'What instrument?' he asked.

She hesitated.

'Brass.'

'My late wife played the flute. Not very well, if I'm being honest. Is that brass too?'

She thought for a moment and answered, 'Of course.'

He came and stood closer to her.

'The modern flute may be made of metal, but it's still woodwind. Any musician would know that. I would not expect it of a television reporter necessarily.' Sordi recalled the single word of Spanish he'd heard when he tried to call Costa on the private phone, the one that was supposed to be their link alone. 'Or someone who was simply a voice in the dark in Tarquinia.'

She pushed him back firmly with her right hand. Her face, which seemed initially full of a simple honesty, was contorted by anger. He fell against a radiator and found himself clutching at a curtain to stay upright. When he regained his balance she was fumbling at the instrument case, releasing the catch so that the front fell down of its own accord. Inside, held by what he assumed to be fasteners for some large instrument, there was a weapon, too large for a pistol, too small to be a conventional military rifle. These things had changed so much since the Second World War and he had never had a great deal of interest in firearms, even then.

The thing looked efficient and deadly.

Her trembling fingers snatched at the barrel, then the stock. The case fell to the floor. Her hand found the butt of the weapon, the trigger guard, and she started to grip it in a way that suggested some skill and intent.

The pistol, almost a child's toy, was aimed his way, though not as directly as her wide-eyed, determined gaze.

'This is the Quirinale Palace,' Dario Sordi told her. 'At any moment there will be security people to interrupt our little discussion. They will not wait to ask questions, signora. They will see you with that thing and shoot you dead.'

'They're all in there,' she retorted, nodding at the closed door into the Salone. 'With the important people. Where you should be.'

'Important?' He frowned. 'You flatter me.'

The barrel moved slowly towards him, like the black nose of a hungry beast. He raised his hands – which was, he supposed, what she wanted.

Her sharp eyes dashed towards the door to the Salone. Sordi caught the reflection in the adjoining window: a tall, straight-backed old man who hated to see himself; a young, plain, yet striking woman, her face distorted by fury and doubt.

He took the opportunity to move a step closer.

She saw his intentions and the barrel swung straight back towards him, dashed forward, stabbed him in the chest. Not a painful blow. More of a prod. A threat.

'Why are you not afraid of me?' she asked, pointing the sleek black weapon towards him again as a warning.

He laughed. There seemed nothing else to do.

'I'm almost eighty years old,' Dario Sordi replied. 'I've been smoking since the age of thirteen, and drinking wine, good and bad, rather longer than that. On occasion I argue so much my blood pressure attains levels my doctor believes physically impossible. If I live another five seconds or another five years, what does it matter?'

She was silent, listening.

'They used to make me read Horace when I was a schoolboy,' he added. 'I remember one line in particular . . .' It was the day of the Via Rasella, and he'd spent the morning poring over a copy of the Odes, struggling with the language. '*Sed omnes una manet nox.* "But the same night awaits us all." What exactly am I supposed to fear, signora? Such a small and commonplace creature as death . . . ?'

He was glad there were no Corazzieri there for some reason. Glad he had the chance to try to talk to her.

'Latin's the language of priests,' she hissed.

'Among others.'

'When I go in there,' she told him, pointing with the gun at the glittering doorway, as if it might transport her to a different realm, 'don't follow.'

'I may be just another citizen in the world beyond this place,' he told her. 'But in the Quirinale I go where I want.'

The barrel rose and pointed straight into his face. She didn't speak.

He held his hands up, smiled and said, 'You asked me a question only a few hours ago. Were you happy with the answer?'

She shook her head, in doubt, not negation.

'These demons that pursue you must be hungry indeed,' Dario Sordi said.

'You don't know my demons.'

'No,' he admitted. 'Not your present ones.' He tried to stare straight at her, but she wouldn't meet his gaze. 'I know the ones to come, though.' His voice descended a little, became gruff, became quieter. 'Here is something I never told anyone before – anyone except my wife, that is, and she's gone.' He stiffened, feeling cold. 'Their faces don't die. They never leave you. I can see those two young Germans I murdered now. The surprise in their eyes. As if everything was a joke, even life itself.'

'I don't want to hear.'

'Perhaps, but I wish to say it. Sometimes I wake up in the night, sweating, mumbling, sad old words from a sad old man, you might say. But it's not fear that wakes me. It's regret. It's remembering . . . It's the fear that, when I die, those faces may be the last thing I ever see.'

The weapon rose and pointed directly at him.

'I lost my family!'

'I lost my father. My uncle. The Germans murdered them in the reprisals. Some would say I helped kill them. Some say that still. Yet today I have a very good friend who is a Berliner, and both of us are much too old and sensible to mention any of this. He served during the war. He was a German. What do you expect?'

Her eyes flared with fury. She snatched a look at the door to the room beyond.

'Do you ever stop to wonder how much blood is on their hands?' she demanded. 'Blood in Europe. In the East. More than I could spill in a lifetime.'

Dario Sordi rarely lost his temper. Anger was, he felt, beneath someone of his age. Also, once lost, his temper proved difficult to rein in. At that moment he was dismayed to recognize a red ire rising in him that would brook no control.

'I never forget that,' he retorted, his voice rising to a shout. 'Not for one second. It's why I am here. Why I made this journey. I lived through a war that ripped apart this world of ours. I watched my father's torn corpse dug out of the Ardeatine caves by men with picks in their hands and tears in their eyes.' His arm came down, his long, bloodless index finger jabbed at her through the bright, golden air streaming from the palace windows. 'You travel the world as if it's a place of no consequence. You play with toys that kill men at the push of a button, miles away. It saves you looking into their eyes, I imagine. How brave. How noble! Do not, signora, seek to lecture me . . .'

'Shut up!' she screamed. 'Shut up—'

The weapon rotated swiftly in her strong arms and the stock flew at him, dashing up to his head. Dario Sordi felt a fierce, sharp hurt in his temple as the blow fell upon him, and stumbled to the floor, shouting, swearing.

Perhaps he blacked out. He wasn't sure. There was a moment when everything seemed to fade, when the bright, beautiful corridor in the Quirinale Palace disappeared for a moment, and in its place he found himself in a narrow cobbled Roman street in front of two men in uniform, found that he was staring at them from behind the eyes of another, younger body, one he had long forgotten – a child, he knew that, a boy who was taking out a weapon from the grey, grubby fabric of his threadbare school coat.

He could hear the dream voice of the German taunting him again.

So you're a coward now, are you? A little late for us, isn't it?

'It's a little late for everyone,' Sordi found himself whispering, his eyes straying fearfully towards the mirrored door that led into the Salone dei Corazzieri.

It was open, and as his eyes began to focus on the stilled bodies in their lounge suits and cocktail gowns beyond the door, he became aware that the soft, simple music of the orchestra had stumbled to an uncertain and awkward halt.

– 4 –

The offices of CESIS, the Executive Committee for Intelligence and Security Services, had not moved in forty years. The organization that liaised between the civilian and military arms of the Italian intelligence services, SISDE and SISMI respectively, occupied a six-storey former outpost of the Vatican bureaucracy in the Via delle Quattro Fontane. It was a nondescript building that stretched from the busy straight road running past Borromini's church to the narrow lane of the Via dei Giardini, which ran the length of the border wall of the Quirinale gardens. The offices possessed one spectacular attraction: a roof terrace with magnificent views of the city, all the way to the Vatican, and, from the very edge, down into the verdant hectares of the presidential palace itself.

Elizabeth Murray had attended countless parties there, for intelligence-community weddings and retirements, and more private engagements, where attendance was tightly restricted to those in the higher echelons of this secretive, though inwardly congenial world. She had little doubt that the place would now be put to good use, and was able to confirm this as her taxi, after a circuitous journey, dropped her at the very edge of the Quirinale security cordon, opposite the Palazzo Barberini, at the head of the Via Rasella.

There was a sniper on the roof, exactly where experience told her to look for one.

She had called ahead to check who was on duty and, after navigating the switchboard, using all the persuasion and name-dropping she could manage, was pleased with the eventual answer: Carlo Belfiore, a junior spook when she first met him, now a senior CESIS official.

A good, honest man, like most of those she worked with. It didn't surprise her to find he was at work. It would have been impossible to persuade him to go home in circumstances such as these.

She waited on a hard leather bench in reception for five minutes until Belfiore arrived. He had less hair and more flesh, but the same broad, easy smile. They hugged, kissed. He looked at her stick and then himself and said, 'We're all getting older, aren't we?'

'So what?' she wondered.

His smile slackened a little.

'This is a busy time, Elizabeth. It's wonderful to see you. But to be honest . . .'

'I'm sorry, Carlo. I should have given you notice. If I'd known I'd find Rome like this. Who could have guessed the Blue Demon would rise from the grave?'

'Not me. That's for sure.'

He looked at her.

'You know more about them than anyone else.'

'Possibly . . .'

'Were you surprised?'

She thought for a moment and then said, 'It never felt quite dead. Did it?'

He seemed disappointed by the reply.

'Come. I have time for a coffee. And something to show you.'

Belfiore took out his security card and flashed it through the machine, ushering her through the gate before him. They hadn't had toys like that two decades before. Then they got in the lift and rose to the fifth floor, the one she knew so well, and walked down a familiar corridor into a large office overlooking the Quirinale gardens.

She peered at the expanse of perfectly kept lawns, flower beds and patches of shrubbery. On the palace roof opposite there was a single, black-clad figure with a rifle in its hands.

'You seem more relaxed than I expected,' she observed.

'We're nearly done for the day, thank God. It's all in the papers. I'm not breaking clearance. I wouldn't. Not even for you. Soon the visitors move on to the Vatican. After that we're done. All those famous guests become someone else's problem. Until eleven, when they want to go to bed, and then their people can take care of everything.' He smiled. 'Tomorrow they go home and we can try to go back to normal. Try to find out what the hell has been going on here. Giovanni Batisti—'

'You knew him?' she asked, unable to take her eyes off the office. It was so different from how she remembered it, and dominated by technology: two computer screens, three telephones, a couple of mobiles on the desk too.

'I worked with him on the preparations. A nice man. Missed his family like crazy. We do this for a living. He did it out of common decency. Look where it got him.'

'A tragedy. Do you like my old lair?'

Carlo Belfiore nodded.

'But it was better with you in it. Queen Elizabeth the Third.'

'You never dared call me that to my face.'

'Of course not. But now I can. It was a compliment, you know. The way you remembered everything. Understood the links. The possibilities. You were a legend, Elizabeth. You are a legend.'

She laughed.

'I'm a distant memory, a name on a dusty plaque. And I was well aware of that nickname, by the way.'

He sat down. She took the chair opposite, facing the window and the empty expanse of the gardens beyond.

She stared into his genial, intelligent face.

'Can I help?' Elizabeth Murray asked.

'No,' Belfiore replied immediately, shaking his head. 'I'm sorry. You have no clearance. Times are different. Rules. Regulations. We are not as free as we once were.'

'You said I knew the Blue Demon better than anyone.'

'If we had the time . . .' He thought for a moment. 'When the summit is over and the circus has moved on. There will be work to do. I could arrange a temporary attachment.' He looked embarrassed for a moment. 'We have accommodation you could use. I heard you were running a farm or something. In New Zealand. On your own. There can't be much money in that. Pensions . . .' He looked around the office. 'One becomes so engrossed in the present that it's easy to forget the future is just around the corner.'

'It is too,' she agreed. 'That's kind. And in the meantime?'

He frowned.

'In the meantime you must enjoy Rome as best you can.' His eyes were watching the messages on his computer, more than her. Carlo Belfiore's face had turned somewhat paler. 'You have to excuse me now. There's something I must deal with. I'll call for an officer to show you out.'

'I can find my own way. I worked here long enough.'

'Yes, yes,' he mumbled, eyes glued to the screen. A phone began to ring. He snatched at it, cupped the handset, looked at her and said, 'I'm sorry. This is important. Please. Call me at the weekend. Come for dinner. We would love that.'

Then he was talking, rapidly, eyeing her in a way she could read. It was a private conversation, one she wasn't supposed to hear.

Elizabeth Murray got up and walked out of her old office. The corridor was deserted. This was the executive part of the building, never a place for much in the way of visible activity.

A narrow set of stairs led to the roof terrace. She could remember walking up it, half-tipsy, so many years ago in the company of beloved colleagues, some gone, some dead on duty, a few in parts of the world where their bodies still rested, undiscovered. The fallen.

Behind an ancient door at the top of the stairs there was a small hut, like a sentry box, a place to store watering cans and gardening equipment for the handful of flowerpots and features that one of the green-fingered intelligence specialists liked to keep there.

The bottom door was unlocked. This was a secure location. There was no need.

Steadily, one step at a time, leaning on the stout shepherd's crook she'd bought at a market in Dunedin, she ascended the stairs, opening the door at the top to find herself inside the little cabin at the summit.

A memory returned: drunken kisses exchanged with a young, pretty secretary towards the end of a retirement party. A rash moment, one that could have been costly. No one liked an officer who stood out from the ordinary, not in the intelligence services. They were under no illusions about her preferences. It was simply bad form to display them. This was prudence, not prejudice. Sexual dysfunction, as it was then perceived, might lead to blackmail or worse.

The secretary had been very pretty, though, and her abrupt move to a more mundane department the following day, on grounds of pure necessity, was a loss Elizabeth Murray had privately regretted for some time.

The watering cans and gardening paraphernalia were still ranged along the shelving on the wall adjoining the exterior door. Next to them was a black nylon jacket of the kind worn by the more arcane security services.

In the right-hand pocket was a plastic, sealed ID card. She held it to the light streaming from the cabin's single tiny window and saw the crest of the Ministry of the Interior and a name: Domenico Leone. He was a senior civil servant in the ministry, it said, and nothing more.

She placed her large thumb over the photo so that only the crest was visible and a lazy man might think it referred to someone else altogether. Then she stepped out onto the terrace of the CESIS building, heading immediately for the Via dei Giardini side, where she had seen the sniper's silhouette from the street.

A tall, sturdy man was stretched out on the concrete there, in black combat uniform, vest and cap. In his hands was a rifle with a telescopic sight.

'Domenico?' she shouted, holding the ID high, still obscuring the photo. 'Domenico?'

She tried to remember what it was like to talk as a true Roman: with a short, guttural accent, and abbreviated diction.

'*Si?*' the officer said, turning, and looking puzzled. 'I'm sorry, signora . . . I don't know.'

'No, you don't. They brought me in from Milan. There's a change of plan. Belfiore wants you to do something else. He needs you to report to his office now.'

He shuffled up to a crouch, took off the cap and scratched his balding head.

'But the roof . . .'

'The gardens can go without sniper cover for five minutes, Officer. Have you seen a thing in any case?'

'No. But in the palace . . .' Another puzzled look. 'I thought something was happening.'

'Champagne and canapés. Wouldn't you need a drink, if you were going to spend the rest of the evening in the Vatican?'

Domenico Leone guffawed.

'You bet,' he answered, then hauled himself to his feet and walked over to the open cabin door.

She came with him. When he got there, something fell from Elizabeth Murray's wrist. The officer looked, saw her stick and said, 'You've lost your watch.'

'Damned strap,' she muttered. 'I must get it changed.'

She eased forward on the shepherd's crook.

'No, no, signora. Please.'

He bent down to retrieve it. She thought of all the training she'd done thirty years ago or more. How they'd practise on one another from time to time.

Then she brought down the shiny oak handle of her stick hard on his head. He stumbled to both knees. She fell on him, crooked her right arm round his neck and brought her left in to pinch on the carotid and the jugular, squeezing them.

Leone went still in a couple of seconds and slumped to the ground in the shadow of the cabin door. She picked up her watch and slipped it back on her wrist. It was a struggle to drag him inside. When they got there, she stripped off his vest and cap. There was a ball of twine in the garden equipment. Carefully – there was no hurry, and he would be this way for a few hours – she bound his feet and hands, then gagged him with her scarf. Finally, to be sure, she passed several lengths of washing line around his chest before strapping him tight against an old sink unit.

He was starting to wake by then, with fury in his eyes.

'*Scusami*,' she said, then went outside and picked up his rifle.

Weapons were weapons. Back home in New Zealand she was used to hunting the wild black razorback pig. It was a monster, wildly aggressive and capable of slaughtering a dozen or more lambs in a single night. The beast's one saving grace was that it tasted good, which was another reason to shoot it.

Domenico Leone's rifle was nothing like the .30-06 Springfield she used to kill Captain Cook's feral boars. The thing was surely far more deadly. But it wasn't hard to work out.

She walked to the cabin to find the jacket hung on the peg behind the door, put it on, and then the protection vest over that. The cap just about fitted if she tucked in her hair. She was about Leone's size. That was as good as it could be. There would be snipers on other rooftops. If they peered at her through binoculars, they'd see through the ruse. But the snipers were looking at the Quirinale and the surrounding streets, not at each other. Or so she hoped.

Elizabeth Murray went back to the corner of the terrace where he'd been stationed when she arrived. There was a low stool there and, on the wall, a black fabric and padding gun rest. The sniper rifle fitted neatly between the two mounts set at each side. She let it fall into place, then leaned down and began to adjust the telescopic sight. It was pretty much set perfectly already.

It took a moment for her to juggle her bulky frame into the right position, one where the weapon felt comfortable. Then she bent down to the eyepiece, peering, squinting, hunting. The cross-hairs ranged the gardens of the Quirinale, from spectacular flower bed to leafy, artificial glade, from classical statue to dainty, ornate pond.

Finally her sights settled on the stone bench beneath the wicker canopy, by the handsome young figure of Hermes.

It would be an easy, clean shot. She left the rifle idly poised against the rest and checked her watch, wondering how long she would have to wait.

– 5 –

Anna Ybarra pushed open the mirrored door, not knowing what to expect. A room full of strangers. A brief storm of violence before her own life was snatched away. She had thrust Dario Sordi's questions from her mind. They were too close to her. They hurt.

With the little Uzi tight in her right arm, her finger on the trigger, she burst into the gilded hall and found herself stumbling noisily into a table laden with glasses and canapés, sending wine and little plates scattering onto the hard, shiny floor.

The *salone* was like something out of a child's picture book, full of paintings and gilt, with high, bright windows to one side.

Beneath a forest of chandeliers sat an orchestra to her left – the women, she could just see, wearing long, dark velvet gowns identical to the one she had found in the stable in the Via delle Scuderie. They had stopped playing, as had the men. In front of them, in the main body of the hall, were figures in formal suits, women in elegant dresses that seemed unsuited for a hot Roman afternoon, all of them frozen in silence.

Every eye in the room was on her.

She scanned them, searching for the words. Some of these faces were familiar: politicians, men mainly, whose features appeared daily on the television, in newspapers, everywhere, usually smiling, always in control.

Now they seemed smaller, more human. A few were moving in front of the women by their sides, as if to block them from what was about to occur. One or two had begun to stride swiftly towards the back. From the corner of her eyes she could see others, anonymous figures emerging from the shadows, starting to stir into action, and she knew who they were, knew what they would do.

There was nothing to say, nothing that had true meaning. Only two things ran through her head, Zeru and Josepe – Zeru more than any – though the words of Dario Sordi continued to haunt her, and she knew she could never, as she'd intended, scream the names of her slaughtered child and dead husband at these elegant strangers as they stood, frozen with fear.

None of them would understand. None of them would know.

The trigger of the Uzi fell beneath her finger, the way they'd taught her in the hot, primitive training camp on the wild stretch of the Helmand river where the NATO forces never dared to venture. Anna Ybarra held the Uzi tightly and began a sweep of the bodies in front of her, not looking too closely at the suits and cocktail gowns, not thinking about what came next.

Her finger jerked the trigger. The weapon awoke. There was a sudden staccato burst of sound, and the Uzi leaped in her grip like a wild animal woken from a terrible dream.

Someone screamed. A woman. A man.

She arced the shuddering weapon once to the right, once to the left, and then it was silent.

Too soon, she thought. In Helmand it had lasted longer.

Desperately, she tried again. There was nothing. The magazine had jammed, perhaps. The thing was dead.

She let it drop from her fingers, to clatter on the shiny, polished floor of the Salone dei Corazzieri.

Dark, anonymous figures from the periphery of the hall were starting to close in. They held handguns the way the Taleban did – in a taut, outstretched arm, threatening death with a fierce, unwavering certainty.

Her hands fell to her sides. Tears filled her eyes, tears of fury at her own failure and her stupidity.

There was not a single casualty among the crowd in front of her. Men gripped women by their shoulders. Some of those who had retreated to the rear of the hall were beginning to return. One more she recognized from the TV: a man who had been the first to flee, Ugo Campagnolo, the prime minister.

No one had died. No one had been hurt. Whatever bullets she'd managed to loose off before the weapon failed had simply disappeared into thin air, as if they'd never existed at all.

Anna Ybarra thought of the Kenyan Joseph Priest and the fiasco at the Trevi Fountain. How he'd fought to do what Deniz Nesin had told him, only to find it didn't work at all, not until Andrea Petrakis, unseen, had pushed the button.

Dead Joseph. Dead Deniz. Dead . . .

The armed men in suits were so near she could see the curling wires emerging from their earpieces. She raised her arms, realizing she was the spectacle now, the intended victim all along.

Quite deliberately she closed her eyes, wishing she could say something that held meaning, if only there was time, and the right words.

A hard and powerful blow caught her, sent her wheeling off balance, down to the polished floor. She looked, found herself thinking, automatically, that she ought to locate the source of the pain.

A tall, stiff, commanding figure was over her, and he was angry, bellowing – at the circling figures, at everyone, it seemed.

It was Dario Sordi, and he was shouting a name she didn't recognize.

'Ranieri! *Ranieri!*'

The president's hands reached down to grip her shoulders, tugging her torso towards him. She found herself reaching for his long legs, holding on to them, like a child seeking protection.

'Dammit. Ranieri!' he yelled again, and finally a man in a blue serge suit forced his way to the front, through the line of figures with guns. Behind him came several officers in ceremonial uniform, shining breastplates, swords, plumed helmets.

There was another individual too, one with a long, angry face.

This one pushed his way to the front, stared at Sordi and said, 'Sir . . .'

'Be quiet, Palombo. I'm in charge here. Ranieri—'

'*Sir!*' the angry one cut in. 'You must leave this to my people.'

'Leave what, exactly?' the president roared. 'An execution? Or rendition, as you call it, to some country beyond our control? I see no casualties here. No danger . . .'

'We were lucky.'

'Good. The state police shall take this woman into their custody. They will decide what charges she must face. Corazzieri!'

The silver uniforms barged through the suits. Anna Ybarra let go of the old man's legs, struggled to her feet, taking the hand of one of the soldiers, finding herself in their midst. The one who'd helped her up did not let go. She looked at him and saw the face of the officer she'd met, and deceived, in the courtyard outside. She glanced at the shining floor, feeling ashamed and lost and confused.

'I cannot allow this,' the one called Palombo declared. 'I must insist—'

Sordi stepped forward and confronted him.

'You cannot allow? I am the president of Italy. This is the Quirinale Palace. These are the Corazzieri, and they do my bidding. Officers!' He turned and gazed at them. 'Take this woman to my apartment to await the police. Allow in no one without my permission.'

'Mr President . . .'

'Those are my orders.'

'Mr President.' It was the one he'd called Ranieri who was speaking. 'You're bleeding.'

Sordi wiped his forehead with the arm of his jacket, then stared at the stain on his shirt sleeve.

'Well, at least it shows I'm alive.'

Then he made his way to the front to address the crowd.

'Ladies, gentlemen,' Dario Sordi told them. 'I apologize for this interruption. We will get to the bottom of it, I promise. And I am grateful that the only injury is a scratch to an old man's head. Now . . .'

He glanced at the orchestra, and then the assembled crowd.

'I think this event is at an end. Your transport leaves for the Vatican very soon, perhaps sooner than originally intended. I suggest you retire to your quarters here till then. My staff will be in touch. Please . . .'

The man in the blue serge suit took her by the arm. They left by the ornate gilt door through which she had entered, never expecting to live for a minute or more. In her head she could hear the sound of the plainchant in the quiet distant monastery she had visited as a child.

The words echoed in her head, her lips moved to match them.

Be not angry, O Lord, and remember no longer our iniquity.

The imposing figure of Dario Sordi caught up with them as they strode along the corridor, matching the younger men step for step.

'Get this woman into the hands of Costa and his friends as soon as you can,' he ordered.

- 6 -

Five minutes later Falcone's blue Lancia set off for the Quirinale. They left Teresa at the church. There was no room in the car, no time for arguments. She was to find her own way back to San Giovanni while the others extracted the woman from the Corazzieri. Afterwards they would attempt to get their captive safely into the maximum-security area in the basement of the Questura in the back streets behind the Pantheon.

Costa took the wheel. Falcone talked his way through the security cordons, more easily than any of them expected, then spent the rest of the journey on the phone. Peroni and Rosa sat in the back, silent, expectant, listening to the car radio. They pulled onto the pale cobbles of the Quirinale piazza to be greeted by a sea of armoured limousines looking as if they were preparing to remove the palace guests elsewhere.

A group of officers in gleaming silver stepped outside the portico as they drew up. Falcone told Costa to deal with it, and quickly.

'Captain?'

Ranieri was at the head of his men. He moved slightly to the left, to reveal a dark-skinned young woman in a long black velvet dress, in the midst of the *corazzieri*. She looked shell-shocked. Her eyes seemed bleary, as if she couldn't decide whether to burst into tears or not.

'This woman is called Anna Ybarra. She is a Spanish citizen. She will confess to an attempted terrorist attack.' He nodded at the palace behind. 'The president wishes you to charge her as soon as possible. Once she is inside our legal system, it will be difficult for anyone to take her out of it. This is important.'

'Is anyone hurt?' Costa asked.

'No,' Ranieri replied quickly. 'Turn on the TV when you have the time. Palombo is about to brief the media. He can't wait.' The tall officer coughed into his hand and stared at Costa. 'The gun jammed, it seems. The bullets didn't work. Something like that. We will discover. Not that she was to know. Perhaps we were very lucky. Perhaps . . . We can discuss this later. You have little time.'

Costa glanced at the woman. She wouldn't meet his eye. He knew why.

'We've met before,' he said, and led her to the rear of the car where Peroni stood, beckoning her to sit between him and Rosa.

Falcone was still on the phone, talking, listening, issuing rapid instructions to someone on the other end.

Costa got in the driving seat and gunned the muscular engine.

'Esposito is at a liaison meeting with the Carabinicri,' the inspect-or revealed when he cut thc call. 'He'll know what's happening by now, but at least he isn't in the Questura.' He reached beneath the dashboard, pulled out the blue light, opened the passenger window and set it on the roof. 'Let's get there before he does.'

Costa wheeled the powerful saloon round the cobbles, sending the limousine chauffeurs scattering, filling the Roman afternoon with the screech of a klaxon.

They roared down a deserted Via XXIV Maggio, into the road-block near the Via dei Fori Imperiali. Falcone had the window down before thcy cven got to the Carabinieri post there, screaming at them to open the barriers into the empty road by the scattered ruins of the Forum.

For once the men in dark blue didn't argue. The street was open to them the moment the Lancia arrived. They were through, racing towards the Piazza Venezia.

Only a few pedestrians wandered across the bare cobbles, anxiously striding out of the way of the approaching police car, with its siren blaring and light flashing.

Costa kept up a steady pace, flung the Lancia round into the main street of Vittorio Emanuele, found a further Carabinieri unit opening another barrier for them, one that would take them back into the traffic beyond Palombo's ring of steel.

'Everyone's very cooperative,' Peroni observed from the back.

Costa glanced in the mirror. The big man and Rosa sat close up to the Ybarra woman, who seemed lost, as if none of this were quite real.

Peroni had a point. This had been so easy.

He forced a half-empty bus onto the pavement, then manoeuvred his way round to the side street leading into the Renaissance warren of alleys and lanes that made up the *centro storico*. The Piazza di San Michele Arcangelo was just a few blocks away. An everyday location. Befuddled tourists who wandered into the piazza, from the Pantheon, the Piazza Navona and all the other great sights, saw nothing special in the Polizia di Stato's little square. Only a small shop, a tiny cafe, some offices and a tall, grimy building surrounded by squad cars parked in a haphazard fashion.

Costa was aching to reach it at that very moment. One more electric bus got forced out of the way. Then he was past Bernini's comic stone elephant with an obelisk on its back, marooned in the Piazza della Minerva, and cutting in to the dark, narrow lane that led home.

They turned the corner, rounding the cafe run by Totti, a foul-mouthed misanthrope whose only saving grace was the quality of his coffee and the cheapness of the *cornetti*.

'Oh . . .' Peroni said simply from the back, as the Lancia slid screeching to a halt just twenty metres short of the Questura's front door.

The entire piazza was packed with black armoured vehicles. Dark-clad figures, hooded and bearing rifles, swarmed everywhere, blocking the way to the station.

Costa was trying to think, when a group of them fell upon the vehicle, ripping open the doors. He felt himself seized by strong arms, hurled out into the street, onto the worn cobblestones he knew so well. Falcone was arguing. So was Rosa. He could hear their voices, angry and shrill as he rolled upright to find himself facing the barrel of an automatic weapon.

They didn't have badges or even an obvious sign of rank. There must have been twenty or more.

'Get up!' the one with the gun barked.

Costa did as he was told and climbed back to his feet. There was a cry. It was Rosa. He looked. One of the men had pushed her back hard against the car. Falcone was remonstrating with him. The inspector got a rifle butt in the gut for his pains and went quiet, clutching his stomach.

Peroni was still in the Lancia, right in the middle seat, his big arm around Anna Ybarra.

'We're Roman police officers performing our legitimate duties,' Costa barked at the faceless figure in front of him. 'I will have every one of your names, and tomorrow I will see you in court.'

There was laughter behind the black wool hood.

A small crowd was gathering. Totti was there, abandoning his doubtless deserted cafe, never willing to miss a fight, though strictly from the sidelines. Some shoppers. A couple of stray tourists and the bent and argumentative old woman they all knew, Signora Campitelli, who came in most weeks to complain of some imaginary misdemeanour. People were beginning to wander out from the station too: Prinzivalli, the uniform *sovrintendente*, was on the steps, arms folded, watching everything like a hawk. Next to him was the gruff and none-too-bright plain-clothes officer Taccone, and Emilio Furillo, Teresa's friend, a one-time cop who'd switched to running systems.

'Tell your gorilla we want the woman,' the lead soldier demanded, waving his rifle towards the car.

Colour rose in Falcone's lean, tanned face. He rubbed his stomach, looked at the man and replied, 'Don't ever speak about one of my officers that way. You will—'

They moved. Falcone and Rosa got pushed out of the way. Armed men closed in on both sides of the Lancia's open rear doors. The one who seemed to be in charge leaned in and bellowed, very slowly, 'Get . . . out . . . now.'

The little piazza was continuing to fill, with police officers and civilians. There was a mood Costa could feel. A pressure building. They'd lived with the ring of steel for too long, lived with seeing these faceless armed men in black everywhere, on rooftops, on street corners. It felt as if the city had been stolen from the ordinary men and women to whom it belonged.

Peroni struggled out of the car, taking care to keep his right arm around the woman.

The hooded figure took a step back. With his huge frame and ugly, scarred face, the big man could do that to people. He looked calm, almost content. The rifles stopped him after he'd taken one step towards the Questura.

'She's in our custody now,' the lead one told him.

Peroni shook his head.

'No,' he said without emotion. 'This woman is the prisoner of the Polizia di Stato. On the orders of the president of Italy. No one takes her from me.'

'We've got orders too—' the man began.

'You?' Peroni interrupted, narrowing his eyes. There was something in them, something about his stance, the size of the man, that gave them all pause. Even with their weapons, none seemed keen to come close. 'Who are you?' he asked. 'A mask and a rifle? I don't hand over my prisoner to a man who daren't show his face. Ever . . . Now get out of my way. We've work to do.'

The Spanish woman stayed tight under his right arm, her eyes on the weapons as they rose again.

'Gianni—' Costa began to say.

Something broke the atmosphere. Signora Campitelli, the little old woman who pestered Prinzivalli and his colleagues on the front desk constantly, about lost cats and noisy teenagers, was moving, with a manic and angry intent he recognized only too well. She began elbowing her way through the crowd of black figures, dragging her ancient wicker trolley behind her, full as usual of old clothes, litter she'd picked up from the pavement, and a couple of paper bags with bread and groceries from the store on the corner.

Behind her came the fat little grocer who had a loaf in his hand, one he kept pressing towards her back while making whimpering noises. She forgot a lot of things.

'Not now, you old witch,' another soldier yelled, and that was it.

She burst into life, with a stream of vivid and ancient curses the like of which Costa hadn't heard in a long time, epithets that mixed the sacrilegious with the scatological in a flowing, near-poetic stream that no mere foul-mouthed teenager could ever achieve.

A shocked silence descended on the piazza. She kept on walking, to the lead figure who'd been haranguing Peroni. With a surprising turn of speed, she was on him, lungeing at his head.

The attack came so much out of the blue that the soldier was utterly lost. The old woman got both hands on him and managed to rip off the hood completely, before he could react. Exposed to the bright Roman afternoon, he looked no more than twenty-five, with a somewhat weak, pale face and a head of curly dark hair.

Signora Campitelli turned and grabbed the loaf still being offered to her by the shopkeeper.

'*No maschere a Roma*,' she yelled, and fetched him a hard blow around the skull with the bread. 'No masks in Rome!'

Peroni glanced across the crowded piazza, caught Costa's eye and winked.

'*No maschere a Roma*,' Costa shouted too.

Others began to take up the cry. The shopkeeper. Totti, the angry cafe owner. A couple of other pensioners he dimly recognized, both of whom were now trying to drag the hoods off two soldiers close to them.

The *sovrintendente* Prinzivalli pushed his way through the sea of bodies and got between Peroni and his prisoner, and the men in black. Furillo, the timid bureaucrat from Systems, did the same, and was immediately joined by Taccone and more officers who began to stream out of the Questura into the crowd.

No maschere a Roma.

You could push the people of this city only so far, Costa thought. The limit had been reached. He went and joined the phalanx of bodies growing around Peroni and his charge, creating a living, shouting, almost joyous barrier between them and Palombo's faceless minions.

Toni Grimaldi, the Machiavellian old Questura lawyer they all turned to when things got awkward, materialized in the mob. Next to him was a tall, elegant woman in a very fashionable light suit. She had chestnut hair, a little too bright to be real, piercing green eyes that were fixed on the young curly-haired officer Signora Campitelli had exposed, and the rather timeless look of many professional Italian woman, one that made it difficult to guess her age.

'I'm the lawyer involved in this arrest,' Grimaldi announced. 'This is the magistrate, Giulia Amato, who is handling the case. If you stand in our way for just one more second, I will personally,' his finger prodded the man's bulletproof vest, '*personally* bring you to court on a charge of obstruction of justice.' He pushed the officer's weapon to one side with his hand. 'And that's for starters.'

'So?' the magistrate asked, coming to stand beside the lawyer, smiling as if she were at a cocktail party. 'May we proceed to the Questura? Or do you intend to shoot us all?' She didn't wait for an answer. Giulia Amato – the name rang a bell for Costa, one he dimly associated with tales of controversy and politics – turned to Peroni and said, 'Take the prisoner inside.'

A gap opened among the mob of police officers and citizens. Peroni and Anna Ybarra walked through it, on towards the steps of the station. The figures in black stood and did nothing.

Costa waited with Prinzivalli until all the other police officers, along with Grimaldi and the woman magistrate, were inside. Then the old, grey-haired officer in uniform tapped the pasty-faced lead soldier on the shoulder and said, 'This is a restricted area, sonny. You can't park here. Now move it!'

Signora Campitelli was wielding her loaf once more. Totti, the cafe man, had found sufficient courage to start yelling abuse in all directions. The figures in black slunk back to their armoured vehicles and started the engines noisily.

As they fled, Commissario Vincenzo Esposito stomped into the piazza, his face like thunder, marching across the cobblestones like a man possessed.

'Good day, sir,' Prinzivalli declared cheerily as he arrived.

The *commissario* turned and stared at the departing troops. They were leaving to a flurry of merry abuse and a series of obscure and frequently obscene hand gestures from the largely elderly mob milling around the square.

'Is it, Sovrintendente?' Esposito bellowed. 'Is it?'

Prinzivalli was beaming from ear to ear as he watched the crowd bid the black vehicles farewell.

'Yes, actually,' he replied. 'I do believe it is.'

– 7 –

Ben Rennick – he thought of himself this way, had done for more than two decades – strode out of the Quirinale, back to Borromini's church where'd been confronted by the state police earlier. He almost felt grateful to them for inadvertently suggesting the location. It was a good, private place for an important meeting.

Behind him in the palace all was well, or as manageable as he might have hoped in the circumstances. The guests were departing for the Vatican. The story Rennick had been aching to release was running everywhere. The emergency was over. A desperate attempt to murder the politicians of the G8 summit in the heart of the Quirinale had been prevented at the last moment, and the terrorist cell behind it destroyed.

Coverage of the events in the Salone dei Corazzieri would be easily controlled, with enough manipulation, enough pressure. The story was set already. The Spanish woman had entered the room with an automatic weapon then been disarmed by security guards after loosing off a few wild shots, which happily caused no injuries. Intelligence information indicated that the leader of the Blue Demon, Andrea Petrakis, had fled the city after the failure of the attack. All exit points would be subject to extra security in an attempt to locate him. There would be disruption to international travellers for some days to come. But a sense of normality would start to return to Rome that very afternoon, and by the following day the city would begin to resemble the place he had loved since the moment he first set eyes on it more than two decades before. A place he felt guilty about despoiling, about using.

There were items to tidy. Eye-witness accounts of events in the

Quirinale needed to be checked and corrected where necessary. The weapon the woman had used was, happily, in Palombo's hands, where the fake shells and the crippling device that had jammed it could be quietly removed, if need be. A standardized version of the attack would soon be agreed and adhered to. Most of those in the Salone dei Corazzieri had witnessed little except a brief altercation, ending in shots, in any case. It would be easy to convince them of what they saw. Even the loss of Anna Ybarra posed no great difficulties, since she knew nothing of what had gone on behind the scenes.

'No opportunity for recrimination, no time for regrets,' the American told himself, and walked back into the darkness of the church, stepping beneath the light of the dome once more, heading for the fluid shadows, the site they'd agreed on.

The building was empty. In the half-light of the nave there was no sound at all, no traffic outside, not even the distant murmur of the city.

Then something touched his arm and Ben Rennick almost leaped out of his own skin.

'Jesus . . .'

He threw up his arms in shock. A soldier was there, close to him. A *corazziere* dressed in ornate regalia, a sword at his hip, a plumed helmet on his head.

'Who the hell . . . ?' Rennick began, then stopped as he looked at the eyes beneath the shining metal. Dark, dead eyes. Familiar.

'Andrea?' he murmured.

The man removed his headgear, stood there, arms open, beaming like a teenager.

'Andrea,' Rennick repeated and embraced him, trying to hide the shock he felt at seeing the man's face for the first time in twenty years.

The lines, the tanned, leathery skin, hair desiccated by sun and worry – it was as if life itself had been slowly withdrawn from Andrea Petrakis. And in its place? A husk. A shell.

'Renzo.' His voice sounded different, not just older, but as if it belonged to another man.

'Renzo's dead,' he told him, stepping back a pace, taking another good look. 'Don't forget.'

'I killed him. How could I?'

'You did,' Rennick agreed. Twenty years was a long time, and neither of them had any idea what had filled that void in their separate lives. 'I owe you an apology. When we put you with the Afghans. No one had any idea it would take this long . . .' There hadn't been many options at the time. After the deaths of the Petrakis couple, and the risk of exposure of the Gladio network, no one else in Europe could be trusted to take a young Italian who knew too much. 'Or that they'd become the enemy. They were ours back then, Andrea. The mujahideen – we made them. If I'd guessed . . .'

Petrakis stopped smiling.

'Please. Those people in Washington knew what they were doing. They put me in there because you needed someone on the inside.'

Rennick sighed and admitted, 'Maybe you're right. I was just a field guy. A foot soldier. What you've become.' He looked him in the eye. 'So you understand exactly how that works, huh? We're always in the dark. If you're right, it was someone else's idea. I was just trying to save all our hides. If what had been going on became public . . .'

He looked at the stranger in front of him.

'We offered to get you out. You know that. All the same, you stayed. We're grateful. It was brave. It was selfless.'

'What else was I supposed to do?' the man in the *corazziere* uniform asked. 'Come back here under an assumed name? Pretend to be someone else? Why? Why should I do that?'

'I'm sorry. This was never going to be an easy conversation. What happened after your parents died was a kind of madness. People were panicking. Everything we'd been doing looked like it was going to unravel. I wanted you out of that. Me too. I wanted us clear so that we could sort things out later.' He frowned. 'I never knew there'd be so much blood along the way. Or that we'd be using a stay-behind man, still needing one, after all these years.'

Petrakis stood a little closer.

'I left you a message. I always leave you a message. Now you don't want me to finish the job, do you? Why is that?'

'You mean those crazy numbers? Jesus, Andrea. Why do you do that? I never understood the need for them back then. Now . . .'

'I like to leave my mark. Something that lingers. Pictures on a wall.'

Rennick laughed.

'You mean like the Etruscans?'

His amusement didn't seem to impress Petrakis.

'Like the Etruscans. I like to finish the job too,' the man in the uniform insisted.

'Well, I guess communication has not been our strong point in this venture. I never got the message. Maybe Palombo was too busy.' Maybe, Rennick thought. 'This job is finished. Done. Over.'

He'd realized that as soon as he saw the final message, in the hands of a cop in this selfsame little church little more than an hour before. Rennick knew *Julius Caesar* almost by heart, had guessed what that coded riddle had to mean, and confirmed it, to his alarm, when he got back to the palace. 'How the hell did you get this idea in your head? Tell me.'

'I thought you put it there,' he answered immediately. 'Or maybe the Blue Demon. Who knows?'

'There is no Blue Demon, Andrea. There never was. We invented all that stuff, remember? Your old man came up with the name when we trying to put together one more lunatic bunch of terrorists to keep Gladio going. When he got killed, we just adopted it as a way of covering up what we'd been doing. If we hadn't, everyone's cover would have been blown. It was the only way . . .'

'He didn't make it up,' Petrakis insisted.

'Excuse me?'

'He . . . didn't . . . make . . . it . . . up. The Blue Demon's real. I know.'

This was crazy. Petrakis was crazy.

'Listen to me. This has gone far enough. The Etruscans. The tombs. The idea someone might fight for some dead race wiped out centuries ago. That was your father's idea. It was one more operation we were going to run. Then, when he died . . .'

They were grasping in the dark that week. Everything – the panic, the fear of the network's discovery, the desperation – remained etched on his memory. Clutching at the idea of another fake terrorist gang, paid for by illicit Gladio money, seemed the only way out, even if it came at a frightful cost. The loss of innocent lives. The end of his own identity. A terrible exile for Andrea Petrakis.

'He didn't make it up. So who really runs the Blue Demon, Renzo?'

The American sighed.

'My name is Ben Rennick, not Renzo Frasca.'

'Who . . . ?'

'Leave all this to me. I'll deal with it. Your work here's done. Excellently done.' He made a grateful gesture with his hands. 'We've reminded people this is a dangerous world again. That they should place their trust in those who govern. Very soon they'll believe you've managed to flee the country, gone for good. You're free. You can be whoever you want.'

'Don't patronize me.'

'I'm not. I'm trying to keep you safe. This has gone further than I wanted. Giovanni Batisti . . .' Rennick shook his head. 'I don't understand why his death was necessary. Or the airport. That was never part of the plan . . .'

'Nor was a bunch of cops prying into what I was doing in Tarquinia. In the tomb. I would have killed them all if you'd let me.'

'You should have phoned me when you were supposed to,' Rennick told him. 'You should have called when you found those officers. We're not murderers.'

The silver breastplate came close and touched his chest as Petrakis leaned into him.

'Are you sure about that?'

'Yes. Those guys stumbling on you – it was an accident. These things happen.' He peered into Petrakis's dark, dead eyes. 'Like Stefan Kyriakis, I guess.'

'Kyriakis was a gun-runner. A thief. He asked too many questions. He *knew*, Renzo. He would have sold us . . .'

'He was one of ours. One of mine. It doesn't matter now.'

'I was out there. In the field. You were behind a comfortable desk.'

'True,' Rennick agreed. He hesitated, trying to ensure Petrakis understood what he was saying. 'I may – I do – regret some of the details of the last week, but there's nothing here that can't be dealt with. We've covered up worse in the past. Everything will work out so long as we stop now. I want no further actions.'

He led the man deeper into the shadows, looking around them.

'You can go wherever you want. I'll see to the money. A new identity. A fresh start. Not Europe, I think. Maybe South America. Australia.'

'I like the East. Afghanistan.'

'Not an option.'

'It's what you want, isn't it? Their heads on a plate.'

Rennick took him by the shoulders.

'Not any more. You've done enough. I won't allow it. I can't.'

Petrakis nodded, as if he were listening. Rennick felt a moment of relief.

'So my mission's ended?'

'Finally,' the American agreed. 'Yes.'

'I don't get to lead you to the high command?'

'It wouldn't work,' Rennick told him. 'They're not stupid. There's not enough . . .'

The show at the Trevi Fountain. A dead politician. A handful of innocent civilian victims at the airport. A failed assassination attempt. If things hadn't started to unravel, perhaps there was a chance. But not now. There was too much risk, and most of that would, he knew, come from the man in front of him.

'Not enough blood?' Andrea Petrakis asked, eyes gleaming, interested.

'I guess you could put it that way. After today the Blue Demon is history. It stays that way.'

Petrakis was shaking his head, looking crazy, saying, 'No, no, no . . .'

'I'll get you out of the city tonight. Out of the country by morning. The further, the better.'

'Easier if you just kill me.'

'Don't say that,' he snapped, aware his own voice was rising. Then, more softly, 'Don't even think it.'

'Easier if you slaughter me, the way you slaughtered my mother and father.'

Rennick blinked.

'The Mafia murdered your parents. They wouldn't stop their little sideline. Dope. That's the truth. You know it.'

The sham *corazziere* leaned forward. He seemed taller than Rennick remembered.

'Don't you see the problem, Renzo?'

'Please don't call me that . . .'

Something stirred above them: a stray pigeon that had flown in from the street, flapping between the darkness and the light.

A feather, pale and downy, floated down gently and landed on Rennick's jacket. Petrakis brushed it aside with a flick of his right hand.

'I've spent the last twenty years with the men who were selling my father that junk in the first place. I've watched their children grow. I've eaten with their families.' His voice fell a tone. 'I've been a part of them.'

He took Rennick by the arm, leaned into his ear, whispering.

'They're animals, Renzo. But like animals, they only know the truth.'

'What truth would that be?'

'My parents, they did stop dealing dope. Both of them. Just as they were ordered. They did it because they were scared. Not of the people you think, either. They were scared. Because they found out who the Blue Demon really was. What this was about.'

Rennick tried to think, to remember. None of this had concerned him. He'd been told what had happened. By the Italians.

'The mob killed them for money,' he said. 'What other reason could there be?'

'Knowledge.' Petrakis had come very close and placed a finger over his lips. 'Please, Renzo. After all this time. No lies. I just want to hear you say his name. Just once . . .'

The American shrugged his shoulders. His body ached. He felt old and exhausted, and out of words.

'You tell me,' he suggested.

Petrakis blinked, then spoke.

Rennick looked at his watch and sighed.

'We can talk about this later,' he insisted. 'I need you to get out of that uniform, out of Rome. When this is over, let me buy you a beer. Somewhere warm and safe.'

'I don't hear you denying it?'

He should never have come alone. He should have foreseen that Petrakis might have become detached from reality over the years.

'Because it's too ridiculous for words. Believe me.' He glanced at the door. 'Believe—'

The words froze in his mouth. A pained sigh escaped his throat. A cold, stabbing agony was rising from his gut into his chest.

Rennick looked down, saw his hands fumbling for the source, recoiling when they found it.

Andrea Petrakis's ceremonial sword was buried in his stomach, up to the hilt.

He was aware of blood rising past his lips in a salty flood, of a buzzing, screaming noise in his head. Petrakis leaned forward, pushed once more, then withdrew, taking the weapon with him in a sudden sweep that made the wounded man moan long and low.

In the shadows of Borromini's church, Renzo Frasca, Ben Rennick – a man with two names – fell backwards, stumbling to his knees against a pillar, clutching at the damp, growing pain in his belly, feeling the life run out of his body.

The figure of a soldier stood above him, his helmeted head silhouetted against the bright, circular dome, a static, descending dove at its centre.

The American said something and didn't even understand the words himself.

Petrakis stepped forward to wipe the bloodied blade against the stricken man's jacket, one damp shiny side first, then the other.

'We shared so much once, Renzo,' he murmured. 'Latin and Shakespeare. History and dreams. Smoke and mirrors.'

The American's vision was narrowing. The ache was turning into something else, a dull, distant sensation, diminished by his weakening condition.

A cold finger touched his trembling, murmuring lips. He could barely feel it, barely think in the swelling darkness that was beginning to embrace him, falling all around from the bare stone folds of the church.

- 8 -

Teresa Lupo was halfway down the Via dei Serpenti, trying to make her way back to San Giovanni, when the shouting and cheering started. It came from a little cafe near the Piazza degli Zingari, a modest, friendly corner of Rome where she liked to drink coffee. It sounded as if Italy had won the World Cup once more.

She pushed her way through the crowd, thought of asking what had happened, then didn't bother. Everyone was glued to the TV. Ugo Campagnolo was there, beaming, his face shiny with sweat, as if he'd run to the cameras, missing make-up on the way.

The prime minister had a message for the nation. The crisis was over. Rome was safe. One terrorist was dead, out in a field near the Via Appia Antica; another was in custody; and the third and final individual, Andrea Petrakis, the leader, was attempting to flee the country, pursued by the Carabinieri, stripped of his cohorts, unable to cause further damage.

Romans didn't like Campagnolo. No, she reminded herself. Most of them positively *hated* him. Even so she could feel there was some grudging gratitude towards the man as he told them their city was safe again, and that the security measures of the previous two days would soon be lifted.

Glasses were raised, beer and *prosecco* ordered. She caught the eye of an elderly man with a grey face and a salt-and-pepper moustache, about to take a long swig of wine.

'You believe a word of that?' she demanded.

'I believe that bastard when he says we get our city back,' he answered straight away. 'He can't take that away from us now, can he?'

He was probably right, though she wondered how Campagnolo and the security services could feel so sure Petrakis was powerless on his own. This seemed presumptuous, she thought, as she wandered back out into the street, to the main drag of the Via Cavour. The roadblock at the foot, near the Forum, was being dismantled already. Life was returning. She hauled herself into the road to stop a cab that someone further up the street had already summoned. The driver looked at her with one arched eyebrow. Teresa flashed her police ID and said, 'I'm doing this on Ugo Campagnolo's orders. Take me to San Giovanni.'

Five minutes later she was outside the former monastery, still feeling grumpy and out of sorts. The more she thought about it, Campagnolo's announcement of victory felt premature and artificial. The men and women in the cafe in Monti surely understood that. Their relief came from nothing more than hearing what they longed for, not any rational consideration of the available facts. Terrorism did that to people. It made them live off their nerves, ignore the usual rules and rituals of everyday life. That was what gave men like Andrea Petrakis – and those behind them – their power.

The apartment appeared to be empty when she marched inside, which did nothing to improve her mood.

'Silvio?' she yelled. '*Silvio?*'

He was in the main bedroom, his podgy form stretched out on the big double mattress, sleepy-eyed, a sandwich and a can of beer in his hands, watching the TV. It was still featuring a grinning, triumphant Campagnolo, with some pompous-looking Carabinieri ass by his side, and Luca Palombo in the background.

'Where's Elizabeth?' she wanted to know.

He shrugged and took a bite of the sandwich, then mumbled, 'Must be a long lunch. Why come back? It's over. Says so on the TV.'

'I don't recall saying it was over for you.'

'Who stepped on your bunions? There's no work. There never was, really. We were just doing some secret stuff on Dario Sordi's orders, weren't we? Speculative. A little crazy.' He hesitated. 'Very crazy. Infectiously crazy.'

She marched over, snatched the can from his hand and would have had the sandwich too, if he hadn't managed to wrest it out of her reach. Instead she grabbed the remote and switched off the TV.

'May I remind you that we have one dead politician, his woman driver, Mirko Oliva and those people at the airport. Do you hear Ugo Campagnolo even mentioning them?'

'Difficult to hear anything with the TV off.'

'Don't be smart with me.'

She launched the TV remote at him. The young pathologist ducked. These days he always looked more offended than scared when she lost her temper. She wasn't sure whether this was progress or not.

'What, exactly, is wrong?' he asked.

'Everything! Nothing! I don't know.'

'That narrows it down . . .'

Teresa took a swig of his beer and waited for him to say something else. He didn't. This was not the anxious, gauche young man she'd taken on seven years before. He'd grown, and along the way found infinitely more subtle ways to infuriate her.

'I haven't done a damned thing to help any of them,' she moaned. 'We might as well have stayed in the Questura, doing as we were told.'

'We were doing as we were told.'

'Huh! Fishing in the dark. What do you mean Elizabeth is still at lunch?'

'Went to meet a friend. I imagine she heard the news. Decided it wasn't worth coming back.'

Teresa didn't like that idea at all.

'Tell me about the numbers.'

'The numbers?'

'The Latin numerals. The ones you were working on.'

'They don't matter now, do they?' he said, looking a little guilty.

'Why? Because Ugo Campagnolo says so?'

'I fell asleep. When I woke up . . .' He gestured at the dead eye of the TV. 'Does it matter?'

'Who knows?' Teresa led him by the arm back into the main room and the computer and ordered, 'Tell me what you have.'

He grumbled something wordless, then sat at the desk, scrabbled through his notes, screwed up his bland, pasty face and announced, 'Twelve didn't mean midday. Noon. Not two thousand years ago when they didn't have clocks. Things weren't that simple. Time was not easily measured. Here's a quote I found from Seneca. *Facilius inter philosophos quam inter horologia conveniet.* It's easier to get agreement among philosophers than clocks.'

'Was that the Elder or the Younger?'

'Um . . .'

He was turning a touch red, which she found satisfying.

'Oh, for God's sake. I was only trying to bring home to you the futility of quoting dead people. Are you going to tell me something useful, or what?'

'The time of day varied according to the season, as did the hours, which also varied in length.'

'Facts . . .'

'Facts.' He glanced at a sheet. 'The number twelve cannot refer to a specific time. Only an hour. Which isn't an hour, not in the way we know it.'

'What hour?'

'*Hora duodecima.* Which in the summer would run from approximately six-fifteen to half-past seven in the evening.'

She thought about this.

'So it doesn't mean it's in the past?'

'If you accept the premise that "it" exists . . .'

For a moment she felt like slapping him.

'This was written on the wall of the tomb of the Blue Demon. It was a message for someone. Between him and them, whoever they are. Mirko Oliva—'

'Point taken. No need to labour it.'

'Isn't there? Here you are, sitting on potentially important information. Then Ugo Campagnolo goes on TV, issues the all-clear and you take a nap.'

'It could indicate something might happen this evening, I guess,' he admitted. 'If Petrakis has become some kind of one-man army.'

'Don't push me. And the other numbers? I told you. If XII at the beginning does stand for a time this evening, it's pretty obvious what the rest stands for, isn't it? What did Petrakis paint on the walls of the nymphaeum at the Villa Giulia?'

He looked at her blankly.

'Refresh my memory.'

'Silvio,' she roared, and was surprised to see his eyes turn damp and unfocused, as if there were tears close by.

'I've been staring at this stupid screen for eighteen, twenty hours a day,' he bleated. 'I feel exhausted. I can't stay awake. If I close my eyes, I get pictures of a computer screen. If I sleep I get . . . bad dreams.'

He stared at her, his face that of a guilty child.

'Really bad dreams. I can't think straight, or remember every last thing that's happened. I'm sorry.'

'Fine,' she said quickly, and patted him on the shoulder before pulling up a seat and sitting down beside him. 'The numbers on the wall at the Villa Giulia referred to Shakespeare. The play *Julius Caesar*. Act, scene, line.'

He murmured an apology, tapped the keyboard lightly and brought up an online version of the play.

Di Capua scrolled down and she found herself recalling the last time she'd seen this dark, compelling story on stage, at an open-air performance in the park of the Villa Borghese. The subject matter – conspiracy, murder, intrigue, assassination, all contained inside the shadowy, grubby and depressingly eternal world of politics – came back to her. The room was too hot from the summer sun streaming through the large windows onto the Via San Giovanni in Laterano. All the same she felt a chill as these recollections returned, and soon found herself shivering in her summer shirt and slacks.

It was a planning scene from the play: Brutus, a good man, in his orchard, reluctantly considering the plot, and finally shaking hands with the conspirators.

'There,' Di Capua said quietly as he reached the right lines. She leaned forward and spoke them out loud.

> '*Let's kill him boldly, but not wrathfully;*
> *Let's carve him as a dish fit for the gods,*
> *Not hew him as a carcass fit for hounds.*'

They looked at each other, then Teresa Lupo glanced at her watch. It was now five-thirty.

'Let me get this straight,' Di Capua said. 'What we have here is something written on the wall of the tomb in Tarquinia where Andrea Petrakis kept his munitions.'

'Alongside his friendly Blue Demon,' she reminded him.

'Quite.' His eyes were suddenly sharp and intelligent again. 'And it's a *message*. There for someone he knows will read it. Someone . . .' He was so pale she felt guilty. Di Capua looked utterly exhausted. '. . . a man, a woman on the inside who'll understand what it means.'

'He likes riddles and codes. He likes playing with people.'

'Elizabeth disappeared the moment I told her about those numbers,' Di Capua murmured. 'I saw her flick through that Shakespeare book I got. Then she was gone. What was I doing? How could I—?'

'You were dog-tired,' she interrupted. 'It takes energy, and a little enthusiasm, to think the unthinkable.'

'Between six-fifteen and seven-thirty Petrakis is going to kill someone. A head of state,' Di Capua said. 'And our trusted companion – who knows everything we've done, every thought we've had – is out there somewhere.' He hesitated before saying what was in his head. 'She understands that and she never told us. Was the message for her?'

'I don't know.'

'So who the hell do we call?'

She gave him the look and said, 'Now that *is* a stupid question.'

Costa was there on the first ring.

'Don't ask why, just give me a straight answer,' she said immediately. 'Where are all the big G8 people, the ones God talks to, between six-fifteen and seven-thirty this evening?'

'In the Vatican. Formal reception. There all night. Why?'

She felt like screaming. There was no way anyone from the police force was going to get inside the private state on the other side of the river.

'You might want to tell them to be careful. We've decoded those numbers on the wall of the tomb in Tarquinia. They seem to be saying there'll be some kind of assassination attempt at that time.'

There was a short silence, then he asked, 'Against whom?'

'Whoever counts as the modern Julius Caesar, I guess. Take your pick. You've got eight to choose from, haven't you? Ugo Campagnolo? Any of them.'

'I don't think Campagnolo is with them. Things get tricky with events in the Vatican. Besides, no one can get in there, Teresa. Not even Andrea Petrakis. The security . . .'

'I know, I know. But I wanted to tell you.'

Di Capua was tapping her shoulder. He was wearing the smug expression he used when she'd made a mistake.

'What is it?'

'Ugo Campagnolo is an elected politician. Julius Caesar was only appointed by the Senate. Strictly speaking, it's a bad analogy.'

'Oh, don't be so damned pedantic, Silvio! We don't do things like that these days.'

He didn't say a word, just leaned on the table, placed a forefinger against his chubby cheek and stared her in the eye as if to say, 'Really?'

'Oh, my God,' she murmured. There was still someone appointed by the politicians alone. She should have seen it straight away. 'Nic. This may not be what we were thinking. Where will Dario Sordi be tonight around that time?'

There was a pause on the line, followed by a barely audible curse, a word she'd never heard him utter.

Then he said, 'Where he always is.'

– 9 –

Fabio Ranieri looked up from his desk in the Quirinale's administrative wing. It was twenty to six. His immediate concerns – for the safety of the president's guests – had been relieved by the transfer of the G8 parties and their followers to the Vatican. The aftermath of the attempt on their lives was now the business of the police. This was a rare moment of calm in a day he would long remember, for all the wrong reasons. The security of the palace had been breached. He had no idea how, nor was there likely to be much opportunity to investigate until late the following day when the summit visitors left for home and the Quirinale would return to his full control once more.

The door opened. Palombo entered followed by a series of Carabinieri officers in full uniform, all of them grim-faced.

'This isn't going to be pleasant,' the Ministry of the Interior officer declared.

'It's that kind of day, isn't it? Make it brief, please. I have work to do.'

'Not any more. You're to be detained. These men will take you into custody. You will be held by the Carabinieri this evening. Tomorrow I will consider charges.'

Ranieri didn't move.

'Charges? What charges?'

'Obstruction of the security services in their legitimate duty. A breach of your secrecy obligations. A loose tongue, which may have cost us dear . . .'

'What in God's name are you talking about?'

'You heard.'

Ranieri had his hand on his phone. Palombo strode across the room and replaced the handset, watching him intently.

'I am formally relieving you of your duties, Captain. Your men have been confined to barracks, except for those on the gate. I don't wish the Corazzieri's failings to be any more apparent to the outside world than they already are.'

'This is a disgrace. You have no right to obstruct the security of the Quirinale Palace . . .'

'I have every right to question the actions of a man who allowed a terrorist to penetrate into a room that held some of the most important politicians in the civilized world.'

'Allowed?'

Ranieri rose to his feet. He was still wearing his plain dark suit, but his height made him stand out as a *corazziere*. Palombo retreated a step. The uniformed officers behind him didn't move.

'There will be a full investigation into how that woman got into this palace, make no mistake,' Ranieri told them all. 'I wish to know the answer to that, as much as anyone. But this is our job. You will not interfere with the role of the Corazzieri in this building. We have our duties and our rights—'

'Do you deny you've been in secret discussions with other parties about the security arrangements here?' Palombo interrupted. 'Do you deny you made a covert visit to the house of an unauthorized individual two nights ago to discuss these things? That you have been making repeated contact with people outside the list of approved officials sanctioned by me?'

It was, Ranieri thought, impossible to avoid their attentions in the end. He'd always known this, and so had Dario Sordi.

'I do not answer to you for my actions.'

'Oh, but you do.' He glanced at the men with him. 'No denial, I see.'

'I confirm or repudiate nothing. I'll come with you for this farce. My deputy shall act in my place . . .'

There was a brief, curt moment of amusement on the man's narrow, cold face.

'Your deputy is confined to quarters, along with the rest of your officers. I act in your absence. I would advise you to admit to everything that has occurred these last few days. It will be easier in the end.'

This was impossible to envisage, and to accept.

'There has never been a moment when the Corazzieri have not guarded the Quirinale, not since we became a nation. How dare you?'

'Tradition is dead, man. You're a fool if you think otherwise.'

Palombo walked round the desk and wandered over to the long window, pulling the velvet curtain wider. There was a wide, angled view of the palace gardens, over to the spot where the president liked to take tea of an evening.

Ranieri followed Palombo's cold gaze. He loved this room, loved being able to watch out over the green space beyond, and the old man with his china cup and plate of biscuits. The Corazzieri's disposition within the palace and its quarters were, to him, a bulwark of safety and stability in an uncertain, fractured world. That was what hurt most about the afternoon's events. Not the abortive attack itself, but the very fact that someone had wormed their way through all his careful safeguards and brought the bloody, cruel business of terror into this oasis of sanity.

Two officers in Carabinieri uniforms came and stood by him. Ranieri picked up his favourite pen from the desk, placed it in his jacket pocket and walked towards the door. Palombo took his chance and fell into his large leather office chair, swinging from side to side, smiling quietly to himself.

The Corazzieri captain turned and surveyed the man, this jumped-up civil servant in an expensive suit. The smirk on Palombo's face was designed to infuriate. It did not miss its mark.

'If anything should happen while I'm away from here,' he warned, 'I will hold you responsible. I say that personally, man to man. Not as a soldier.'

'You've spent too long in fancy dress, Ranieri. Your world is gone, never to return. After what we've seen today, I will make sure the Corazzieri never again strut around this palace as if they own it. You can go back to being real soldiers, not toy ones. Detain him in a room somewhere until I decide where to take him.'

'I will not allow—'

Two strong arms held him back. Palombo sat there, leering. It was done, Ranieri realized. There was no way to protest, or fight.

The ring of Ranieri's mobile phone broke the silence. It was still on the desk. Palombo leaned forward and picked up the handset, peering at the screen. Then he hit the red button to reject the call.

'It's private,' Ranieri insisted.

'It certainly is. No caller ID.' He pressed a few buttons. 'No address book. Lots of calls, though. In and out.' He turned the thing off and pocketed it. 'I'll get my people to take a look at this later, I think.'

– 10 –

It was getting cooler on the roof of the outpost of the CESIS offices overlooking the Quirinale gardens. Elizabeth Murray hugged her stolen protection jacket for a moment and checked her watch one more time. Just past six. Leone, the officer she'd slugged, was still in the little cabin on the roof, securely gagged and bound next to the watering cans and tubs of fertilizer. He wasn't going anywhere. But perhaps he had people to meet, people who'd worry about where he was. Perhaps they even went through some kind of automated checkout procedure these days, a smart card that logged you in and out and started to scream when something went wrong.

Machines, she thought. There were too many of them, and too few human beings. That was all the services seemed to rely on now. Computers and procedures. Rule books and protocols. It hadn't been like this in the 1970s and 1980s. In those days everything was more flexible, open to interpretation.

A lot easier to hide too.

That thought prompted her to go and check out Domenico Leone one more time. Judging by the fierce look in his eyes, he wasn't getting any less livid as the hours went by. She pushed some more furniture against the door, blocking the stairs from the floor below, then went back to her viewpoint at the edge of the roof.

It was time for one more dry run. She spreadeagled her large body over the concrete, legs akimbo, and brought the firearm up to her right shoulder. The bulk of the weapon was leaning correctly inside the folds of the rest. The sniper's rifle felt steady in her arms. She squinted through the telescopic sight, scanning the grounds of the Quirinale gardens, across flower beds, ornate classical fountains, stretches of perfect green lawn and dark patches of shrubbery.

It was empty. She almost believed the palace was too. No one moved anywhere, not even in the windows, as far as she could see.

Another minute passed and then, against all custom and practice, she took out a packet of cigarettes and lit one, sucking the smoke all the way down.

Not that she was supposed to. The doctor back home had told her that repeatedly. He was insistent. An annoying little man.

Elizabeth Murray took a long, satisfying draw of the thing and blew a grey cloud out into the cooling evening air. Rome was just as beautiful as ever, she decided, watching her faint smog disperse against a background of the palace roof and the city skyline beyond. It had been a mistake to leave.

Something drew her attention to the expanse of green in front of her. With the cigarette still in her mouth, she bent down and peered through the scope again, scanning the palace gardens.

A tall, slightly stooped, elderly figure was walking the main path from the side of the Quirinale, a cup and a plate of biscuits held awkwardly in one hand, a book in the other.

She knew already where he was going. The scope ranged the flower beds and fountains again and found the marker she'd already set for herself.

It was a handsome old statue, somewhat worn by decades out in the grubby Roman rain. But the wings on Hermes' feet made good sighting points, and when she fiddled with the focus a little she could see the delicate stone feathers there, clear as day.

– 11 –

Costa slammed the phone back into the cradle. They were in Falcone's office, digesting the warning from Teresa Lupo, trying to work out how to respond.

The inspector stood up.

'You say Sordi is in the garden around six-thirty?'

'Usually. Same place. Creature of habit.'

'Habits can kill,' Peroni cut in. 'We've still got half an hour or so. How about I check the outside? Those gardens have to be overlooked. Someone might get on the roof.'

'Check it out,' Falcone ordered. 'Get two or three officers you can trust. Take a separate car. We'll go straight to the Quirinale and see if we can argue our way in. Tell no one.'

A few minutes later they were back in the Lancia, trying to squeeze the big saloon out of the massed tangle of badly parked police vehicles swamping the cobblestones of the Piazza di San Michele Arcangelo.

There was a quick, sharp rap on the driver's-side window.

It was Signora Campitelli, the old woman who'd set about the security men earlier. She seemed insistent, so much so that she was blocking the only way out.

Costa wound down the glass.

'Signora, please. We're in a hurry.'

'Showed those bastards, didn't we? *No maschere a Roma!*'

Falcone was getting furious in the passenger seat, about to say something that might have persuaded her to stay where she was, out of nothing more than bloody-mindedness.

'We did indeed,' Costa said quickly. 'Excuse us, please. We have to go show them again.'

'Hah!'

Her stick rose triumphantly towards the soft evening sky. She stepped back, still shouting, dragging her shopping trolley sufficiently to one side to allow the wide saloon to squeeze through.

'May we now depart?' Falcone asked, removing the blue light from beneath the dashboard again, then placing it on the roof and activating the device.

The shriek of the klaxon echoed off the high terraces of the *centro storico*. The Lancia criss-crossed the warren of narrow streets as rapidly as Costa could manage, finally screeching into the broader thorough-fare of the Corso, where the shoppers were now wandering down the middle of the road, starting to revisit stores that had been empty or closed for days. The Piazza Venezia was returning to its normal state of chaos. Workmen were already dismantling one of the high check-point towers that Palombo's men had erected earlier in the week.

It took little more than a minute to climb the Quirinale hill and abandon the car in the street next to the piazza.

The bell of *Il Torrino* was finishing its mark of the hour, the sixth peal dying over the hill.

There were two *corazzieri* in regal uniform on the gate, and a third in the pillar box. They all looked as miserable as sin for some reason.

Falcone marched up to the sentry in the cabin, Costa in his wake, ID card out, and demanded to speak to Fabio Ranieri.

'Not available,' the man said, and nothing more.

'Ranieri is a friend of mine,' Costa added. 'This is important. You must find him.'

'Not . . . available . . .'

'Then call the duty captain. I need to speak to him.'

One of the others came over, sensing trouble.

'Something wrong?' he asked, in a gruff northern voice.

'We need to see the duty officer now,' Falcone began.

'You can't,' the *corazziere* in the box repeated. 'That's final.

Come back tomorrow. Maybe by then someone can tell us what the hell's going on here . . .'

Costa marched into the office and began to pick up the phone.

'Cut that out!' the man there yelled, slamming his fist hard on the handset. 'What's wrong with you people? Don't you know who's boss around here now?'

'Who?' Falcone asked.

He nodded in the direction of the Ministry of the Interior.

'Those grey-faced bastards around the corner. Not us. Not any more.'

'We're state police officers,' Costa told him. 'We've spent the last few days investigating the Blue Demon on the personal orders of Dario Sordi. We now believe there will be an attempt on the president's life, within the next half-hour.'

The others had joined them. The three tall figures in silver breastplates looked at one another. The officer behind him took off his helmet and said, 'You'd better not be jerking us around.'

'Andrea Petrakis is planning an attack within these walls,' Costa insisted. 'Very soon. With help from someone on the inside.' That quietened them. 'Someone let that woman in this afternoon, didn't they? I don't think it was one of the Corazzieri.'

'No. I don't think it was.' He stared at the oldest of the three. 'Ranieri's in custody somewhere and every last *corazziere* apart from us is sitting on their backside in the barracks till someone lets them out.'

The higher-ranking officer didn't look them in the eye when he said, 'You heard our orders.'

'Your orders are to guard the president, aren't they?' Costa asked, trying to push a button that might work. 'Who's doing that now?'

'We are,' the talkative one said straight away. 'Three of us. Plus a bunch of waiters and a few goons from the Ministry. It's a tomb in there. I've never seen anything like it. That Palombo bastard has taken over Ranieri's office as if he owns it. God knows who else is in the building. Except,' he thought for a moment, 'some other *corazziere* I spotted wandering down in that direction a couple of minutes ago.'

He stepped in front of the senior officer.

'Something is wrong, and you know it.'

The *corazziere* in the box looked Costa in the eye.

'If you're mistaken about this . . .'

'Take us to Palombo now,' Falcone ordered. 'Get Ranieri free. We'll bear the responsibility.'

The man didn't even move.

Then the officer behind him, the man Costa was starting to think of as the awkward one, stepped into the cabin and grabbed a set of keys.

'For God's sake. If you won't do it, I will. Follow me.'

- 12 -

A good book, a cup of Earl Grey tea, a plate of English biscuits. These familiar items seemed, to Dario Sordi, comforting signs of a world beginning to find some kind of equilibrium. He sat in his usual shady spot in the deserted Quirinale garden, content, almost at ease.

It was earlier than normal, but the palace was unusually empty save for a few servants. He'd spent the last forty-five minutes alone in his apartment making discreet phone calls to men and women who mattered. Politicians and judges, allies, the uncommitted, and the occasional foe. It was important they heard the truth about the Ybarra woman from him, and understood his insistence that she be dealt with inside the Italian judicial system, investigated by the police and no others.

There would be arguments. There always were. This was the world of politics, and he was only the president – not, as Ugo Campagnolo constantly reminded the media, a politician elected by the masses. Nevertheless, Sordi felt, as he finished the final call, that he might win this particular battle. The Questura's rapid decision to bring in the combative Giulia Amato as investigating magistrate had been a wise, perhaps decisive move. The woman was not the type to be diverted by a quiet word from some party hack and the promise of preferment. Even with his growing ranks of supporters placed in the political hierarchy and the law-enforcement agencies, Campagnolo would be hard-pressed to seize Anna Ybarra from the grip of the police and the magistrate.

He found himself staring at the expressionless face of Hermes. The handsome young god always seemed distracted, a little fey as he stretched down to tie the ribbon on his sandal.

'Do you have any messages for me, I wonder?' Sordi asked.

There was silence, punctuated only by the distant sound of a jet wheeling high overhead, something he hadn't heard in a while. Sordi placed the teacup and biscuits on the stone table.

'Another Etruscan in our midst,' the president murmured, recalling a little of his school-days mythology. It was the lot of his native city to inherit the past, for good and bad. History always emerged like a foundling, anonymous, unclaimed, impossible to control, like the Blue Demon itself. Alone now, able to think clearly for the first time in days, Dario Sordi felt he could finally begin to understand a little of the original inspiration for that terrifying image on the subterranean tomb in the Maremma, and the effect it had on the unfortunate Andrea Petrakis. For the doomed Etruscans – for Petrakis too – the Blue Demon was Rome, with her rapacious, insatiable hunger for domination, for territory and power, at any human cost. That ceaseless greed, a burning desire to own and rule, was one more gift his ancestors had handed down to the modern Western world, alongside more noble ideals about law and charity and God. Which of them was now uppermost? Sordi didn't wish to consider this question too closely. He felt his answer might tally too easily with that of a confused and embittered individual like Andrea Petrakis. The Etruscans, with their worldly, hedonistic attitude to life, had invented for themselves a bright and fleeting paradise, one that was stolen from them, then destroyed by the men from the south who brought guilt and responsibility, democracy and order into an enclosed, interior society built on nothing more than a lust for the immediacy of existence.

This endless argument was, in a sense, the very same squabble he had pursued with Marco Costa over the years – one that had, in the end, driven two dear friends apart. Should a human being choose the dull, dead round of pragmatism and responsibility against the brief and brilliant spark of individual satisfaction, the ecstasy of the moment? Was a life that spanned eight decades of duty and routine and service really more worthy than some briefer interlude that lit the sky with fireworks and then was gone, leaving the stage to others dazzled by the intensity of its departure?

He waved the book in his hands at the mute statue.

'If you could read, my friend, you'd know these choices are made for us. By nature, not intellect.' Sordi frowned. 'They always have been. They always will.'

It was the visit to Marco's son that had prompted him to pick up his own copy of Graves's *I, Claudius* again. There'd been little time for reading of late. Besides, he knew the work so well that he was able to turn directly to the parts he loved most, skipping over the author's occasional historical peregrinations.

His bookmark stood at chapter thirty-four, a few pages from the end. Gone was the flowery language and philosophy. This was a plain retelling of the climax of this first part of Claudius's story. How a man regarded by most as a stammering, slobbering cripple – an idiot, worthy only of ridicule – would rise to the emperor's throne, against his own most fervent wishes.

Sordi wondered if he loved this story so much because, in some ways, it mirrored his own. Claudius was a republican, a believer in democracy, not the dictatorship of the imperial family. He spent years in the wilderness before being thrust into power by a quirk of fate, only to find that the demands of being head of state circumscribed and made impractical the very principles he held so dear as a power-less, ordinary citizen.

The president recalled the old copy he'd found in Marco Costa's library, a gift to his former ally, a kind of apology. And the inscription.

From Dario, the turncoat.

Was this what, in truth, he'd become? Through compromise and pragmatism, a traitor to his own beliefs?

Claudius, in the second volume, had come to feel that way towards the end of his life, when the intrigue around him reached a feverish intensity. Graves, basing his story for the most part on the account of the emperor's reign given by Suetonius, had him murdered at the hands of his own wife, Agrippina, acting in concert with her son, Nero, the emperor's chosen successor. The author's fictional but all-too-realistic Claudius went to his fate with his eyes wide open, praying that his own end, and the accession of the monstrous tyrant Nero, would bring about what he had failed to achieve in his lifetime:

the ruin of the tyrannical imperial family, the restoration of Rome to republican democracy.

Politicians, much more than ordinary men and women, agonized long and hard over what they might leave behind after their deaths, perhaps because they realized only too well their failings in life. Claudius's modern successors were little different and they, too, often came to count their legacies for the most part in blood. Tiberius Claudius Caesar Augustus Germanicus spilled more than his fair share in his sixty-four years. Yet perhaps he would never have created such a lost and malevolent creature as Andrea Petrakis. Sordi was reminded once more of the old saw: what we learn from history is that we learn nothing from history. The constant battle between liberty and security, democracy and the need to safeguard a broken and imperfect state, seemed as real and as undecided now as it was when a frightened, uncertain cripple of the royal family cowered in an anteroom of Nero's palace on the Palatine, another Roman hill, a short distance away across the Forum, 2,000 years before.

He sat down and found the page, feeling both a little distracted and disturbed by these thoughts. The tale of Claudius's conversion, from terrified bystander to reluctant emperor, was so amusingly written that he could read it again and again. But there was a prerequisite to its denouement. Before the new king could be crowned, the old one had to die.

– 13 –

There were buildings in Rome that a wise police officer never asked about. The high, anonymous block at the back of the Quirinale was just such a one. There was no sign on the door, just a fancy, high-tech entrance with a man in a dark uniform beyond the glass and a trickle of nondescript people going home for the evening.

Spooks, Peroni thought. Another outpost of Luca Palombo's Ministry of the Interior, this one with a roof terrace overlooking the palace gardens. A viewpoint that still had a dark figure at the corner, even though the emergency was supposed to be over. It was probably nothing.

One small thing made him uncomfortable. Peroni had brought a pair of small binoculars with him. He wasn't able to see the face of the sniper on the roof, only the long barrel of a rifle and a pair of strong arms on the perimeter wall. But there'd been a cloud of cigarette smoke rising from the unseen space behind and that didn't ring true at all. He had no idea what secret-service officers did during the long, boring hours of waiting for an event that rarely materialized. But smoking out in the open air . . .

He looked at the entrance. The man behind it, a bored-looking, lean individual with black, greasy hair and heavy spectacles, was already eyeing him. This was, Peroni considered, an invitation. So he walked up to the glass door, took out his ID, pressed the bell and said, very firmly, into the speakerphone, 'I'm from the police. I need to speak to the duty officer immediately.'

'Do you have an appointment?' asked a tinny voice from the speaker on the wall.

'This isn't that kind of business. Just call someone, will you?'

A brief argument ensued, and it was not one Peroni intended to lose. Eventually an individual who seemed boss class came and allowed him into the building. He looked like someone recently relieved of a burden. Balding, middle-aged, congenial, with his dark silk tie tugged down to hang around his flabby neck, he resembled a doctor more than the Ministry agent Peroni suspected him to be.

The man introduced himself as Carlo Belfiore and asked, 'How can I help?'

'I'm just checking. You've got an officer on the roof.'

'We *had* officers on the roof. The emergency is over. Didn't you hear?'

'I heard. You still have someone up there. I saw him with my own eyes. Not his face. But I can see his rifle. And . . .' This still irked. 'He was smoking.'

The man laughed.

'No one smokes on government property. Except for Dario Sordi. And he's not on my roof. '

'I know what I saw.'

Belfiore's face clouded with puzzlement. He pulled out a phone and called someone, asking for the name of the officer who'd been assigned the roof duty earlier. Then he made another call, to the man himself, Peroni assumed. There was no reply.

He looked at the security guard on reception.

'You know Leone?'

'Good guy,' the doorman said straight away. 'I see him at Roma games sometimes.'

'Does he smoke?' Peroni cut in, hoping.

He thought about it and shook his head.

'I don't think so.'

Belfiore scratched his chin.

'I'm under orders,' Peroni lied. 'Plus, I have the nastiest *ispettore* in Rome on my back and he doesn't like second-hand news. I want to see this man up there for myself. I'm not leaving this building till I do.'

The boss-class spook didn't seem so congenial any more.

'Do you have any idea where you are?' he asked.

'Not really.' Peroni pointed at the lift doors. 'Are we going up there, or what?'

– 14 –

'Where's the president?' Costa asked.

They were striding down the corridor next to the Salone dei Corazzieri. The palace seemed deserted. There was no one anywhere, not on the security gates, in the offices.

'Still in his apartment,' the first *corazziere* said. 'He doesn't go out there till six-thirty. You can set your watch by it. The deal was we talk to Palombo. Stick to it. If Ranieri says otherwise . . .'

'You don't even know where Ranieri is,' Rosa Prabakaran pointed out, and got a caustic glance from Falcone for her pains. Costa understood why. They were lucky to get this far. It could still, so easily, go wrong.

They rounded a corner past the *salone* and climbed a short set of winding marble stairs.

The men in uniform stopped outside a mahogany door at the summit and glanced at one another.

The senior officer rapped on the polished wood with his knuckles and called out. Nothing. Then he shouted again, his rank and name, demanding that Palombo answer.

Rosa leaned forward, turned the handle and pushed. Costa and Falcone took out their guns, edged in front of the *corazzieri*, who had no other weapon than their swords, still sheathed, and slowly made their way into the room.

From behind them, one of the men in uniform murmured a low, shocked curse.

Automatically, Costa shoved his way to the front and entered the office, gun high, scanning the space ahead.

Luca Palombo was motionless in a leather chair behind the

desk, body thrown back at a crazy angle against the bright, sunny window. His chest was a sticky red mess of blood and gore, his head was bent forward, mouth gaping open, eyes shocked, dark, unfocused.

Falcone strode across the office and bent down over the stricken figure, peering at his face.

'Dead. Can't have happened more than a few minutes ago. Who's had access?'

'I told you I saw another *corazziere*,' the northern officer complained. 'Everyone was supposed to be confined to barracks except us.'

The older one seemed lost, for words, and for action.

Costa kept looking, caught Falcone's eye, motioned to him to move back from the desk. Then he turned round and glanced at the uniforms there, got the message over to them too, with a hand gesture, a look in the eye.

At the end of the wall, by the side of the purple velvet curtains, in an office surely made for the courtiers of a pope, was a narrow door, just ajar. In the reflection of the window Costa could just make out the shape of a pair of shiny leather shoes, black, smart, the kind a soldier might wear, behind the polished wood.

An arm tried to drive him out of the way. He turned. The senior *corazziere* had caught sight of it too, stared at him, mouthing the word 'Us'.

Costa brought the gun up to eye level, glimpsed the drawn sword and raised his eyebrows.

Not waiting for another word of protest, he moved forward, slowly, deliberately, until he was beyond the curtain. His left hand pushed back the door, his right held the service revolver tight and still, where he expected the man's head to be.

There was a shout of pain as his effort collided with something physical on the other side. Dazzling sunlight streamed into the room. He could hear the *corazzieri* assembling behind him, prepared, alert; could hear too the gasp of surprise that greeted the figure cowering on the other side, who was shaking like a leaf, holding his shoulder as if in pain.

Ugo Campagnolo's too-tanned features were wreathed in sweat. There was terror in his face.

'He's gone?' the prime minister cried, his voice breaking. '*He's gone?*'

'Who?' Costa responded calmly.

'Him!' His eyes peered cautiously into the larger officer, and at the dead man at the desk. 'The monster!'

'You mean Andrea Petrakis?' Falcone asked.

'I mean . . . I mean . . .'

His eyes, bright and beady, had begun to veer between fright and cunning.

'I was talking to Palombo. It was a discreet conversation. There was a knock on the door. So I stepped in here.'

They listened, and said nothing.

'I heard.' Campagnolo's eyes grew bright with remembered terror. 'I *heard*.'

The man stank of fear and perspiration, yet even at that moment there was a sly, conniving expression in his taut, smooth face, one that spoke of an imminent attempt to control and defuse this situation.

'You should find this intruder. Not waste time in here. Those are my orders. There. You listen to me.'

Costa's eyes strayed to the verdant palace terraces beyond the window.

In the distance, by the statue of Hermes, sat a familiar figure, seated, hunched over a book, entirely focused on its pages, a white teacup held idly in his right hand.

A shape was slowly coming into view from the palace patio. A man in the silver uniform of a *corazziere*. In his right hand was a long, shiny sword, half its length dark with blood.

– 15 –

The Ministry man Belfiore led Peroni to a small, slow, rickety lift. They made their way in silence to the top floor of the building. There was a narrow concrete staircase to the roof. The door at top of the steps was closed. Locked, or so it seemed.

'This is more my line of work, than yours,' the cop said.

He set his shoulder to the old, flimsy wood and pushed and heaved with all his weight. He'd taken down plenty of doors in his time and he knew this one wasn't going to pose a problem. The lock was feeble and soon gave way under the force of a couple of prolonged kicks. That was only the start. Someone had piled a stash of objects behind, blocking any entry. Twice he heaved with his shoulder and just managed to get the door back by the width of a hand.

He paused, thinking, then asked, 'There's no other way?'

'None,' Belfiore responded. 'I'll get help.'

There was a sound from the other side. A man's voice, angry, muffled, still full of concern, even though there were no words.

'Dammit,' Peroni muttered, feeling the heat rise in his head.

He went at the door again, with all his weight and force. This time it moved further. Belfiore, who was a little slimmer than him, said, 'Let me try and get through.'

It was a squeeze, but he got his hand round and managed to dislodge whatever was on the other side.

Peroni burst through and found himself surrounded by ancient garden objects and old junk. In the dark corner ahead lay a man in the anonymous black clothing of the security services, a guise he'd seen too often these last few days in Rome. He was bound and gagged.

Something else. A smell of tobacco on the air. Familiar. One that reminded him of what Teresa had told them when she called, speculating a little, as they all were, constantly.

'I'm not armed. Wait for my people,' Belfiore ordered.

'I don't think so,' Peroni said and strode out through the little cabin door onto the roof of the spooks' building behind the Quirinale.

The figure was where he'd seen it from the street, in the far corner, overlooking the palace gardens. Stretched out, legs akimbo, heavy, stiff, but intent on the job. The rifle butt was hard in the shoulder, the sights up to the face.

He used to smoke himself. Loved it. Only age and a new-found interest in his own health, which came from meeting Teresa Lupo, had changed things. But a good smoker never forgot.

'Elizabeth,' he yelled, and took out his gun.

He was too far away to shoot. Even if he wanted to. Peroni hated guns, weapons of all kinds. There had to be another way.

'Elizabeth,' he repeated. Then, to himself, 'Don't make me shoot you. Please.'

The Englishwoman turned for a moment and shook her head.

Then she huddled over the sniper's rifle, intent on the distant target.

Peroni kept the gun by his side and walked across the roof.

He watched as Elizabeth Murray let loose a single shot, the rifle kicking hard against her shoulder, then murmured a low curse.

– 16 –

'A fool?' Petrakis found himself saying as he stared at the old man on the stone bench, amazed that still there was no fear in his pale, exaggerated face.

'You heard me, Andrea,' Dario Sordi said. 'A foo—'

There was a sound like the crack of a whip. Petrakis watched as the foot of the statue of Hermes disintegrated into a grey cloud of dust.

The man in the *corazziere* uniform raised his bloodstained sword, aware that somehow the time available to him was fast vanishing. It never occurred to Andrea Petrakis that the second shot might be his. The force of its impact sent him reeling back on himself, deafened by the arrival of the sniper's bullet, shuddering from its shock.

The pain was odd, a sort of revelation. It felt as if some kind of vast celestial hammer had beaten on his chest, iron against iron. His entire body ached. Blood was beginning to spurt through the ragged hole the shell had made in the shining carapace covering his left shoulder and, unseen, in the flesh beneath.

As the agony grew, he fought to retain his balance and found himself staggering backwards, struggling to stay upright, wishing for a moment in the shadow, a brief pause to think, to find himself again.

There was something he needed to say.

- 17 -

Peroni wanted to scream, to swear, to leap on the prone English-woman with the rifle on the ground, shrieking: *why, why, why?*

Wanted to know why, too, he hadn't done what duty demanded. Shot her straight out in cold blood.

There were people at his back now, a commotion. Violence loomed, that curt, dark confrontation he'd come to know too well.

Then, as he got to her, the sniper's rifle barked again and she let loose a squeal of satisfaction.

He was cursing, pointing his pistol at the long, corpulent form on the concrete roof, ready to fire until Elizabeth Murray rolled over, let go of the black rifle, held her big hands wide open, looked him in the face and grinned.

Peroni kept the gun set straight at her face, unable to think of a sensible thing to say.

'Oh, don't look so cross, Gianni,' she said, still beaming. 'A couple of minutes earlier and you could have got us all into real trouble, my boy.'

The weapon wavered in his hand. She stretched out her right arm.

'Now. Will you help up an old lady? Please? I really am past these games, you know.'

– 18 –

It was as if they were in a movie, events shifting rapidly, frame by frame. The first shot splintered the foot of the statue next to Dario Sordi, raising a cloud of fragments and dust. As Andrea Petrakis struggled to finish the final act of his adventure, of what he surely regarded as the purpose of his life, a second crack rent the air. This time the arrival was different: the clatter of metal meeting metal, of a powerful, violent impact shattering the evening calm.

The man in the ornate uniform jumped back, a look of agonized astonishment on his lined face. It was only at that moment that Dario Sordi realized they were no longer alone. Beyond Petrakis, Nic Costa was sprinting down the path from the palace, pistol in hand, starting to cry in a voice full of righteous anger, one that reminded the old man of the friend, the young officer's father, he'd lost years ago. Behind him came a group of *corazzieri* and other men, swarming into the gardens, Fabio Ranieri at the rear.

He looked at his assailant again. The shot had entered the breastplate somewhere near his left shoulder. There was a dark hole torn in the shiny metal there, and blood pumping through. The glistening sword hung loose in the man's right hand, ineffective, though still a part of him. His eyes were glassy with pain and shock. He was stumbling round and round on himself, heading back towards the palace, making hurt, whimpering noises, as if pain were a stranger to him except in its infliction.

Sordi stood up.

'Take this man into custody,' he ordered, then, slightly ashamed of the note of triumph in his voice, added, more quietly, 'and . . .'

What?

'Thank you,' he muttered, mainly to himself. He felt a little giddy, heard some more words escape his lips unbidden. 'I'm safe now.'

That grim day in the Via Rasella was rising again in his memory. In his mind's eye he was seeing the faces of the two Germans, the speaking one from his recurring nightmare brighter than the other.

Safety was what everyone sought in the end. A private place to call their own. Shelter from the storm. The young never quite appreciated this. To them the world was a place to be fought for, to be won. For some, like Andrea Petrakis, it would remain that way for ever, which was a very personal and dangerous tragedy. Age never softened their sharp ambitions, diminished their appetite, whispered the great secret: that life was brief and fragile, a gift to be cherished, not thrown away on a whim or some obsession.

Costa got to him first, face anxious, watching the rooftops. Soon he was met by a crowd of others, *corazzieri* crowding round like some ancient Roman phalanx in silver, a growing human shield of tall men, one that Ranieri soon reached out of breath, uncharacteristically wild-eyed.

'There's someone else out there,' Costa said quickly. 'We need to get you inside immediately.'

Sordi found it difficult to hear, to comprehend. He couldn't take his eyes off the other figure, the one clutching the bloodied sword, who'd now staggered to the steps in front of the cool, shady terrace, with its long evening shadows, only to turn back, mouth open – eyes too – in shock, at his own injury and failure. Sordi wondered which was the greater suffering: the wound or the sudden, brusque collapse of his mission. Wondered too how he might have felt all those years ago in the Via Rasella if matters had turned out differently.

He shook his grey head, hoping to clear his thoughts. There was time to work, to prepare. Perhaps, finally, to discover something tantamount to the truth of the Blue Demon.

'Don't you see what this means?' Sordi said. 'We have someone. Alive. A witness. I want Falcone. I want . . .'

The lean inspector was there already. Sordi realized he should have expected no less.

'Deal with him,' he began, pointing at Petrakis, half in the darkness of the terrace, leaning against a column, lost and hurt. 'As you dealt with the Spanish woman.' Sordi found some grim satisfaction in the situation. 'This one can tell you something. Everything. We shall have answers, important ones. Do this now, please. Quickly. No need to inform Palombo for the moment.'

They fell silent. No one looked at him.

'He's got a gun,' someone said.

Sordi looked. It seemed impossible. The wounded man in the silver breastplate leaking blood had somehow exchanged the sword for another weapon. A black pistol. It was half-erect in his shaking right hand, as if it had found its way there without the man's knowing.

Andrea Petrakis stared straight at him across the verdant space that separated them and shouted, 'I know who you are.'

'I know who I am too, young man,' Dario Sordi whispered, watching him prepare to move.

Sordi blinked, trying to comprehend what he was seeing, hearing.

Petrakis snatched off his plumed helmet, lumbered down the path back towards them, the revolver rising, repeating over and over, 'I know, I know, I know . . .'

Behind him was a second figure. A familiar one.

Ugo Campagnolo stepped out into the sunlight. There was a gun in his hand too. A small weapon, almost insignificant. Sordi watched aghast, knowing what he was about to see.

Campagnolo walked up to the side of the man in the *corazziere*'s uniform, extended a shaking arm, then pumped a single bullet into his bare head. Petrakis fell down to the lawn on one knee, screaming. They watched as his assailant took aim and fired once more.

The shot man leaped sideways, as if hit by some electric shock, and his broken frame tumbled to the ground, arms outstretched, unmoving.

Dario Sordi shook himself free of his guards and marched across the perfect green grass of the Quirinale. There was a scarlet fury in his head, one he knew and hated.

'Give my officers the gun,' the president ordered. 'The police will need it. Evidence. This is too far. Even for you.'

'Evidence?' There was a wild look in the prime minister's eyes, and a fierce, determined demeanour.

'The gun,' Costa demanded, then walked up and removed the revolver from Campagnolo's trembling hands.

'Evidence?' Campagnolo asked again, more quietly, as he recovered a little of his composure.

He took one step forward, his features taut with hate and anger, and stared into the president's long, pale face.

'I saved you, Dario. Don't you realize, you old fool? He had a weapon . . .'

'Which came from where?' Sordi interjected.

'He had a weapon and he'd have used it.'

Ugo Campagnolo looked at each of them in turn.

'I saved the president today. You all saw it. You're witnesses.'

He raised himself up on his heels and brushed down the front of his jacket, as if it were covered in dirt.

'Soon you shall hear about it too. In the papers. On the TV. One call is all it takes. Soon . . .'

His voice froze, recognizing something on the faces of the men watching him. Unseen by Campagnolo, something had travelled towards him. A bright red mark, like a scarlet beauty spot on a movie actress from another era, had briefly brushed across the prime minister's sweating temple, then disappeared, as if dashing away in search of another target.

Sordi stopped breathing. All eyes had turned until they were upon him. He looked down. The livid spot, some sighting aid from a twenty-first-century weapon hidden away on a distant rooftop, had ranged across the grass to climb his arm and begin moving steadily towards his head.

Ranieri yelled something. Sordi found himself surrounded by a pushing, arguing phalanx of bodies, men dragging him to the ground, trying to cover his frame with theirs. He briefly saw Costa's anxious face. Then Ranieri's. A shot rang out. A man's pained shriek rent the air. Then another.

'My God . . .' Sordi cried and found himself swamped again by the crush around him.

Still afraid?

It was an old, dead voice. German. Clearly audible in the crush of struggling men around.

There was a time to stand up, he thought. A time to face the Devil.

Sordi pushed and yelled and screamed and fought his way against their well-meant intentions. Finally, his anger and what little strength he possessed had some effect. He found himself free of their arms and scrambled to his feet to see three silver-clad *corazzieri* bent over the still frame of Fabio Ranieri, tears in their eyes.

Sordi tore himself away from the broken form of the Corazzieri captain and turned to look at the bright blue sky and the buildings around them.

'Bastards!' he screamed. 'Do you think I fear you now?' He pounded his chest with his fist, looking for something, anything, seeing only the skyline of Rome, its ancient buildings and church towers, a horizon imprinted on his memory since he was a child. 'Do you imagine after all these long, bloody years . . . ?'

'Dario.' It was Costa beside him, his face pale and pleading, his eyes round with shock yet filled with some determination. 'You must—'

The red dot returned and ran up the young police officer's sleeve. Sordi elbowed him out of the way and let the deadly bead fall on him, bellowing, 'Take me. Take me if you dare!'

He waited. Nothing.

Then a low, worried sound came from the officers crouched by the unmoving Ranieri. Sordi followed the direction of their gaze. The sighting point had moved on and was now travelling along Ugo Campagnolo's right arm. The prime minister saw it too, shrieked and stupidly tried to rub it off with his hand. The scarlet mark rose to his brown, stocky neck, higher to his cheek, then rested above his right eye.

Campagnolo howled with fear, clutched at his face with his hands, stood still for a moment, and then was thrown backwards by a single sniper shot, one that caught him straight in the head, with an effect that Sordi could not bring himself to witness.

The president turned to one side and looked at this cherished oasis of green in the heart of the overcrowded, overburdened city. The still Roman evening was broken by the urgent, hurt cries of the men around him.

Il Torrino began to toll the half-hour. On the third stroke the sonorous tones of its chimes were drowned out by another noise, a deep, baritone bellowing like the roar of some subterranean monster shaking itself awake. They all turned towards the building and watched. A black and yellow storm cloud was beginning to tear through the palace behind them, right to left, a rolling ball of thunder that picked up debris, stone and fabric and canvas, in its maw, and burst out of the porticoed arcade like a fiery tsunami shrieking as it travelled, tearing down columns, turning this visible side of the palace – a view Dario Sordi had come to love – to rubble and chaos.

The final resonant chimes of the campanile were faintly audible as the noise of the blast abated. They were replaced by the harsh mechanical chatter of a million alarm bells strewn somewhere inside the shattered Quirinale. Sordi watched the flames start to recede and the garden edge of the building begin to crumble and collapse into a tumult of disorder. The *corazzieri* left the broken, shattered body of their leader and began to stumble mindlessly towards the place they were sworn to protect.

Duty followed a good man forever, from the first dawn of consciousness all the way to the grave.

Sordi watched the palace of the popes begin to disintegrate before his eyes. This was what they wanted all along, he thought. Not blood, not vengeance, but anarchy over order, the sharp, bright fury of the moment victorious over the slow, pained progress he knew as civilization. It was the lesson Andrea Petrakis had learned from the Etruscans, and perhaps the man had a point.

The Blue Demon was everywhere and nowhere, eternal, invisible, waiting for its time to come.

Part 7

THE WAY SOUTH

- 1 -

Costa was woken by the smell of tobacco smoke drifting into the bedroom from the patio outside. The acrid aroma mingled with the fragrance of jasmine blossom clinging to the wall of his country home off the Via Appia Antica.

A familiar stench. Black Russian. He got up, dressed slowly, thinking.

It was six days since the bloody events at the Quirinale. Normality, of a kind, had returned. An interim government was in power, awaiting elections that Ugo Campagnolo's heirs, shadowy men of more dubious provenance, were expected to win with a landslide. The prime minister had been accorded a state funeral, which Dario Sordi, looking frail for the first time, attended in silence. Afterwards he had gone to the private ceremony for Fabio Ranieri, one that had attracted no publicity whatsoever, at the insistence of the dead Corazzieri captain's family.

No one in Italy quite believed they had heard the full story. No one expected to. The Spanish woman, Anna Ybarra, remained in police custody, charged with attempted murder and numerous terrorist offences, seemingly unable to shed any useful light on the men who had brought her to Italy. An attempt by the divided opposition to force an investigation into the affair had failed. After that Dario Sordi had retired behind the shutters of the Quirinale Palace, refusing to appear in public. The natural Italian penchant for cynicism towards politicians had come into play too, filling the Web and the scurrilous prints with rumours and suggestions. The identity of the final sniper remained a mystery. Only his location was known, through the discovery of a set of shell cases in the campanile of *Il Torrino*.

The previous afternoon Costa had passed the old, crumbling statue of Pasquino near the Piazza Navona and found the base plastered in fresh posters making any number of allegations about the political classes – a few about Sordi himself. There was a febrile mood in the air, along with a sense of guilty gratitude. Whatever had happened behind the ring of steel surrounding the Quirinale Palace, the emergency was over. The status quo – awkward, imperfect, fragile – had returned. In a sense the Blue Demon had won. No one questioned the present state of the nation at that moment. The average Roman lacked the energy, and saw no point in attempting to summon up the necessary courage. These matters were covered up in the end. It almost seemed routine.

Costa had read the scabrous messages on Pasquino on his way back from the Questura after some nameless official from the Ministry served suspension notices on all those who'd worked in the apartment in San Giovanni in Laterano, even Teresa and her hapless assistant Silvio Di Capua. Commissario Esposito was hanging on to his job by the skin of his teeth somehow. It was unclear what would happen next. An investigation would have proved too embarrassing for the Ministry. Some swift judgement – a loss of pay, demotion perhaps, even ejection from the force – would be handed down to the police officers involved, probably in a matter of days.

This no longer concerned him. After they handed out the notices he turned down Falcone's offer of a consolation lunch with the others, walked into a stationer's shop, bought a few sheets of notepaper and some envelopes, then sat in the belly of the Pantheon, listening to the echoing voices of the visitors, entranced as always by the light falling through the oculus, the eye in the centre of the dome, which dispatched a shaft of bright sun directly into what was once the hall of a pagan temple built by the emperor Hadrian. This was a building with memories, of a time when he felt some kind of hope and ambition, for himself and the world. A period of love, too, something that had slipped between his fingers like dust almost as quickly as it had arrived, unbidden, almost unwanted.

Beneath the great span of Hadrian's sanctuary he penned his resignation from the police. It was a short, unapologetic, practical note, which he delivered by hand to Prinzivalli, the desk officer on duty at the Questura, one hour later, asking that he pass it on to whoever was in charge at that moment.

He had no plans. Some part of him that had been slumbering for a decade or more whispered reminders of a dream he'd almost forgotten: taking a bicycle onto the ancient cobbles of the Appian Way, the old Roman road at the foot of his drive, which ran, straight as a die mostly, all the way from the capital to Brindisi in Apulia, moving from modern Italy into the lost past of fable. He'd never allowed himself that kind of freedom. There had always been cares and duties that got in the way as he slipped from a quiet, introverted childhood into the sudden demands of a family falling apart beneath the weight of controversy, illness and death.

Costa made two cups of coffee and poured a couple of glasses of orange juice, then went outside. Elizabeth Murray was basking in the hot morning sun. She wore sunglasses, a blue checked cotton shirt of the kind farmers liked, and a baggy pair of jeans. The cigarette went out the moment he appeared, ditched beneath the wooden table that had been used for outdoor meals for as long as he could remember. He saw, now, that the oak was rotten, and perhaps had been for some time, without his noticing.

There was a black briefcase on the surface and a mobile phone.

Elizabeth grabbed at her cup, took a swig, closed her eyes and said, 'You know, there's nowhere else in the world where coffee tastes like this. Rome. It must be the water.'

'Why didn't you tell us?' he asked. 'That you knew what Petrakis's message meant?'

She squinted at the horizon: the ruins of tombs, the roofs of the nearby mansions, a fringe of trees waving in the soft morning breeze.

'What would you have done?'

'We could have talked to Ranieri.'

'You would never have got through. So who else? Palombo? Dario himself? You should read history more. These things don't happen by accident. They're conspired at. Plotted. Planned. They knew exactly what they were doing from the moment Andrea Petrakis left Afghanistan. Dario was isolated as soon as the G8 parties left for the Vatican. I know. I tried to call him myself. It was never going to work.'

She shrugged and a brief, self-deprecating smile creased her face.

'So I did what you can't. I took matters into my own hands.'

'You might have failed.'

'I might,' she agreed. 'I didn't feel I had much of an option. It was obvious they'd try to attack Dario while he was in the garden. I know his little tea ceremony well myself. Where do you think the old boy gets those English biscuits he loves so much?' She frowned. 'I was sure Petrakis would try to do the job in person. He had a theatrical streak to his nature, in case you didn't notice. I reasoned that in those circumstances I could take him out. I would have done, too. I wasn't trying to wound the bastard. I wanted him dead. So did Ugo Campagnolo, of course, though for entirely different reasons.'

'Petrakis wasn't alone.'

'No. I'm old. Out of practice. Twenty years ago I might have seen a barrel poking out of *Il Torrino*. Not now. Sorry!'

'Peroni could have shot you.'

A look of puzzlement crossed her face.

'Is life meant to be led without risk? I didn't know that. Never occurred to me. How boring.'

She patted the briefcase.

'Before I open up this thing, do you want to tell me what you think happened? Then we can compare notes.'

'I don't know,' Costa said emphatically. 'The truth is, I don't care any more.'

The answer surprised her.

Elizabeth Murray gazed at him and there was something in her friendly, mannish face he couldn't interpret. Sympathy? Reluctance? Some slow, subtle anger?

'But you do, Nic,' she said quietly. 'I'm going to make sure of that, I'm afraid.'

She snapped open the case, reached inside and came out with some kind of report. The paper was yellowed with age, the words clearly typed, not printed from a modern machine.

'This is the submission your father produced for the Blue Demon commission. I suppressed it, with the backing of Dario Sordi, before any other member could see it. Or so we thought.'

'No, Elizabeth. You can't do this. I won't become involved . . .'

'Nic!' She looked furious, and for the first time since they met he realized he could imagine her in the security services, an active participant in some live operation; could see her as Peroni had described, spreadeagled like a professional on the rooftop overlooking the Quirinale gardens. 'May I ask you a personal question?'

'Can I stop you?'

'No.' She watched him intently, curious to see his reaction. 'Tell me. Your parents died of the selfsame cancer eleven years apart. An identical disease. Did that never strike you as a very unfortunate and unusual coincidence? Are you perpetually incurious? Or simply down-right naive?'

The bright morning seemed to pall, the vivid country colours leaching out of the fields and flowers and vines around them. He couldn't hear the birds singing. It was impossible to think.

'What did you say?' he murmured, shaking his head.

'I'm going for a smoke. In what passes for your vineyard.' She threw the report at him. 'Read this. Then we'll talk.'

- 2 -

There was a voice inside the words on the fading pages and it was that of his father: precise, impatient, penetrating and angry. The submission ran to ten sides and described the relationship between Ugo Campagnolo, the Gladio team led by Renzo Frasca, Gregor Petrakis, the father of Andrea, the network's place-man, and the three principal crime organizations in Italy: the Sicilian Cosa Nostra, the Camorra of Naples and the 'Ndrangheta of Calabria.

Costa read the accusations his own father had put down on paper two decades before and found himself wondering, with the distance of time and his experience in the police, what, in truth, they were worth. Everything was circumstantial, the sources anonymous, the links intangible.

The charge was simple: Gregor Petrakis and Campagnolo met through the covert Gladio organization, set up initially to provide a network of stay-behind agents in the event of a Soviet takeover of Italy. The Blue Demon was one of several fake terror groups envisaged by the two as a way of meeting Gladio's demand for a 'strategy of tension'. But the pair soon discovered a mutual taste for illicit income. At the time Campagnolo's legitimate businesses were beginning to fail. He and Petrakis quietly made themselves small fortunes worked through the supply of hard drugs – not just in Tarquinia, but in Rome and Florence too – by using the Greek's links with Afghan sources to channel heroin and marijuana directly to customers outside the usual networks controlled by the mobs.

Over time, Campagnolo came to understand the risk he was running by undercutting the gangs. His solution was to persuade the three normally independent crime organizations to pool their resources, take over the Blue Demon's drug network and use him and its resources as a conduit into the world of politics. Slowly, Campagnolo subverted the political ambitions of his NATO handlers and shifted his allegiance to the mobs in return for their support. The Blue Demon became a conspiracy, a consortium dedicated to a covert attempt to fund, shape and control the political future of the nation, infiltrating its institutions, creating parties and groupings that would quietly work in the interests of organized crime.

Petrakis and his wife, idealists at heart, died when they realized what was happening and threatened to inform their original paymasters, the Americans and the British running the Gladio operation. Campagnolo's response was to inform the consortium that Petrakis was still involved in direct drug-trafficking on behalf of the Afghan gangs, against their direct orders.

When the couple were murdered, Renzo Frasca, the US handler for the couple's work with Gladio, was panicked into inventing a solution that would prevent discovery of the network. Petrakis's original plan for the Blue Demon as a terror group became the answer, and his son – a minor participant in his parents' schemes – was talked into fronting the imaginary cell as a way of getting him out of the country safely and saving what reputation his parents had. The deaths of Frasca and his wife were faked. Those of three students whose only interest had been drugs, and of a hapless *carabiniere*, were all too real, props to lend the story a terrible credence.

And Ugo Campagnolo escaped, to rise and prosper through the world of Italian politics, the frontman for the conglomerate of crime interests that took on the name that the late Gregor Petrakis had given his fledgling terror group, the Blue Demon.

Costa finished the report, his head spinning. There was nothing there but supposition and hearsay. Not a single statement from a named witness or a piece of paper that could link Campagnolo's companies to the Petrakises' illicit operations.

Yet it was true, and he knew it. His father was a careful, fair-minded man. He would never have put down on paper suspicions that were mere gossip and rumour.

These were events that began in Nic Costa's childhood. Much of them passed him by. There were reasons: the sensation the Blue Demon generated in the media had come to an end once Andrea Petrakis disappeared. More personal grounds too. Not long afterwards his mother had become sick, falling into the long, slow, debilitating illness that would take her life, slowly, day by day, as the rest of them watched, distraught and impotent.

The words Elizabeth Murray had uttered brought back a thought that had dogged him for years: why should they have been so unlucky? What savage quirk of fate meant that both his father and mother should fall victim to the same disease?

He was lost in his own memories. Only the smell of smoke told him, in the end, that she'd returned to sit at the old table again, where the family used to eat together, laughing mostly, even in the dark days.

– 3 –

'Why did you bury this?' Costa asked.

'For his own good. Ugo Campagnolo was a member of the commission. Your father would have been serving his own death warrant had we allowed that report to be presented.'

'You could have done something.'

She closed her eyes for a moment, exasperated.

'Listen to yourself. You're a cop. How many bent politicians do you have in Italy? How many have seen the inside of a jail cell these last thirty years? Besides, they'd covered their tracks so well. There was nothing we could do. It was impossible . . . So we tried to keep Marco safe, in spite of himself.' She waved at the report. 'We had to make sure Campagnolo's people never knew any of this existed. It was dangerous. For Marco.' Her bright, serious eyes never left him. 'For his family.'

He could hear the sound of a tractor working in the adjoining field, the distant voices of the farm labourers going about their work.

'Do you want me to go on?' she asked softly.

'She had cancer. They both did.'

He could picture them wasting away and recall so sharply the impotence he felt as he watched.

'I was out of the service by then,' she went on. 'Marco kept on nagging people. He wouldn't let go. They were bound to find out in the end.'

She took some more papers out of the briefcase.

'I was in touch with Dario throughout, discreetly. The idea that the crime gangs were deliberately infiltrating the political process, not just buying off individuals along the way, it terrified us. The mobs were weaker when they were rivals. If they came together, made a concerted attempt to infiltrate the process of government . . .' She stopped for a moment. 'It doesn't bear thinking about. When your father became sick, we sent some friends into his office. They were looking for bugs. They found some. They also found this.'

He stared at the report. It bore the letterhead of a private laboratory in Milan and a few paragraphs of text that seemed mired in scientific jargon. One thing he could understand: the recurring term 'radiation'.

'These people have friends everywhere. Among them are some ex-secret-service agents in the former Eastern Bloc. They used junk like this long before it occurred to anyone else it might disguise a murder. What they put in the desk in your father's office,' she stared at the report, 'must have been there for months, if not years. Long-term, low-level exposure to radiation is very difficult to detect, unless you know that's what you're looking for.'

He got up and walked to the corner of the patio, scanned the drive. It was empty except for the small red Fiat she must have used. Costa wiped his eyes with his sleeve, then came and sat down.

'What about my mother?' he asked.

She reached for another sheet of paper. He could see it was from the same company.

'When we realized what had happened – the similarity between her symptoms and his – we managed to get someone into her office in the university. Radiation lingers. There was still a faint trace there. The same kind.'

The Englishwoman frowned.

'I'm sorry. Maybe they warned your father. Maybe not.' She glanced at the farmhouse behind them. 'They were bugging this place. You know that. You also know threats would have made no difference. The way your father was . . .'

'You could have told me this.' Costa felt like screaming, like running away.

She sat still and silent, waiting for him to calm down. After a little while she asked, 'Told you what? That we believed these people – Ugo Campagnolo among them – had your mother and father murdered, in the cruellest way imaginable, and there was nothing in the world we could do about it? We can't link him to the radioactive material here. We can't even prove an organization called the Blue Demon exists.' She hesitated. 'Not yet.' Elizabeth Murray watched him closely, then asked, 'Why do you think Andrea Petrakis came back?'

'Is this a test?'

'You could say that.'

There could be only one reason.

He thought for a moment, then said, 'He was ordered back. They were worried about something.'

'Exactly.' Her eyes never left him. 'A few of us have been quietly working on the Blue Demon for years. It's not easy. I moved to New Zealand for a reason. To stay alive principally. In our favour, there is the simple matter of human nature. This is an awkward arrangement. The members have detested each other for decades. You can't bury all that hatred overnight, even when the prize is an entire nation. Now they're winning, it's worse. There are even more arguments to be had over how to divide up the spoils. Some of those who signed up find it deeply boring too, and much prefer the old ways. In the end they wind up marginalized. Left out of the loop. They don't like that.'

'You have someone?' he asked. 'An informer?'

'I wish it were that simple. Some months ago there was word that one of those involved was willing to turn himself in. We don't know who. We don't know why. We were told he would give us everything. Names, bank accounts. The structure of everything Campagnolo and those behind him worked to establish. If we could bring in this man alive . . . keep him that way. Get into court. That's a big if. Particularly now they know. They'd kill him without a thought, of course, the way they were content to shoot Ugo instead of Dario when they saw the endgame was falling apart. No friendship among thieves.'

He remembered those few grim, bloody moments in the garden of the Quirinale.

'Who was it?'

'Someone in the campanile. That's all anyone knows. All they're likely to know. The same goes for the bomb in the palace. It was in a room in the basement. My guess is someone placed it there after Palombo detained all Ranieri's officers. I don't see how it could have happened any other way. They weren't trying to kill the G8 people. They weren't that interested in assassinating Dario, at least not in a personal sense. They were making a statement. Trying to tell us they knew we were chasing them and they wouldn't allow it. That was why they summoned Andrea Petrakis back from Afghanistan.'

A car stopped in the road at the end of the drive. She watched it for a moment, then said, 'Rennick was fooled into thinking this was one last false-flag operation to keep the public on side. He didn't realize Andrea was seriously damaged goods by that stage, more damaged than even Luca Palombo appreciated. Andrea had come to believe all that nonsense his father invented about the Blue Demon. Except that for him it didn't mean a bunch of murdering criminals. It meant . . . some bloody retribution against Rome, against Western society. As if he were some avenging angel from Hell.'

She drained her coffee.

'He was a leaky weapon, one that might go off anywhere. Rennick was willing to contemplate some small-scale display of terrorism in the heart of Rome, with a handful of casualties, just enough to keep the hoi polloi in its place, and maybe even send Andrea straight back into the arms of the leadership in Afghanistan. He didn't tell his superiors. I know that. I checked. They would have stopped it the moment they heard. Those days are over. Besides, it was never going to happen. You understand why? Andrea said it himself. You heard him. He didn't come here for the reason Rennick thought. He came here to kill the Blue Demon.'

Costa's mind returned to those last few moments in the palace gardens. Petrakis approaching Dario Sordi, his face full of fury and a passion for revenge.

'Andrea had no idea what the Blue Demon really represented,' he said quietly. 'For him it was the man who betrayed his parents.'

'Quite. So Palombo conveniently put none other than Dario Sordi in the frame, which happened to fit very neatly with the world view Andrea had come to develop over the years. The lunatic craved a target and, when he had it, nothing was going to stop him. Not Renzo Frasca, not us, not you – certainly not that poor fool Giovanni Batisti, who opened his mouth to Palombo the moment Dario tried to sound him out.'

'Are you sure of this?' he asked.

'Pretty much. Ranieri had a wire tap on Palombo for a while. He thought he could control Andrea. He didn't realize Petrakis intended to destroy everything, and everyone, he associated with Rome. Dario. Palombo. Ugo too probably, if he'd got the chance. If you tell a man to pretend he's a monster, place him among monsters, then demand that he act, in word and deed, like a monster, only a fool should be surprised if in the end he becomes a monster himself.'

Costa felt as if the world had turned upside down, rearranged itself into a form that was different, unrecognizable, yet one that made a terrible kind of sense. All the self-hate he'd recognized in his father over the years. All the pain and the internalized agony. It was, he now saw, a form of self-recrimination, the knowledge that his own dogged integrity had brought an untimely death upon his wife, and then, in a way Marco Costa probably regarded as a deserved form of retribution, upon himself too.

'Can you prove any of this?'

Her pale, very English face fell.

'Not a thing. Sorry.'

'I need to think,' he said, and got up from the table.

She didn't move.

'There's no time for thinking,' Elizabeth Murray observed, sounding a little cross. 'Don't you understand?'

'I'm sorry . . .'

'Listen to me, Nic. I've been chasing the ghost of the Blue Demon for twenty years. I used to think it was Ugo Campagnolo himself, and now I wonder how I could ever have been so stupid. This is the dark side of Italy, the part that's always there, as much as we try to pretend it doesn't exist. They made Campagnolo prime minister and murdered him when they thought he might prove a liability. They will pack the government that replaces him with their own men, loyal to the organizations, not those who elect them. They're inside the Carabinieri, the police force, the judiciary, the entire process of government. As every day passes they become more powerful, their influence more corrosive than ever. This is my adopted country and I had to abandon it because these sons of bitches made me fear for my life. Did you hear what I said? *This all happened because they think we may finally have them*. And your response is going to be to walk away? Your name is Costa, isn't it? Or were you adopted?'

'Don't push me, please.'

She reached into the briefcase once more and removed something. Costa saw what it was: the resignation letter he'd handed to Prinzivalli at the Questura desk the day before.

'I gave that to a police officer . . .'

'A damned good one too,' she interrupted. 'He handed it straight to Leo. It never went any further. We're not totally alone, you know. We have a few select friends. And this is your answer, is it? To hide your head in the sand. To flee. Just as Dario and I did twenty years ago, burying the evidence your father was pressing upon us. Looking the other way for no other reason than cowardice dressed as convenience.'

She stood up and came to face him beneath the uncut, overflowing vines of the terrace.

'Marco was the only man alive who had the guts to stand up to these crooks. If some of us had shared his courage, perhaps he'd still be here today. And your mother. Maybe this place,' she threw an arm towards the honey-coloured house beside them, 'would feel like a home instead of a tomb.'

'That's enough.'

The anger left her red-faced. She looked a little ashamed of it.

'It's not even close. How many people know what you just heard, do you think? How many dare we trust?'

The thought hadn't occurred to him.

'I've no idea. There must be some kind of specialist group . . .'

She laughed at him.

'Where? To do what? Are you hearing what I'm telling you?

Twenty years ago, when these people raised Ugo Campagnolo out of the gutter and put him into power, they were the conspiracy. Today the conspiracy is us. A handful of people who hardly dare pass the time of day with a stranger. Why do you think I told you so little in San Giovanni? I didn't know for one second whether one of you would run back to Palombo and tell him every word.'

She threw the envelope on the table.

'Well, I know now. We have a meeting this afternoon. If you want to come, bring a suitcase and some things. I don't know when you'll see this place again. But,' she nodded at the table, 'if you want to stay here and watch the grass grow, then good day. You're no use to us.'

There was so much to take in and, staring into her big, friendly face, so little time to think.

Costa found himself wondering what his father would have done in such circumstances, and knew the answer immediately, almost as if he'd heard the old man's cracked, gravelly voice in his ear once more.

He picked up the envelope and tore it to shreds. She watched him, expressionless.

'I have one more favour to ask,' Elizabeth Murray said. 'Dario's in that car. He doesn't know whether you want to see him or not. This has been eating at him for years, Nic. Talk to him. The last week . . . Ranieri's death – this has all taken its toll on the man. He needs you.'

- 4 -

Dario Sordi emerged from the car at the gate with the tall figure of Leo Falcone by his side. The old man waved at the police inspector to stay back as he began to walk slowly towards the house.

The two men met halfway, next to the bench seat they'd installed when Marco Costa's illness made it difficult for him to walk. Sordi looked grateful for the chance to sit. He seemed so much more frail than a week before. It was the first time Costa had ever seen doubt, and perhaps a little fear, in his eyes, and he felt guilty for being in some way responsible for the change in this decent old family friend.

'I'm sorry. I am so very sorry,' Sordi said in a faltering voice, one that betrayed his age. 'I apologize that I lacked the courage to tell you to your face. Forgive me . . .'

'Dario, there's nothing to forgive.'

'I wish I could believe that. I've always tried to think the best of people, Nic. I hoped, I believed for a while, that Ugo Campagnolo and the men behind him would be satisfied with what they had. It is a nation, after all. Few own such a jewel as Italy. Few get it handed to them by the weakness and petty divisions of their opponents.'

He shook his head, as if fighting to clear his thoughts.

'But I was a fool. There's no accommodation to be made with thieves. For an atheist, your father had an extraordinary knowledge of religion, you know. He quoted Augustine at me on this subject once, and I never forgot what he said about,' his mouth became narrow, almost cruel, 'kleptocracies. "If justice is taken away, then what are states but gangs of robbers? And what are gangs of robbers themselves but little states?"'

Sordi looked him in the eye.

'This is not ordinary politics. Far from it. This is criminality posing as democracy. The men behind the Blue Demon are quietly seizing every institution, every element of the state they value, carving up the proceeds between them, hoping to make sure this nation will remain theirs for generations. My God . . . I was born into a nightmare like that. I don't wish to die in one.'

His voice broke, his hand shook as he pointed at the house in the field behind them.

'I wish I could have saved Marco and mother,' Dario Sordi whispered. 'And poor Ranieri. I wish so much . . .'

Costa reached out and embraced him, holding his stiff, bony body firmly, in a way he had never managed with his own father. Sordi's chin, bristly and dry, brushed against his cheek. Then the old man pulled back and gazed away for a moment, ashamed of his tears.

'No one could save my father, Dario. He lived as he saw fit. That was who he was. We all knew that. None of us could have changed him one iota. Perhaps now . . .'

He stopped himself. There was a stray thought rising in his head – that perhaps Marco Costa's spirit did live on somewhere, and might notice this moment. It seemed unnatural, and so inimical to the way in which he was raised in the house a few short steps away, that he felt almost guilty to have entertained such a notion.

There was a sound. Elizabeth Murray was walking up the drive, looking like a mountain shepherdess who'd lost her way.

Then he heard something from the road. Two more cars were moving slowly towards them. He could see Gianni Peroni at the wheel of the first, with Teresa Lupo by his side and Silvio Di Capua in the back. Rosa Prabakaran, her face dark and pretty and serious at the wheel, was driving the second. In the passenger seat next to her was the magistrate Giulia Amato.

Peroni drew up by the gate and winked at him.

'Hop in then,' the big cop told him.

'Goodbye, Dario. Take care,' Costa said quickly and strode to the rear of Peroni's vehicle. There he opened the door for Elizabeth Murray, helping her onto the seat, passing over her crook, before returning to climb in the other side.

They set off to the south, away from Rome. He reminded himself that, for the last few days, he'd been fantasizing about a journey such as this. Down the Via Appia Antica, to an unknown destination, a different Italy, a land he knew only by reputation, not experience.

It seemed he was going there anyway.

– Author's note –

The events and characters portrayed here are entirely fictional. However, Operation Gladio and its networks of clandestine stay-behind partisans were very real and operated for two decades or more with the secret support of successive Western governments fearful of a Soviet domino effect in Europe after the Second World War.

The CIA's founder, Allen Dulles, was instrumental in the formation of Gladio, and it was his organization that paid for most of its operations in both NATO and neutral countries. Their existence was nothing more than a rumour until the 1980s, when the Italian judge Felice Casson discovered archive documents which clearly showed that some elements in the intelligence community had links with right-wing terrorist groups.

Gladio's initial brief was to provide the basis for a network of partisan opposition in the event of a Soviet takeover. Power was usually devolved to those involved in the covert movements, men who, in the case of Italy, tended to be recruited from within the ranks of former fascists and the criminal classes and were often left to devise their own strategies of action.

Casson told a BBC documentary that the aim was '. . . to create tension within the country to promote conservative, reactionary social and political tendencies. While this strategy was being implemented, it was necessary to protect those behind it because evidence implicating them was being discovered. Witnesses withheld information to cover right-wing extremists.'

A 1972 attack in Peteano, in Friuli-Venezia Giulia, was a rare visible example of Gladio's apparent links to terrorism in Italy. Three members of the Carabinieri died in a car-bomb explosion, which, for years, was blamed upon the Italian left-wing terrorist group, the Red Brigades. When Casson reopened the case, he discovered that the explosives used came from a secret Gladio arms cache. Vincenzo Vinciguerra, a former member of the neo-fascist groups *Avanguardia Nazionale* and *Ordine Nuovo*, received a life sentence for the attack and went on to speak openly about connections between terrorism and the secret services. He claimed that he had been able to escape and hide after the outrage because of support among the Italian security community for his anti-communist stance.

Vinciguerra recalled, 'A whole mechanism came into action . . . the Carabinieri, the Minister of the Interior, the customs services, and the military and civilian intelligence services accepted the ideological reasoning behind the attack.'

He was later to tell the Swiss historian Daniele Ganser, author of *Nato's Secret Armies, Operation Gladio and Terrorism in Western Europe*, 'You had to attack civilians, the people, women, children, innocent people, unknown people far removed from any political game. The reason was quite simple. They were supposed to force these people, the Italian public, to turn to the state to ask for greater security. This is the political logic which remains behind all the massacres and the bombings which remain unpunished, because the state cannot convict itself or declare itself responsible for what happened.'

At his trial, Vinciguerra was to add, 'With the massacre of Peteano and with all those that have followed, the knowledge should by now be clear that there existed a real live structure, occult and hidden, with the capacity of giving a strategic direction to the outrages. [This structure] lies within the state itself. There exists in Italy a secret force parallel to the armed forces, composed of civilians and military men, in an anti-Soviet capacity, that is, to organize a resistance on Italian soil.'

On 24 October 1990, the then Italian prime minister Giulio Andreotti astonished the political establishment when he finally confirmed the existence of Gladio, in testimony to an Italian senate subcommittee. Andreotti had been forced into making this admission by the discoveries of Felice Casson in the archives of the state's secret services. Gladio was, Andreotti said, a 'structure of information, response and safeguard'. Some 622 civilians belonged to Gladio units in Italy. He denied that the organization had any involvement in terrorist activities, but confirmed that 127 separate arms caches used by Gladio had been dismantled. It was from one such cache that the explosives which killed the three Carabinieri officers in Peteano had originated.

According to Giulio Andreotti, all incoming Italian prime ministers were informed about Gladio. This was challenged by the former socialist prime minister Bettino Craxi, who said he only knew about the secret organization when shown a letter about it that bore his own signature. Aldo Moro, the former prime minister who was kidnapped and murdered by the Red Brigades, was closer to the political establishment of the time than Craxi, and doubtless knew of its existence. According to one of his kidnappers, Alberto Franceschini, Moro had helped set up the Gladio structure in the first place. However, Moro's keenness to embrace a reformed communist party in a coalition known as the 'historic compromise' (*compromesso storico*) offended many on the right, and has proved the basis for frequent conspiracy theories surrounding his kidnap and assassination.

Some of those with possible answers did not, however, survive to give them to subsequent parliamentary inquiries. The Carabinieri general Alberto Dalla Chiesa, who led the anti-terrorist campaign in the 1970s and captured two key members of the Red Brigades, was assassinated in Palermo in 1982, along with his wife, on the orders of the Mafia boss Salvatore Rina.

Among the cases Dalla Chiesa was investigating at the time was the murder of the journalist Mauro De Mauro. According to a Mafia informant, De Mauro was killed because he had learned about the planned 1970 *coup d'état* known as the *Golpe Borghese* involving the right-wing 'Black Prince', Junio Valerio Borghese. The plot involved the occupation of the Quirinale Palace and Ministry of the Interior by army dissidents, with the support of Mafia backers. Borghese was an aristocrat and fascist soldier who had been rescued from partisans at the end of the war by the US agent James Angleton, later a long-serving chief of the CIA's counter-intelligence staff. Known to many as the 'mother' of the modern CIA, Angleton grew up in Rome, where his family owned a business, and returned to the city on one of his first CIA postings. Borghese fled Italy after the collapse of the plot attempt. In spite of several years of trials, no one was convicted of any crime over this very real attempt to overthrow a democratically elected European government.

A second journalist to suffer from the fallout of the 'Years of Lead' was Carmine 'Mino' Pecorelli, a specialist writer with extensive contacts inside the secret-service community. Pecorelli had written an article warning that Alberto Dalla Chiesa was in danger of assassination four years before the Carabinieri general was murdered. Pecorelli published a number of private documents relating to the Moro case, drawing a connection between the death of the former prime minister and Gladio. He had also linked Giulio Andreotti himself to the Mafia.

In March 1979 Pecorelli was murdered in the Prati district of Rome. The distinctive ammunition that killed him proved to be easily traceable. The journalist was assassinated by the *Banda della Magliana*, a group involved with all three arms of the Italian organized crime community, the Cosa Nostra, Camorra and 'Ndrangheta, as well as a number of fascist groups and the notorious P2 Masonic Lodge. The four bullets that killed Mino Pecorelli came from a cache of arms hidden in the basement of the Italian Health Ministry in Rome. The Mafia informant, Tommaso Buscetta, who grew up in Palermo and was later associated with the New York Gambino crime family in the US, testified in Palermo in 1993 that Pecorelli was killed as a favour to Giulio Andreotti, on the orders of two Mafia cousins, Nino and Ignazio Salvo, who were the linkmen between organized crime and Andreotti's Christian Democrat party.

Buscetta was one of the first and most important Mafia members to break the code of *omertà*. His testimony, to two judges who would later be murdered by the Mafia, resulted in the imprisonment of almost 350 gang members. It also served to increase the pressure on Giulio Andreotti.

The former prime minister denied ever having met the Salvo cousins. However, two photographs showing him with Nino Salvo were found in the archives of Letizia Battaglia, the legendary Sicilian photographer who has spent a career documenting the lives and deaths of the Mafia and their victims.

In 1995, five years after he first confirmed the existence of Gladio, the man who was a giant of post-war Italian politics was charged with ordering Pecorelli's assassination out of fear that the journalist was about to reveal damning information confirming his links to organized crime. Andreotti was acquitted in 1999, but found guilty on appeal in 2003. At the age of eighty-three he was sentenced to twenty-four years in jail. He was then immediately released pending a further appeal, and one year later was acquitted of all charges.

After Andreotti finally confirmed the existence of Gladio, the European Parliament drafted a resolution criticizing the fact that 'these organizations operated and continue to operate completely outside the law since they are not subject to any parliamentary control'. It went on to call for 'a full investigation into the nature, structure, aims and all other aspects of those clandestine organizations'. Since that call was issued in 1990, only Italy, Belgium and Switzerland have carried out parliamentary investigations.

Apart from the Quirinale Palace and the Ministry of the Interior, most of the government buildings featured in this book are imaginary. The Quirinale is open to the public once a week, on most Sunday mornings. The visit includes the Salone dei Corazzieri and is one of the great sights of Rome – a free one, too.

The real-life tomb of the Blue Demon lies close to the Etruscan necropolis site on the outskirts of Tarquinia, and was discovered in 1995. At the time of writing it is one of the few tombs on the site that is closed to the general public.